Repair 3/20

50

The Snowfly
a novel

Joseph Heywood

THE LYONS PRESS

To Bullshidos Al, Reg, Bob, Dick, and Lars for more than twenty great years on the Pere Marquette. To G2 for our Michigan meanderings. To Sandy and my family for enduring a writer's stubborn ways. To my agent "Mambomama" Betsy Nolan, and to "Catskill" Lilly Golden for her skillful and delicate scalpel; editing is an art. May your rivers flow clean and cold and the flies hatch at your convenience.

Copyright © 2000 by Joseph Heywood

Printed in the United States of America

10 9 8 7 6 5 4 3 2 1

ISBN 1-58574-020-9

Design by Compset, Inc.

The Library of Congress Cataloging-in-Publication Data is available on file.

The Snowfly

Other Novels by Joseph Heywood

The Domino Conspiracy
The Berkut
Taxi Dancer

PROLOGUE

I am standing in life-water clear as vodka and cold as Kelvin. The trout rise. They are small, but they rise, which is all I care about. I have no further interest in large fish with jutting kypes. I heard that siren and followed that track far beyond the last station. It is written: We are born to die. Between these events we may cover a lot of water. Some may argue that this is a trouter's memoir. I say it is something more and something less. I never felt the chill of running water, only its heat. Most of what I have written is factual, but two writers can order the same facts into diametrically different tales. The story I tell is mine as I prefer to remember it, and am able.

It is autumn in all ways. This river, like all rivers and lives, holds secrets. How we handle the secrets of our lives defines us. Rivers define themselves and do not willingly surrender their mysteries. Some of us cover sweetwater in search of trout, but covered waters remain ever so. There is staghorn sumac behind me, rusty and blushed brilliant orange under a falling sun. The lack of light degrades chlorophyll, but knowing the science does not change the splendor. I am tired. Plaque collects where genes decree. I need to sit in the sun and let my mind have its head. Sleep comes easily in Indian summer on a rock beside a river with no name, but life comes hard in any season and truth comes even harder.

Bowie Rhodes
September 4, 1999

PART I

"Damn fools," the old man said.

I noticed he had grouped the floater into the broader category to which he consigned many people he knew or encountered.

"What do you think happened?" I asked.

The old man lit a cigarette. He smoked Chesterfields, but only outside the cabin. Queen Anna didn't abide smokers (or most anyone with habits and values that differed from hers, meaning virtually all males). The old man cupped the butt to protect it from the sleet.

"Lotta stupid people in the world, Bowie. They're not stupid all the time. Most of the time they do just fine, but they've got weaknesses and blind spots. Like trout fishermen. If I told you there were diamonds in the back forty you wouldn't go running out there to dig like a maniac because you'd know that this isn't the right kind of land to make diamonds. Right?"

"Yes, sir," I said, knowing full well that if I didn't get into a digging frenzy I'd certainly give the back forty a thorough going-over just in case a few of the gems had worked their way to the surface by pure chance or God's plan (which were about the same to me). The old man was a practicing pragmatist, as was my mom; in later years I'd learn that this genetic default skipped me and landed squarely in my sister. A time came, in fact, when I wondered if I had been adopted, because no matter how hard my parents tried to inculcate certain values in me they never seemed to take. I tried, to be sure, but something always came undone. I didn't see what diamonds had to with a drowned man or trout, but the comparison only added to the delicious air of mystery.

The old man continued. "See, that gent there on the rocks is a fool. You can see he's a gent by his clothes. Spent a lot of money to look like a trout fisherman. In England they even wear coats and ties when they fish."

I tried to picture fishermen in coats and ties but couldn't get full resolution. Was trout fishing a form of worship? The old man only wore a tie and coat to church.

"Trout fishermen have all sorts of knowledge," he said. "They're loaded down with information, but they don't always use it. Whirling Creek's killed fifty, sixty people in my lifetime. If you fish upstream, it'll kill you. Everybody knows that, but still they go. That's a fool for you."

"Why was he up there?"

The old man flicked his cigarette into the creek's wintry black water. "Looking for diamonds," he said with a sort of clucking sound. "Fool."

This turn flung me off the old man's logic trail. The dead gent was fishing for diamonds? I needed clarification, but the old man didn't like being

1

I was eight when the floater drifted past our cabin on Whirling Creek and hung on the rocks. It was late September and most of the leaves were already down, the creek awash with early-autumn debris. My sister, Lilly, was sixteen and crashed through the front door to announce the find, but when she opened her mouth to speak, she vomited and fainted.

My mother, Queen Anna, whispered, "Please God, don't let it be morning sickness." It was years later before I understood the significance of that remark.

My father and I went outside to look around. Actually, he told the rest of us to stay inside and went to investigate alone; naturally, I followed. We were two males in a household of two strong-willed females and at eight I was already trying to assert my gender. Whatever had put Lilly down was outside and if the old man was going out, it was my duty and my right to be beside him, but the old man was a strict constructionist about his rules so when he went out the front door, I crept quietly out the back and circled, Indian style. What I imagined to be Indian style.

It was ten o'clock in the morning and sleeting. The barren ground was iced and slick; the stiff browned skeletons of ferns crackled when I brushed past them. The old man made straight for the creek bank. Years before, he had stacked boulders upstream and down to create a swimming hole for us. Summers I caught brook trout and browns from the hole, mostly on worms and crickets. I often went out early on Sundays and caught enough for fresh-fish breakfast. I did not fish anywhere else along the creek because I didn't need to and because the old man said it was too dangerous. Such declarations did not welcome requests for explanation.

When he got to the embankment, the old man hunkered down. He was small and wiry with knots of hard muscle and no fat. In deer season he could squat for hours and not move. He never complained of being hot or cold. At times I was sure there was nothing he couldn't do.

"I know you're over there," the old man said without looking in my direction. "You might as well see this, son."

I approached warily. The body had tumbled over the spillway and hung on ragged downstream boulders. I didn't need to be told I was looking at a dead man.

questioned. He did his own thinking and expected others to do the same. I shifted gears.

"We gonna pull him out?"

The old man gave a long, reflective look. "Think you could deal with a corpse?"

"It's just a stranger," I said.

This got me a peculiar grin from the old man. "You're a hard-nosed little shit," he said proudly.

The old man did not retrieve the body, but he did crawl out onto the rocks to secure the dead man so he wouldn't float away. Then the two of us walked out to Chickerman's General Store in Pinkville to call the sheriff. Queen Anna did not believe in telephones and even if she had, we couldn't have afforded one. I walked beside my father, feeling his equal and swollen with the knowing.

Gus Chickerman did not talk like the rest of us. He had come to the U.S. sometime during or after World War II, been sickened by New York and Detroit and moved on to upper Michigan. Facts about Gus were cloudy and often butted against each other, but I assumed this was how it was with all adults and paid no attention. Gus had a wife and an eight-year-old daughter formally named Raina, known to everyone as Punky. She was my best friend.

Chickerman's was our local lodge. You didn't have to carry cash in hand to be welcome. Gus Chickerman himself had a scraggly gray beard. He did not limp but his back was bent and he always carried a cane. It was as black as obsidian and crooked with an ivory handle inlaid with three gold diamonds. Raina's mother, Ruby, had a wide smooth face bathed in a perpetual smile. Usually Gus and Ruby were happy to have children in the store, but this day they were focused on my old man and the news we had brought.

Punky found me and plopped down beside me. "You see the dead guy?"

I nodded solemnly, savoring my newfound importance.

"I wanna see him."

"Girls can't take it," I said. No insult intended. I'd already seen the effect of the dead body on my sister.

"I can," Punky said. "I can do anything."

It was well established that this was true. Raina Chickerman was an antisocial "brain." She also was the best athlete in the third grade, got the best report cards, drew the best pictures, had the finest singing voice, and was best among us at just about everything except making friends. Worse, she did everything without apparent effort. The rest of us had to work at things, but Punky seemed to get and do everything with ease and confidence. She was scary for a girl and a lot of kids made fun of her, but she and I had always been comfortable together and I had been her only friend.

"Sheriff's coming," I told her. "Otherwise I'd give you a look."

She shoved me gently. "You think you own the goddamn thing?" She also swore more than anybody in the third grade.

"It's in *our* swimming hole."

Sheriff Bielat did not come. Instead he sent his deputy, Roger Ranger. It always sounded funny, a joke, to have a lawman called Deputy Ranger, but Roger Ranger was no joke to me. My old man owned two hundred acres; on paper it was his, but I thought of it as equally mine and spent most of my time exploring my wooded kingdom. The thing about exploring is that you never know what you'll find. Twice I'd been treed by a mama bear with cubs. Another time a stranger stopped to take target practice with his deer rifle and knocked loose a dead branch, which hit me in the head and earned me thirty stitches and a scar that forced Queen Anna to part my hair differently.

My most puzzling discovery involved Roger Ranger and my sister, Lilly. I found them with their clothes off. He had hung his uniform and gun holster on the open rear door of his cruiser. I'd slipped up for a look. They were wrestling, sort of. He was smack on top of her and she had her legs wrapped around him and they were rocking fast and grunting, not talking. I emptied Roger's gunbelt and dropped the bullets down a woodchuck hole. I'd found the two of them for the first time last summer and many times since, though they never knew. Deputy Ranger stopped at our house a lot to brown-nose Queen Anna and flash stupid grins at Lilly.

One day the old man said, "I know what that jamoke has in mind." He didn't elaborate and I didn't enlighten him with what I knew. Whatever game they were playing, Lilly was at least as enthusiastic as the law officer.

Three years after the floater, Lilly and Roger got married and everybody seemed happy. Many years later Sheriff Roger Ranger was found in another county, hog-tied, shot once in the back of the head. The murder was never solved. The loss hit Lilly hard. I suspect she has never gotten over Roger.

This time, though, the deputy was all business. The old man and I got in the cruiser and rode with him to the cabin. He didn't hesitate, but went right to the dead body and announced, "Looks like he drownded."

I was surprised when Roger left the body where it was and went back to use his car radio. By midday we had a black hearse and attendants from a neighboring town's funeral parlor, more policemen, and a young doctor from Ludington. We also got a visit from a woman in a red Cadillac El Dorado convertible who identified herself as the dead man's wife. I expected her to be sad, but she seemed more angry than anything.

"Fucking men are so fucking stupid," the woman told me. "Fly fishermen are the fucking worst. Pure assholes. No sense of reality. You ever hear of the snowfly, boy?"

"No, ma'am." She used language I'd never heard from a grown woman.

She gave me a crooked grin. "That's because there's no such thing. You think that jerk Chuck would believe it? No way. He says, 'Baby, I gotta do this.' And now he's gone. Isn't that about the stupidest thing you ever heard?"

Adults said a lot of things that struck me as stupid. I didn't rank them or answer her because I knew she was talking at me, not to me. Before she departed, she called me over to her Caddie. The door was swung open. She wore a bright red dress and red leather boots. She was sitting sideways. When I got close she opened her legs and I saw a patch of flaming orange hair.

"You know what this is, boy?"

I shook my head.

She laughed. "You will and when you do, you keep your mind on that and don't run off and do something stupid like my Chuck did. Hear?"

"Yes, ma'am," I said.

The old man came up to me after she was gone. "What did she say?"

"It didn't make any sense," I told him. "What's a snowfly?"

The old man rubbed his chin, thought for a few seconds, said, "Beats me," and left me to wonder.

A month or so later Deputy Ranger stopped in with a wooden apple crate. In it was all the dead man's fishing gear, a vest, a bunch of small metal boxes with flies, waders, a small knife, a wooden-handled net.

"The widow said she don't want this stuff," the deputy announced solemnly. "Said we could 'just chuck it.' " He held the box out to me. "But I thought maybe Bowie would like it." I wasn't fooled. The gift was a gesture aimed at Lilly, and shortly after the presentation I saw them at their favorite parking spot. This was getting to be old hat. The cruiser shook and rolled steadily. I was more interested in my new treasure. I had seen fly fishermen on Whirling Creek before and had always admired the quiet way they went about their business. I liked their vests and the colorful little flies and their wicker creels and rubber waders. Now I had most of what they had, all but a genuine fly rod and reel, and I spent all winter examining my unexpected windfall.

Queen Anna took me to the Pinkville village library on Sunday afternoons. I found everything I could on fly fishing and, in doing so, began the formal part of a hunger for information about trout that has lasted the remainder of my life.

The following spring I found the dead man's fly rod. It was jammed along a cedar sweeper two hundred yards downstream from our place, like it was a naturally growing branch. The straightness of the rod caught my eye and I crawled out onto the sweeper to fetch it. The reel was a mess, but the old man put it right with oil and a thorough cleaning. The rod was made of split bamboo that was green and brown when I found it, but the old man cleaned it and waxed it until it shone a deep yellow-orange. I nicknamed it the Golden Rod, but never told anybody about this. What amazed me was the feel of it. I couldn't get over how light it was compared to my old steel rod and bait reel.

"Lotta wand for a kid," the old man said. I caught my first trout on an Adams that May. It was a nice thirteen-inch brown. It rose as a gray shadow, a submarine from below the boulders in our swimming hole. The family witnessed my catch and they all looked at me like I was crazy when I let it go.

"Why'd you go and do that?" Queen Anna demanded.

"So I can catch him again."

She grunted, which was her well-established signal of disapproval. "First, you don't know it's a him. Second, you can't catch the same fish twice."

I had no idea why I'd done what I'd done and I didn't care. That day, at that moment, having caught my first fish on a fly, it felt right to let it live. From that day on I spent my every spare moment casting flies for trout, letting most of them go and still wondering what a snowfly was. I asked a lot of people about it, but nobody seemed to know, and it would be a long time before I found anyone to even bunt at an answer.

Some days after I found the rod and caught my first trout with it, Punky biked over to our house and saw me practicing casts with the bamboo rod. "Want me to show you how?" she asked. She was always cocky.

I thought it was pure bravado, but with Raina you never knew. I wasn't sure I wanted to surrender the rod, but I ended up handing it to her.

I saw right away that she could cast a lot better than I could.

"You fly fish?" I asked her.

"No law against it," she said, "and I'm good at it."
I did not doubt her for a moment.

My mother was big-bone tall and towered over the old man. She was one of those people certain that God had ordained her to provide direction to the rudderless and exquisitely ruddered alike. She had the answer to everything and quixotic and mercurial methods; her natural voice was loud, her tone hectoring. With her voice she could rattle windows and freeze the most facile minds with terror, but she could also modulate to a tone as soft as cumulus, pat a cheek with love tender enough to melt the hardest skin, then backhand it black and blue in a wink. We simultaneously loved her and feared her, praised and cursed her, emulated and scorned her, followed her and fled her, but we never messed with her. She believed in matriarchal power, meaning raw female force, fully exercised. She did not suffer fools or pay heed to any view but her own. As would be said of such individuals in later years, she walked the talk.

Only the old man would stand up to her and sometimes Lilly and I, cast as spectators, would watch and with certainty know the old man had carried the day, but Queen Anna would never cave to defeat. I once thought I heard her tell him that perhaps they both had valid points. I no longer remember the subject being debated, but the Queen's admission was tantamount to conceding defeat and I headed for cover. A draw with the old man presaged a burning need for a victory elsewhere and I didn't care to be a conquest of convenience.

She was not cruel, just unpredictable. She would catch houseflies midflight between her forefinger and thumb, then catapult them carefully out the kitchen window. She would not kill until food was at issue and then she would kill with the steady hand of a practiced assassin. She raised chickens and named them, but when it came time to eat she would helicopter them and take the cleaver to the remains. Whatever name the bird had worn would never be used again, her way of paying homage, I supposed.

When I was six or thereabouts, she shot a spikehorn through the kitchen window. The old man was off hunting and the buck had wandered under the clothesline and she popped a slug in the .16-gauge and blew out the windowpane, dropping the animal and severing the clothesline all with one round. This happened without warning and gave Lilly and me nightmares for days afterward. By the time the old man got home, the venison was gutted and hung, the lines and pane replaced.

"Like the damn Queen of the Amazons," the old man had declared proudly.

The name stuck.

Queen Anna was partial to long-bladed sharp knives and could dice and chop and slice and hack while she scolded and lectured. Talking was important to her. At meals she'd take a portion of everything, cut it up, and mix it all so that she didn't have to look at what she was eating or make choices. She didn't want anything to interfere with her monologues.

We were a family of few means, meaning we lived on the margin, but the old man and Queen Anna were frugal and clever and Lilly and I never truly went without. The old man never had a steady job; I doubt he could tolerate laboring for the same person for too long. But he always had work, especially when we needed something. Queen Anna shopped the way a trophy hunter passed up bucks in anticipation of finding the biggest, and she made it clear that our poverty did not demean us. "There is no shame in being poor, as long as you are clean."

I used to go along with the old man to hunt, but he always carried the weapon. He had taught me to shoot and said I had a real knack, but the killing part never set well and he did not press it. I gladly ate whatever he managed to get, but I could not shoot at living things.

One autumn he shot three deer, a buck and two does, and as we cleaned them he lit a smoke and looked troubled. The law entitled him to one deer.

"Ordinarily, I follow the rules," he said. "But the winter ahead feels like a bad one and we'll be able to use this meat."

"What will Queen Anna say?"

"She'll huff and puff and say a prayer for me leading you astray, but she knows our need well as I do, and in the end she will take the meat and move on. Your mother has some strong notions about right and wrong, but she's not the kind to follow a rule if it might hurt someone, especially her kin. Do you well to remember that."

"You could say I shot one of the deer." I thought this would ease the Queen's anger.

"I could, but your mother knows you as well as I do. If you can't kill, you can't. But you need to understand, Bowie, that there's all sorts of hunting, and killing is a relative thing. I've watched you out there in Whirling Creek and you hunt trout as hard as I hunt other things. Sometimes it's the hunting that does the real damage, not the killing. That's just sort of the end of the road."

At the time I thought he was saying that I hurt trout by hunting them. Later I would realize that by hunting he meant pursuit, that anytime you pursued anything with unswerving purpose, damage would be done. It took me a long time to learn this.

It was my sophomore year of high school. I had discovered basketball in the fourth grade but had always been gangling and more than a little clumsy before I finally began to grow into my body. The old man had rigged a backboard and hoop near the house and I spent years shooting away. I still could not kill, but I loved to win. I made the varsity as a tenth-grader, but barely. A couple of games into the season I got put into a game at the start of the fourth quarter when we were down twenty points, and I took this as a sign that the coach was throwing in the towel. But I viewed no game as ever lost and I went into a frenzy and potted twenty-four points in one quarter. We lost the game by three, but that eight minutes changed my life. I was moved off the bench into a starter's job, which I never relinquished except for one game in my junior year, and that because of Raina Chickerman.

Raina and I were only a month apart in age, her being the elder, and she held this over my head just like every other edge she had, imagined or otherwise. While we both had our licenses to drive at sixteen, she had her own car, a wallowing black Buick she called White Whale. I was curious about the name, but she refused to answer most of my questions and I was left to guess.

Raina had been a skinny kid and a certifiable tomboy, but by tenth grade she had developed into a shapely young woman who seemed more mature than anyone in our school, including most of our teachers. They just looked old. She often drove me to basketball games while the Chickermans hauled my family. Some years we had a junker for transportation, and some years we didn't. The Chickermans monitored our current state of wheels and stepped in to help when we were vehicleless.

Just before Christmas of our junior year, the team had reeled off eight straight wins with no losses and we had climbed to eighth in the state polls.

We were to play Gaylord, which was ranked second in the polls, and even the *Detroit Free Press* did a little write-up on the showdown.

Raina arrived early that night and I threw my gym bag in the backseat and we headed for town. It had been a light fall and there was little sign of winter, which meant she could take dirt roads all the way to town. Given her choice and cooperating weather, Raina would always drive the dirt. This night she headed down a narrow two-track and suddenly stopped, dropping the gearshift into neutral.

"I've been watching you," she said.

"Watching me what?"

"Your butt, stupid. You've filled out nicely."

I blushed. "You too," I managed to mumble.

I had virtually no experience with girls. We lived in the woods and Punky was my only close female friend. In fact, she was my only friend.

"*C'est l'heure bleu,*" she said, staring at me.

"What?"

"That's French. It translates to 'the blue hours' but means dusk or twilight, which the French say is the best time for romance."

"You've been to France?"

She rolled her eyes. "I read."

"I read too," I said in my own defense. Though my reading tastes ran toward Tom Swift.

"All you read are your press clippings."

This made me uneasy. How did she know? It was true: I read everything written about me, which wasn't much but seemed to be growing.

"Physiologically, we're grown up, Bowie. Emotionally, women mature before men. But physically we're both there. In two years you'll be at your sexual peak and the rest of your life it will never be as good. Doesn't that scare you?"

I didn't know where she was heading with this, but my stomach was fluttering and I was sweating. "You're crazy."

"I won't dispute that possibility," she said. "But that's off the subject. I have in mind that we should engage in some osculation, perhaps in the French style."

"Some what?" It was not unusual for Raina to bring some strange subject out of left field. And to do the unexpected.

When we were thirteen or so Raina came over to the house and was waved upstairs by Queen Anna. She entered my room without knocking and flopped on my bed, her eyes dark and cloudy.

"What's wrong?" I asked.

She answered by peeling off her T-shirt to reveal budding breasts with coral-pink aureoles. "What the hell am I supposed to do with *these*?"

I could not take my eyes off them. "All girls have them, even my sister."

"Well, I ought to have a choice," she said. "You want to touch them?"

I declined, but still remembered that moment when something began to change between us. Until we reached the end of junior high school we had been inseparable, best friends, coexplorers, competitors, but always thinking of ourselves as a team.

That was then. "Osculation is kissing," she said. "God, Bowie! How will you get into college with such a lackluster vocabulary?"

I heard only one word in this statement: *kissing*.

Which we clumsily attempted and stayed at until my mind melted and I felt like gravity had abandoned the earth.

"Oh shit," Raina yowped in the middle of a long kiss, "we've got to get you to the gym!"

At that moment I would have junked my basketball career and everything else I held dear, but Raina had other ideas and once her mind was set, you had no choice but to go along.

On the way into town she asked, "You dated anybody yet?"

I shook my head.

"No coitus then."

"Caught us?" I looked around with paranoia.

"Gone all the way," she said. "Done the deed, made the beast with two backs."

I stared straight ahead. Why was she like this?

"You don't have to answer," Raina said. She looked over and winked. "Your secret's safe, but this is so sweet, Bowie. Tonight I am going to watch you run up and down that court and all the girls and even some grown women are going to be watching your butt and lusting for you and I'll know that your lips have never tasted any but mine."

"I didn't say I hadn't kissed a girl."

She rolled her eyes. "Actions speak, Rhodes. You're a virgin by all counts."

"And you aren't?"

"Wouldn't you love to know."

The whole thing left me out of sorts. Part of me was still with Raina and the other part was trying to get me focused on basketball.

Coach stared at me from across the room. "What the hell is that on your collar and neck, Rhodes?"

I didn't know until I stood up and looked in the mirror. Lipstick. Smeared all over my shirt and neck. "Blood," I said. "Must've cut myself shaving."

Coach grunted skeptically.

We returned to the dressing room after warm-ups and Coach went over the game plan. He didn't look at me until he had finished. "Find yourself a seat on the bench, Rhodes. A man who's lost that much blood can't play a big game like this. I'd be morally remiss to risk your health for a mere sporting event."

I was sick. I was angry. I was also still thinking about Raina's kisses.

At halftime we were down seven points. "Still bleeding?" Coach asked.

"No, sir."

"Okay, you're going in, but don't ever cut yourself shaving before another game or I'm gonna have to tell your folks to have you checked for hemophilia."

I played like a demon and we won by fifteen and jumped to the top of the polls, but of that night, it is the kissing that still stands out in my memory.

After the game, I dumped my soiled shirt in my bag and wore a basketball warm-up jacket.

Raina was standing with her folks and my parents. Queen Anna gave me the once-over. "How come you sat so long? You feeling okay?"

I said I was fine and when Raina and I got in the White Whale I told her what happened and I thought she was going to pass out laughing. Her laugh was like a hyena's bark.

A week after school ended that year I went down to the Rock Socket River and had a great evening on gray drake hatches. I didn't consider myself an expert fly fisherman, but I was learning and most times I could get into fish if I just thought through what I was seeing. When I got back to the old man's latest beater, I found Raina Chickerman sitting on the right front fender, her fly rod across her lap. She wore a black bathing suit and hip boots and was smoking a cigarette.

"What's the matter?"she asked. "Jocks look down their crooked noses at smokers, or is it just at women who smoke?"

"Neither," I said. "Let me have one."

She raised an eyebrow, flipped her pack of Luckies to me, and studied me while I lit one. "I am at a loss for words," she said, "which is truly rare. That is obviously not your first coffin nail. How long you been on the weed?"

"Long enough, but I always quit during basketball season. How'd you find me?"

"The mere fact that we are co-located geographically does not mean that I am following you. Geography is often a false explanation of intent. Do you also swear off screwing during basketball?"

I laughed. "You don't have to quit what you haven't started."

She chuckled. "Don't lose heart, Rhodes. You know what they say about big dogs."

"No."

"Big dogs walk last, but they walk best."

It seemed a bizarre metaphor. "Why are you following me?"

"Not for kissing practice," she said. "So how'd you do?"

"Not bad. You?"

"Just pulled in. I like to fish after dark."

"Kind of risky."

"Only for a gimp," she said.

"I'd think your parents would worry."

"Of course they worry. All parents worry about their progeny. But they don't stand in my way. They know I am going to do what I do. You're out here. Why shouldn't I be?"

"I'm leaving at dark. You're just starting."

"We could always fish together," she said.

"Queen Anna expects me back."

"She would."

"Besides, I can't see well enough to fish at night."

"Blind people fish," she said in her lecturing voice. "Doesn't matter to them if it's night or day. If the eyes don't work, the ears do."

"Bull."

She said, "My father knows a blind man who fishes alone at night, from a boat."

As usual, I wasn't sure if I should believe her. She was not above fabricating facts to carry an argument or make a point. "You're full of it," I said. It's funny how the mind works, but years later I would remember her telling me about the blind man her father knew and it would help confirm my suspicions in the mystery that dominated a great part of my life.

Raina stared down at the river. "Yes, I suppose that's true. You and I are so alike, Bowie. And we're so different and I don't refer simply to the obvious plumbing disparities. You like order and predictability. I like excitement and living life in big chunks. Circumstances conspire to hem women in. If we pick a safe, narrow trail at the start, we'll end up at a safe, narrow destination. I'm not going to be trapped like that."

Did Queen Anna feel trapped? I doubted it. "Like a beatnik?"

She smiled and shook her head. "Beatniks have their own narrow paths and never mind what others say about them. I don't plan to fit any

category." She slid off the fender. "Time to get wet," she said, "no innuendo intended."

Innuendo? What did she mean now?

Raina walked several steps, stopped, leaned forward, and thrust out
her behind. "The adjective is *callipygian* and it's top drawer, you agree?"

I nodded. Context was all I needed to understand.

I half followed her to the water's edge. "You remember that dead guy
back when we were kids?"

She looked over her shoulder. "I never got to see him." Her tone said
she still had hard feelings about this.

"His wife came down to identify the body and she was mad as a hornet
that he drowned. She drove a red El Do. She said he was after something
called a snowfly. You ever hear of that?"

"No," she said curtly and waded silently into the river, not looking back.

Punky and I had known each other all our lives. This time I knew she
was lying, but I could not imagine why.

Raina was indifferent about grades and grade points, at least on the surface, and had little tolerance for other school measures that she referred to
as "pedestrian pseudo-academic trifles." She also had a perfect four-point all
the way through school.

At graduation I got the Markham Award for writing. It brought with it a
scholarship that would go a long way toward paying for college. With work
and the scholarship I figured I could get through. There was no way my parents could afford it. The prize was one of the few gewgaws not collected by
Raina, but I knew she was miffed and no doubt offended. She had her
exquisite vocabulary, which she used like a weapon, but I could write things
that my teachers could comprehend and even enjoy. Others couldn't see
Raina's anguish over my winning the prize, but I could and I liked knowing
I had bested her at something. It had happened only one other time, in the
elementary school spelling bee when she missed *systalic,* mistaking it for
systolic and forever after blaming the teacher's mispronunciation. I got
syzygy on pure guesswork and won and was never forgiven. Raina was not
the sort of person who could live with losing.

She was, of course, our valedictorian and gave a curious speech about
dreams and determination, the hidden but polite competition between gen-
ders, and how no genuinely educated person ever got much from formal
schooling, which played to the middle, unable to recognize—much less

serve—the gifted. Then she thanked her father and mother and named every teacher she had ever had and all of us were left to wonder if this was gratitude or one of her subtle put-downs. With Raina there was a fine line between the two.

We all scratched our heads, but we were all of a common mind about one thing: Raina Chickerman was headed somewhere to be someone. Only where and what were up in the air.

My parents and the Chickermans held a joint graduation party at the store. Raina and I hung to the side while our parents basked in the glow of hearing what fine young people they had raised.

We slipped outside during the festivities. It was a muggy night with a white moon covered with gauze. As she had years before, Raina removed her blouse. Only now the buds of then had grown firm and prominent and her breasts glowed in the moon's reflected light.

"Since this seems to be a night for finishing, I thought you should see how my girls turned out."

"Nice," I said, fumbling for something to say.

"Just *nice?* That's *all* you can say? God, you are such a jerk when it comes to women, Bowie." With that she turned away from me.

It was one of those clumsy moments in life and I tried to recompose myself. "Have you decided on a college yet?"

"Didn't you hear anything I said at graduation?"

"Of course I heard."

"If you did, you would know that there are certain people who cannot possibly benefit from the stilted education imposed by institutions. *Life* is education, Bowie. Learning is a way of life."

"Well, what kind of living will you do?"

"The most that I can," she said. "Remember that woman who said something about a snowfly?"

I remembered and I had searched the library and talked to people, but nobody seemed to know what I was talking about. Eventually I'd written it off as the ramblings of a sad and angry widow.

"I remember."

"Tell me exactly what she said," Raina said, turning back to face me.

I did, leaving out nothing.

"She hiked her skirt?" Raina asked.

"She did."

"Was she wearing drawers?"

"Nope."

"Have you followed her advice?" she asked. Then, just as quickly, "No, don't answer. It doesn't matter. I think the snowfly is actually a white mayfly, *Ephoron leukon*."

This was the second time we had talked about snowflies. The first time, I had opened the subject and she had claimed ignorance. But this time it was her initiative and I wondered why. She had long ago passed me in the entomological knowledge needed to fish flies.

"So what?"

She shrugged and her breasts rippled in the light. "I thought you would want to know. Think of it as a graduation gift."

"Some things I prefer to discover on my own."

"Don't get into one of your snits," she said, sliding her blouse back over her head.

Her tone bothered me. "I'm sorry."

"Apology accepted. You remember that night you cut yourself shaving?"

I grinned. "Yeah."

"I would have gone all the way with you that night, Bowie. If only you had shown the courage to take the initiative. That night is both a wonderful memory and a great disappointment to me."

"I'm sorry." She had me groveling again.

"It's just as well. With our luck, we'd have had a dead rabbit to contend with."

"What?"

"I would have gotten pregnant, dummy. I thought for the longest time we were meant to be together, but now I know that's not true . . . at least not yet. There's too much we each have to do and we'd just get in each other's way and be holding the other one back. I think maybe we're too much alike. We have too much fire in our hearts, but I doubt you realize that about yourself yet."

These were disconcerting words. Was she declaring the end of our friendship? "We'll always be friends," I said.

She sighed and the sound was barely audible. " 'Things sweet to taste prove in digestion sour.' "

"Shakespeare," I said.

"That's not a citation."

"Richard the Something."

"Second," Raina said. " 'And therefore, since I cannot prove a lover . . .' "

"I don't know that one."

"Look it up sometime."

She kissed me chastely on the cheek and went back inside.

It would be a long time before I remembered this quote again.

The day I left for college Queen Anna was cutting scallions and green peppers and brandishing her knife like Toscanini with his baton. College was not going to be easy financially. I had the small scholarship, which would help, but I was going to have to work as well and I needed to find something that would provide a good hourly rate so that I would not be tied up working all the time.

"Keep your nose in your books," she said. "It took your father and me a lot of effort to make you who you are and I don't want it undone *down there*"—this her term for anywhere she wasn't.

I had once heard her tell my sister, Lilly, to "keep your knees together and your mind on Jesus."

To me she said, "Jesus taught us to fish, that we might feed others. College is where you're going to learn to fish in the waters of life, and life's *filled* with temptations." She looked me in the eye. "Steer clear of women, Bowie."

"But *you're* a woman."

She gave me a rare smile and a gentle touch on the cheek. "I'm not a woman, Bowie. I'm your mother."

I supposed that every freshman in America would be having similar talks with parents, but the Queen's send-off left me feeling uneasy. She went to the bus with me and handed me something wrapped in brown paper, tied neatly with purple string, and a cloth sack filled with apples.

On the bus I opened the package to find an old and worn copy of Izaak Walton's and Charles Cotton's *The Compleat Angler*. I wondered where she had found it and where she found the money for it, but it was one of my favorites and the gift made me teary. Inside the front cover she had written, "Simon Peter said, 'I go a-fishing,' and they said, 'We also will go with thee.' " She added, "We are all with you, Bowie, wherever you go."

After my freshman year at Michigan State, I went west to Idaho to fight fires for the summer. I had done all right with my grades and scraped by financially. The chance to go west offered me an opportunity to bank enough money to take care of a couple of years of school. When I wasn't on fire duty, I was fishing for rainbows and cutthroats and hanging out with a twenty-seven-year-old schoolteacher named Rose Yelton. We met in a bar. In Idaho the legal age was still twenty-one then, but the reality was that if you were tall enough to stand at the bar you could get served. I wasn't yet nineteen.

"You must be a virgin," a woman said to me.

"What?" I felt my neck go red. How did she know?

"Your hair hasn't been singed. Obviously you haven't had your fire-cherry busted yet." She had a mesmerizing smile and the diaphanous hair of an angel.

We left the bar together that night and I admitted to her that it wasn't only my fire-cherry that was intact and she kissed me and told me that she couldn't do anything about the fires in the woods, but she could do plenty with other kinds of fires and she proved true to her words.

Her father ran beef on a scruffy, open-range ranch near Weippe and was also a trout fisherman. When I asked him about the snowfly he grinned and shook his head.

"It's a destroyer, son. Some men go plumb crazy chasing the snowfly."

"Then it's real?"

"I can't honestly say."

"Where can I find out?"

"I don't know, son. You might better put that question to Red Ennis."

Ennis, I learned, was a professor emeritus of history from the University of Idaho in Moscow. He had retired to a cabin on Peavine Creek up in the panhandle near Pierce. Rose and I went to visit him.

Peavine Creek was not large by Rocky Mountain standards, but it was clear and quick, with moss-covered boulder steps and deep pools gathering wads of foam. The professor's clapboard cabin was built at the edge; a platform jutted out to the lip of a dark pool and Red Ennis sat on the platform in a metal rocking chair, which had so oxidized to rust it looked like it might turn to powder any second.

"Professor Ennis?"

He did not look toward us. "You hear him?" he asked, gesturing toward the pool.

Rose said, "Far side."

The old man smiled. "Howdy, Rose." He had white hair and slow, gentle eyes.

"Nice fish," he said.

Rose nudged me. "Professor Ennis, I came to ask you about the snowfly."

"Did you? And who might you be? A friend of Rose? One of her curled-toes club?"

Rose looked at me and rolled her eyes. She had told me during the drive to the cabin that Ennis was "not all there." His specialty was the history of the Rockies. He had spent a lifetime tracing the movements of mountain men, spending several winters alone in the Rockies to better understand his subjects.

"What's he mean?" I whispered.

"Talk to him," she said impatiently.

"I'm Bowie Rhodes."

Ennis smiled and cocked his head in my direction. "Any relation to Grizzly Rhodes?"

"No, sir," I answered without knowing who he was talking about.

"He came out of Pennsylvania around 1800. Merchant family, well-to-do people, but he was the black sheep and a bad fit for the self-styled civilized East. He lived to be ninety and he was quite a man. Unusual in that he could write, but he didn't much bother. Married a Crow woman and taught her. They had a dozen kids, all of whom lived, which was unusual in itself. The woman's name was Red Face. She and those kids were writing fools. I located forty journals written by various members of the family. What we know about the lives of mountain men sits squarely on the shoulders of Red Face Rhodes and her spawn. Helluva lady, she was. Sure you're not a relation? The Rhodes family had iron blood and molten fire in their hearts, that's for damn sure."

"Not aware that I'm related."

"Too bad for you," he said. "Why do you want to know about the snowfly?"

"I heard about it once."

"Par for the course. It's one-a those things that doesn't get much talked about. Lotta people say it's myth, but me, I say myths're usually based on something. Smoke from fire, right? That's what history's taught me."

I wanted more, but Ennis only stared out over his pool.

"You believe it's real?" Some people needed prompting.

"Doesn't much matter what I believe."

"But I'd like to know more."

"Someday maybe you will and maybe you won't. The snowfly's a peculiar slice of life. Some are meant to know. Most aren't and those who do know usually end up sorry for the knowing. The snowfly's a burden, son, and I wouldn't put it on so young a man. Best keep your attention on Rose there."

In August my roommate, Larry Showly, was killed during a fire in the Bitterroots. We were bunked two to a room and Larry was a quiet guy from Kansas who wanted to be a forester, did his job, and got along well with everyone on the fire team. He'd crossed a log in his corks, which was against procedure. The rotted bark gave way, he fell seven or eight feet onto a stob, was impaled and bled to death. I was the one who found him and the vision of him lying there with his unseeing eyes staring up into the heavens would not leave me.

I did not fish much after that. Rose and I spent most of my free time in her bed. Rose taught me about making love. "It's like basketball," she said. "You can't win in the first five minutes. You need to play the whole game." When I got into my VW in September for the trip back to East Lansing, I had pretty much forgotten the snowfly. It took forty-nine hours to make the drive. Life lay ahead and I was eager to get on with it. I arrived just as registration began, secured my classes, and headed for a friend's house to sleep. I had an apartment leased, but was too early to take possession. I felt empty without Rose. There had never been anything like what I imagined to be love between us, but we had been fine companions. The last thing Rose said to me was that I would never be comfortable again sleeping without a woman at arm's length. She laughingly called it her legacy. She also said that wherever life took me, no matter how many women I loved, I would always think of her.

I slept for twenty-four hours after I got back to East Lansing and then went to claim my apartment, the top floor of an old house on Michigan Avenue. It didn't take long to unpack, but it was another day before I found the envelope stuck between two shirts. It smelled of Rose and made me smile.

Sweet Bowie: I guess I get the last word in. I know how bad it was for you on the Bitterroot fire. It changed you. I like to think I changed you, too. You changed me. I guess that makes us even. While you were in the Bitterroots I went to see Red Ennis. He says the snowfly legend is probably baloney, but here it is. The snowfly hatch takes place every ten to fifteen years. Nobody knows where it will happen or when. Never the same place twice. You know that trout don't live that long. That's what the fish biologists say. But Red says they do. He says some fish with particular genes can live forty, fifty years. They find themselves a great place where nobody can find them and grow fat and old. Only the snowfly brings them out. They risk their lives then. Nobody knows why, but it's prolly no diff than college boys trying to keep a bunch of trees in nowhere-land from burning up. Knowing you, there's a hundred questions you'd like to ask, but I've given you all that Red gave me so it's in your hands now. I worry about you, Bowie. I keep thinking what Red told us about Grizzly Rhodes and I wonder if the blood of that family flows in you. You have certainly got a fire in your heart and it's a thing that keeps people from ever getting too close. I suppose that will never change, which is sad. We are all who we are. I won't say be careful because I know you will, to the extent you can, but I also realize that when a man so young seeks out fires to fight, he will probably be fighting one sort of fire or another for the rest of his life. I wish you a great life, Bowie. And true happiness. I don't know about this snowfly thing. Please know what it is that you want, my darling. Life is too short to waste. My love forever. Rose (P.S. We sure didn't waste our summer!)

I spent the day in my front window watching the traffic pass. I wanted to know more about the snowfly. During the next few years I didn't think about it all the time. But there were moments. Which is how an obsession takes root.

2

LONG before I arrived at Michigan State I knew I wanted to write. I didn't tell people about it, but I knew and the Markham Award had strengthened my conviction. I had no idea what I wanted to do with my writing, but I had bested Raina Chickerman at it, which reinforced both my interest and my resolve. I did not resent the life our parents have given Lilly and me, but neither did I want to relive it. They were happily rooted to Michigan, but something inside me wanted more and to have a job that gave me the means to enjoy it. I settled on journalism as a major and in my junior year at the university I signed up for a course in science writing; it turned out that I was the only student and I figured the class would be canceled, but Professor Luanne Chidester was a woman with a mission and if there was only one student, so be it.

"People lose interest in science," she announced to me at our first session, "because too many teachers learn by rote and pass it on the same way and that's a shame. A newspaper's a business," she added. "You'll hear a lot of righteous, pompous piffle about public service, but it's the bottom line that drives news. People ought to be interested in science because it's at the root of understanding life. I want to produce reporters who understand how science works so they can cover it properly. If reporters can write interestingly about science, it'll become an important part of the news."

Professor Chidester was in her midthirties. She had worked for papers in Miami and Sacramento before going back to school for her masters and doctorate at Northwestern. She was tall, a shade over six feet, thin, and not unattractive. I had grown an inch the year after I finished high school, topping six-five, and her reedy figure made her seem nearly as tall. She always wore high-heeled shoes and baggy dresses. When she talked, she looked right into my eyes, and she seemed to sense my curiosity early on and did all she could to encourage it. Her class was one of the few I had that didn't seem like a class. It was more like we were colleagues trying to understand things together.

The first week we met in her office in the journalism building. After that it was at her house or on the road. We drove every other weekend to Chicago or Detroit or Cleveland to attend scientific symposia or trade shows.

We usually stayed with friends or colleagues of hers, which kept expenses down. She took me to an autopsy and seemed pleased when I didn't flinch. She took me to an Air Force museum near Dayton where a retired colonel gave us a half-day lecture on aircraft design.

In October we drove down to Kentucky, where she took me to a church in a small town on a Saturday night. A gnarled minister with bad breath explained something called creationism. We met with the Reverend for an hour after the service. His name was Jerboam and though he didn't have a beard, there was something about him that reminded me of Abraham Lincoln. He was passionate in his beliefs and tried his best to use logic to convince us, but his arguments didn't work for me.

We had rooms in a boardinghouse in a town called Greenhill, which was in a gray, hilly area denuded of trees and vegetation by strip miners. After our meeting with the minister, we went to a small restaurant where the food was greasy but the servings large.

"Do you believe in God?" Luanne asked over dinner.

"I don't know."

She smiled. "You don't give up much of yourself."

"It's the truth. It's not like I haven't thought about it, but I just don't know."

"Religion is like science," she said. "There's a central hypothesis. Believers test the hypothesis by making observations and trying to prove what they believe. Do you buy this creationism thing? I'm afraid it's just getting up a head of steam again after several decades in hibernation."

"Well, it runs counter to evolutionary theory, doesn't it?"

"Evolution is *fact*, Bowie. A lawyer might say we have an evidentiary trail. There is no scientific basis for creationism. Still, people believe it. Why do you think that is?"

"I guess people want to believe in something. They want somebody to tell them this is how it is."

"Why not believe in science?"

"Because it keeps changing. We know one thing today and another thing tomorrow. Science is the search for answers. Religious beliefs are answers. Or what passes for answers. And they don't seem to change."

"Why aren't you a believer?"

"I don't have enough information to believe in the literal creation, but I believe some things." Queen Anna believed and never questioned. This always bothered me, but I never felt it my place to question her.

"Such as?"

"I think life's precious. We only have so much time and we ought to do what we think is important. We ought to use our lives to make things better, not just for ourselves, but for everybody."

"What's guilt, Bowie?"

"To me?"

She nodded. "Do you ever feel guilty?"

"Not really."

"That doesn't worry you?"

"No."

"Some would say that guilt is a signal from your conscience. Sort of a GO SLOW sign on a dangerously curving road. There's pathology connected to the total absence of guilt. It can be sociopathic. Do you heed traffic signs?"

"Most of the time."

"Why?"

"Common sense."

"Do you always use common sense?"

The conversation was making me uncomfortable. Was she trying to dig into me? "Do you?" I asked her. We had never talked so personally. Usually there were other people around us and my job mostly was to listen to what they had to say.

"Not always," she said. Then she chuckled. "Sometimes not at all."

She stared at me a long while and I stared back and sometime during that long look I began to see her as pretty and to think of her not just as a professor, but as a woman. I wondered what she thought of me.

We left long before daylight on Sunday. She had to get back to East Lansing for some sort of late-afternoon meeting. We trooped silently out to her station wagon and she tossed me her keys. "Will you drive?"

"Do I have to obey the traffic signs?"

She clutched my arm and laughed. "You have definite charm, Bowie Rhodes."

We weren't far out of town before she was asleep against my shoulder. She had a soft snore. It felt good to have her so close.

It was still dark when she awoke and rubbed her eyes. She was still on my shoulder and snuggled closer. "Need a break?"

"I'm okay," I said. She closed her eyes and soon her breathing told me she had fallen back to sleep.

I had a fair number of fantasies about Luanne Chidester after that drive, but our relationship remained formal. I got an A from her and she sent a letter to the dean of the College of Communications Arts & Sciences recommending me for a scholarship that would pay for my entire senior year. My job out west had earned me a sizable nest egg, which had taken the pressure off for a couple of years, and if I got the new scholarship I knew I would get through without much worry. I would still have to work, but mostly for expenses.

The class finished before Christmas and I moved on to other courses with other teachers, but I made it a point to stay in touch with Luanne. About once a month, usually on a Sunday afternoon, I was her guest for brunch. These were wonderful sessions, filled with discussions of arcane science and an incredible range of tangential subjects. Over time, we became friends. By late March I was bubbling with anticipation for the opening of trout season.

"Tell me about this fishing," she said. We were in her solarium. She had her legs tucked beneath her and she was settled in a huge soft chair. "You have a passion for it?"

"I love it."

"Why?"

"I guess I never thought about it that way."

"That's not an answer."

"I just like to fish for trout."

"You say 'trout' a certain way, as if there's a distinction and hierarchy between trout and other fish. Is this a snobbish thing?" She flashed a mischievous grin.

"Probably."

She smiled. "Are trout good to eat?"

"Yes, but I usually don't kill them."

She sat up. "What's the point then?"

"The search, I guess. The pursuit."

"You catch them to let them go."

"Pretty much."

"You don't like to eat fish?"

"I like fish fine."

"Is it that you feel sorry for them?"

"No. I don't have any feelings for them. They're just fish."

"Then why let them go?"

"To catch them again."

She giggled. "How would you ever know if you caught the same fish?"

"I wouldn't and it doesn't matter. I let them loose so they can be caught again by somebody. It doesn't have to be me. It's just so they're there. I guess I like knowing that."

"But somebody else will probably kill them."

"I can't make decisions for others. All I know is that I don't want to kill them."

"It seems to me that if you really cared about their well-being you wouldn't catch them at all. You'd just leave them alone."

I couldn't argue. "Okay, it's a selfish act. I get what I want, but the way I see it, the trout also benefits. Each time a fish is caught and released, it gets harder to catch. Trout learn and pass their lessons on. In England they say that brown trout pass along their experience genetically."

"That's not possible. Mutations are critical to evolutionary theory, but they don't work like this."

"I don't know what the science is. I don't think anybody really knows for certain, but if one fish is better at recognizing food than another, it's going to thrive, and if it thrives it will pass this on. Look at athletes. How many times are the sons of great athletes also good at their fathers' sports? All I know is that in England and other places there are trout that are extremely difficult to catch."

"But people still try."

"Naturally."

"Do you think you could show me?"

The following Sunday she met me at my place. We went to a parking lot behind the house. I used a black cast-iron skillet as a target, strung up the old bamboo rod, and demonstrated the cast. At twenty yards the fly landed in or close to the pan about half the time.

"Wanna try?"

She cast until her elbow got sore.

After about an hour, she said, "I want to do this for real."

"You mean it?"

"I mean everything I say," she said solemnly.

"When?"

"Soon."

"The season opens at the end of the month, but it'll be crowded then and the weather's usually lousy, especially up north."

"I don't care at all for crowds," she said.

We settled on a Thursday in mid-May. She had no classes to teach and I was happy to cut mine.

I took her north to the Brother River. It was shallow, wide, open, a good place for a beginner. Luanne swam in my waders, which were far too large for her.

She hooked her first fish on a tan caddis soon after we started. These were hatchery fish reared on pellets and hand-fed, so they weren't picky about food. I had her play the trout to the shallows and got my hand on it. She got down on her knees and stared, openmouthed.

"Bowie, it's *fantastic*." The eight-inch rainbow squirmed. "The color is indescribable!"

"Shall we keep it?" I asked her.

"What do you mean, 'keep'?"

"Kill it, gut it, cook it tonight."

"I can't kill anything this beautiful."

I held it in the stream, keeping its head into the current and moving it back and forth to get water moving through its gills; when it was sufficiently revived, it flitted into deeper water with an energetic spurt and disappeared.

Luanne sat down on a rock. "Now I want to watch you."

I caught four fish out of the same run, the first one a fifteen-inch brown. She didn't say anything for a long time.

"Stop," she said. "Please."

When I turned, she splashed clumsily over to me, threw her arms around my neck, and kissed me so hard we both collapsed onto the gravel bar. "I understand now!" she said. "It's not just the fish. It's the music of moving water, the smell of clean air, the scenery, the pull on the line, it's the whole thing. You're a romantic, not a sociopath!"

She did understand. Rather, she had a start at understanding. On the other hand, I kept wondering if she had really considered that I might be demented. A sociopath? It was a disturbing thought.

"I want to do this again sometime! Can we?"

Of course we could. The heat of her kiss had inflamed me and I seized on the thought that maybe our friendship could get more intimate.

She looked at the bamboo rod. "How old is this?"

I told her the story of the floater on the way back to East Lansing. When we got to her place she kissed me again and I thought I might get invited in, but that was not to be.

In early June she went to New Orleans for some kind of academic conference. After she was gone, I came home to find a package. It contained a new fly rod made of fiberglass, and a new reel. There was a note inside. It said she was taking a job at Tulane and that she was sorry to see our relationship end so impersonally, but she hoped we'd always be friends and she thought it was time I stopped fishing with a dead man's "pole."

I felt abandoned and sad to lose her friendship. Maybe I still hoped for more and this was the source of my disappointment, but all I knew was that her news left me swimming in self-pity.

She called me in late June. Her words slurred. Sleep, emotion, booze, all of this? I couldn't be sure.

"Bowie? Did I wake you? I'm sorry, but I wanted you to know."

"Know what?"

"I'm getting married."

I felt a knot in my stomach. "That's good." She had moved to New Orleans early in the month and she was already getting married? It hit me that she had had a boyfriend there all the time and this bothered me, though I knew I had no right to such feelings.

"I hope so," she said. "I truly hope so."

What more was there to say?

"Have you tried the new pole?"

"Yes," I lied. I didn't know why, but I had put the new rod in a closet and left it there. It's never been used.

"I'm so glad," she said. "Listen, there's something I forgot to tell you in my note. There's a professor in the entomology department. His name's Nash. I hear that if there's anything to know about trout, he'd be the one to know it."

Another silent interval followed.

"Well," she said, finally breaking the silence, "I guess that's it. Bowie, there's a force inside you. You can use it or it can use you. Remember, we all get to choose."

After I entered college, I never went home to live, but I did visit every few months. After talking to Luanne for the last time, I headed home to spend several days with my folks. On Independence Day the old man and I fished the creek below the cabin and Queen Anna sat on a cedar log on the bank, shucking corn, telling us how hungry she was for fresh trout.

Dad used worms and I used the old bamboo rod with an Adams on a long leader and caught nice-sized browns more often than I deserved and Queen Anna complained bitterly that releasing the fish was "stealing from her stomach." My old man laughed out loud at her and told her to watch me and she'd see that I had become an "artiste" with my rod and artistes didn't concern themselves with their bellies. He added that he had eight browns in his creel and she wasn't going to starve.

"I don't recall anything in the Good Book about letting God's fishes go," Queen Anna proclaimed in her own defense.

"That Good Book of yours don't say anything about V-8 engines, airplanes, or apple pies with sharp cheddar cheese neither," came his rejoinder.

She was quiet after that and I was amazed to witness him challenge her and prevail.

Roger and Lilly came over late that afternoon with their year-old son, Roger Junior. Roger brought beer and when we opened a couple of bottles, Queen Anna scrinched up her face and declared for all to hear that "college is leading my son astray."

Roger said, "I never went to college."

My mother looked over at him and rolled her eyes. "*You* were always a lost cause."

Roger laughed and held a bottle up to her in salute. Queen Anna stomped into the house.

During dinner, Lilly asked what I had planned after college and I told her I'd probably look for a job with a newspaper.

"Gossip chasers," my mother announced. "You can't believe anything you read unless it's in a book. Newspaper people drink and have loose morals."

I held up a beer bottle. "I guess I'm halfway there."

My mother grimaced, my father laughed out loud, Lilly looked shocked, and Roger Ranger slapped my back in good fellowship.

I expected verbal retaliation, but instead my mother came over to me and kissed the top of my head and patted my hair and said, "You were born good to the core and that will never change."

"What about me?" Lilly asked in mock indignation.

"We'll deal with you later," my mother said in a jocular tone. I never remembered her kidding around before and it made me happy.

Lilly and I did dishes after dinner. She and Roger lived only a few miles away from the folks and I knew she would be up on local goings-on.

"Anybody hear where Raina is these days?"

Lilly frowned. "You still carrying a torch for *that* one?"

"No, I'm curious."

Lilly let the denial pass. "She left when you left and nobody's seen or heard from her since. Gus says she's off 'chasing the dream,' whatever that means."

"The" dream, not "her" dream? Odd language, but that was Gus for you. "Well, I hope she catches it."

"All that one's likely to catch are nightmares," Lilly said. "More likely, she'll be the cause of them for others."

"That's pretty harsh," I said.

My sister turned to face me. "I know you thought she was your friend, but her kind doesn't have friends. She kept you close to make sure you didn't beat her out of anything. You never thought with your brain when it came to her."

"That's not true," I insisted on Raina's behalf. And mine.

Lilly shook her head.

I felt the levity of the evening leave me.

Queen Anna came into my room as I prepared to go to bed. "I don't want you traipsing around the world," she said. "God gave me only one son."

"I have to go where the work takes me," I told her. "But I'll be careful."

"Like hell!" she said. It was the only time in my life I heard her use such language.

3

AFTER classes began in September, I called on Professor Lloyd Nash, a Lilliputian man in his early sixties with long snowy hair, a flushed face, and a soft voice. His office was in the fifty-year-old Natural Sciences Building on the old campus.

"You're the student Luanne mentioned."

I shouldn't have been surprised that she had talked to him, but I was.

"She said you'd want to fish with me."

"No, sir. The fishing I can take care of myself. What I want is to learn."

"Bugs, eh. You tie your own flies?"

"Not yet. I don't know enough."

"Boring stuff, bugs. But if you want to learn about nature and trout, I can teach you."

I had gotten the scholarship Luanne recommended me for and had a fairly substantial courseload that fall term, but in fact I spent a great deal of my study time learning about insects and fantasizing about trout fishing.

I wanted to learn, and Doc Nash was patient with me. The first thing we addressed was life cycle: how some species went from egg to nymph to adult and others from egg to larva to nymph to adult. Over the weeks we talked about size and color, shape and behavior and habitat. I had always thought that weather played a big role in fishing and Nash said it did, but mainly because meteorological conditions affected water temperature and clarity. In time I came to understand where certain insects would appear and when and how to look for them.

Nash's offices and labs were in the basement of the Nat Sci Building, just down the dingy hall from a huge, poorly lit room with a collection of entomological specimens that looked even older than the building. The Collection Room's clutter was beyond description. Display cases had been knocked over, spilling their contents. Wooden storage boxes were coated with dust and huge cobwebs that looked like muslin. The air was stale and dry. Nash called the room "the purest of chaos." We went down to the room from time to time so that he could show me something to bring home a point he had been lecturing on. He told me that the collection had been neglected for years and that time, disorder, and inattention had rendered it pretty much useless to the academicians. It would cost more to clean it up than to leave it, so there it sat. I volunteered to organize the room and Nash offered me twice the minimum wage to inventory the specimen collection. I agreed. I would have done it for nothing.

I also had a new job that term with a chain store called Discount City, a huge expanse of can't-live-withouts spread over several acres under one roof. My job was to be visible in my off-the-rack cop suit, but it was also made clear that I was not to *do* anything, my first experience with the principle of deterrence. I had no idea if my presence dissuaded shoplifters, but I tried my best to look fierce when people acted suspiciously. The pay was steady, I could pretty much name my own hours, and when I was on the job and things were slow I could hide out and study. It was one of those places where nobody talked about careers. What we had were jobs, a means of making the money we needed for what was important in our lives right then.

Over time, I gravitated to working nights at Discount City. I had classes in the mornings, and studying and bugs and working in the Collection Room in the afternoons until it was time to go to work.

It was Lloyd Nash who told me about the salmon "fiasco" (his word). The Department of Natural Resources had planted cohos in a couple of Upper Peninsula streams and they had taken hold, which apparently came as a surprise. There had never been salmon in the Great Lakes. The state's fish biologists had been rearing salmon fry in a hatchery on the Upper Peninsula to plant elsewhere to relieve the alewife problem. Back in the 1940s and 1950s alewives—small, prolific Atlantic Coast fish—had moved up the Erie and Welland Canals to propagate in the Great Lakes. This wasn't a problem at first because there were huge populations of lake trout to keep the alewives and smelt in balance. Smelt had been introduced accidentally into the Great Lakes from a private rearing pond in upper Michigan and also taken hold. Then, following the same route alewives took from the Atlantic, lamprey eels moved up and began to kill off the lake trout. As the lake trout died, alewives overpopulated and began massive spring and summer die-offs, washing up onto beaches by the tens of thousands to rot and stink, driving off tourists and disgusting locals. The cohos were intended to take care of the alewife and smelt populations for another state but some got out of the hatchery, swam out into Lake Michigan, and began to come back after that. The brood stock was from Washington State, where the fish were born in rivers, moved into the ocean to grow, and came back up the freshwater rivers when it was time to spawn. Here they were in fresh water all their lives and the fish biologists were astounded when the salmon thrived.

"When man begins to tinker with nature, the results are not predictable," Nash declared. "And they are invariably disastrous."

"Do the salmon take flies?" I asked Nash.

"You should see for yourself," Nash declared with a harrumph and told me where to find the fish. That was the end of that conversation.

I knew a couple of guys majoring in forestry, Mike McGinn from Vermont and Eddie Moody from Georgia. It's funny how people with similar interests gravitate to each other. I had met several guys during my years at MSU who were trouters and I had fished with some of them. Mostly I fished alone, but occasionally I went with McGinn and Moody, who were inseparable pals, good fishermen, and pretty good company. I mentioned salmon to them and both of them had heard about the fish but didn't know much about them. I suggested we head north to take a look, so we loaded McGinn's Volkswagen bus and drove to the U.P. It was mid-October.

According to Nash, the fish were spawning in Thompson Creek, a two-hour drive west of St. Ignace and the Straits of Mackinac. There was a village where the creek dumped into Lake Michigan; upstream the DNR had a hatchery where the fish had been raised. We were miles away when we began to see campers parked along U.S. 2. There were lights and fires on the beaches and the running lights of boats off shore. The village of Thompson had a population of maybe a hundred people, but it looked like a Saturday-night crowd at Olympia Stadium when we pulled in around midnight. The boat launch was backed up for miles to the west. State troopers and county cops tried to direct traffic but were obviously overwhelmed by the crowds. Shadows crossed the road in front of us. We saw people running, shouting, and laughing boisterously. It was a grand and ugly carnival.

At daylight we made our way down to the big lake. We had to hike over an expanse of dunes and when we got closer to the water we heard a low buzz, like a huge bee, and when we stepped over the last sand barrier I stopped and sank to my knees. There were hundreds of fishermen in the surf, all of them shoulder to shoulder, with long stiff rods. You could hear their lines buzzing as they threw heavily weighted lures. The air sounded like there was an electric current whipping around. Now and then someone would scream, "Fish on!" and the snagged salmon would cut across dozens of lines, tangling them all. Despite the mess, fish were being landed and tossed on the beach, where they flopped around, flashes of dying silver in the morning light, sand clinging to them like bread crumbs.

There were two pickup trucks on the beach with aluminum beer kegs in their beds; beer went for a buck for a small paper cup. Guys in rubber hip boots stumbled around, screaming like animals. I saw two behemoths in red plaid hunting jackets suddenly grab each other and fists flew and so many other people were so close that they started punching out of self-preservation. I backed away and stood there with my mouth agape. A cop car wallowed through the dunes with its siren wailing, only to get stuck. The deputies scrambled out and threw themselves into the brawl with their billies and I saw somebody grab a fish by the tail and smack one of the cops in the side of the head, spinning his hat away like a Frisbee. McGinn shouted, "Un-fucking-believable. This is *great!*"

I did not fish. The surf fishermen were slinging treble hooks the size of walnuts; the hooks had been soldered to pyramid-shaped one- and two-ounce lead weights that cast like bullets and hit the water like depth charges. Several men had bloody arms, having been snagged on sloppy backcasts, and there was one man—somebody said he was a doctor—who stitched several wounds while the victims sat on blue-and-white ice chests filled with fish, their tails sticking out, shouting, "Hurry up, for Chrissakes, the fish are out there!" His fee was one dollar a stitch and he had a huge jar filled with dollar bills and dark bloodstains on the sand by his cooler.

This was not fishing and these were not human beings.

Not long after the sun came up, the wind began to blow at near-gale force. There were hundreds of boats off the beach, some barely beyond the reach of surfcasters. At the mouth of Thompson Creek there were so many boats that the surface of Lake Michigan nearly disappeared. There were thirty-foot cabin cruisers and varnished wooden Chris Crafts and aluminum boats and prams and two red-and-white dinghies that bobbed like corks and wooden rowboats and dented canoes, craft of every description mixed together in a giant flotilla. The bulging, rolling surf banged them together and metal thumped and scraped and grated and a pall of blue-gray exhaust raced over them as the wind intensified. Ragged whitecaps rose up and began to break against the beach. Boats began to roll and pitch as the swells grew to more than six feet and canoes flopped toward the beach like abandoned surfboards. The surfmen kept casting and reeling. A small cabin cruiser began to smoke and more cop cars and even a fire engine tried to come through the dunes, but sank to their axles. Uniformed men stumbled out of the vehicles and through the dunes, their service revolvers drawn, shielding their eyes against blowing sand.

I had no idea where McGinn and Moody were and didn't much care. When I got up to the road, there was a faded red bus with a hand-painted sign on the side that said PUSSY: $20 and a woman grabbed my arm as I

THE SNOWFLY ❖ 39

passed the bus and said, "You want some?" As I pulled away she said, "You're beautiful, honey, I'll blow you for nothing." I kept going until I found the VW and got in as the sky darkened. Ambulances and fire engines began arriving from the east. I lay in the van and I knew I had seen something that I did not care to ever see again.

This was not sport. It reminded me of accounts I had read of buffalo hunting. I had witnessed something I'd previously only heard and read about: mob mentality, where some sort of group psychology overrides individual conscience. Intellectually I thought I could comprehend the mind-set of a lynch mob, or similar group, pursuing a killer, but a bunch of men chasing fish? It was frightening and I wanted no part of any of it.

Most of the fish were being taken with snagging rigs. In the years that followed, snagging would be outlawed and the blood-crazed insanity of Thompson Creek would become a thing of the past.

My companions eventually came back, dragging four huge salmon. There had been no room for them on the beach, but they had bought a few of the lethal weighted hooks, called spiders, off some of the butchers on the beach and, not wanting to risk eyes and ears, had gone upstream and made their luck there. The salmon were black and where the spider hooks had caught hold, there were gaping pink-and-white tears, chunks gone. They claimed to have tried flies to no avail and quickly abandoned them for spiders, reasoning that a twenty-pound salmon was a good reason to choose effectiveness over sport. When we returned to East Lansing I would never fish with them again. I thought I was immune to big-fish fever and didn't want to be contaminated by those who lacked the willpower to resist. I was a self-righteous fool.

Back at school when I next saw my bug mentor, Nash asked what I thought about what I had seen. There was so much inside me that I stood mute while he looked me over. He gave me his sternest look and said, "Therein lies the road to trophy fish. When the state gives the people what they want, this is how it turns out. Salmon don't belong here. When we start to mess with the natural order, it always turns bad. Trust in nature, son. She provides all the miracles we can handle. If you want to chase big fish, you're on your own."

The period before Christmas at Discount City was shoplifter season. A state trooper briefed the security team on surveillance procedures and once again we were told that despite our elevated knowledge, we should continue to refrain from any in-store confrontations. If we saw a theft, we were to call the Ingham County Sheriff's Department and they would take care of it. Like many plans I've confronted in life, this one was solid on paper and that's as far as it went. Ingham County was financially strapped. Cop patrols were reduced. Bodily harm might get a response in ten minutes, but shoplifting? Not a chance.

There was a small employee break room in the rear of the building. It had picnic tables and several vending machines. As a rule, most employees were not friendly. We were paid barely more than the minimum wage, and turnover was high. Over the months I saw a few faces that seemed to endure, and we who endured naturally gravitated to each other. As with trout chasers.

Security worked in pairs. My partner, Rick Fistrip, was a senior from Flint enrolled in the criminal justice program at State. I usually saw him when we punched in and again when we punched out. He was always in a hurry and worried about scuffing his gleaming black Corfams.

From time to time I saw customers acting suspiciously; eventually I decided they were mostly just normal people made nervous around uniforms and badges. I'd relate what I saw to Fistrip at punch-out and he'd say, "Yeah, yeah, I saw."

The first time we met he asked if I was a student. I confirmed I was in journalism, which elicited a look of the sort reserved for a dog rocket on a Grosse Pointe sidewalk.

"Why would you want to be one of those assholes? Reporters obstruct justice or get in the way."

We did not care for each other and over several months we rarely spoke. The funny thing was that even though we worked the same shifts I never saw him from punch-in to punch-out. It was one of life's small mysteries, the sort that make you scratch your chin for a moment before you move on to other concerns.

One Friday night I was in the break room when a woman from the jewelry department came in. Her name was Spruce Graham. She was thirty-one and had three kids. She didn't look much over twenty. She had a fully developed figure, with a soft-roundedness I found appealing. Her husband was a Bootstrapper at the university, an Army enlisted man of promise sent off to get a college degree at taxpayer expense. Spruce had never finished high school. Married at sixteen, she was clearly awed by her husband's current undertaking. She was from rural Alabama and had a slow drawl and relaxed air.

"Nice uniform," she said, lighting a cigarette. Her long fingers had perfect nails.

"Clown suit," I said.

"No, it looks real nice, you bein' so tall and all. I like a man in uniform."

I smiled and thanked her.

"Seen your partner lately?" she asked.

"Fistrip? He's around somewhere."

It would be some time later before I would realize that she had been trying to tell me something.

Spruce and I didn't run into each other every night at first, but eventually we seemed to arrive at breaks at the same time. When she wasn't there I wondered what happened to her.

"Had a sick kid," she'd say the next night. Or, "The cellar flooded." She talked a lot about her children, three boys; the oldest was fifteen. She worked part time, six to midnight, Monday through Friday. "My man's home by six. I make supper, but he feeds the boys and puts the youngest to bed and then he studies. He has to study hard. I can pick up a few dollars to help out and he gets the quiet he needs to hit the books."

At the end of the shifts, I'd change out of my uniform and walk out to the nearly empty parking lot. I began to notice that after work, Spruce would go out to her car and sit there alone, smoking.

I asked why.

"Well, I sit here another hour to give my husband his space. School comes first, after the kids. It's his future." His, not ours, a curious word choice.

I invited myself to smoke with her after work one night. A few days later we repeated the episode. By then I knew her pretty well. Her father owned a paint store in Eufala and was a part-time Baptist minister. She had enjoyed high school, had been a cheerleader, two years varsity, "before I got knocked up." I sensed unspoken regrets.

She lived in married-student housing in a section reserved for Bootstrap families. The government paid their rent, which helped the students immensely. Of military life Spruce said, "It has its points. I can't complain." They had lived in Spain and Panama and in Texas just before her husband got his Bootstrap assignment.

Several times she came to work with puffy, red eyes and was less talkative than usual.

Nash, meanwhile, had stopped lecturing me. Instead he gave me books and handed over his dog-eared fishing log, in which he had recorded every detail of his outings, including sky conditions, wind direction (and sometimes velocity), air temperature, hourly water-temperature readings, estimates of water level, flow (in feet per second), and clarity, for which he had his own descriptions. He did not reveal where he caught fish. All streams and rivers were coded and the key wasn't in the log, which I observed with interest. Nash meticulously used a stomach pump to check the feeding habits of his take and gave the usual details about length and girth. He did not specify which artificial flies he used; rather, he recorded which species were actually hatching and when and on what kind of water. It was a journal devoid of color and touched by paranoia. Passionate trout fishermen, I was learning, did not willingly give up their secrets.

I continued my efforts to return order to the cluttered Collection Room in the Natural Sciences Building. I tried to convince myself that I was driven by simple curiosity, but the truth was that I hoped that somewhere in that chaos lay a specimen called a snowfly and, if it was there, I was convinced I would find it. I wanted to ask Nash about the snowfly, but couldn't bring myself to do it. He was a gentle, scholarly entomologist who liked to cogitate before he talked. It was as if words were too expensive to spend thoughtlessly. He seemed feeble and cautious and I had a hard time picturing him in a trout stream, much less feeling in his gut what gripped me when I was thigh-deep in fast, clear, cold water.

The collection of specimens was immense, but I was patient and methodical, starting just inside the door and working my way along the east wall. I pulled out every case, opened it, cleaned it, and made a list, numbering each box and specifying its contents. Some were already labeled; I used Nash's texts and reference books to verify these as accurate and several times found mistakes and reported these to him, which seemed to please him. "Becoming a real bug man," he told me. I also used the references for unlabeled specimens but many times I had to take these to Nash. He wouldn't tell me what they were; rather, he would take me through an entomological checklist so that I could get the family and then he would leave it to me to go from there. It was slow going and it consumed me.

I was barely into the mess when I hit several boxes of arachnids, mostly tarantulas collected in Central America. In another case I found a family of mice that scampered for cover, but eventually came back to see what I was up to. I talked to them as pets. It occurred to me that I should get somebody in to eliminate them, but they were doing no harm I could discern. Those were the days when the term *peaceful coexistence* was in vogue, and I simply extended the concept down the evolutionary ladder.

Despite it being my senior year, I was also having second thoughts about college. I had been busting my ass for four years and it was not at all clear where this was going to take me, and I naturally began to wonder why the hell I had endured it. I had completed the basic J-school courses, which were heavy on writing, English literature, poly sci, and history, all of which required a lot of tedious reading. I also decided early on to learn Russian and was in my fourth year with the language. The Cold War was on, and it was real to all of us. As far as the world was concerned, there were only two major countries, the Soviet Union and the U.S. It made sense that if I wanted to travel as a journalist, I ought to speak Russian. But it was a grueling routine: sleep, school, Nash, work, study. Balanced, it wasn't. And there were days when the point of all the effort eluded me.

One night I joined Spruce in her car after work. She was chain-smoking, which was unusual.

I was getting to know her pretty well and I liked being able to read her moods.

"Problem?"

She glanced at me then looked straight ahead. "I don't think we should be doin' this," she said. "Anymore."

I thought she was joking. "Sitting in the car together?"

"Yes."

"Why not?"

"Because I don't think it's best."

I was amused as much as anything.

"Best for what?"

"You ask too many questions, Bowie. I think it would just be best if we don't."

She was nervous and tight. "What's going on, Spruce?"

"*Him,*" she whispered.

I had to think. "Your husband?"

"Right." She rolled down her window, tossed the butt, and lit another. "He's crazy."

I suddenly had no further curiosity. "Okay." When I reached for the door handle, she caught my arm and pulled me back.

"He's real jealous."

"Of me?" I felt queasy.

"He doesn't even know you exist."

This was good news in an otherwise bleak moment.

I didn't have a lot of experience with married women. There was Lilly, but she was about all, and Spruce seemed at least as happy as my sister. I'd never heard anything but respect for her man in Spruce's voice.

"He thinks I'm foolin' around. Somebody told 'im that every night I sit in my car with a man. I think maybe it was Rick."

"Fistrip?"

"Yeah, he's been hustlin' me and I haven't given him the time of day and I think he's seen us and he's jealous."

"Fistrip? What is that guy's problem? We haven't done anything," I said.

"Facts don't matter to jealous men, Bowie."

I felt uneasy again and quickly said, "It's not like we sit together every night." Panic can make us nitpickers. I hated riding the guilty seat when I was totally innocent.

"Don't worry," she said. "He doesn't know your name. I said you were just a friend, but he's always been real jealous. He scares me when he gets like this. He was a sniper in the Army and you know what they're like."

I said, "I don't want to be the source of a problem for you. If this is mis-interpreted, then that's easy enough to fix."

She looked at me. "You don't understand. I *like* talkin' with you. I love sittin' here with you. You always listen to what I've got to say, as if you're really interested in me, and part of me would surely like to do more than just talk."

Full panic set in. I opened the door. "I'll just get out. I'm sorry about this."

She grabbed my arm again. "I'm real sorry. I wish there was somewhere else we could go."

It took a few seconds for her words to sink in. I looked back at her, but she was fumbling with the key. It was time for me to go.

New Year's Eve afternoon I was back in the secure environs of the Collection Room.

I breathed in the musty air and found it mildly calming. I spent most of the day checking the identities of grasshoppers (Acrididae, Tettigoniidae, et cetera) and took a lot of time looking at them and thinking about what Doc Nash had said about them as trout bait. They start to show up in late June and tend to be dark and small, and by summer's end they tend to be light in color and large. Nash loved hoppers and called them "caviar for trout." He reminded me to always make sure a hopper fly had some red in it, and sure enough I found that all the naturals had some red. It was fascinating to see the reality of insects beginning to merge with my knowledge of artificial flies. And to begin to recognize cycles: Fish grow over the course of the season, and so do the crustaceans, minnows, and insects they eat.

About ninety minutes before I had to report to work I found a box with six unlabeled, very large artificial flies. The box was on the floor in the corner along the west wall, buried under a pile of cardboard boxes filled with specimen boxes and capture jars. I saw the corner of the box because it threw a knife-shaped shadow onto the floor, seemingly out of darkness. Naturally, I had to find out what it was. The bugs were white and a little yellowed with age but way too big for *Ephoron leukon*. There were no labels. Between my Sundays in the library back home as a kid and my time with Nash I had a pretty good sense of what was what. I searched all around for labels but all I found, scored into the bottom of the case with a woodburner, were the initials MJK.

I opened the box and studied the six flies; they were very different from each other and all of them old. A couple of them were attached to flimsy-looking green hooks. After a few minutes, I realized the hooks had to be made of brass. Somewhere I had read that brass hooks were used around the turn of the century, which convinced me these flies were ancient. One of them still had a couple of inches of gut attached to it as well, and gut bodies had gone out—when, the 1930s? Not academic specimens, but a box of fishing flies. Not much value scientifically, perhaps, but they'd have worth to a tackle collector or museum. What were they doing here? I imagined one of the bug docs had been in a hurry one day and left them in the room, and I laughed when I thought how pissed he would've been when he got to the river and had no flies. I toyed with the notion of liberating the flies, but decided that this would violate Doc Nash's trust. What I did was bury the box in the clutter. As far as I knew, nobody but me went into the Collection Room, but I had a hunch about the gargantuan white flies and I wanted them safe until I could talk to Nash. I hid them in such a way that nobody was going to accidentally find them: I placed the box inside a box inside a box and then stacked other debris on top.

I spent a lot of time thinking about them after they were hidden. What weight of line and leader would be needed to cast such things? More important, what size of fish would rise to them? Maybe the flies were an elaborate joke from a former time. Or not a joke at all. I had never seen a fly in nature even a third the size of these. Even the huge and nocturnal *Hexagenia limbata*, what Michiganders called a "fishfly" or "Michigan Caddis," were dwarfed by the mysterious white flies. Nash and his wife were in Florida for the holidays; I couldn't wait for him to get back to campus. Surely he would know what they were.

There were days in the years ahead when I would wish I had never found the damn things.

I was in a pretty fair mood when I got to work. As soon as I punched the clock I went looking for Spruce, but she wasn't in the jewelry section. It was a night when we were shortstaffed in anticipation of low customer interest. It didn't make sense to be open at all, but the company was willing to pay and I was happy to accept its money.

All the sales clerks were wearing party hats to put customers into a celebratory state of mind. My uniformed status made me exempt, which pleased me. I had never been one for forced joviality; in fact, I had always found that fun and trout fishing had much in common, not the least being that the best times seemed to arrive by serendipity.

At break there was still no sign of Spruce. I went back to the jewelry department. The clerk there was a young, rotund student with a pink party hat. He was wearing makeup, including blazing red lipstick, false eyelashes, and earrings. He saw me staring.

"Do I look okay?"

"That has to be your call, not mine."

He chewed his top lip. "It's New Year's Eve. I'm going to a costume party."

I said, "Good for you. Missus Graham got the night off?"

He gave me the once-over. He looked puzzled. "You mean Spruce?"

"Right, Missus Graham."

"She's in back, doing inventory."

"I thought inventory was done on the floor."

"Every department except jewelry."

I didn't ask where to find her, but felt his eyes on my back as I walked away. I didn't know why, but I had doubts about whether she would want to see me. More important, I wasn't sure I wanted to see her. Our last conversation had left me shaken, yet here I was seeking her out. I was Icarus ascending. I pushed all the alarms aside and decided I needed company.

Our night manager was a former navy petty officer and retired Oldsmobile worker named Jolson. People were always saying "Mammy" under their breath when he went by. Most nights he stayed in his office, but tonight he was on the floor and cruising directly at me.

"Mister Rhodes, there you are. I can't find Mister Fistrip. Hike back to the cage. Missus Graham has informed me that there's a problem with the lighting. Skeleton staff tonight, Mister Rhodes. You know where the electrical panels are?"

"Yes, sir."

"Good. Go and do your duty, Mister Rhodes." He dismissed me with a wave of his hand, pivoted, and swooped back toward his office.

The cage was a secure room surrounded by floor-to-ceiling walls of heavy-gauge black wire. The warehouse was even larger than the sales floor and one side seemed to be dark, but there were a few lights on nearest the cage. I wondered what the problem was.

I had no key for the secure room. "Spruce?" I rattled the wire walls with the palms of my hands.

"Don't be making such a dang racket."

The voice was behind me, in the darkness. "Spruce?"

"Hush and come on over here."

"I've got a flashlight."

"We won't need that."

"Mammy said you had a light problem."

"I made that up so you'd come on back."

"Coulda been Fistrip as easily as me."

"God, Bowie. You are so dang *thick* sometimes. Rick clocks in and leaves the store. Then he comes back to punch out," she said. "He gets paid for workin' when he's not even here."

I stared at her for a long time, trying to grasp all that she was telling me.

She rolled her eyes. "You're *so* blind, Bowie."

"He leaves every night?" I still couldn't believe it. Didn't want to accept it. How had I missed this?

"Just about. He's a real creep, Bowie. Do you know he's gonna be an officer in the army when he graduates?"

"I thought he was going to be a cop."

"He wants to be an army hero first and get what he calls merit badges."

Queen Anna and the old man had taught us that when you worked for someone, you did the job to the best of your ability. To do less, they said, was theft, which by their measure made Fistrip, the would-be cop and officer, a practicing thief.

Spruce Graham smelled of fresh lilacs and was so close I felt cocooned by her perfume.

"How's your husband?" I asked.

"Not here," she whispered.

The alarms sounded in my head again. I was shaking. "He's not Super-man."

"Not hardly," she said. "He can't see through cinder-block walls."

I could barely hear her.

"Alone at last, but we can't smoke," I said, trying to make a joke.

She didn't say anything. We were both tense with anticipation and lightheaded. I needed words, the *right* words.

"Maybe there's something we could do here that we couldn't do in the car."

"Could be," she said. "Were you thinking of something in particular?"

You learn by experience. With some women, it's the man's job to make the first move.

I put my finger under her chin and lifted gently.

Our kiss was soft and sweet and long. When it was finished, she put her hands on my chest and pushed me gently away.

"Sorry," I said. A programmed response.

She touched her finger to my lips. "Hush," she said. "I never cheated before."

I felt a surge of guilt and tried to apologize again, but she stopped me. "It's not like it feels like a sin or anything. I just don't want to get caught. Can you understand that?"

I understood her husband was trained in the use of weapons. I didn't want to get caught either.

"Bowie, my husband hasn't touched me since last June. Do you think I'm ugly?"

"No way."

"All he thinks about is school and becomin' an officer. Here it is New Year's Eve and he's *studyin'*. Dammit, I've got needs, Bowie. Big needs. It's healthy to have needs. Maybe when school's finished, things'll be better for him and me, but right now I've just got these-here needs and he's studyin'. Y'all understand?

"I got this girlfriend," she went on. "Julianna? Her hubby's also a Boot-strapper and she's goin' through the same thing so she took her a boyfriend on the side? She keeps tellin' me go ahead and do it, but I just don't want to get caught."

"Well, if you're not sure," I muttered, stepping back. What was I sup-posed to say?

"Geez, Bowie." She let out a loud sigh. "You're thick as cold chicken fat."

Which was her final comment of the evening. I had blown it. She retreated a few steps and tripped the circuit breaker so that the warehouse was bathed in light. She went back to her inventory and I went off to patrol the floors with rubber legs and a pounding heart.

Nash returned three days later and invited me over to his house on Friday night to eat some redfish he had brought back with him. I went to the Collection Room to retrieve the white flies. I looked at the hiding area and it looked undisturbed, but when I dug down into the pile, I could not find the wooden box. At first I thought I'd misplaced them, but that couldn't be. I tried to remain calm and began moving everything in sight, but the flies were gone. I had Nash's key. As far as I knew, only the janitor had another key. There was no other conclusion: Somebody had broken in and stolen the fly box.

When I got to Doc Nash's house I was in a lousy mood. I should have stolen the white flies. At least I would still have them.

Nash grilled the redfish and told me about fishing he'd done in Florida. "Bonefish," he said. "Talk about energy and efficiency. Like catching an artillery shell."

This was as lyrical as I'd ever heard him on the subject of fishing. He was peeling from sunburn and his hair seemed whiter.

I told him about the white flies.

"What species?"

"Not specimens, trout flies. Huge things."

"In with the specimens?"

"In a wooden box marked on the bottom with the letters *MJK*."

He nodded solemnly. "It's been a long time since I was familiar with exactly what's in there. A lot of my colleagues dump stuff there. Always have. Entomological detritus. All faculty members have keys."

My assumption of a break-in wasn't necessarily right. Still, they didn't fly off on their own: *Somebody* took them. That fact was indisputable. I got paper and rendered some sketches.

He looked at them and shook his head. "Insufficient data," he said.

"They were there," I said. "Now they're gone. I thought they might be snowflies."

I watched him closely to gauge his reaction. Nash grinned, "Snowflies, eh? Maybe it's nothing, but a scientist learns to embrace coincidence." We went to his library and withdrew two thin volumes from a shelf. The first was called *On the Habits of Trout & Their Environs*. The author was M. J. Key and the publication date was 1892. The second volume was called *Trouts of the Americas* and dated 1943. The author was also M. J. Key.

The publication dates were more than a half century apart.

"Key," he said, "was a controversial professor here when we were still an agricultural college. That's about all I know about him. Key's trout works were ahead of their time. Barbless hooks, light tackle, catch-and-release, and habitat management rather than hatchery fish. He was a genius and outspoken in his views, and because of this, a lot of people thought he was a nut case. Maybe he was."

What did this have to do with white flies? I said, "He wrote two books, fifty-one years apart?"

"Who knows? There aren't many people left now who knew him, but those who did say Key was a mistrusting and almost pathologically secretive individual. He left the college under some kind of scandal in the late nineteen-thirties. Some say FDR called him to government duty, and others say he was run out. Nobody knows for certain. The college was informed by the government that he died during the war, but there were no details, not even a date. He was a foreigner and spoke German, so maybe he was a spy or in the intelligence business. His second work could've been posthumous. I guess we'll never know."

"The flies could have been his."

Nash nodded solemnly. "That's one hypothesis among many possibilities."

"Did he write anything else?"

"Nothing I've read," Nash said. "You can borrow my copies of his books if you like."

I did.

Several weeks passed and I had worked hard to get more information on M. J. Key, but I hadn't assembled all that much. On microfilm at the university library I managed to find some clippings from the *Lansing State Journal* saying that Key had been accused of Nazi sympathies and had been asked to leave the college. While there wasn't much on Key the man, his work—despite its consisting of only two books—was cited and quoted just about anytime somebody wrote seriously about trout fishing. I read the books rather quickly because they were pretty thin with tight, sparse sentences. Whoever Key was, he seemed to be a shade, a figure from the past, lost forever. But I kept thinking there had to be more about him somewhere. There was no mention of the snowfly in his books, but I had found the flies and the box with his initials; it had to be more than a coincidence.

The state of Michigan had a massive central library in downtown Lansing. I often went there for books because it was closer to my apartment and a lot less crowded than the university's facility. Buddy Wilihapulus worked in the research section. He had come to East Lansing to play football for Duffy Daugherty, the first recruit out of Duffy's fabled Pineapple Pipeline, but Buddy had blown out a knee, which ended his football career. He had lost weight since his football days but remained an astonishing specimen at six-four and 250 pounds Coke-bottled around a narrow waist. Buddy's hair was cut short in a severe flattop, and he had bad skin but a perennial smile and a soft voice. We had been in some journalism classes together.

"Bruddah Bowie," he greeted me. "What're you thinking about this Vietnam business?"

I knew Kennedy had sent a bunch of army advisers into the country and that some sort of civil war was going on. "I haven't," I said.

"Maybe you should. They could draft your *haole* ass."

Draft? I had done two years of mandatory ROTC, my class the last to have to suffer through it. We had taken it as a joke and massive waste of time.

"Head of the state draft board comes in here to hide from his old lady. He say numbers be goin' up, bruddah. *Serious* numbers. Blood gonna flow."

My last night at Discount City Spruce Graham sought me out. We had not smoked together in weeks and had barely talked. She looked tired.

"It's nearly graduation?" she asked.

"End of the term."

"What're you gonna do afterward?"

"I'm not sure yet." The truth was that I was so caught up in classes, M. J. Key, and the subject of snowflies that I hadn't really gotten around to looking for a job. I could smell her lilacs.

She hesitated. "This is your last night?"

I nodded.

"Do you think I can have your address?"

"Are we going to be pen pals?" I blurted out. It was a cheap shot, born in frustration, but she ignored it.

"I was thinkin' I can get tomorrow night off from work and come on over to your place. I promise I won't go loony. About six be okay?"

I nodded dumbly.

Spruce arrived promptly at six and ten minutes later we were undressed and in bed, where we stayed until midnight. We made love like neither of us would ever get another chance. We both knew, without talking about it, that this was our one time and we made the most of it.

On her way out she said, "My husband's not gonna go through the graduation ceremony. He says he has the paper and that's all that matters.

We're headed out a week after the last exam is done. Back down to Texas. He's got more trainin' ahead of him."

I wished her well and meant it. I learned from Spruce that people can be very different in different circumstances and that some people become trapped in their own lives. Back then I thought maybe that getting trapped was more a problem for women, but I was young. Now I know it can happen to anybody. And that there are all sorts of traps, the snowfly being just one of them.

Queen Anna died suddenly the day after Spruce and her family left for Texas. She and the old man had made it to East Lansing for my graduation and she had cried all weekend and gone home and died. Her heart stopped and her death nearly stopped mine as well. Doctors could not figure out why she died and in the end, what did it matter?

The call came from my sister, Lilly.

We did not go to a church for the funeral.

Father Luke was a retired Episcopalian priest who lived a mile down Whirling Creek. He drove up at noon, still wearing his waders. The grave would be on a knoll on the north end of the property. The old man said it was what Queen Anna wanted. Lilly and I had our doubts because, unlike our father, our mother was a regular churchgoer, but we were not willing to challenge the old man. He'd let her have her way as long as we could remember and now he wanted to have his way and that seemed fair. Besides, he knew her better than anyone.

The Chickermans came in the company of a dark-haired beauty with wild blue eyes and sharp features. It was Raina and I could not take my eyes off her.

Father Luke read a prayer and once stopped to pick a large yellow stonefly off the Good Book. He held it up and examined it studiously before flicking it away. When the prayer was done, he looked up.

"Anyone care to speak?"

There was an astonishingly large crowd at the ceremony. My mother had done good deeds all her life and only then, at her funeral, did I realize the impact her life had had on others. People began stepping forward one after another and after a while I had to sit down. My mother hadn't been a queen; she'd been a saint.

When the last person had spoken, the priest looked expectantly at my father.

"Poor bastard," my old man muttered.

"Who?" Father Luke asked. He looked worried.

"God. She'll turn Heaven to Hell."

"You have no cause to say that," the priest said.

"What do you know?" the old man shot back. "I lived it."

Lilly and I just smiled at each other. After we got through greeting mourners, I looked for Raina and the Chickermans but they were gone. I drove over to the store hoping to catch them, but they weren't there either.

Raina's sudden appearance and disappearance left me wanting to reconnect with her. I didn't care what Lilly thought of her. She had been my friend. I knew that in my heart. In the years to follow I would learn that what's in our hearts may not be in others'.

4

IT was early August 1966, nearly midnight on a Saturday night. The temperature had been in the nineties for ten days, humidity thick as Saran Wrap, unrelenting even after sunset. I was working part time at an auto parts store called Sulac Automotive and also getting sporadic assignments from the *Lansing State Journal*. It was stringer's work, paid by the published inch, but I thought it would look good in my portfolio. Other professions emphasized résumés and academic records, but if you wanted a reporting job you had to have proof that you could write. And the only proof that mattered was what actually made it into print.

A small flat roof outside my bedroom served as a porch. Some nights I slept right there, where a little movement in the night air made the humidity tolerable. I had a phone installed illegally by an acquaintance in electrical engineering.

I was in no mood to go out when the call came, but neither was the heat conducive to sleep.

"Rhodes?"

"Talking."

"Madill. Get your ass down to the Bellamy Building. You know where that is?"

"Yep." Madill was an assistant city editor and my benefactor at the *Journal*.

"Got your credentials?"

"Somewhere."

"Find them and go get me a story, Rhodes."

The Bellamy Building was the major landmark a few blocks north of the Capitol. The area had once been home to Lansing's elite. Now it was the anchor of a sort of quasi-middle-class neighborhood, a mix of black and white families, some on their way up, others headed in the opposite direction. I found trucks and buses unloading dozens of cops who formed a serpentine single file, making their way past dozens of anodized trash cans stuffed with new ax handles. They looked like cans of kindling. Each cop took a handle out of a can and moved on. The cops wore military helmets with stainless-steel covers, heavy black leather jackets, and black gloves.

Shoulder patches told me that the officers were from departments all over the area. Something big and sinister was unfolding. There is no sweeter scent to an aspiring reporter.

I saw Reg Bernard, a Lansing cop I knew.

"What's up?" I asked him.

"Race riot."

"What's that mean?"

"It means some boofers have fucked the pooch. There was a party. It got noisy and out of hand. Deputy Chief Williams went over there to tell them to keep it down and some splib hit him with a brick. Fractured his skull."

There were cops strung out to the left and right of me. Every fifth or sixth man carried a powerful flashlight. The cops with the ax handles were banging them on the asphalt.

"What're you going to do?"

"Sweep the area," he said with a shrug. "Our orders are to disperse the crowd and collar resisters."

The area west of us looked dark. House lights were out and many streetlights weren't working.

"Don't get out in front of the line," Bernard warned me. "This will not be pretty."

The sweep commenced with a babel of whistles to my left and right.

The cops continued to hammer their clubs on the street, against trees, on everything in their path. The vibrating clamor reminded me of a rattlesnake's final warning to intruders.

Cops in the street waited for those going through yards to re-form the line, which advanced quickly and relentlessly.

To my right I heard shouts and some shrieks, and the ever-present tattoo of ax handles.

Ahead there was darkness.

Eventually I left the main formation and worked my way into a group of cops moving through backyards; from there I raced ahead of them to see what it was they were actually after.

I ran to get breathing room and didn't stop until I was a block ahead.

"What the hell you doin', kid?" a voice asked nervously from a driveway.

"I'm a reporter."

"You fucked. Shiny hats be catchin' your ass out here."

"What's going on?"

"It got to have a name? It the same thing always goin' down here."

"I heard a deputy chief got hurt."

"Hear lotta shit when big sticks be goin' bip-bap, man. Ain't no hurt depatee chief. They just got the bloods worked up. You best step on over here wid us."

What happened next has never been entirely clear to me. Behind me there was a fracas, several scuffles, curses, the sounds of sticks. Police lights knifed through the darkness. I had always imagined that a head struck by something solid would have a mushy, hollow sound. It didn't. It sounded like the ax handles were striking oak beams.

The sound of struggles grew steadily like a night hatch of skittering flies and hungry fish. Shadows melded with shadows. I sensed hurried movement all around me, but no sounds of fear. Men cursed and shouted, grunted and barked, all the sounds muted and workmanlike, the sounds of commitment. On both sides.

A light beam swept me seconds before someone shoved me from behind, knocking me down, then there was the leaden stamp of feet around me and I could smell hate and sweat and a light beamed into my face and an angry and surprised voice said, "*Rhodes?* You piece of shit! Still porking that good old southern poon? Hold that asshole right there."

There was no mistaking the voice or the message. Rick Fistrip. I had no time to contemplate my recognition because fire erupted in my forearms. Then in my head.

I awoke in white. A man in white speckled with blood sat in a chair nursing an unlit pipe. "How you feelin'?"

"I'm not."

"That's the dope," he said. "You will. Concussion. Both your arms are broken. No ID. Who are you?"

I gave my name, explained that I was a reporter.

"How'd you get caught in that mess?"

I wasn't sure I could explain it. I had pushed out ahead and gotten myself enmeshed.

"Gonna have to get positive ID on you," the man said apologetically.

I gave him the name of my contact at the paper.

Madill showed up with his tie tucked between the third and fourth buttons of a starched white shirt. He had yellow-green sweat stains under his arms. "He's mine," he told the doctor and a cop, who was standing at the door.

He turned to me. "I said *get* the story, Rhodes. Not *be* the story. They really worked you over, son."

I told him to write down what I said. The lead began, "Tonight police swept side by side through West Lansing, using pristine ax handles to club anybody in their path. They came, they claimed, to restore peace. From where I stood, it looked like they destroyed it. A lot of people are concerned about our deepening involvement in Vietnam, but it looks to me as if the real war could be right here, and just as nasty." It was one of the most prophetic statements I ever authored.

Madill looked at me. "Jesus Christ, kid. I like the 'me' angle. Keep it rolling."

I did.

The story made the *Journal*'s front page. It wasn't the precise story I wrote, but my facts and most of my observations were there and I got a check for fifty dollars and a prognosis of full recovery, casts off in eight to twelve weeks. I left out the part about Fistrip. I wanted to handle that separately.

The paper covered all my medical bills. The morning I got out of the hospital I went directly to the police station and learned that Fistrip, who was part of some sort of police auxiliary that had been mobilized for the event, had indeed been involved. I filed a complaint. I told a lieutenant that Fistrip had put a light in my face, spoken my name, and then I had been beaten. I also told him what Fistrip had said about reporters when we first met at Discount City. I said nothing about Spruce Graham. The lieutenant nodded with mock interest and nothing more came of it. At least not then.

I had seen the heart of two mobs in my short life; I didn't like either one and had no inkling that the worst was yet to come.

Labor Day week I got my draft notice and called home. The old man talked to a friend at the local draft board, told him what had happened, and got my government physical postponed until I had a medical release from the riot injuries.

A week later I had another visitor.

Grady Yetter wore a suit like it was a vise. The fingers of his left hand were yellow from nicotine, his voice hoarse.

"You Rhodes?"

I nodded.

"Madill called me. We did Korea together. Read me the story you wrote. Piss you off, they didn't use it the way you wrote it?" He didn't pause for my answer. "That's a local rag for you," he said with a sarcastic chuckle. "Guard the status quo like a virgin's cherry. The first-person wrinkle threw them for a loop. It was a damn good story, Rhodes. I talked to Joe Lawler out at the college. He said you've got talent. You want a job?"

Joe Lawler was my academic adviser at MSU. "Doing what?"

"UPI, Rhodes. War correspondent. You say yes, we'll ship your young ass to Vietnam. Nothing like a war to kick-start a career. I should know."

"I got my draft notice."

"Good, that makes your decision easier. Either way, Rhodes, when your arms heal, your ass is headed for Asia. You can go and find out what the fuck is going on, or you can go over there and have some pimple-faced brown bar from Bumfuck, Iowa, lead you through the jungle."

"If they draft me, I've got to go. That's the law."

"Horseshit. The law don't apply to everyone equally. You say yes to us and we'll take care of Uncle Sam. Whaddya think?"

"How much does it pay?"

Yetter grinned crookedly. "Some days you'll wonder why you're not paying us. Other days you'll think about coming back and slicing my throat." He cited a figure and detailed benefits and other arrangements. He also gave me the name of another doctor who would look after my injuries.

"Don't you need a transcript of my classes and grades?"

"We're hiring talent, Rhodes. Not sheepskins."

I accepted. Trout and white flies were put aside. I was moving on.

I called my old man and broke the news to him.

"Are you crazy?" he asked, not wasting words.

"I'm not going in uniform."

"Going is the problem," the old man said curtly, "not what you'll be wearing."

5

I T was 1967, I was twenty-three and in the second year of my war. Most of the details don't matter now. They didn't then, either, but I had to learn that for myself. I had no big picture to orient me; my war amounted to a series of snapshots, most of them unpleasant and out of wider context, much less any real focus. I met other correspondents, many of whom had spent their entire professional lives chasing wars, and even they were at a loss to explain the mess. I operated out of Saigon but spent as much time as I could in the field.

UPI was a screwed-up organization. The Saigon bureau chief had been medevacked back to the States the day before I arrived. Bloody hemorrhoids took him home and left me reporting to a telephone voice in Manila. UPI had a half-dozen reporters and several contract photographers dispersed around the country. I think I drew Saigon as my operating base because I was new and would need an overseer, but my would-be boss's medical problem left me pretty much on my own. UPI kept telling me a replacement bureau chief was on the way, but one never arrived.

The Manila voice belonged to Del Puffit, who gave me orders and assignments without a clue of what I was facing every day. I met him only once, in a skin bar in Manila. He was obese, inebriated, and spewing projectile sweat. This graduate of some small private college in St. Louis kept telling me that I needed to develop an intellectual's view of the world and grow out of the rubber-stamp education I got at a state farm college. To my credit, I held my tongue and my fists and after one drink, I paid the tab with my own dime and left him perched precariously on a barstool.

His telephone contacts were erratic. I'd hear from him four days in a row, then nothing for weeks on end. The calls had a set script.

He'd bark, "Find the outrage. We need to tug heartstrings." This was the intellectual view I was supposed to aspire to?

I almost always countered, "Come on over and show me what you mean."

He never did. Outrage in Vietnam had no context when you were in Manila. Was it spending a hundred grand to mine a dirt road the NVA cleared with water buffalo dragging garbage can lids? Was it a squad of

Marines wasting eighty-three old folks, women, and children in a village in II Corps? Or was it a squad of VC wasting eighty-three old folks, women, and kids in a ville in the Delta? There were no reliable points of reference and good and evil defied definition.

Morality was a moving target.

The South Vietnamese government lied. The North Vietnamese government lied. The American government lied. Reporters lied. Civilians lied. The way I saw it, only I dealt in the truth, but now I realize that, because I never knew what was really true, my presumed truths were also lies.

Only the South Koreans (ROKs) seemed forthright. They were renowned for their methods of pacifying areas that MACV (Military Assistance Command Vietnam) briefers labeled "politically ambiguous." The Koreans would ride American-flown slicks into an area, dismount in force, and kill the first twenty or thirty locals they encountered. There were no interrogations, just summary executions. They were not seeking truth, only symbols. The heads were staked around the area as warnings to the politically unambiguous. The Koreans did not suffer OLs—op losses—because their brutal arrivals assured that all folks of differing political flavors would expeditiously relocate to safer, more ambiguous environs. Korean efficiency was recognized by all sides, if not universally admired.

I interviewed an ROK captain one rainy afternoon in a camp not far from the Mekong Delta.

"Why are Korean troops here?"

"U.S. is our ally. They ask help, we come. Someday we will kill North Korea communists. We practice now on South Vietnam communists."

The essence of war is simplicity.

I found myself spending longer and longer periods of time in the bush and, afterward, longer and longer intervals rejuicing to return to the bush. It got more difficult every time. Harder to pull myself out, harder to put myself back in. The first year was bad, the second worse.

The things I saw in the war sometimes defied description, but still live in my mind. I do not have night sweats or nightmares, but I have plenty of ugliness floating around in my subconscious.

I went out with the troops every chance I could finagle, and over time my stories reflected my state of mind.

Today was like yesterday for Bravo Company. Captain Walter Stiff led his company slowly through a reptile-infested swamp searching for Viet Cong storage sites. Two men were bitten by poisonous snakes. One man had heat-

induced convulsions. One man got lost and remains missing. And one man was wounded in what he told his captain was a one-on-one encounter with the enemy; the company commander is calling it a wound of unknown origin, which means a Purple Heart is unlikely. Just before sundown, Bravo's survivors shotgunned a colony of reddish black monkeys that were declared a potential "nocturnal security threat." Human casualties were medevacked out. Primate casualties were roasted for dinner. Tomorrow will be just like today, only one day closer to each soldier's ticket to the Freedom Bird. The noblest cause in this war is getting out with all your parts intact. Said a platoon sergeant, "We're all in this war separately together."

About the time I got to thinking I had seen everything I discovered I had barely scratched the surface.

In September 1967 I arranged a hop out to the USS *Snow,* a hospital ship named for a Korean war surgeon who had died as a POW in that so-called police action. The hospital ship operated south of Da Nang in the South China Sea; I had heard that the ships' surgeons out there were doing new procedures that were producing miraculous medical results. In any war, all miracles are welcomed, real or imagined. I'd also heard something else, and that's what pushed me to take a look. If my leads on this were solid, Del Puffit would have the outrage he wanted.

The ship was a brilliant white and glowed as my chopper approached just after sunrise. We came in high and my first view of the *Snow* was a white speck on a blue-green carpet; as we got closer she looked like a toy. For some reason I thought of a snowfly rising off a smooth river.

Everything in and on the ship was scrubbed clean and white, including the medical personnel, which was just as I had been told. The doctors on the ship were said to be very good, pushing the envelope of risk with their patients, all of whom were black men. I had learned this from an enlisted medic I met during one of my field excursions. He claimed that two men from his company had been wounded and flown out of the field and moved onto the *Snow,* and that there they had died.

I uttered my sympathies, which made the man angry. He grabbed the collar of my jacket and nearly choked me.

He said, "You don't get it, man! They only take brothers out there and a lot of them don't make it."

"How badly hurt were the guys from your company?"

"They were fucked up, but not ready to buy the farm, dig? I'm just a medic, see, but I know when a man is going to die. My brothers shoulda made it, man."

I began asking around in other outfits after this and heard enough similar stories that I wanted to go out to the *Snow* and see for myself.

"You Are My Sunshine" was blaring from the ship's loudspeakers as the chopper waddled onto the helipad. The song played over and over in a closed loop. The noise from the ship's belly was a soft and steady hum. Pungent salt spray and disinfectants permeated every corner of the vessel.

I had breakfast with a Marine surgeon, Colonel Johnson Quick, the ship's lead thoracic surgeon, a tanned, muscular man who neither smoked nor drank and made sure everybody knew about it. Over eggs Benedict and fresh whole milk he talked me through all kinds of surgical procedures, addressing me as if I had fifth-grade comprehension. He told me repeatedly that "his people" were "results oriented" and that back in the States he had enjoyed a "hugely successful" practice, which I interpreted as his having made a lot of money.

The surgical procedures were interesting, but not my main reason for visiting the *Snow*.

"Colonel, why are all the medical and ship's personnel on board white, and all the patients black? Don't wounded white soldiers need your help?"

He stared at me and joined his hands to make a small wall between us. "We do not pick our patients."

This seemed a fair-enough answer. "Who does?"

The joined hands grasped each other tighter. "This is an egalitarian service. We take care of who is sent to us. Surgery, Mister Rhodes, is color blind and all humans are the same color inside."

I changed directions. "What you and your colleagues do here is largely experimental, am I correct?"

"Not to us," he said.

"But all the procedures you've described to me aren't used in hospitals back home. They're not standard, right?"

The colonel's lips pursed and his neck turned red. "Here is here," he said. "There is there. We set standards here that will eventually become the standards there."

I kept my voice calm. "If you are experimenting here, doesn't that require the patients' permission?"

"This is the military," he said. "There is no time to ask permission of a dying man. And . . . it would be unethical to do so. Out here, time is life."

I would not be swayed. "What's your overall success rate?"

He blinked and scowled. "We have achieved *unprecedented* successes."

"Granted. I've heard lots of good things about your team, but what about an overall percentage?"

He kept blinking.

"For example," I said, "what is the survival rate for a kind of procedure you do here, versus a similar procedure done at field hospitals in-country— or back home?"

He said, "You can't compare durians and mangos."

I said, "Okay, just give me an overall percentage, a batting average. Of the men who come to the *Snow,* how many leave alive?"

"All we are capable of saving," he said.

I never did get answers to my questions and was invited to leave and placed on a chopper heading back to Da Nang before lunch.

I didn't need an answer or a number to write my story. The USS *Snow* was black and white to the eye, but all gray ethically.

My story about the *Snow* ran and created a brief furor back in the World. One of the information pukes from MACV's Information Office made a point of sending me a message letting me know that "the general" (name unspecified) considered my story an act of treason and that while my credentials were not being pulled, I could not count on a great deal of cooperation from the military.

Del Puffit called me and threatened to "have me fired" if I pursued "any more stories of this ilk."

Have me fired? This meant he couldn't do it himself and somehow I knew Yetter would be in my corner. "I thought you wanted me to find outrage?"

"You cannot destroy confidence in the medical service," he blared, lecturing in his most officious voice. "The boys in uniform need to believe that if they're injured, they'll be made whole again."

I said, "Goddammit, Del, they're taking black kids out to that ship and using them as lab rats."

"There is no government conspiracy against *Nee-grows,*" Puffit said. "Don't do this again."

"The story ran. Didn't you review it?"

"I was indisposed." He had been drunk. This story and phone call freed me from following any further direction from Puffit.

In 1972, a few years after I left Vietnam, Americans were shocked to learn about the federal government's forty-year-long "Tuskegee study." Black men diagnosed with syphilis had been intentionally not treated so that doctors could study the natural course of the disease. The *Snow's* outrage had not been the only one against some of our own people.

During my two years in Vietnam, the hospital ship story was the only one I wrote with real political intent. Before and after that I tried to keep my focus on what the individual soldiers were doing to stay alive and get home.

I met some genuine crazies and too many assholes to count, but mostly I met duty-bound young people doing what they thought their country wanted and doing it the best they could.

I hated the war. But I hated what America was doing to our soldiers even more. The troops had a word to cover the situation there and back in the World: *FUBAR*, Fucked Up Beyond All Reality.

In November 1967 I caught a hop on an air force C-130 to Da Nang in I Corps, in the northern part of the country. I wanted to spend time with a Marine unit that made long-range reconnaissance sorties into enemy-controlled territory. The long-range recon guys were called Lurps. They were taken by helicopters into the bush and left in place until their mission was done or their food ran out and their clothes rotted off, even their jungle boots. I wanted to go out with one of these teams and tell the story of what they did, but my request initially had gotten mired between Saigon and Da Nang. The military made an art of delays. After pressing several times, I was told that I could visit the base, but would have to remain there, for "safety and security reasons." I accepted. In northernmost South Vietnam, the war featured fixed lines and was more like the classic them-against-us scenarios of previous conflicts; down south was more of a guerilla and terrorist business, which made it impossible to draw distinctions. From Da Nang I rode west into the mountains to the Marine operation at Camp Jolly with ten taciturn Marines in a lumbering, yawing CH34C Choctaw. Until I got clearance to go out with the troops, it was better than nothing. I always hated sitting around.

Camp Jolly sat within sight of the Lost Mountains, a name bestowed by Americans, not the Viets: The story was that if you wandered into the mountains, you were doomed to get lost. Most troops called the place Camp MagNo (for Magnetic North), because any iron shot in the air by either side's artillery seemed to be drawn directly to the camp. Black humor kept more soldiers alive than prayers, never mind what the God pilots claimed. In two years, much of the time with troops, I never heard a soldier praying in a foxhole. Or a bunker. Or an APC. Or a chopper. They were too busy and scared to pray.

I had been at the camp four days. My Marine hosts were polite, efficient, and aloof. Some of them spent time showing me how to rig night
warning systems with snare wire, tin cans, and stones. And how to use camouflage. I knew they taught me these things so that I wouldn't stand out and
become a target. If I became a target, they might also get it. In war personal
survival drives a lot of what goes on. I had a bunker to sleep in, complete
with a python the marines kept to hold the rat population down. I had shelter, clothing, and food and not much to do while I waited for the brass
to decide if risking a reporter's life was worth the theoretically beneficial
publicity.

The troops at Camp MagNo were businesslike and on alert at all times.
There was no dope that I saw and no booze. I could feel the continuous
pressure of anticipation.

There were rice paddies along the eastern perimeter of the camp. At
times a wind would blow out of the north and, when it did, chubby yellow-
and-green birds would dive into the water, carrying away small, silvery fish.
As bored as I was, it was too much to resist.

I scrounged a long piece of green bamboo, unraveled some parachute
cord to make line, got a hook from a survival pack a jet jock had given me
several months before, got some bread, made them into gluey little balls,
walked down to the water's edge, and waded in. It felt great to fish, but
impulse can feel good and be all wrong.

The fish were small, shaped vaguely like stunted bluegills. They turned
their noses up at the bread. I tried bits of Vienna sausages from K-rats and
they ignored these as well. I looked around to see if there was some sort of
insect hatch. The wind, I figured, had pushed the fish into groups, which
brought the birds. But what pushed the fish together? Wind, fear of preda-
tors? I loved trying to figure out the puzzle and I was in deep cogitation
when a voice sounded behind me.

"Hey, pal."

Two heavily muscled, shirtless Marines were squatting on dry land.
One was black, the other white, and they were both huge. They had sawed-
off shotguns across their thighs and reminded me of my old man and how
he could hunker like that for hours. They wore helmets with camouflage-
cloth covers and matching sunglasses with electric pink rims and yellow
mirrored lenses.

"Me?" I asked. They were about thirty yards away.

"Catchin' anything?" the white Marine asked.

"Not yet." Ever the optimist.

"That's 'cause there's nothin' to catch," he said.

He was probably toying with me, I decided, yanking my chain. Good-natured verbal and mental jousting were common fare between reporters and soldiers.

"I saw birds catching fish out here."

"They can fly," the man said.

"The point is, there's fish here," I insisted with a nod toward the water, which extended above my knees.

"Not for you."

I turned around to face my hecklers, lost my balance on the soft bottom, stumbled forward, and landed facedown, bracing the fall with a hand on the soft, mucky bottom. My two watchers threw themselves flat on the ground and covered their heads.

This was not a good sign, I thought. *What?* I asked, spitting foul-tasting water.

"You're in a minefield," the black soldier said.

My heart started backfiring. "It's not marked."

"This is fucking I Corps, man. What the fuck good's a minefield, you put a sign up for Charlie?" This from the black marine.

He had a point.

"How do I get out?"

"Follow your tracks," the black soldier said. He looked at his partner and they both smiled and nodded.

I was in water the color of dry straw. There were no tracks. "That's a problem," I said.

"That would be a rog," the white guy said.

"Seriously, is there a trick to getting out?"

"Jes' luck," the black soldier said.

Great. My options were all bad and my legs were shaking. I couldn't believe I had been so stupid.

In a war it doesn't pay to agonize or delay decisions. I sucked in a deep breath, let it out, and started wading awkwardly through the muck-bottomed water toward the Marines, who got up and fled, clasping their helmets to their heads.

There were no explosions except in my chest.

I caught up with the Marines a hundred yards from the paddy. They were hunkered under a small tree, crowding each other for shade.

"You guys were joking, right?"

"We don't joke about mines," the black man said. "Who *are* you, man?"

"Rhodes, UPI."

"A pencil?" he asked.

I nodded.

"It's your job to ask questions, right? They pay you to ask questions, am I right?" He didn't wait for my response. "You'd better get better at your job, man."

I took out a drenched pack of smokes and tossed it on the ground in disgust. The white soldier offered me one of his and lit me up.

"Where are you guys from?" I asked.

"Michigan," the black man said. "Both of us. Different families."

I laughed out loud and I told them I was from the same state and we began the game called Small World.

Over the next two days I got to know the two sergeants. The white one was Grady Service, who had been raised in the Upper Peninsula, his dad a game warden. The black man was Luticious Treebone, a Detroiter with a perpetual and infectious smile. Grady and Tree. They were friendly and wired, their eyes never still, as if they expected to be assaulted at any moment.

"Why're you hangin' around MagNo?" Service asked one afternoon.

"I want to go out on an op with you guys. I made a formal request through channels, but you know how that goes."

They both nodded. "Why you wanna go?" Treebone asked.

"It's my job to go and see."

"You'll never get approval," Service said. "No way, Jose. What we do is in the black."

Treebone chimed in. "And black in this context definitely *ain't* beautiful."

"You want a story?" Service asked.

Of course I did.

"This is righteous, okay? Up north on the En-Vee-Lao border there are animals that few people have ever seen and most scientists in the world have never heard of."

I probably grinned. "Like some kind of Shangri-la."

Service gave me a harsh glance. "No, man. This is for real." His tone was earnest.

"You've seen this place?"

"Once," Service said, staring off into the distance.

"Where is it?" I asked. "Exactly."

I followed them to a bunker with thick walls of iron sheeting and sandbags. Service got a map out of a musty leather case. The area he pointed to was at least one hundred miles north of the Demilitarized Zone, that belt of land that separated the two Vietnams and, contrary to its title, was more militarized than just about any locale in either country.

"You were all the way up there? On foot?"

Service smiled and said, "I can neither confirm nor deny."

"Doing what?"

"Peepin', lookin' around, shit like that. The details are classified."

I couldn't read him. He could have been yanking my chain. I still had my doubts about the minefield. "How would I get up there?"

Treebone smiled. "You wouldn't, man. After the war, maybe. But now, no way."

"That's not much of a story."

"Suit yourself," Service said.

That night the two men came to my bunker just after dark, their faces streaked with vertical lines of black and green camo paint, their eyes blazing, nerves taut.

"That place we told you about," Service said. "It's real. Tree and I were both there. There's a lot of stuff on this planet still to be discovered."

"Why tell me?"

"I thought you might write about the unexpected costs of war. Here's a place that may have things that exist nowhere else on earth and we're bombin' the shit out of it and the NVA are using it to hide the shit they're haulin' down from Hanoi."

"Do I quote you?"

"You do and our young asses will be cooked. Only Tree and me ever been in this place and if you say we told you, they will royally fuck us both over."

"Why?"

"Because of what we were doin' up there."

"Peeping."

He shrugged. "It wasn't a Boy Scout camporee."

I thought about what he had to say. "I appreciate this, but it's still hard to believe. Put yourself in my place."

Treebone laughed bitterly. "We'd love to, man! But we gotta split." Service placed a crinkled snapshot on the cable spool that served as a table. It was some kind of antelope and not anything I recognized.

"Show that around and if you can find anybody who can ID it, I'll make sure Tree kisses your civilian ass."

The next day the two Marines were gone and word came down that my request to go out with the Lurps had been officially rejected due to the area's "tactical instablity."

I figured the two sergeants had been toying with me, that they'd been bored and I had been the handiest entertainment. A secret place in North Vietnam with undiscovered animals? I doubted it, but I also remembered what Red Ennis had once said about the snowfly, that there was usually some kind of fire where there was smoke. Okay, the photo was more than smoke, but I wasn't ready to buy the story. This was one bait I wasn't going to take. While I waited for my chopper, I saw a water buffalo wade into my fishing paddy. I paid no attention until I heard shrill voices and a sharp thump followed by a geyser of pink-and-green water. A mine had exploded, leaving chunks of buffalo floating in the discolored water.

The Marines had been serious about everything.

When I got back to my office in Saigon, I sent a letter and the photograph to Lloyd Nash. I told him about the claim but not my sources and asked him to show the photo to some of his colleagues to find out if the animal was known.

Then I forgot about the episode. I had wasted days with the Marines and all I had to show for the effort was one stupid move on my part, because of some fish of all things. Even if the secret place existed, I decided it was not my job to pursue it.

For years after, I would wonder if the two Marines got out of the war alive. In my two years immersed in violence I often wondered this about the many people I encountered. I knew that not all of them would get home alive, and that this possibility also applied to me. Not that the odds against a reporter were as high as those against a grunt, but there was always a chance.

There were many reporters, some of them quite famous, who rarely left the areas where they felt the safest and I couldn't blame them. Queen Anna and my old man had always warned me to not go up the creek, but they also had also instilled in my sister and me an almost religious fervor for not buckling to fear.

Queen Anna would say, "Bowie, God gave us imaginations in order to test our courage. Adam and Eve were afraid when they were cast out of Eden because they could imagine all sorts of horrible things. We're all like that, but you can't let your fears hold you back from doing what you think you need to do." I never forgot her words. I felt fear many, many times in

Vietnam and usually I could push through the veil of terror. Beating fear became a great part of what my life was all about.

Soldiers on a yearlong tour in the combat zone got a two-week R&R break during their year. Two weeks out of thirteen months. I was more fortunate.

For escapes I went to Bangkok, a city where you could walk faster than you could drive and everything and everyone was for sale. The Thai were devoted to their king and to literacy, but neither devotion seemed to move the country in any discernible direction. Spicy Thai food was created by ingenious sadists for insatiable masochists. Buddhist monks in saffron robes roamed the city begging alms. Prostitutes cost less than a gallon of gas in Detroit. The sprawling city's ubiquitous canals, called *klongs,* were clogged with wooden speedboats and fecal matter. I was fascinated and repulsed by all of it.

The Florida Hotel was ocher colored, seven stories, a U built around a small, long pool an even twenty feet deep. There was a bar in the basement. Reinforced windows in the bar allowed patrons to watch live underwater sex shows. After midnight it was amateur hour. You could sit and watch GIs and pilots on R&R screw fourteen-year-old hookers who took Americanized names like Wendy Sue and Zoe, which means "life." As in the war itself, there were no rules on its periphery.

There was no point in searching for a different kind of establishment. Every hotel and establishment in the city had its own version of the Florida's erotic entertainment. I sometimes amused myself topside at the pool. Three very drunk F-105 pilots stumbled in one night and began stripping, staring down at unclad women in the pool. I was the veteran in this environment. "First time here, guys?"

"Yes, sir."

"Stay away from the black-haired one, she has the clap."

"Hey, thanks." They dove in.

There was a couple at the table beside me.

"You're a naughty one, aren't you, Yank?" said a gent in a double-breasted blue blazer festooned with brilliant gold buttons. He had a wide flat face, blond hair, and a ruddy complexion.

"You're not military," the man continued. "Journo?"

"It shows?"

"Have a tonic, mate?"

I moved to their table. A waiter brought a huge bottle of Foster's.

"Name's Dickie Goodwin," the man said. "Wife's Gillian. Tazzies."

Which I eventually learned meant Tasmanians.

Dickie Goodwin was fifty-seven, Gillian thirty-six. His fifth marriage, her second. His vocation he described as "a bitta," meaning he had a lot of irons in various commercial fires, including a coffee plantation in South Vietnam, near the resort town of Da Lat. Thus far, he explained, his operation was producing without interruption through increased bribes, which he called "grease to the monkeys."

"Won't last," he added. "Northies are mobbing up all over. First Law of Business, mate: You don't accumulate inventory if there's no campaign in the offing."

"How do you know?" The brass in Saigon were paranoid about an enemy thrust out of their ubiquitous sanctuaries in Laos and Cambodia. There had been rumors of a major enemy offensive for nearly a year, but there had never been confirmation from intelligence, military or otherwise.

"Simple, mate. I pay and they say. If they won't, I don't. Information is always available at a price, even from Reds. I'd think a journo would know that. Your shout, Yank."

It was my turn to buy a round. This led to another and another. The Tazzies were a gregarious pair with an astonishing capacity for alcohol.

I awoke the next morning with a searing headache and a very naked Gillian Goodwin snoring lightly in my ear. Our clothes were nowhere to be seen. We were on a huge cushion on a wooden-plank verandah over green water. I watched a dark, waterlogged rat paddling frantically below us.

I nudged Gillian.

"Again?" she mumbled.

"Gillian, where's your husband? We need our clothes."

"Dickie's in his bedroom, I should think," she said sleepily. She had thick brown hair and high cheekbones. Her smile made long sliver-moon dimples appear. "Not to worry, mate. Dickie's got a soft pommel. He doesn't mind sharing a bit."

I slid off the cushion and looked around. "Our clothes?"

"Later, love. Shall we celebrate the glorious sunrise?"

There were boats passing by. "Where are we?"

"The Klong House," she said. "Probably. I don't really remember. Did we have loads of fun before we got here?"

She wasn't the only one with a blank memory.

She patted a pillow. "Don't be paranoid, love. It's the boy's duty to do what his hostess wants."

Eventually we showered and dressed and joined Dickie Goodwin for a late brunch at a glass-topped table in a lush garden on top of the house. Frangipani perfumed the air just enough to overpower the river's bouquet of garbage, oil, gasoline, and human waste.

"You two don't look so crook," Dickie said. "Have a good go, did you, old girl?"

"Quite," Gillian said enthusiastically. "Legendary Yankee stamina."

"Good show," Dickie said, slapping the table mirthfully. "Bit out of practice, Gil?"

"Fair dinkum," she said, feigning discomfort. "Feel absolutely deflowered."

A servant brought champagne in long-stemmed crystal flutes.

"What do you write, mate?" Dickie Goodwin asked me.

"War correspondent."

"Slog around in the bush with the lads, do you?"

"Of course he does, Dickie. I can tell a bush slogger."

I nodded.

"Been in the shit, have you?"

"Some."

"Good-on-you, mate. Our own journos scribble from Bangkok. They are not a credit to their bloody race, I should think."

I had never thought of journalists as a race, but I had to concede he might be on to something. An increasing number of people certainly thought of us as a lower order, the so-called fourth estate.

War, like politics, makes strange bedfellows. Literally and figuratively. Having superficially gotten past the discomfort of the peculiar arrangement with the Goodwins, I found Dickie and Gillian to be interesting and charming companions.

A week after I left Bangkok Gillian unexpectedly showed up at my place in Saigon, on *pho x con nhen cay go*—the "Street of Spider Trees." To find the gate into my garden, you had to negotiate a long, narrow, unlit alley. The seven-foot-high stone walls were topped with jagged shards of broken bottles and tight-packed coils of gleaming razor wire; the inner wall was bolstered by a double layer of sandbags. The garden itself was hard-packed sand. Somehow Gillian had found the place, which was not easy, even when you knew the way. She was sitting at the garden table under a single naked lightbulb when I dragged in around midnight. She wore a short skirt and had her legs crossed. She was restlessly jiggling a leg as clouds of insects fluttered around the lightbulb and crickets chirped incessantly.

"Bloody crickets," she said by way of a greeting. "Worse than our cockatoos."

"Gillian?" I was shocked to see her.

"I'm dreadfully parched," she said. "Had a thought you might be on the roger tonight with some libidinous doughnut dolly."

"Just working," I said.

"All work and no play," she countered, teasingly.

"Pays my bar bill," I said.

She smiled approvingly and patted my behind. "I *adore* common sense. One tends to admire most what one doesn't possess, d'ya think?"

"It's as workable a theory as any. What're you doing here?"

She beamed her infectious and mischievious smile. "Dickie said, 'Old girl, you ought to pop over to the Trout, harvest what you can, and kiss the old spread good-bye.' Dickie says the Red invasion's imminent, Bowie."

The Trout? I wasn't sure what she was talking about. It was often like this with her. "And he sent *you?*"

"Dickie's not the adventurous sort nowadays but I do *so* adore the Trout. Some boys have no sense of romance. To Dickie, the place is purely a bloody asset."

"The Trout?" She had said this twice.

"Yes, dear. The coffee plantation is called the Trout House on the River of Trout, which the Vietnamese call *song ca qua*. Their word for 'trout' is the same as their word for 'eggplant' or some such thing," she said with a deep laugh. "Such an imprecise language. It's no wonder they've been fighting for centuries," she added. "The Trout's up in the central highlands, darling. It once belonged to Sir Thomas Oxley, an Englishman raised on the Test. And elsewhere, I should think. Rich bastard. Planted trout, he did. Absolutely pots about them. Must've cost him a bloody fortune, I should think, but fair dinkum, he pulled it off. The spread's not quite a rajah's jewel, but it's splendid and the best trout fishing between here and India. Naturally, I adore it," she said dramatically.

"Are you telling me there are trout in Vietnam?"

"Ah!" she said gleefully. "Only a devout Brother of the Angle would sound so incredulous. Of *course* there are trout and we can thank Sir Thomas for that! It's quite amazing. Pine trees, cool nights, cold water, four seasons, perfect acidity, and such. The eggs came from stock in Uganda, can you bloody believe it? The Ugandan eggs were from brood stock originally from England but packed into South Africa by Sir John Parker and the

Drakensbergers in 1890. From South Africa up to Uganda, and Oxley sent Ugandan ova to Vietnam in the nineteen-twenties. His stubborn English mind was set on propagating trout. Bloody miracle, indeed, but you know the Poms. Right or wrong, when they decide something will be, then it shall come to pass."

"I've never heard any of this." I was astonished by the information, but retained a modicum of skepticism. Trout in Vietnam? I thought about the two Marines and their claims of unknown animals in the north. Perhaps war made peoples' imaginations run amok.

"I'm not the least surprised," Gillian said. "But it is a matter of public record that the Poms and Krauts put their beloved trout everywhere they could. Our little River of Trout is no doubt the only place on the subcontinent that could sustain them, but sustain it has for a good long while now. And, I must say, our dear fish rise to a dressing as politely as one could ask."

I remembered Dickie Goodwin mentioning in Bangkok that his rubber plantation was near Da Lat. This was a resort area developed by the French at the turn of the nineteenth century. It was the place where Vietnamese royalty went to escape the heat of the lowlands. It was also rumored to serve as an in-country R&R center for combatants on all sides, and there was said to be tacit agreement by belligerants to leave it alone. So far, all sides had. The only military connection I knew of was that South Vietnam's version of West Point was located in the area.

She stood up, hooked her arm though mine, and made a pooch-face. "This geography conversation is becoming exceedingly boring, Bowie. Aren't you glad to see me? Let's have a sexploration of Gillian's geography, shall we? I've come a long way in bloody awful heat and a nice fuck would settle me nicely. Yes?"

"Does Dickie know you're here?"

"Not technically," she said sheepishly. "Here, yes. With you, no. He said to check the spread and the spread's in Vietnam. You're also in Vietnam, which makes for a wonderful coincidence, yes?"

The whole thing seemed ludicrous, but ludicrous was often the norm in Vietnam. We started undressing on the way to my bedroom.

After making love frantically, we sat on my roof and smoked in the middle of the night. Saigon was never silent. Trucks with bad brakes wheezed through the streets. Horns honked. Military and civilian police sirens wailed plaintively. Motorcycles and Vespa scooters without mufflers roared up and down the streets, howling like wild animals. Formations of helicopters pounded overhead. The afterburners of departing F4 Phantoms rumbled in the distance as attack formations left Ton Son Nhut, the airfield that served military and civil aviation in Saigon. We heard the chuk-chuk of artillery batteries putting rounds out from the edges of the city—rounds leaving, not arriving, a good sign. The prevailing scent was tropical, all things rotting.

"Like to pop over to the Trout for a look?" Gillian asked.

"You bet. When do we go and how do we get there?" Getting around in the country was not easy unless you were connected to the military.

She rested her head on my chest and chewed my left nipple. "Leave the details to Gillian, darling."

She had a driver deliver us to Ton Son Nhut early the next day. We were dropped at an unmarked Huey piloted by an Australian with a waxed handlebar mustache. He was busy with checklists and not introduced. There were two blond door gunners wearing Bermuda shorts, distressed green-and-yellow aviation helmets, and flak vests. Somebody had painted SURF OR DIE on the backs of the vests. The gunners were suspended from umbilicals that let them swing 180 degrees to get a good look at the ground below. Fortunately, there was no shooting en route. We flew more or less northeasterly out of the city, the prevailing terrain slowly gathering altitude as we got farther north. Eventually we began to pass over a series of rugged valleys, most with silvery ribbons of streams gleaming deep at the bottoms of them. The area was dotted with many small reflective lakes. About an hour into our journey the sun went away and we moved into islands of rain clouds with tattered bottoms and continued dodging our way north in limited visibility. This was an area I had never visited; there was very little action here.

The scenery below was attractive, but I couldn't see it that well through the rain and in any event, scenery no longer held any allure for me. At the heart of rich green beauty below was the ugliest of realities.

The Goodwin "spread" amounted to twenty thousand acres on terraced ground ringing the Blue Flower Mountains. The house was a sprawling one-story affair with stucco walls painted a soothing turquoise with pale yellow shutters and awnings. The roof tiles were also yellow with some orange ones here and there. A lawn was manicured down to the river. There were wide stone paths along both banks. The river itself was wide, perhaps one hundred yards by the house, and gently riffled with vegetation undulating in the flow. Behind the house and across the river a mountain rose precipitously into mist. Above me I saw enormous outcrops of white and gray rock. The sides of the hills were packed with fragrant straight-trunked pine trees and the scene about as peaceful as I had seen in the war-torn country. A convoy of civilian trucks was gathered around the main house and several outbuildings, and dozens of Vietnamese men and women were loading them.

I walked down to the river and watched several fish feeding among the riffles. Gillian was squatting Asian style on the lawn, engaged in an animated conversation with an old woman with an ancient double-barreled shotgun slung over her back. When the talking was done, Gillian joined me. The mist was thickening into a cool drizzle and I was cold, a first for Vietnam.

"You speak the language?" I asked her.

"Just pidgin really, a little Viet, a little French, a little mountain lingo. They're Montagnards. Some of the families have been with the Trout since Oxley's time. They're hardworking and loyal. That's Granny Rat," Gillian said with a nod toward the woman she had been talking to. "She's a tough old girl. The 'Yards love fresh rat and she's the main provider for her tribe, which has a village up the mountain. Her shotgun shells are packed with rice, not shot. Doesn't shred the meat so bad," Gillian said with a grin. "Granny says that the North Vietnamese are gathered about eight kilometers up the valley. Fourteen tanks and several hundred men. Apparently they've been up there several days and seem to be waiting for something; Dickie was right, of course, but the 'Yards are taking care to remove things and we don't need to concern ourselves with such matters at the moment. It's just as well because we have our own things to do. Are you ready to cast feather bits on Asian waters?"

I was curious about the enemy troops, but I had come with Gillian to fish and I had never been readier. All the gear was stored neatly in a stone hut with a thatched roof beside the river. There was no need for waders or hip boots; the riverbanks had been sculpted and shaped to accommodate dry-fly fishing and we had nets with six-foot-long handles. The drizzle intensfied as we selected and assembled bamboo rods.

"How high are we?" I asked.

"About sixteen hundred meters," she said. It was easy to see why the hoi polloi used to flee up this way in the warm season down below.

"English rules," Gillian said, false-casting her rod to limber her arm. "One must present only to a rising fish. Upstream only. Dries, please. A fish in net must be killed."

"There's no point in killing them."

"Sorry love, but tonight we will dine on *my* trout from *my* river. Perhaps for the last time," she added, a bit teary. "Makes me feel crook and quite sad."

Her casts were more accurate than mine and I saw that she mended automatically and effortlessly to give her fly long drag-free drifts. We were using small orange-and-red attractors, flies she called Hens.

Rarely did ten minutes pass without a fish on, but at least half of them fought their way free by breaking off the tippets on sharp-edged green rocks in the river.

At our latitude, and with so many mountains around us, there was little twilight. The sun set with a sort of no-notice, perfunctory plop. By dark we had ten fish and the surrounding forests were alive with the screams of insects, birds, and monkeys.

Gillian cooked the two largest trout over coals with bacon and fresh lemon slices. We had a chilled Sancerre with the fish and, afterward, a sweet yellow fruit in thick clotted cream and syrup.

We did not talk a lot. Gillian was pensive and sad. It was downright cold after darkness came. The servants (I assumed they were servants) made a fire in a bedroom that looked down on the river. We made love on a mat in front of the fireplace; Gillian was usually in a hurry, but this time she took her time and seemed to make the moment last and, afterward, we fell asleep in each other's arms.

I rolled around restlessly, couldn't sleep, and finally got up. I tried to get Gillian to move into the bed, but she sleepily waved me away and muttered, "Bugger off, Yank."

I found a light blanket and covered her. I needed to stretch tight muscles and I was curious about the Trout House.

There were several lanterns hissing in the house; outside, the drizzle had melted into a thick night fog that diffused the light and made it shimmer. The house was filled with shadows.

There was a study off the bedroom and a lantern in one corner that cast a golden glow through the room. Two walls of the study had books on shelves made of a fragrant, shiny wood that smelled of incense. The shelves were packed with books and I perused them halfheartedly until I discovered one entire shelf lined with books on angling and trout flies. I couldn't resist.

I began to reach for a book but stopped myself. These were ancient tomes, with faded bindings, some of them in leather. Many had no titles on the spines, and some of the books lay on their backs rather than standing upright. One section of a bookcase was built into cubicles into which the books fit. Custom-made, I decided, with each book measured by the carpenter. I had never seen anything like it and, after getting up my courage and hoping I was not transgressing, I began to pick up the books and look at them. It was hard to believe. The titles were in modern English, Old English (maybe it was Middle English; I had never been able to distinguish the two), French, Latin, Greek, and other languages I couldn't recognize because of the strange and antiquated type fonts. *Reliquiae Antiquiae,* 1845. *Livre de Chasse. The Book of St. Albans,* whose faded date read *MCDXCVI,* or 1496. Could it be I was holding a book created only four years after Columbus blundered into the Americas? My heart was pounding. The miracle of old books had always fascinated me, how knowledge could be imparted over centuries. I next picked up *A Booke of Fishing with Hooke and Line.* It was dated 1590 and in fragile condition, and I carefully replaced it after examining the flyleaf. There were also editions of Ovid, Pliny, Socrates, Thoreau, and Shakespeare.

Trouting on the Brule River, 1880. *Driffield Angler,* 1890. *The Fly-Fisher's Entomology,* 1836. W. J. Turrell, *Ancient Angling Authors,* 1910. Hills's *A History of Fly Fishing for Trout,* 1920. The books all seemed to be original printings, first editions. I had never seen a collection like this, never imagined such a thing existed. I was fascinated.

Then I saw M. J. Key's books and I felt a strange light settle around me like a caul. M. J. Key: From Lloyd Nash's study in East Lansing to a coffee plantation in Vietnam. It was unreal. I pulled the two volumes out of their places and set them on a table. The room had a stone floor with thick reed mats and a huge divan made of rattan and covered with thick cushions. I wished for an electric light but knew there was no hope for this. I went back to the shelves.

Several minutes later my hand settled on a manuscript that had been inserted between two hard leather slabs. It had once been bound by string, but that had broken.

I lifted the leather cover and read the title. It was typewritten. *The Legend of the Snowfly.* The author was M. J. Key. There was no date. I felt a catch in my throat. Key? Something by Key never published? About the snowfly. My hand trembled and my heart raced as I stared at the title. I lay the book gently on the table and started to carefully lift the title page, but it was brittle and I did not want to damage it. Not now, not at the moment when a dream was within reach. How could I do this safely?

Before I could decide, an explosion shattered the windows in the study and rocked the foundations of the house; I stumbled into the other room to find a dusty, angry, and disoriented Gillian on the floor, tangled in the blanket I had put over her.

"Bloody fucking savages," Gillian cursed, hacking and coughing to clear her lungs as she clawed frantically at the blanket.

I freed her, hoisted her to her feet, and tried to brush her off. "Are you hurt?"

She shook her head. "I'm not ready to go," she said. "It's my night. *Ours.* Bloody bastards can't just walk in and take over."

Another explosion rattled the walls. Bits of stone zinged around like angry wasps. More explosives popped outside and I heard several incoming artillery rounds strike close. "There's no choice," I said. "We have to get out *now!*" The distinct sharp crackling of AK-47s peeled in the distance.

"There's always a choice, darling," Gillian said calmly.

She was wrong. "Not this time."

Another round hit near us, knocking a wall down and filling the room with a nearly impenetrable cloud of gray plaster dust and flames.

Gillian looked at me with tears in her eyes. "Well, we did try to do it right, didn't we?"

I slid my arm around her waist and moved her along. "Yes, we did."

We hurriedly stuffed our feet into our boots and fled the burning house carrying our clothes. As we passed the study, I stopped. The room was an inferno and in it I saw faces of fear and laughter, faces I thought were mocking me. The Key manuscript and all those wonderful books would soon be ashes and lost forever. Gillian jerked me by the arm and we made our way out of the burning house to the chopper, whose rotor was screaming.

We clambered aboard and Gillian shouted, "Eddie, give us a spin over the old place!" The helicopter leapt off the ground. The pilot bent the Huey in a tight, ascending turn to the north, then veered back south.

Both door gunners shot white flares into the darkness. I watched them ignite and sputter as they floated earthward under tiny parachutes.

I saw a dozen tanks fording the river adjacent to the Trout House. Hundreds of infantrymen were wading resolutely across shallow riffles in the wakes of the tanks. There were sparkling star-shaped muzzle flashes from the river and the area around the house. I wondered about the servants, Montagnards, and other people I had seen loading vehicles when we arrived. I could only conclude that what I was seeing was the start of a major military operation, perhaps even the major uprising feared so long in Saigon and Washington, D.C.

"Throw them some candy?" one of the door gunners shouted.

Gillian answered angrily, "Bloody fucking right! Give it to the bastards!"

Ejected brass cartridges rattled around the belly as the gunners strafed troops caught in the shallow river. The cool night air raced through the open bay and I smelled gunpowder and aviation fuel and my own sweat.

I begged a drop-off at an artillery camp about twelve miles south of the Trout House. My gut told me that the enemy action was huge and I wanted desperately to file a story and beat the competition. The Huey bumped the ground hard. Gillian kissed me quickly and pushed me away.

"Bloody fools, you men," she shouted before the helicopter smothered her voice and climbed away.

The firebase was built on a treeless ridge and surrounded by wire, fire pits, and bunkers that stretched along the spine as far as I could see.

"Who the fuck're *you?*" a sergeant asked. His M-16 was pointed at my head.

"Rhodes, UPI. Get on your radio. NVA tanks are crossing the River of Trout."

"The River *what?*"

"Get me a map."

He looked at me with bulging eyes. "Man, you might want to holster your Johnson."

Only then did I realize I had on my boots and nothing else. In other circumstances, it might have been funny.

It was several hours after I was dropped at Camp Gates before there was an attack, but once it began, it was brutal and the camp took a terrible pounding. I had no way to call in a story, and it didn't take long for me to forget about journalism and concentrate on staying alive.

A Russian tank fired at the camp and the camp fired back. A light colonel shouted frantically into a PRC radio, "Get that tank, get that tank!" It became his mantra.

I couldn't separate the tank's gun from other incoming rounds, but I sensed waves of violence. First came heavy incoming, followed by a pause, then even heavier outgoing. I had no doubt that the North Vietnamese had us zeroed in, and I suspected our outgoing fire was mostly guesswork and helter-skelter in its effect. The ground around me shook like a continuous earthquake, raising a huge cloud of dust in the bunker where I took cover. Outside it was like a fireworks display on an unlimited budget. A lethal show.

Shrapnel sometimes whizzed by the opening to the bunker and smacked dully into things outside.

The dust inside was so thick that I soaked a kerchief and held it over my nose and mouth to keep from choking. I crawled cautiously outside during one of the brief lulls between artillery exchanges and made my way over to a pair of troopers in a slit trench firing an M-60 at the treeless rim of a clearing slightly downhill of us. I watched spouts of dirt erupt under the machine gun's steady pounding. The ammo feeder's face was red with dust and sweat and he had loud hiccups that sounded like mortar rounds going out.

I never saw anybody get hit, but I saw the results. A soldier farther down in the slit trench was holding his left arm in his right hand. The left arm was no longer attached and he looked puzzled more than hurt. I had seen enough wounded during the war to recognize shock.

Journalists pride themselves stupidly on their professional neutrality. We're supposed to be dispassionate observers and seekers of facts that lead to the truth, not participants. I heard my voice yelling, "Medic! Get me a fucking medic!"

"There ain't none," somebody shouted to me.

I did not think. I acted. I took the soldier's severed wet arm and set it aside. He objected, "That's mine, man!" Blood spurted from his armpit and pink bubbled from his mouth. I had no idea what to do to stanch the blood and all I could think of was finding somebody who could help. I picked up the soldier in a fireman's carry, bent under his weight, then picked up his severed arm and started through the camp with the man on my back. "Medic? Medic?"

Soldiers pointed and yelled, "That way, man. Keep going! Move, move, move!"

There were explosions all around me, but I couldn't stop. Red dust hung in the air and things whooshed through it. Fumes of cordite hung heavy. My ears rang. I felt like I was going to choke and sneeze all at once. And die. My eyes burned and tears ran freely.

All-out combat is pure chaos; when you are in the middle of it there is no strategic point, only the immediacy of where you are and what you are trying to do. Motion and time slow down. I passed the helipad I had arrived at that morning. Three Hueys were broken skeletons, black against hot tongues of orange flames, ammo from their guns popping.

All along my route troops kept pointing the way to an aid station, which was downhill. Behind me, the explosions continued. Ahead, beside a bunker, I saw a woman smoking a cigarette. Her surgical scrubs were purple, red blood mixed with blue-green cloth and dust, blood in her hair, on her forehead.

"Hospital?" I said.

"There," she said, pointing to a bunker entrance. "Put him down." I held out the severed arm, which she ignored as she knelt and felt the wounded man's neck.

"Ernie!" she shouted into the bunker opening. A cigarette stuck to her bottom lip.

A squinting soldier came cautiously out of the bunker. "Take the arm," the woman said.

"Okay, doc."

"You're a doctor?"

She looked up at me with glazed eyes. "No shit," she said, flipping the cigarette away. "Help me get him inside. Buddy of yours?"

Because I was so often in the field, I was dressed in green army fatigues. "No, I'm a reporter. There was nobody else to bring him."

A bullet whacked the door frame of the bunker, spitting dust and some small splinters of wood. She never flinched. The man who had taken the arm came back, carrying a stretcher, which he unfolded.

I helped slide the wounded soldier onto the stretcher and watched as another man came out of the bunker and helped take the soldier down into the darkness. I was tempted to follow.

Another soldier arrived, carrying a wounded man, lowered him gently, and looked at me. "Can you help me, man?"

"Help you what?"

"Move wounded. We got beaucoup down and we're short of guys."

The doctor touched my arm. "See you later?"

I nodded and turned to follow the Good Samaritan, but the doctor held on to me and pulled hard enough to turn me around. "See you later," she repeated. "Here, *okay?*"

My new partner had GEMTFOOH written on the back of his helmet liner in nail polish. "Gemtfooh? What kind of name is that?"

"Get Me The Fuck Out Of Here," he said as we jogged uphill.

We carried wounded all afternoon and left the dead where they were.

A huge round exploded as I tried to scoop up one GI with a stomach wound and knocked me flat, taking my breath and leaving me gasping like a trout on a riverbank. The middle of my back throbbed, I had an erection unlike any I had ever had before, and my testicles ached. The soldier I had been trying to lift was no longer breathing but stared dead-eyed up into the sky. I moved on, aching, stumbling, gagging, fighting to reclaim my breath.

The attack finally slowed late in the day, but the pain in my back remained. As did the erection.

I was hurting and tired and went looking for the doctor I had met earlier. Someone at the aid station directed me into another bunker. Blood was everywhere, the interior lit with arc lights that were hot and made clicking sounds. The smell was terrible. There was a lot of talk, but it was subdued, not panicked.

"Scrub there," a soldier said to me.

"I'm not a doctor."

"Who is?" he said grimly.

He showed me how to scrub and helped me into gloves, a mask, and a silly little hat like the doo-rags some of the troops wore.

"Over here," a voice said. It was the doctor I had met earlier. She was wearing a mask, which was splashed with blood.

"I'm not trained."

"Got all your parts?"

"So far." My back ached and so did my balls.

"Good, just do what I tell you to. No more, no less. Got it?"

I did. I saw the insides of dozens of bodies. My doctor was calm, decisive, and worked fast. I clamped arteries, put my gloved hand on warm living organs, and did whatever I was told to do.

Some time later a gravelly voice said, "Take a break, Louie."

The doctor nodded to me. "Let's blow this pop stand."

We walked outside, shuffled quickly across open ground, and ducked into another earthen bunker. This was was filled with broken wooden ammo boxes. There were sporadic shots outside now, not many. No big stuff.

"Dworkin," the doctor said, lighting a cigarette and offering it to me. Then she lit one for herself. "Louise . . . Louie to the others." She held out a canteen. I took a long pull. "What happened to your back?" she asked.

"What?"

"You were bent over like Quasimodo the whole time we were working down there."

"Something knocked me down."

She said, "Let's have a look. Peel 'em off," she added with a tug on my belt.

"Peel off what?"

"Your clothes. Off."

I did as I was told. Her hand felt cool on my skin and I was embarrassed as she bent close to examine my genitals. The inspection done, she picked up my flak vest and ran her hand over it, then clucked and held the vest out to me. "Feel." I felt a lump of something inside. "Whatever it is, your vest paid for itself today," she said. "You're probably going to hurt for a few days."

I stared at the vest, then at my penis, which stood like a flagpole.

She took the jacket, put it on the ground, piled my soiled fatigues on top, quickly shed her own clothes, added them to the pile, took my hand, knelt, and said, "We don't have a lot of time."

I sat down clumsily. She did not move fast.

"I thought we were in a hurry."

She laughed mischieviously. "Who's the doctor here?" Her hair was short, the left side caked flat with dried blood. I smelled blood, cordite, dust, urine, our sex.

When we finished, we lay on the pile of clothes. "God, I could go to sleep now," she said. She sat up, dug through her shirt for cigarettes, lit two, and passed me one.

"We both needed that," she went on, sitting beside me, relief in her voice. Then in a clinical tone, "Back injuries can cause priapus, which is the fifty-cent word for an endless, painful hard-on. You took a bad whack in the back." Her hand continued to fondle and examine. "It'll go down," she said. "Which is too bad," she added.

"You're putting me on?"

She laughed out loud. "Medically no. I don't know if ejaculation eases the condition, but why waste the opportunity, right? We've got to reaffirm life in the face of so damn much dying." Her voice turned serious. "All these kids," she said. "*Kids,* for God's sake. This isn't like the World. So much pointless death here. Hell, all death is pointless. We were here on an inspection, can you believe that? Stopping for a few hours. You have a name?"

"Rhodes, Bowie."

"You did good things today, Rhodes, Bowie. I'll be going back to Cam Ranh when this shit is over. You come see me so I can check your medical progress, okay?" She exhaled smoke. "I can smell us over the rest of this shit," she said, "life over death."

"Thanks," I said.

"For balling you?"

I smiled. "For making an insane moment seem sane in the middle of so much insanity."

She placed her hand on my chest. "It's crude out here, filthy. Our medicine is less than basic under these conditions." She kissed me slow and long, then pushed me away playfully. "When I get you into a real bed,

I'll show you what I great physician I *really* am." She grinned. "Cam Ranh, got it?"

"I'll be there."

"You'd better. The sooner, the better . . . medically speaking." We dressed slowly in clothes that were both wet and stiff.

It was quiet outside the bunker, but dust lingered in the air like fog. "Be careful," she said over her shoulder as she scuttled back to surgery.

I returned to the upper camp, found a sergeant, and told him I needed to get a story out. I figured I could hand-write it, send it by chopper to Saigon, get it on a commercial flight to Manila, and get it on the wire there.

"Is it over?" I asked the sergeant. He had a new scab stretching across most of his forehead.

"Who the fuck knows? You can't predict these assholes." He looked at me. "Where's your weapon?"

"I don't have one."

He handed me a rifle with a scope. "Can you shoot?"

"I'm a reporter," I said.

"That's not what I asked."

"I've shot targets," I said, "but I don't know if I can shoot another person."

He put his hand on my shoulder. "I like an honest man. Take it." He gave me a canvas bag of clips. "If you have to shoot, you'll be glad you've got it."

"Is there a way to get a message out?"

"Not until we start getting dust-offs when this shit dies down." Dust-offs were helicopters used to remove the wounded. I would not be getting a story out anytime soon.

I found a bunker and went inside to try to get some rest. At four o'clock the next morning the rockets started again and were followed by salvo after salvo of mortars. There was a captain and a lieutenant in the bunker with me, and a buck sergeant with a radio. The captain's head was bandaged like a mummy and he was on the radio jabbering coordinates. And swearing incomprehensibly.

"What's happening?" I asked the lieutenant.

"Maneuvering in force," he said wearily. "The LBMFs, not us." LBMF meant Little Brown Mother Fucker, one of many terms the grunts had for the enemy. "Our asses are stuck here. Our LPs have been reporting heavy troop movements all night."

"Are they coming in?"

"We're not sure yet. Stay tuned," he said, trying to smile.

Outside the bunker the night turned white as flares popped and floated slowly down under tiny parachutes.

"We're gonna keep it lit bright as hell," the lieutenant said. "They come, they're gonna get fucked over. At least for a while," he added.

But the enemy did not come and I never had to face a decision with the rifle. Instead snipers popped away at us from nearby positions, keeping our heads down, harrassing us. The camp commander figured we were a minor obstacle the enemy had brushed against on its way to something of greater strategic value.

In the morning I carefully made my way back to the aid station. The destroyed choppers on the helipad were smoldering. I wondered how long before we could get medevacs in. Helicopters were lifelines in this war.

I asked for Dr. Dworkin.

A heavy man immediately shuffled over to me, put his arm around my shoulder, and steered me toward the bunker in which Louise and I had made love. It stank of death. A naked lightbulb illuminated a slapdash pile of muddy body bags, some of them torn. The wooden boxes were gone.

"You the reporter?"

I nodded.

He exhaled loudly, painfully. "She told me what you did to help." His eyes were listless, sunk deep in their sockets, his skin gray. "Thanks."

I stared at the bags of remains and knew why we were there. "Is Louise dead?"

"I'm sorry," the man said. "It was a fucking sniper."

"When?"

"First light today. We worked all night. She went out for a smoke. I told her to be careful. She was, but it didn't matter." His tone was one of barely restrained anger. "The round wasn't meant for her. She was down low, well protected, out of the line of sight. A soldier near her stood up and was hit in the temple. The bullet went into his head, exited his throat, and hit Louise here." He reached over and touched the knob of bone at the base of the back of my neck. "Instantaneous. Doesn't take much to break the spine right there. She was a great surgeon and a great gal. This fucking war sucks and if this is God's plan, he sucks too."

"I want to see her."

The man knelt, opened a bag, and stepped back. I saw for the first time that he wore the black eagles of a full colonel on his left collar along with a caduceus, the emblem of doctors and the medical corps.

Louise Dworkin looked asleep.

It took three more days before the choppers returned and I got a hop out. The belly of my bird was stacked two deep with body bags and the inside of the chopper was coated with splotches of dried blood and what I knew were bits of human tissue. The gunner gave me cotton to stuff in my nostrils. I strapped into a web seat and tried to figure out where to put my feet.

The door gunner looked over at me and shouted, "Those fuckers can't feel it, man."

I gingerly put my feet on the remains and stared down. Beside my foot there was a single dog tag covered with red mud. I picked it up, scraped it clean, and read the name. FISTRIP, RICHARD L. 1ST LIEUTENANT. BLOOD TYPE: O+.

My mind swam. I felt dizzy.

"You okay?" the gunner yelled over the whine of the turbine engine.

I held out the dog tag.

He shook his head. "Pitch it," he said.

"Is it from here?" I shouted.

The gunner shrugged. "No, man. It's been rattling around in here since last night when we were picking up bags from a camp east of here. How the fuck it didn't fall out is beyond me. I guess his ghost wanted somebody to have it."

Yeah, I thought. I tried to convince myself that Fistrip had gone to Hell, but I couldn't. He was a creep, but nobody deserved to die here, not like this.

I didn't get back to Saigon until a week after Gillian and I had fled the Trout House. My place on the Street of Spider Trees had been ransacked, all of my belongings stolen. The outer walls were pocked by bullet marks. My office in the press center had plywood where glass had been and everybody had a Tet story to tell.

I was certain that I had seen Tet at its seed, and, as it turned out, I probably had. The countrywide attacks were supposed to begin several hours after the assault on the Trout House, but for some reason attacks around Da Lat and Nha Trang had been launched early and far ahead of the rest of the country. The North Vietnamese Army and Viet Cong had risen up in hundreds of locations and struck simultaneously across the length and breadth of the country; from what I could tell, most of the attacks had been failures, but a major fight still raged in Hue, the country's historic capital. Such was the fog of war. You could never extrapolate. You saw what you saw, experienced what you experienced, and that was that. In the years ahead historians would try to make sense of it, but they wouldn't. There wasn't much sense to be made.

There was a telegram waiting for me at MACV after the fighting relented in Saigon. It was from Lloyd Nash, who said that the photograph I had sent to him was being "passed around by colleagues" and that there was "every reason to believe that this is a new and heretofore unknown species." His excitement was clear and he had numerous questions, none of which I could answer.

I gave much thought to unknown animals after that and, later in my life, would encounter something I would never have dreamed of back then in Vietnam. There's one hell of a lot to learn about this earth of ours.

But Nash's letter was nothing compared to the Trout House manuscript. The combination of the two events brought the snowfly into a new focus. Because it seemed mostly myth and baloney, this did not necessarily render it untrue. Besides, I had held Key's manuscript in my hands.

I had a couple of long, mostly unfruitful assignments in II Corps after the Tet mess. In August UPI asked me to extend and offered a substantial raise, but I refused. The accumulation of experience was too heavy to carry any longer. The deaths of Louise Dworkin, whom I'd known intimately but only superficially, and Rick Fistrip, whom I'd once hated, were too much. A telegram from Yetter told me to take a month's vacation and then we'd mutually decide my future.

On my way home to the States I flew to Hobart, Tasmania, and spent a week fishing for trout with Gillian at her place in the highlands. Dickie Goodwin was there, too, but busy with business and Gillian and I enjoyed ourselves. We fished every day and I commiserated with her loss of the Trout House. She explained how her husband had purchased the coffee plantation from the Oxley Trust of London. At the time this information didn't really mean much. But it would. I was twenty-four. UPI got hold of me and wanted me to go to Northern Ireland, but Lilly sent me a telegram telling me the old man was sick. It was time for me to go home.

6

MY mother had withered with age, but the old man had always seemed immune to the ravages of time and, over the years, Lilly and I had assumed he'd outlive us both.

I flew into Pellston, which several times each winter is the coldest locale in the lower forty-eight. Lilly handed me a beer when we met in the terminal. These were the days when airport security consisted almost exclusively of trying to prevent overcurious paying customers at rural airports from wandering into moving propellers.

At thirty-two Lilly looked barely out of her teens unless you looked into her eyes; being married to a cop and trying to raise three young children was no picnic.

"I'd kill for your tan," Lilly said.

You could get killed for my tan, I thought. "How's Dad?"

She shook her head. Her eyes were dry. "They wanted to keep him in Traverse City, to treat the pain, but you know how he is."

Lilly gave me the medical details as we drove home. Our father's cancer was inoperable, which meant terminal unless a miracle happened. It rarely did in such cases. Not too many years later impending deaths would be described in much more refined detail and this would be hailed as progress. I did not ask how long he had to live. In the war I had seen doctors succeed and call it skill, and fail and discard it as bad luck. Ballyhooed advances aside, the practice of medicine remained largely a crapshoot.

The house looked larger without my mother filling the space. The old man was splitting wood outside. He paused to glance at me and went back to work.

At dinner he hardly ate. His face was drawn. "Returned for the wake, I see."

"A bit early, I'd say."

He grinned and nodded. "Staying long?"

"Thought I'd take it a day at a time."

"Only way it can be. I'm glad you're home from that mess."

The old man refused pain medication and went about dying the way he went about living, one thing at a time and when everything was done save dying, he did that.

I had been home nearly three months. Lilly had gone back to Alpena with her children. Her husband, Roger Ranger, had moved up in the world and was a trooper in the Michigan State Police, an agency well known for taking only the best. The old man and I settled into a routine. He chopped wood most mornings, but one morning I heard only silence. Cutting wood, I knew, was his way of showing that he would not knuckle under to the disease, but some mornings he could hardly move and it was rare when he split more than a few small logs. I found him by the woodpile, sitting on a stump. It was snowing and his face was blue.

"Dad?"

His eyes flickered.

"You need to get inside, Dad."

"I'm fine right here," he said in a barely audible voice.

I squatted beside him and we looked down on Whirling Creek.

"Burn the house when I'm gone," he said. "Only the land has value. And no reading from your mother's Good Book."

I didn't offer supportive words. There was no point and I didn't know how.

"You never listened," he said in a mildly scolding tone. "You went up the creek."

"No, Dad." It was his one rule that I had never broken.

"Your life is going up the creek," he said. "I always admired that and feared it too."

"I love you, Dad."

His hand touched my shoulder. I could not draw a breath. And he drew his last.

We buried my father beside Queen Anna. I could imagine her demanding to know where he had been and him shuffling his feet. They had had their differences, which came and went, but they had also had love, I supposed, from start to finish. I wondered if I would ever be so lucky.

All the neighbors came to the funeral, including Gus and Ruby Chickerman. All of the visitors hauled food for the customary potluck and many of them spoke fondly of my dad and none of them used the Bible. Father Luke was there and said my father had had his own ways, but was a man to be counted on when it mattered.

After the funeral, I returned to the house. Lilly and Roger took what they wanted and after they left, I burned the place. The house had been my parents' creation and now they were gone. I thought I understood my father's reasoning. It did not deserve to outlive them.

I stood by Whirling Creek and watched the flames.

A dark-haired woman appeared nearby. "Bowie," she said. "Your father was a wonderful man."

Raina Chickerman had grown even more beautiful. "I was too late for the funeral," she said. "I am really sorry, Bowie. You're all alone now."

I don't know why, but I didn't want her pity. "I still have Lilly."

Raina smiled the way she smiled when we were kids. It meant I was nitpicking and she would not descend to my level.

"How are you?" I asked. I had a million questions but all that I managed was, "What're you doing these days?"

"Living life the best I can."

"The most or the best?" I asked.

"It's the same thing, Bowie. You should know that, running off to a war. I'd say senseless or stupid war, but that would be redundant." She tilted her head slightly. She was as arrogant as ever. "What will you do now?" she asked.

"Go up the creek," I said.

"Don't forget your paddle," she said with the hint of a smile.

A crash of collapsing timbers from the fire caught my attention and I turned to make sure it wasn't getting out of control. I wanted to talk to her, get to know her again, but when I turned back she was walking with her purposeful stride into the forest near the creek and although I tried to follow, I did not catch up and could not find her. Had she really been there?

In some ways I was more disturbed by her departure than by my father's death. There had been no choice for him and I had resigned myself to his passing, but I had never dealt with my feelings for Raina and how we had drifted apart. Standing there by the roaring fire I realized I had always loved her and I mourned my losses, all of them at once.

7

G RADY Yetter was waiting for me in the dimly lit La Guardia terminal. My father had passed away in mid-November and I'd spent Thanksgiving with Lilly, Roger, and their kids, but I needed to get back to work and I wanted time and space alone to mourn my father. Northern Ireland seemed just far enough away. I had called Yetter and he asked me to come to New York. I shouldered my way through the crowd in the narrow brown hallways and found him leaning against a wall of dented, gray public lockers, reading the *Daily News*, which he had meticulously folded vertically into two-column sections. Yetter was an inveterate reader with an unerring nose for news in the form of emerging hot spots; he was called Spook behind his back at UPI, and so accurate were his predictions that it was not uncommon for employees to wonder out loud if he was on the CIA's payroll.

Grady's other gift lay in his ability to recognize talent for UPI's insatiable human pipeline. Wire service work burned out reporters fast, which made turnover a perennial problem. It was Grady's job to find new blood for UPI and to pick places and situations about to emerge as newsworthy. Some bureau chiefs saw Yetter as a meddler in their domains, but the company brass had him pegged as their chief talent scout, and as long as he kept producing they would keep listening to him.

Nobody talked about mentors in those days, but I felt like Yetter was my personal booster at UPI and, for reasons I could not understand, I was his anointed protégé.

"Have you had that suit cleaned since the last time I saw you?"

He lowered his paper and squinted at me. "How long's it been? More'n two years? I probably had it cleaned at least once since then." He carefully folded the paper into a small square and extended his hand. "You did a damn fine job," he said.

"Too many of my stories got spiked in Manila."

Yetter grimmaced. "It's just politics, kid. You can't take the bullshit personally. Your job is to get the story and get it down as good as you can. Everybody has a boss, even the free press. This country wasn't ready for reality, but they're getting hit right in the kisser with a shitpot-full now. You wanna grab something to eat?"

"No thanks."

"I do," he said. I followed him outside the terminal to a hot dog vendor with a battered pushcart. Grady had two greenish franks slathered with pale brown mustard and seared blue-gray onions dredged out of grimy, tarnished metal boxes. I had rancid black coffee. Light snow fluttered around us, like spinners falling back to the river, their cycle complete. I remembered something Lloyd Nash had told me. "Bugs are born to die," he said. "Just like people, only faster."

"Sorry about your father," Yetter said, interrupting my reverie.

Cabs were lined up. Horns honked. The air was filled with a haze of blue exhaust. People shouted angrily at each other in several languages. Aircraft departed in the background, their engines roaring as they lifted off the ground.

With his mouth full, Grady said, "There's a story going around that you burned down your house with your old man's body inside. People think you're crazy." He glanced at me for a reaction. "The way I see it, crazy's an asset in this racket."

"There wasn't anyone in the house."

"Which says you torched it."

"Yeah. It's what my old man wanted."

He picked at a piece of food caught between his upper lip and gum. "Is this like some sort of Indian thing?"

Yetter was one of those New Yorkers who looked upon the Midwest as still being populated by savages. "Something like that."

"You like basketball?" he asked between mouthfuls.

"No."

Yetter grunted. "Contrary prick, aren't you? Sure you do. You scored seventy-six points in a high school game. You were first-team all-state two years in Class D."

"You've been snooping."

"That's what they pay me for, pal."

"I just played to attract the girls."

"Guy scores seventy-six points in a game ain't ambivalent about the game. B-ball get you a lot of cooz?"

"Some," I said. Which was a lie, of course, but in the male world, such lies are permissible.

"I was never a jock," Yetter said. "I had to work for ginch my whole life. Still do. Hookers are more efficient. You pay, you do, you move on."

We took a cab into Manhattan.

Crossing the Tri-Borough Bridge, I asked him, "Why Northern Ireland?"

"Because I think there's a helluva storm brewing up there," he said, with his voice tapering off, "only you're going to London."

"London?" This was a surprise and I noticed that he avoided my eyes. There was a gob of mustard at the corner of his mouth.

"Yeah, there was a real nasty debate about what to do with you. Your story on the hospital ship yanked a lot of political chains. And this thing about burning your old man's house down doesn't help. What I've never understood is how you got out to that damn ship in the first place."

"I told them I wanted to do a story on how surgical practice jumps ahead during wartime."

He looked at me with what I took to be admiration. "Tell them what they want to hear," he said, flashing a grin and nodding supportively. "Misdirection is the cardinal rule of investigation. Smart. Point one way, go another. Just like a fake in basketball."

He made it sound Machiavellian. "Why London?" I asked again.

"It's a great assignment, lots of good stuff happening. You know, youth movement and that bug band?"

"The Beatles?"

"Yeah, yeah, yeah," he said, grinning at his own lame joke. "You're gonna cover cultural changes and that includes the peace movement."

"In England?"

"Right."

"What happened to Northern Ireland?"

He said animatedly, "Hey look, we're at your hotel and I gotta run. We'll talk tonight."

The hotel was the Tudor on Forty-Second Street, a few blocks west of UPI's offices. It was seedy by city standards and palatial in a Vietnam context. My room was in back, away from the boisterous street.

I had agreed to meet Yetter at Madison Square Garden for the Knicks-Celtics game that night, which gave me the better part of the afternoon alone. I was glad for the time. After the River of Trout, Key's manuscript and the story the two crazy Marines had told me, my curiosity about the snowfly had grown into a hunger; I was like a famished trout rising to a hatch after an endless, barren winter. I needed to find out more about the snowfly and to do that, I needed to know more about M. J. Key.

It was a cold, blustery day and the acrid stench of garbage wafted down brick and stone canyons, but it smelled positively civilized compared to what I had experienced the past two years.

The New York City Public Library was a landmark, reputed to have a collection that surpassed many major universities. Unfortunately, it was closed. With dozens of other people, I sat on the steps in a brief respite of sunlight and smoked. A woman examined me carefully before sitting down nearby. She wore a full-length charcoal gray car coat and black wool scarf tied under her chin in a nondescript knot. After so many years of fishing with flies I paid attention to knots and it occurred to me that noticing the knot on a woman's scarf before looking at the woman wearing it was not a particularly healthy sign. She opened a sandwich wrapped in reddish brown butcher paper.

"Come here often?" she asked.

She had a soft, friendly voice. "Just today, but it's closed."

"It'll be open tomorrow. You can come back then."

"I'm afraid I won't be here. It's one of those now-or-never things."

She smiled. "Passing through?"

"More or less."

"Ah," she said, " a man of mystery." She flashed a toothy smile between bites of her overstuffed sandwich.

I smiled back, wondering if we had entered some sort of negotiation. I had to remind myself that I was no longer in Asia, where there were no rules about anything.

"What is it you're looking for?" she asked. "In the library," she added.

An interesting distinction. "It's pretty obscure."

"I'd like to know," she said.

What the hell, I thought, and told her some about M. J. Key. I told her I'd heard about the possibility of a manuscript, but nothing of my experiences on the River of Trout or that I'd held the Key manuscript in my hands. She listened attentively while she steadily whittled the sandwich down to nothing.

"You're a fisherperson?" she asked.

It was a stange way to put it. "Yes, but I don't get a lot of opportunity."

"It's not healthy to let your life become unbalanced." She neatly folded her sandwich wrapper and placed it in the huge bag slung over her shoulder. "I'm Danny," she said. "I work here and I'd love to let you in, but I can't. There's a dreadful plumbing problem and we've been closed by Public Health for a couple of days. I could do some looking for you."

"You're a librarian?"

"A law student masquerading as a librarian," she said in a whisper. "The work is similar, when you think about it. I'd love to help. It sounds interesting."

"It's a long shot," I said. I didn't want to put her to the trouble.

"Well, there are no patrons inside today, so I have plenty of time on my hands and I hate to just sit around. Where are you staying?"

I gave her the name of my hotel; she said she would call me there and I thanked her again for her willingness to help me.

"A library's main product is service," she said with mock pride.

We shook gloved hands to seal the arrangement. As we started to separate, she said, "You have a great tan. Have you been down south?"

"Asia," I said.

"I see," she replied pensively. "The war?"

I nodded.

"Soldier?"

"Reporter."

She stared at me for a moment, then stepped closer, put her arms around me and gave me a hug. "Welcome home."

This was my first time in New York and as I wandered the cold and windy streets, it struck me how people went about their business as if there were no war in Vietnam. I moseyed around for the rest of the afternoon, taking in the sights of the city. Near the UN building there was a small, loud crowd carrying signs. STOP THE WAR NOW. They chanted, "Hey, hey, LBJ, how many kids have you killed today?" I moved on, knowing full well that there would never be demonstrators in Hanoi chanting, "Oh no, Uncle Ho, how many more of our kids will have to go?"

The game that night was a sellout. The New York fans seemed to hate the Celtics. Boston scored off the opening tip-off and went on an eighteen-to-two-point run.

"Fucking spastic sadsacks," Grady muttered. "Let's go find a brew."

There was a short beer line in the upper concourse. We leaned against a nearby wall. The crowd's moaning and shouting gave life to the building, the sound passing through in anguished, ragged waves.

"Why London?" I asked him.

"Because you're my go-to guy. I don't want you in another Manila crossfire. Your bureau chief in London is an old hand and one of my boys. His name's Daly and he's a Mick and don't be asking me which flavor because I don't know and don't give a shit."

"What if I'm not interested?"

Yetter coughed and grinned confidently. "London, the city of youth and free love. Don't be an asshole. They've all got dirty feet, but who cares when you're in bed, right?"

"Level with me," I said.

Yetter didn't respond right away. After a long pause, he patted his belly. "Northern Ireland is gonna go hot. I can feel it. It'll become a bloody cesspool and you've just gotten out of one. You don't need another war, kid. I don't want you to become a blood junkie."

"I hated covering that shit," I said defensively.

He glowered at me. "That's what junkies always say." He raised his chin, as if his mind was set. "Go to London, kid. It's a sweet assignment and it'll give you a chance to see what Americans didn't want to become."

I was not going to complain. I had found M. J. Key's manuscript among Sir Thomas Oxley's books in Vietnam. Oxley was English and at one time, at least, there had been a trust in his name—and the Oxley Trust was a trail to the manuscript. A cold trail, but a trail nevertheless. I should have been questioning my motivation, but I didn't, for reasons not at all clear to me. All I knew was that solving what I thought of as the mystery of the snowfly had become very important to me. London was the next logical choice in an illogical search and I wasn't going to turn down the assignment. I agreed to go there. Yetter was visibly relieved.

There were details like a visa and work permit to finalize, but Yetter would handle them. He gave me my ticket. "Daly will meet your plane." We shook hands. "Let's get back to the game."

"You go. I need sleep."

Yetter looked shocked. "You know how much these tickets cost me?"

"Not out of *your* pocket," I said sarcastically.

Yetter's face hardened and he stuck out his hand. "Be careful, kid. Cowboys die ugly."

There was no word from Danny when I got back to the hotel from the Garden. Life was a series of disappointments, large and small. I tried to watch TV, but I'd never appreciated the medium. I liked my entertainment on a big screen and my news on paper. I decided Danny would not be calling. I was asleep when the phone rang.

"Mister Rhodes? This is Danny. Did I wake you?"

I looked at my watch. It was two A.M. "I was just catnapping."

"I'm sorry to take so long. When are you leaving?"

"Tomorrow, late afternoon out of La Guardia."

"Super! Do you think we could meet?"

"How about at the library when it opens?"

"How about breakfast at your hotel?" she countered.

"Delish," Danny said with her mouth jammed full of western omelette. She ate more in one sitting than most Vietnamese families.

"You're not hungry, which doesn't surprise me in the least," she said. "I looked you up. Awful stories." She immediately winced, rolled her eyes, and circled her forefinger around her temple. "Call me Dumbo Danny. I meant to say your stories were great, but your experiences must have been awful. Datelines suggest you were there quite some time. I guess this is all a major readjustment for you. How do you feel about all the protests?"

I didn't answer and she politely moved on. "Want to know what I found?" she asked.

A straight-backed waiter interrupted us and poured more coffee.

"Your Mister Key is *exceedingly* obscure and biographical information is difficult to come by, but I found a book called *Scholars or Charlatans?* It was published in 1939 and barely mentions Key, but it's indexed and there he was. He had a doctorate in biology from Princeton and taught for a time at Michigan Agricultural College, now Michigan State. The author contends that Key was interested in eugenics and was a Germanophile. The not-so-subtle inference is that Key was pro-Nazi."

I knew about Key's teaching. I tried to remember what Nash had said about Key's leaving. Sometime before World War II and either resigned or forced out? That question seemed to be answered.

"There's more," she said, plowing on enthusiastically. "I mined our so-called morgue as best I could and found a story out of Detroit. Key resigned from the college in 1938. He wasn't the only academic under fire back then. There were a dozen or so others from Michigan colleges forced out because of alleged pro-Nazi sympathies. In the clipping Henry Ford defended the professors and the Nazis, maintaining that Nazi efficiency was to be admired, not their ethics. This isn't much, but what struck me is that the other ousted professors protested and vehemently denied the allegations, but your Mr. Key said nothing. He was the only one to remain silent. If I dug more and had more time, I'm sure I could find more."

"I appreciate this," I said. Key was a Nazi lover. What did that have to do with trout and snowflies?

"I love to dig," she said. "My mother says I was born nosy and I won't deny it. I found more, but I'm not certain it applies. There was a journal published by the University of Chicago math department. It was called *Vari-*

ables. I found an article by a man named Vijver and coauthored by M. J. Key of MAC. This was in early 1937 and I assume this is your professor, but I can't verify it."

"A math article?" By a biologist? I wondered.

She glanced up and her eyes narrowed. "Not exactly. The article talks about the use of plain language codes in the field of cryptography. The authors claimed they could write clear-text messages that professional cryptoanalysts would not be able to decipher."

Danny wiped her mouth with a cloth napkin and inhaled deeply. She dug into her bag and extracted a dusty journal, propped her eyeglasses on top of her head, and began to read.

" 'Shakespeare wrote: "Brevity is the soul of wit," and in this regard the most effective codes reside in clean, plain language. Poets have comprehended this for centuries. Rhyming schemes devised in Ireland in the seventh century have never been equaled anywhere in the world since. Not only can a code exist in the most mundane language, it can also exist in the meter of the language, meter serving as a kind of cryptographic Morse Code—to employ a crude metaphor.' "

She continued reading: " 'The monks of Greavy achieved the penultimate of linguistics in the seventh century and their work gave rise to English poetics, of which the Great Bard, Mr. Shakespeare, is the crowning example, his work more than adequately demonstrating the use of double and triple entendre, which is, loosely speaking, a form of code intended for those few in the audience knowledgeable enough to comprehend the entire content.' "

I interrupted her. "What's Greavy?"

Danny said, "I did some snooping and even called my friend at the Medieval Center at Yale. There are no references to Greavy and my friend says she's never heard of it. You think the name is somehow connected to a code?"

"I don't know." In fact, the more I learned, the less I knew.

Danny paused at this juncture and said, "I'm skipping ahead here. 'One could pen a daily column in the *New York Times,* for example, that could convey information diametrically different from the apparent content. In fact, this article may contain such a code and if so, we challenge our colleagues and readers to read the true content.' "

Danny briefly looked up at me to see if I was still tracking and, apparently satisfied, resumed where she had left off. " 'Information can be conveyed most efficiently in language,' " she read, " 'which means that the true and ardent study of cryptography should rightfully fall into the realm of poets, not engineers or mathematicians.' "

I couldn't sort it all out. Key was a biologist, trout fisherman, conservationist, German-speaking Nazi sympathizer who happened to dabble in writing codes? Who the hell was he, James Bond? He had left the college under a scandal's cloud, but what had happened to him after that? Nash had suggested matter-of-factly that Key might have been a spy. Maybe Nash had been right, but on whose side was Key? I didn't know whether to laugh or cry. I saw in my mind the woman in the red Cadillac and tried to figure out how one stupid statement had led me down this bizarre, twisting path.

"You look confused," Danny said.

"I am," I admitted.

"There's a bit more," she said. "I found references to the 1892 and 1943 books you mentioned and I got them off our shelves and in one of them, the 1943, I found a partial note, unsigned and handwritten. It said a new manuscript by Key was nearly done and that a working title had been assigned: *The Myth of the Snowfly*. The note wasn't dated, but it was on H. Hixson letterhead. Hixson was the publisher of the second Key book in 1943, so it could be a note from an editor or someone in the house around that time."

"You got all this in one day?"

"I'm sorry there's not more. If I just had more time."

I laughed out loud. I had no idea how any of this fit, but she had just pushed me forward by a huge margin in my quest for Key. In one night. "This is amazing," I said. "Is Hixson still publishing?"

"I anticipated you'd ask that," she said with a flash of her eyes. "The firm went out of business in 1947. It was not bought or absorbed by another publisher, it simply folded. And," she said, "it only began to publish in 1938. It was *very* unusual for a publisher to have such a short business life in those days."

"What are you suggesting?"

"I don't know, but my instincts say that a publisher being in business only during the war years is an interesting fact that should not be ignored."

I agreed with her and tried to sort through what she was telling me. I had held Key's snowfly manuscript at the Goodwins' Trout House. It sometimes seemed unreal to me: While knew I had had the evidence in hand, I had not gotten more than a glimpse at the cover. Danny's findings at least confirmed that the manuscript had not been a hallucination.

"Thus endeth the take," she said, sliding the dusty journal across the table.

"You're letting me have this?"

"Well, it's not strictly according to Hoyle, but I trust you to send it back. I pride myself in judging character, and you seem trustworthy." She handed me a piece of paper with an address and phone number. "Home," she said. "If you let me know where you are, I'll send along anything else I dredge up. You would like for me to keep digging, wouldn't you?"

If Key had been forced away from the college, where had he gone? "Is there a way to find out if Key left the U.S. after he resigned from the college?"

"If it's findable," she said, "I'll find it."

"You'll be a great lawyer one day. Can I pay you?" I asked.

She gave me a dismissive wave of the hand. "*Hush* about money. This is an intellectual challenge."

That afternoon I left for London; I read the Vijver-Key article several times during the flight and with each reading became more and more confused. The more I learned, the less I knew. What the hell was I chasing? More to the point: Why?

UPI's bureau chief in London was Joe Daly, a Bostonian, barely five feet tall, stocky and freckled with a broad flat face, bushy red hair, and a long shiny forehead. He was standing outside immigration with my name scribbled almost illegibly on a piece of cardboard.

We traded names and shook hands hard and he growled, "Follow me."

Daly had a small dark high-roofed sedan with numerous dings and scratches. The thing tipped like it would roll at the slightest provocation. Stability wasn't helped by my driver's rough manners with the clutch and gears. He had short, thin fingers with thick pads that flattened at the ends, an almost nonexistent chin, and small dark eyes covered by thick eyelids that opened and closed lugubriously. The overall effect was that of a small toad.

"Good work in Vietnam," he said, *nam* rhyming with *lam,* a pronunciation that grated on my ears.

He continued, "There're two schools of thought in the wire service business. First school says that they want people who can dig up facts and let editors and rewrite yoyos polish the words on paper. The other school says that diggers ought to be able to write what they find. You got a position on this?"

"School two," I said.

Daly nodded his approval. "Good answer. That saves me work. I don't mollycoddle my people, Rhodes. We're all pros. You know anything about the peace movement here?"

"Not really."

Daly hardly waited for my answer. "This country," he said wistfully. "It's a *beaut*. Flower power moved across the Atlantic. Dope, free love, peace, the whole shebang. In the States there are always people with a beef and looking for a fight. The younger generation back home doesn't trust older generations and nobody except cretins trusts our government. Here? Too much respect!" He laughed out loud and banged the heel of his left hand on the steering wheel. "Back in the States students take to the streets and the government shits its pants. Here the government says, 'By jove, we'd best hear what the young blighters have to say.' The peacies here are left, socialists, commies, who knows what all? The average Brit wants peace, racial equality, Eden on earth. 'Veddy' left, you see? 'Veddy propah, old boy.' "

The bureau chief looked to see if I was paying attention and rambled on. "Naturally the pinky peacies here figured to link up with the lefty unions, only the unions here are up in arms over immigration, very pissed that wogs are taking proper English jobs. The lefty unions here are fascist when it comes to skin color. They hate everything but white. Result? The peace movement here is stillborn and the country is headed downhill."

"Not a story, then."

My new boss cleared his throat. "Maybe. This country's going to hell fast. Rule Britannia and all that folderol. In their hearts the Brits remain certain that the empire exists and the sun never sets on it. The silly sods live in the past. Meanwhile, across the channel, the rest of Europe is fashioning itself into an economic union. The Brits, of course, want no part of it. Things have been good here for a long time, but deep down there's big trouble. The Brits are losing capital fast. Immigration is stirring serious discontent. The students here are very elite. Not like back home, where just about anybody can get into school somewhere. Here you're in by blood or big smarts, period. This is a class society. Per capita income doubled for the middle class after the big war. But that's not going to last. The damn country's caught in a time warp. The Brits look at how their music has moved into America and become the rage. The queen gave medals to the Beatles, can you believe that? Members of the British Empire. Geez. The Brits think this music thing and the fashion industry, which you will not believe, prove that they are still top of the heap. What the Brits don't recognize is that American culture has a powerful beachhead here. We're dug in and we're gonna get deeper and deeper. Rest of Europe too. What I want you to do is to go among the people, find out what they're thinking. Let them tell their stories in their own words. The way you did with soldiers. This is the world capital of eccentrics, Rhodes. Peculiar ideas abound and virtually all of them get automatic respect because that's how Brits are. Get your talented butt into the streets and countryside and write about what you see and hear."

"It's not exactly a breaking news beat."

Joe Daly frowned. "Breaking news? Anybody can cover that shit. TV will kick our asses on a breaking story every fucking time. We have to put words in print and that takes time. They just have to break into their programming. To survive, we have to go deeper than breaking news. The world's shrinking like a tomato in the sun. Homogenizing. It's happening slowly, but it is happening and *that's* news. Hell," he added, "a lot of reporters would kill for an assignment like this."

"I had thought I was going to Northern Ireland."

"You were, but I waylaid your ass."

"I thought the shift to London was Yetter's idea."

Daly guffawed and shook his head. "That's Grady for you. He fought like hell to put you over there, but I read your stuff. Great reporting. I want you to take people on patrol here. Besides, there was a better candidate for Ireland."

"Who?"

"Benita Hamill. She was born there, educated in the States. Boston College and Columbia. Smart as they come and she's one of them. She's as ruthless as Churchill and writes like Keats," he said. "She's also my daughter," he added. "I met her mother during the Blitz. We never married, but I made sure my kid got taken care of." He looked at me and wagged a stubby finger. "She belongs over there and you belong here. This isn't nepotism, it's professional judgment."

"Yetter said he didn't want me to become a blood junkie."

Daly's shoulders sagged. "I put that idea in his head."

"Why?"

"Because that's what Yetter is and I knew it would hit home." Daly looked over at me again. "Don't misread this, Rhodes. I want you here. My daughter got the job only because I wanted you."

"Should I feel grateful?"

He cleared his throat. "I don't give a shit how you feel. I just want you to know how it is."

I appreciated Daly's forthrightness. After Del Puffit, he would be fresh air in my working life. Besides, this might be an easy tour of duty and I had personal business here. At this point my interest was more in the line of the mystery, but in the back of my mind I knew that once it was solved, I wanted to fish the snowfly hatch—if such a thing existed. Why else would I go to all this trouble?

"You were here during the Blitz?" I asked Daly.

"Came over in '39 and pretty much been here ever since."

"Do you know much about the codebreaking effort during the war?"

Daly smiled. "No, but I know somebody who knows all there is to know about that stuff. Why?"

"Something I scraped against in Vietnam," I lied. I was thinking about Vijver-Key. They said they could write codes. Had anybody believed them? "Can you arrange an introduction?"

"I can try," Daly said, pulling into a parking lot. "Here's home, Rhodes."

We left the car in a lot with a female attendant in a black uniform and walked down Fleet Street, home to most of Britain's major newspapers. About halfway down Middle Temple Lane we turned left into Wine Office Court. The building housing UPI's offices was an old structure, four stories high with a nondescript entrance and no signage to indicate who or what might be inside. We trudged up narrow, dark stone stairs, worn in the middle by what I imagined to be centuries of foot traffic.

"Expensive real estate," Daly said as he huffed and puffed. "But it's owned by an old broad who worked for us during the war and she leases it to us for next to nothing. Brits are loyal. Remember that."

I liked the building.

The offices were on the top floor. They were small and cramped with high ceilings and a heating system that clanged and coughed and hissed like a living thing. There was a small garden on the roof where we could take tea, "when it isn't raining or the soot won't choke you, which is about a half-dozen times a year," Daly said.

There was a receptionist sitting behind a low barrier, holding court over an ancient switchboard with all sorts of colored wires. She smiled dutifully at us. "This is Dolly," my new boss said. "Do what she says if you want to be linked to the outside world. In fact, just do what she says," he added.

The floors of the office were filthy, caked with grease and dirt, the air heavy with stale smoke.

The bureau chief's office was small, the same size as the others, and across a narrow hall from the tearoom. "Elevenses," he said with a nod toward the other room. "Whole fucking country stops at eleven A.M. to have its tea. Dolly makes it every day." He seemed amused by this.

I saw no photography equipment and no lab. "Do we have photographers?"

"Not on staff. The company's got most of its resources elsewhere. We hire local talent as we need it, fly somebody in, or use some of the crap Fleet Street shoots. It's cheaper this way. The local talent can hack it, but make sure you plan ahead. Talk to Dolly. She has the list."

I nodded agreement and took out a notebook and began to make notes.

"Dolly's booked a flat for you." He looked at me. "It'll get you started and we'll pick up the rent. You don't like it, you're free to find something on your own. If what you want costs more, you pay the difference. Dolly has the key."

"Fair enough."

"The bureau owns four cars," Daly went on. "The one we were in is mine. The other three are up for grabs as you need them."

I said, "Talk to Dolly?"

He grunted. "You're catching on. She'll help you work out a driver's license. We've got a deal where we can drive on our American licenses and not have to go through red tape for the locals, but let her handle it."

He took me to an office at the end of the hallway. It was crammed with boxes and piles of curling yellow dog paper. There was a Royal upright type-writer that had lost a corner support and listed. The room seemed cold and I must have shivered.

"We call this the Fridge," he said. "Low man on the totem, Rhodes. No choice. Good incentive to be out in the street doing your job."

I pecked at a couple of keys on the Royal. It worked fine.

"Staffers are all out working," he said. "You can meet them later. Dolly's already put out a note telling everyone you're on board." Office assignment made, Daly camped me in front of Dolly's station and left us alone.

"Cuppa?" she asked.

"Pardon?"

"Would you like a cup of tea?" she asked, carefully enunciating each word.

I laughed. "That would be great."

"Follow me," she said.

Dolly Aster was a tall, big-boned woman with a leonine head and a huge mane of hair. She wore a short skirt, loose blouse, and satin vest festooned with rhinestones. She was married to a London cop, a detective. She had been with UPI for more than twenty years and was proud of it. She gave me Earl Grey tea and explained that this was the only proper English tea; she had no use for the fruit-flavored "concoctions" that were beginning to emerge on the market.

"Your flat is clean," she said. "I've seen to that. Wouldn't do to have you in filth. You get enough of that in your work. I expect conditions here to be a bit better than your last assignment." Daly had obviously told her something about my past.

She gave me a list of the other UPI reporters, their addresses and phone numbers, and the key to my flat with directions for finding it, including a city map she had carefully and precisely marked.

I thanked her for everything and she assured me I could call her at any time and that I should bother Daly only when circumstances were "dire."

"You're in charge around here." I meant it as a compliment.

Dolly stiffened. "Mister Daly is the regimental commander. I am merely the regiment's sergeant major."

"But sergeants actually run the armies of the world," I said. She rewarded me with a smile.

I walked to my apartment, which was on Rupert Street in Soho. UPI's offices were in Holborn and to get to Soho I had to traverse the Covent Garden district. Soho had once been open fields and home to foxes, which royalty chased on horseback. Later I learned that the name came from an old hunting call, *So-ho!* Now the area was a crowded jumble of old buildings in every imaginable architectural style and people sardined into small flats above seedy commercial establishments. There were bright new signs and old faded ones for cafés and pubs and nightspots, and the streets were filled with hawkers and buskers and hippies and young people decked out in electric colors. London's Chinatown was one block away from my place, on Gerrard Street. The bustle and noise of Soho reminded me of Saigon, without the threat of somebody tossing a grenade in my face.

My flat was small: a kitchenette, an ancient bathroom with a huge claw-footed tub, a small bedroom, and a living area with a fireplace that no longer worked. The wallpaper was clean but peeling and there were a few threadbare throw rugs on a worn parquet floor. The place was furnished with an eclectic collection of items, including a huge painting on one wall of five naked women making love, twisted into various positions so that the shape of the bodies formed a star. The predominant colors were red and peach; the figures were cartoonish. None of the women had a right breast.

My telephone was already connected, attesting to Dolly's efficiency.

Not remembering that London was five hours ahead of New York, I called Danny's home number in New York and got no answer. Then I called the New York City Public Library. She was out to lunch, but I left a message for her with my new phone numbers.

I did not have many possessions to unpack. A few clothes, a fly rod, some fly boxes, some books, a well-worn fishing vest, and a small net.

Nolan's Pub was a few doors from the flat. I stood at the bar and had a pint of bitters and fish-and-chips served in a newspaper funnel. People were friendly but left me alone and after four pints, I returned to my new home and fell into deep sleep, wondering what lay ahead.

As a reporter you learn that, more often than not, you get the nexus of an idea for a story, then have to scratch and excavate for facts to flesh it out; sometimes, though, a story lands in your lap and leaves you anxious and suspicious. About a week after I began work in London, I had an unannounced visitor. I had arrived at the office early and was alone except for Dolly, who seemed to be there at all hours. I was ensconced in my office reading one of the morning papers when Dolly suddenly appeared in my doorway, looking exasperated and perturbed, but before she could say anything she was pushed aside by a tall gaunt man with a ruddy face and a disabled left hand that curled like a claw.

"Rhodes?" the stranger said curtly. "Christian Shelldrake here." He showed no inclination to shake hands and offered no immediate explanation of what he wanted or who he represented.

"Can I help you?" I asked.

"I daresay that determination will be made forthwith," he said.

His officious tone grated at me. "Who are you with?" I inquired.

"Affiliations are less important than the individual," my strange visitor said with a wince, and sat down. He had intense, darting gray eyes and sat tentatively on the edge of his chair as if he might have to spring away at any moment. "Let me be direct," he added. To save his time more than mine, I thought. "I know that you served in Southeast Asia and I presume you are familiar with flutes."

"The musical instruments?"

Shelldrake sucked in his breath with an agitated hiss and flashed an anguished look. "You are reputed, Mr. Rhodes, perhaps erroneously, to possess a high level of intelligence. If I sought a fool, I would visit Fleet Street."

"I'm sorry, Shelldrake. I didn't mean to make a joke at your expense, but I have no idea what you're talking about. Should I?"

I sensed his veneer of formality was no more than a flimsy firewall against violence. I had met similar characters in Vietnam.

Shelldrake studied me the way a predator examines its next meal. "I refer to baton rounds, used for crowd control, most recently employed in the nationalistic disorders in Hong Kong."

"Baton rounds," I repeated to let him know I was listening. This was a new term to me.

"Yes, teak the length of a man's member and weighted with a metal core. Some call them flutes because the rounds are more or less rifled, but they are also more crassly known as Flying Rogers."

I decided to be as direct as my unannounced visitor. "What does this have to do with me?"

"Everything," Shelldrake said. "Perhaps. It depends on your critical abilities. *They* obviously cannot employ flutes against their own people. The Chinese, even in Hong Kong, are one thing, but against white Englishmen? Unthinkable. It would be political suicide, you see?"

" 'They'?"

"The Home Office, the government. I would say Her Royal Majesty's government, but the monarchy is a sham, inbred show dogs lacking claws, morals, teeth, or backbones."

Shelldrake was certainly free in sharing his opinions.

"The baton device is bad?"

"It is quite lethal at close range and entirely indiscriminate and inaccurate at any distance. Fired into the pavement, the wooden shell and metal cores break up and spray pieces around like shrapnel."

GIs in Vietnam fired their M-16s into roads and hardscrabble dirt to achieve the same effect. Military experts called the practice multiplying firepower. "Why are you here, Mister Shelldrake?"

"You are reputedly a politically sensitive man, Rhodes, apparently that unique journalist with ethics, which in this country is as rare as a royal with a brain. I read a cutting of your story on the racist experiments with wounded black soldiers on your government's hospital ship, the *Snow*. I reiterate, these heinous weapons are not intended for use on *white* Englishmen, but they will be employed without conscience on the coloreds flocking to Great Britain and no doubt will find extensive use in the colonies as well."

"Governments decide how to handle such problems."

"Do you trust *your* government to take such decisions honorably and correctly?"

I immediately recalled that night in Lansing when cops were issued brand-new ax handles from gleaming garbage cans. I also recalled the summer of 1967, during my first year in Vietnam, when American cities errupted in race riots that led to dozens of fatalities, mass arrests, and untold damage to private and public property. It had been strange to be covering a war and reading about violence back home.

I did not trust any government, including my own. "You want to speak out publicly?"

Shelldrake glared at me. "I want the issue thoroughly and properly aired before these weapons are employed. For very good reasons, my identity must be protected."

"And if your identity should become known?"

"I will be promptly rendered incapable of further communications," he said gravely. His meaning was clear.

"How do you know the government's intentions?"

He leered at me. "You may assume that I know well of what I speak. The authorities dare not use teak here; because of this, they are now developing rubber bullets, very hard, equally lethal, and even less accurate. You see, *rubber* sounds better than *teak,* yes? It's a mere subterfuge, porridge words meant solely for public consumption."

"If these things are still under testing, how do you know they're lethal?"

"They're testing bullets made of various substances against sheep. If I decide you're the man to do this, I assure you that you will see evidence that will convince even the most recalcitrant skeptic. When you see, you will understand."

"Aren't there ways to express such concerns through the government?"

"This has been done and led nowhere."

"By you?" I asked.

"I am neither courageous nor stupid, Mister Rhodes."

I mulled over his proposition. "I will need some evidence to proceed."

Shelldrake gave me an envelope that contained a thick wad of newspaper clippings.

"These," he announced theatrically, "are from the Hong Kong riots of 1967 and earlier. The riots in Hong Kong were fomented by Peking, but that's irrelevant. The constabulary used baton rounds indiscriminately and now British authorities are preparing to do the same elsewhere. It *must* be stopped, sir. *Must* be! If you are interested, I will provide you with the compelling evidence you require."

"I'll want photographs," I said.

"This has been anticipated."

By whom? I wondered. "Photos taken by a photographer of *my* choice."

Shelldrake studied me. "You will, of course, be discreet in your selection."

I had no photographer in mind, but I wanted our people doing this in order to be sure of the authenticity of the pictures, whatever "this" turned out to be.

Shelldrake sat quietly for a moment, then got up and nodded. "I will be in touch, Mister Rhodes. Thank you for your time." The sudden shift from brusqueness to formal politeness was odd. I decided that he was less aggressive than frightened and I wondered what of? His own government? If so, did I want to be involved? I had accepted risk in Vietnam, but this was London and I was looking forward to living without carefully evaluating every step I took.

Shelldrake departed without further comment and I immediately sought Dolly. "Your husband is a cop?"

She nodded solemnly.

"So was our visitor."

"He presented credentials?"

"No."

"The laws require it," Dolly said emphatically. "What makes you think he's attached to the constabulary?"

"I don't know. He had a certain attitude. What was your impression?"

"I'm not a reporter," Dolly said, "but I do have have a bit of a nose for coppers and your officious visitor doesn't fit. I daresay he's more in the mold of Special Air Services."

I vaguely remembered reading about SAS in the context of World War II, and hearing of it from Green Berets in Vietnam who admired their British counterparts. "Commandos, right?"

"Of sorts."

"Do SAS personnel have anything to do with riots and civil disturbances?"

"Certainly not on the homefront."

"What about places like Hong Kong?"

"That would not be unheard of," she said.

"Have you ever heard of baton rounds?"

Dolly paused before answering. "Yes. They are sometimes used for crowd control in the colonies and protectorates."

"I understand that some people object to the use of baton rounds. Do you?" I asked.

"I am the wife of a copper. If a weapon keeps him safe, why would I object? Most police in this country still do not carry firearms. I understand their reasons, but I do not share them. If criminals are armed, so too should be the constabulary."

"Would the police use baton rounds to break up riots here in England?"

"I should think not," she said. "We *English* do not riot." After a long pause during which she stared up at the ceiling, Dolly said, "These weapons are not new. If memory serves me, they were first employed right here in London in the late nineteen-thirties. You see, there were provocateurs and pro-fascist Black Shirt groups in the country then who favored Hitler, and there were many vehement anti-fascists. There came a time when the Black Shirts were supposed to march for their cause but decided to change their plans. The anti-fascists had pledged to disrupt the Black Shirts and showed up for the demonstration armed with petrol bombs and rocks and clubs and in nasty moods and the police were forced to deal with them. Baton rounds were used against the anti-fascists, which is heavy irony, if one thinks about it," she said in conclusion.

I decided to keep an open mind about my mysterious visitor and his story.

"Who's our most reliable photographer?" I asked.

"Personally or professionally?" Dolly answered with a playful grin.

"Somebody I can trust to do what has to be done."

"I know the perfect person," she said. "Crackerjack with a camera, though a bit off in his own world, if you take my meaning."

"Somewhat individualistic?"

"To the point of certifiable eccentricity," she said. "Which, praise God, is not yet a crime in England."

Three days later I met Charlie Jowett, an elfin man with a jutting jaw and fiery eyes. When I telephoned him, he suggested we get acquainted over a hop-pop, which I would come to learn was a beer. Charlie Jowett had his own language.

I suggested we meet at Nolan's and he readily agreed. I had just walked into the pub when I heard a ruckus in the corner and saw a huge man punch a smaller man, who went flying backward over a table, spilling glasses of beer. Based on Dolly's precise description, I recognized the smaller man right away: Charlie Jowett. I also observed that the beer glasses hit the floor and bounced without breaking, sounding like heavy brass bells. It wouldn't do to be hit by one of those. I stepped into the fray, scooped a pint glass off the floor, intercepted a kick from the big man aimed at the little man on the floor, and, using the leverage of his own kick, spun the big man around sharply and pushed him off balance.

"Sod off," the big man said menacingly as he stumbled around to face me. "This is none-a your bleedin' business."

I matched the man in size and was quite a bit younger and ready to take a shot if he made a move, but there was no retaliation. The man glared at me momentarily, took a halfhearted kick at Charlie, fetched his hat and overcoat, and stalked away.

"You didn't have to do that," the man on the floor said. "I was settin' 'im up."

"For what? Homicide?"

He looked at me, then laughed out loud. The laugh reminded me of a horse's nicker. Charlie Jowett brushed himself clean of floor dust and checked his jaw several times. He had a bruise, but there was no blood. "Shouldn't have jumped in," he said. "You know who that was?"

"No idea."

"Name's Thigpen, stuffer for the Motuzas Brothers."

"The Motuzas Brothers?" *Stuffer?*

He grinned. "Listen and learn, Yank. The Motuzas Brothers lead a quite notorious gang of very nasty bastards. Thigpen's the muscle."

Not good news to hear. "Why did he punch you?"

"I bettered the bugger in a wager, see? I bet Arsenal over his club and gave him two goals and Arsenal won by three. Not a lot of quid; I expect it's the principle of the thing. The Motuzas Brothers control the full menu for depraved appetites in the West End: boosted whiskey, pay-birds, drugs, and so forth, but gamblin' is by far their biggest earner. I think Thigpen suffered a bit of angst over losin' to an amateur."

I knew vaguely that Arsenal was one of the country's top soccer clubs, a sport the Brits called football.

In thirty minutes I heard Charlie Jowett's life story. Born in Cornwall, apprenticed to Arsenal's youth development team at sixteen, he had moved up to the professional side at eighteen and scored seventeen goals in his first season only to have his back broken just before a European tournament; doctors feared for his future and, after that, no club would touch him because he had become a medical liability. He told the story straight on, evincing no bitterness.

"What do you do now?"

"Take a few shots, chase birds, fish."

Shots were photos, I knew. "Hunt and fish?"

He smiled. "No mate, birds're for bed, though it's okay to eat 'em!" he said, breaking into his nickering laugh again.

"Women."

"Right, ridin' punt," he said with a suddenly thick accent.

"What?"

"Cockney, Yank. *Punt* rhymes with *cunt*, see? Gotta think."

I could only laugh and offered to buy him a beer and then he bought me one and over the rest of the evening we discovered that we were both "mad about trout."

He asked me about the job I "had on" for us and I told him about baton rounds and sheep and the things Shelldrake had said. Charlie nodded attentively and told me that he would be privileged to be not only my photographer, but my ghillie as well, which he explained meant "guide"; the term was usually reserved for professional angling guides.

We migrated from Nolan's to a dark, smoky cellar where several musicians with electrified instruments were knocking out loud, discordant riffs. The sweet smoke swirling above us did not emanate from regular cigarettes. The dance floor was filled with men and women in outrageous and gaudy costumes. The women favored mini skirts, skin-tight satin or velour tops with bare midriffs, and patent leather boots with high heels or platforms. The skirts were garments in name only and it seemed to me that there was an unofficial contest to see who could get by with wearing the least cover without resorting to nudity. One woman near the musicians danced topless. I didn't notice any dirty feet.

Sometime during the night we left the bar with two women and took them to Charlie's place, which turned out to be a four-story house complete with servants and a fire raging in a huge fireplace in a room where the walls were covered by mounted fish and the floor carpeted with something as thick and soft as a cloud.

The women were gone when we awoke the next morning and we sat down to what Charlie's cook called a "proper English country breakfast"— eggs fried sunny-side up, fresh tomatoes, pork sausages he called "bangers," dark toast and orange marmalade, tea and honey.

"Informative night?" Charlie asked over tea.

"What I remember of it."

"You've seen it all, old boy: men, women, pot, beer, loud music, darkness, bad air, easy fuckin'. That's Dear Old London."

I liked Charlie Jowett and had a feeling there was much more to him than he was letting on. How did a freelance news photographer afford servants and a house like this?

"Like to hunt the trout when spring rolls around?" he asked.

"Love to. Where?"

"Southwest. To my mind it's the only tolerable place to angle, eh? The browns there are small and reclusive, but feisty when engaged. And few anglers. I so loathe crowded waters."

"I look forward to it."

Charlie Jowett was a thoroughly professional photographer and over the next few weeks I took him on several assignments and learned that we worked well as a team. I told Dolly I wanted to work with Charlie as often as I could and she looked at me and said approvingly, "I *knew* you lads would get on famously."

Having seen the books in the Trout House, and my UPI duties notwithstanding, one of my first concerted efforts was to try to get a lead on Sir Thomas Oxley. Gillian had said he had "oodles" of books like the ones I had seen and naturally I wondered if there was another copy of the manuscipt somewhere in his collections. The Oxley Trust, I quickly discovered, still existed, but had a private, unlisted phone number. I enlisted Dolly's help and she used her husband's contacts to get the number for me. I took the underground north to Hampstead and emerged to find myself on a tree-lined ridge in a small, tidy village, looking south over the city of London. Before making the journey, I weighed my options and decided that arriving unannounced might produce better results than trying to arrange a meeting.

A short walk from the tube took me to the Oxley Trust, which was in the center of Church Row, a short street of narrow Georgian homes pressed tightly together like bread slices and set off by ornate wrought-iron fencing.

I was met at the door by a young woman with thin lips, crooked teeth, freckles, and red earrings the size of fried eggs. She wore thick white lipstick.

"Sah?"

"My name is Rhodes," I said, handing her one of my business cards. "UPI."

She squinted at the card. "I see," she said thrusting her hand out awkwardly. "Freegift Heartfield."

" 'Freegift'?" I said.

"Yes, sah, it was me mum's idea. Throws people, it does. At first. Can I help you, sah?"

The woman was genially formal, with the hint of a playful smile ready to erupt.

"I'm interested in the Trust's collection of Sir Thomas Oxley's angling books."

"Are you now?" she said. "Why would that be, sah?"

"I'm considering a possible feature story. Great trout-fishing traditions of England and so forth."

"Can't help you," the woman said. "So sorry, sah."

"No?"

"The Trust is soon to be no longer. I've been 'ere six years and meself have been given notice."

"The Trust is folding?"

"I don't know the technical term," the woman said. "I'm just one of the girls, see?"

"Secretary?"

"That's a Yank concept. Here I'm just a girl, sah."

"What about the books?"

"Everything to be flogged off," the woman said. "Liquidated."

"When will they be sold? Is there an inventory?"

Too many questions all at once. The woman made a face. "I think you'd best talk to the trustees, sah," she said, suddenly turning wary.

"Are they here?"

"No, sah, they comes every fortnight or so. For meetings, you see."

"Frankly, it's only the books that interest me. I've been told that Sir Thomas built an amazing collection."

"There were some books," she said tentatively.

" 'Were'?"

"Are, I should say. They're on consignment for sale."

"On consignment to whom?"

"I really couldn't say, sah."

"Won't tell me or can't?"

"Can't, sah. Truth is," she whispered, "I don't know, do I?"

I was disappointed. The Trust was folding and there were books, but they were to be sold. I left Hampstead thinking that my hoped-for lead had fizzled out before it even got going.

That evening I got a call around ten o'clock. There was a tremendous racket in the background.

"Mister Rhodes?"

"Yes?"

"Freegift Heartfield. We met this afternoon at the Trust? Is this a bad time, I'm so sorry to interrupt, sah."

"I remember you and you're not interrupting." Mostly I remembered her unique name and white lipstick.

"Bleedin' bastards," she said. "I'd been given notice for next month but this afternoon Sir Sinjin Wonbrow—he's the director—called me on the carpet and sacked me on the spot. Like a bleedin' execution it was. One minute I was employed and the next minute I wasn't, was I?" The woman sounded very upset and her speech was slurred. I guessed she had been drinking or smoking dope. "Bleedin' buggers," she repeated. "Those books you was inquirin' about?"

"Yes?"

"I no longer feel compelled to maintain confidences. The books you seek, Mister Rhodes, are on consignment with the firm of Broker, Brogger and Grant, New Row, Covent Garden. Do you dance?" she asked.

Dance? "On occasion."

"I never get enoof dancin'," she said. "I'm with some of me mates at the Kitty Kat Klub in Soho. You know it?"

I had seen the facade. "I know where it is."

"And where might you be?" she asked.

"Rupert Street."

"Loovely," she said. "Fite, you think, both of us in Soho at this very minute? Shall I pop on over to your place?" she asked. "Dancin' in private is much less inhibited than in public, do you agree?"

I more or less stared at the phone, not sure how to reply. "I suppose." Was this the wide-open London of current legend?

"Is half-eleven too soon?" she asked.

"No, that's fine."

"Right, then," she said brightly. "Half eleven and we shall dance, yes?"

"Yep." I had no radio, tape recorder, or phonograph. "It's number fourteen," I said. "First floor."

I would learn that *dance* was one of many street terms for "sex" and that Freegift Heartfield was laboring under the misconception that sharing information with me would somehow enable her to strike back at her employers. While this was a possibility, it was not a likelihood, but I did not try to disabuse her of her logic or her hope. I wanted to know the secrets of the snowfly and if I had to tell a few small lies, so be it.

She knocked on my door precisely at eleven-thirty. She wore a red mini skirt, red patent leather boots, and a huge red hat with a wide floppy brim, a gold band around the crown, and a tuft of bright feathers extending out the back. I opened a bottle of red wine for us and after several clumsy kisses we sat on my bed, using it as a couch.

She was all smiles. "I like a bitta chat before dancin'," she said. "It's very old fashioned, very civilized."

She was from South London and had ended up at the Trust after three years of working in city government. "Treat you worse than day labor," she said. She told me trustees had done all they could to keep Oxley's sole surviving relative from squandering the Trust's resources, which were reserved primarily for buying prime trout beats around the world.

She also said that the Trust had severe financial problems and the trustees needed desperately to sell Oxley's book collection, but were "frighteningly aquiver" over possible government intervention.

Why would the government intervene in a book sale? "You said the consignment is with Broker, Brogger and Grant. Which one do I talk to?" I asked her.

"Mister Brogger," she said with open disdain.

"Why do trustees fear government intervention?"

"Something about antiquities and law," she said, sliding her arms around my neck and looping a leg over my hip.

After a while she jumped up and shed her mini skirt to reveal crinkly black panties.

"Those sound like paper," I said.

"Aye!" she said with a squeal of delight. "You see, paper wears to cover a girl's wares. Called Tear Wears, they are. Very groovy, the very latest. Like to rip 'em off?"

Several days later I was in Covent Garden. The office was in a small building flanked by exclusive shops and restaurants. The business was called Broker, Brogger & Grant. It had a small brass sign, tastefully done, and an immaculately appointed interior. I had called ahead and made an appointment with Brogger on the subterfuge of doing an article about rare-book sales in England. I'd gotten a less-than-enthusiastic response over the phone but persisted and used what charm I could summon to eventually talk myself into an appointment. A receptionist with silver hair showed me to a seat and got me a cuppa and there I sat for thirty minutes past my appointment.

A heavyset man with pink skin and a perfectly pressed suit finally emerged from an office and looked at the receptionist, who nodded in my direction. I could tell by his expression that he was hoping I hadn't waited.

"Bowie Rhodes," I said, introducing myself.

"Brogger," he said gruffly.

I followed him into a well-appointed office devoid of personal mementos. There was a fireplace and high ceilings.

Brogger sat behind his desk, his hands clasped on a thick black leather desk pad.

"Rare books?" he asked cautiously.

"Specifically, the Oxley collection."

He blinked several times. "Quite minor in historical significance. Hardly worth a newshound's interest."

"We have lots of collectors in America interested in angling."

"You don't say?" he said.

"Some with plenty of money to pay for the right things."

I saw him edge forward in his chair. The hint of sales potential had captured his interest.

"You've taken the Oxley collection on consignment."

No blinking now. "May I ask the source of your information?" His voice was cool and edgy.

"You can ask, Mister Brogger, but in my business—as in yours—certain sources must remain confidential."

His pink face and neck reddened.

"What is it you want, Rhodes?" he asked impatiently.

"It's the books I'm interested in." He did not look even a little relieved. "If I could just see the books, or have a list of the titles."

"Am I to understand that you're interested in purchasing?"

"I might be," I said, lying.

"Then you must send 'round your solicitor. This is England, sir. We do not engage in commercial intercourse face to face. England is *not* a nation of shopkeepers. I represent a seller and you as a potential buyer also must be legally represented. Much cleaner that way, you see?"

"Is it possible to get a list?" I pressed.

"Your solicitor may obtain one."

"No solicitor, no talk, is that it?"

"This business depends on discretion."

I thought about making a smart-ass remark but held my tongue.

I left the meeting frustrated, but at least I had confirmed that some of the Oxley collection still existed and that it was in the hands of Broker, Brogger & Grant and awaiting a buyer. This was better than nothing. All I had to do was get a solicitor. And check into the sale of antiquities laws.

It was a Friday night at the end of my second month. I had been through a long, tedious week of uninteresting stories and dropped in to

Nolan's for a bite to eat. My plan was to turn in early and get some much-needed sleep.

I was working my way through a shepherd's pie when the bartender, Allan Admiral, informed me that I had a phone call.

I was shown to the pub's office and a private telephone.

"Rhodes? Shelldrake here. You'll be fetched outside Nolan's at twenty-two hundred hours."

I tried to get my mind focused. "What about a photographer?"

"Yes, of course, your colleague Jowett. He has been alerted and is standing at the ready."

Shelldrake's voice and timing gave me the willies. It was a bone-eating cold night with a heavy blanket of fog and mist. He spoke in military times, knew I was at Nolan's, and already knew I planned to use Charlie Jowett. Was I being followed and monitored? Dolly was right. Shelldrake was SAS, at the least, and perhaps some other sort of intelligence type.

I stepped outside the pub for a cigarette moments before the appointed pickup and wondered what Charlie would think of all this cloak-and-dagger stuff.

The pickup vehicle was a small dark lorry, a sort of panel truck. It pulled quietly to the curb, the back doors swung open, and I got in. Shelldrake perched on a bench seat by the door. Farther in I saw Charlie, who flashed a smile and gave me a Churchillian V. Then the doors were closed.

I sat beside Shelldrake. We drove in silence for nearly an hour. We could not see into the cab of the vehicle and were forced to ride in virtual darkness.

Eventually the lorry lurched to a stop. Shelldrake gave Charlie and me black wool hats and black rain slickers and told us to put them on.

We clambered out of the lorry and stretched our muscles. The damp, night cold was penetrating. I tightened the hood of my slicker.

"The two of you are now trespassing," Shelldrake said when we stepped outside. "If pinched, you'll be on your own. Understood?"

Charlie cocked an eyebrow. "Wish I had my Wellies."

We were both in street shoes on wet, muddy ground.

Shelldrake began walking into a copse of trees, not looking back. It was dark and nearly impossible to see. Charlie fell in beside me, his camera bag thumping his side as we stumbled down an uneven, muddy trail through the trees.

"Smashing adventure, eh?" Charlie whispered happily.

"We'll see," I said.

We eventually emerged from the forest onto what appeared to be rolling meadows with high fencing. To our west I saw the glow of lights in the low sky. London, I guessed. I had no idea where we were. The fencing alone suggested a military installation to me, but there were no electric lights. As we approached the wire in darkness, Shelldrake whispered, "Through here, boyos. Step lively now!" I immediately thought of mines as Shelldrake used a small flashlight with a red lens to show us where an opening had been cut in the fence.

"What about tracks?" Charlie asked.

"Everything is arranged," Shelldrake said with a clipped voice.

We eventually entered a building built low in the sod like an old Quonset. When Shelldrake opened the door, the smell inside overwhelmed both Charlie and me.

"Testing room," Shelldrake said. He turned on an overhead light, glanced at his wristwatch, and said, "We have precisely eight minutes."

Sheep carcasses hung from stainless-steel metal hooks fixed to the walls on either side of us. There was blackened blood in their wool coats and on the cement floor. The sweet, malodorous smell of death crawled onto us.

"Positively graveolent, eh," Charlie said, stifling a gag and sinking slowly to his knees. I grabbed one of his arms but couldn't hold him up. He looked up at me with a miserable face and said, "Good place for a nuke, yes?"

"Puke?" I said and Charlie grinned crookedly and exclaimed, "Explosive, I should think," as he lost the battle with his gag reflex and vomited for more than a minute while Shelldrake stood over him looking askance.

Shelldrake suddenly had a riding crop in his hand; he used it as a pointer.

"See," he said to me, stepping up to the first carcass. "Rib cage shattered, compound fractures, bones extending through flesh, this the result of a rubber bullet unloosed at ten feet. This creature did *not* expire swiftly. You see, a projectile either crushes tissue or stretches it. Either mechanism can result in death or serious injury. Many forensics people and the medical community at large are under the misimpression that low-velocity missiles are less problematic than high-velocity projectiles. They are wrong, Rhodes. A baton round is technically characterized as low velocity, and it *is* that if and when compared to today's modern weapons—but the muzzle velocity closely approximates bullets used during the Great War. I would remind you that a great deal of killing took place with such antiquated weapons in that conflict."

He stopped to see if I was following him, saw that I was scratching notes, and talked on. "Even low-velocity projectiles can stop the heart, lacerate the liver, break bones, blind, shatter teeth; the list of potential injuries is endless. Consider this. The modern hunting arrow strikes with less force than a .22 short round, yet it is lethal. You see, power is not the only measure of killing strength or stopping power."

Charlie had recovered, had his camera out, and was already methodically shooting without benefit of a flash. I followed Shelldrake along, listening to him describe wounds and types of bullet materials and all the while Charlie's camera clicked busily in the background. "The baton round is large, heavy, and unstable in flight," Shelldrake said. "A bullet causes the most damage at the point where it strikes with the highest velocity; the greater the area of contact, the greater the force imparted and the greater the resulting damage. Are you following?"

"Yes," I said. I had counted thirty dead sheep. "When was this done? And why sheep?"

Shelldrake gatherered a deep breath before answering. "Sheep are easy to acquire, not missed, and provide some body mass to simulate *Homo sapiens*. Other simulants are used from time to time: gelatins, soap, other animal cadavers, even human cadaver parts in dire circumstances, water-soaked telephone books, and so forth, but sheep are the cheapest to use for this sort of mass testing program."

"What happens to the meat?"

"Buried," Shelldrake said. "The creatures before us were dispatched this afternoon," he continued. "This sort of thing has gone on every day for months. You see this disarray? They have moved past the careful experimental stage, that is, have abandoned whatever impartial scientific procedure might initially have been employed. They now look simply for stopping power and destruction. This is all vile and has no place in a civilized country." He pointed to another carcass that was badly broken with bits of bone sticking through exposed muscle. "Case in point," he said. "A baton is fired at forty feet or so. But it flies erratically, and instead of hitting head-on to temporarily stun the target in a nonlethal location, it may flitter and flutter about and come in all-aside, causing massive damage, such as seen here. You can see that teak is out of the question. All right for shooting Chinese, but perhaps not other races."

"As with anti-fascists before the war?"

Shelldrake nodded. "Done some investigation? Good man. But teak is no longer the weapon of choice. They are now looking at rubber and plastic made from polyvinyl chloride. Thus far all substances show the same horrendous results."

Shelldrake stopped and pointed to a sheep head that had exploded like a watermelon. "Imagine this as a human being, a child, perhaps," he said solemnly. "Destruction is the only goal of this bloody business. The experts speak of Relative Incapacitation Index, but we are not fooled by the use of language to disguise true intent."

In Vietnam I had known a major whose job it was to travel to the site of recent battles to autopsy dead Allied soldiers in order to determine if the North Vietnamese were employing any new weapons. I had seen reams of color slides of the major's work, but most of the wounds I had seen paled next to the gruesome things Charlie and I witnessed.

After precisely eight minutes, Shelldrake announced it was time to depart and we did. Riding back to the city in darkness and silence, we listened to large raindrops pock-pock against the lorry's roof and sides. When we got out, Shelldrake said nothing and Charlie headed for his lab to develop his film. I knew I couldn't write a story right away.

A couple of weeks after I'd met Freegift Heartfield I called the Trust and was informed that it was closed. All inquiries would be handled by former trustee and managing director Sir St. John Wonbrow, who was now representing the trust as its solicitor out of his professional offices on Rose Street in the Covent Garden district. His offices were in a small glass-and-steel building, his entrance several doors down from a pub called the Lamb and Flag.

A receptionist showed me into the office of Sir St. John Wonbrow. He was a much younger man than I had anticipated and presented a scrubbed, overly groomed appearance, too young for peerage, which I thought of as an old man's reward.

"Good morning," Wonbrow said with a slight bow, extending his hand and giving me a crisp, viselike squeeze. His voice tended to rise as the words piled up. "Please call me Sinjin."

"Bowie Rhodes," I said.

"Working on a nostalgic tome, are you, or is it more instructional?"

"History, not nostalgia." I spun a description of trout and historic personages who had advanced the sport.

"Fantastic. I assume you indulge in the piscatorial pursuit."

I nodded. "At every opportunity. And you?"

"Never," he said. "Lack the patience, bugger-all. Perhaps when I've accumulated a suitable layer of years."

Fly fishing as an old man's sport. I didn't like Wonbrow, but I stayed on task and began by trying to knock him off balance.

"I've been told that Sir Thomas assembled a fine collection. I saw some of his books in South Vietnam at the Trout House. I was there as a guest of the owners when the North Vietnamese Army destroyed the estate, including the library."

Wonbrow raised an eyebrow. "Dear me. The Trout House is gone? There were *books* there? Are you certain? This is bloody awful." He seemed quite irritated.

"Knew about the property," he continued, recovering himself. "Always struck me as the whimsical name for an eccentric's dream. Are you *certain* that some of Sir Thomas's books were there?"

Books the Trust obviously knew nothing about. This had horrified him. "There were several dozen volumes in Vietnam and, to be frank, I'm wondering if there are more books in the Oxley Trust."

"There are. What we have is considered to be the main body of the collection," he said slowly, as if still recovering from surprise.

"There may be certain works in the collection I would like very much to see."

"Do you allude to M. J. Key?" Wonbrow asked.

"How did you know?" I felt weak.

He gave me a sly smile. "You're the second American to inquire this week."

I must've looked devastated. "Who else?" It was a clumsy question, but he had caught me off guard.

"Sorry, Rhodes. I'm sure you can understand that I'm not at liberty to disclose that. I will only relate to you what I told her."

Her? Shit.

"Sir Thomas's collection has been sold," Wonbrow said. "The sale was handled by Broker, Brogger and Grant."

"Yes," I said, "Mister Brogger himself handled it." I was trying to create the impression that I knew more than I did. "Did the Trust sell parts of the collection or the entire body?"

"Sir Thomas's collection was sold in one piece," he said quickly.

I had a bit of momentum back. "It's my understanding that the sale was made because the Trust is having severe financial difficulties and desperately needs to raise cash for its creditors."

This time Wonbrow blanched. "I thought your interest was books?"

I leaned forward into his space. "It is, but, as a reporter, I am also interested in understanding how an old and revered trust goes into the loo."

Wonbrow tightened his eyes. "That's confidential business, sir."

"You're certain that the entire collection was sold?" I wanted desperately to see an inventory and hoped against hope to locate a second copy of
the Key manuscript. Given some other American's inquiry, perhaps I was
not the only one with such an interest.

"You may be assured that certain stipulations were made to assure that
Sir Thomas's collection would not be scattered like so much dust before the
wind."

"It's all gone to one buyer?"

"Yes."

I tucked this away and tried to decide about where to go next. "But you
have no idea where the books are now."

"No, sir, I do not."

This was pure lawyer talk. "Meaning you know who purchased them
and technically can't say what the purchaser has done with them since then."

St. John Wonbrow glared at me.

Another American had come looking for M. J. Key. *Her.* My stomach
squirmed and I fought to calm myself. Obviously I was not the only person
to have an interest in Key. His known work was seminal, far more important
to the sport than Izaak Walton, whose *Compleat Angler* was no more than a
travel writer's gregarious ramblings; Walton had stumbled his way through
pubs in English trout country. I had loved the book when I was young and
still felt affection for Walton, but it was M. J. Key who had looked into the
future and showed the way, shone his light on how it had to be if trout were
to survive. Walton wrote as if fish were an endless resource, but M. J. Key
knew better, that abundance was only an apparition. More important, I suspected that Key held the secret to the snowfly. At least he had had enough
interest in the myth to write about it. I had no choice but to keep chasing. I
had built too much sweat equity in finding the answer to give up now.

I had not gotten all that I wanted from Wonbrow. So far I had learned
that the entire collection had been sold. The existence of a second copy of
the Key manuscript remained an open question built mostly on wishful
thinking. It was time to push Wonbrow to a new level. As I moved to depart,
I acted as if I had just thought of another question and turned back from the
door as he edged me toward it.

"One more thing?"

"Of course," Wonbrow said. Clearly he thought I was going to throw him an easy one.

"Was the sale of the Oxley collection proper?"

"I beg your pardon?" His eyes rolled like a broken slot machine. "Sir?" Trying to buy time, trying to figure out where I was taking him.

"I assume that the sale conformed to statute."

"It was entirely legal, if that's your destination.'"

I was ready for him. "There are different degrees of legality. I'm particularly interested in the provisions of Britain's Literary Antiquities Act. If one owned a Shakespeare folio or the Magna Carta, one could not sell them without state approval. Correct?"

"Fish books ain't Shakespeare, Rhodes." He had dropped the *mister* before my name. A line had been drawn between us.

"In terms of theoretical value, I'd agree. My point is that literary works of art require state authorization for sale. An affidavit, I believe."

My line of attack was part truth and part fiction. Some digging had revealed that there was a Literary Antiquities Act that dated to 1946 and concerned the acquisition and disposition of works "liberated" by Her Majesty's troops roaming the world during the war. The Russians, Japanese, and Germans had stolen everything in the path of their war machines and the Crown, ever proper, wanted to make sure that British war dogs did not exercise their finders-keepers when it was their turn at the loot. How the law applied to anything else was anybody's guess. I didn't have enough time to go deeper with my research, which reduced my approach to no more than a bluff. But I was not done bluffing or pushing.

"You insist that the books were sold as a collection, but I've been told that only an unpublished manuscript by M. J. Key was sold. The title is *Legend of the Snowfly*. If true, then you may have a lot of problems with the government. If the affidavit claims all of the materials were sold, but in fact only an unpublished manuscript left the country, then the sale would be illegal. This assumes of course that there is an affidavit."

I had my fingers crossed.

Wonbrow studied me for a long time. His hands were pressed hard against a table by the door.

"You're making a lot of trouble," he said.

"All I want is information."

He frowned. "The books are gone, the manuscript included, and if you persist in this I will be forced to take action. What's so important about these books? The world is filled with books."

"As I explained, I'm primarily interested in Key."

"The collection is gone. Accept it."

"I would if you could provide a name or an affidavit."

"Like I said, they're gone. Out of reach." The managing director gave me a malevolent smile. "Did you notice the adjacency of the Lamb and Flag on your way in?"

"The pub?"

"Yes. You're familiar with its history, perhaps?"

"I'm afraid not."

Wonbrow sighed. "It's quite interesting, actually. You see, the writer John Dryden wrote some things about a woman who was the king's mistress. Scandalous, actually. As Dryden left the Lamb and Flag one evening he was fallen upon by unknown assailants and severely beaten. I should think this an object lesson on the importance of a writer's maintaining good judgment."

Wonbrow sucked in a deep breath. "I've said what I have to say. This has been quite . . . entertaining, Rhodes. Now, you really must excuse me."

I smiled inwardly when I got outside. Wonbrow had pretty much confirmed that there was another copy of the manuscript and that it was with the collection. I left the meeting feeling optimistic.

I had a lot to learn.

The proofs and contacts of Charlie's photographs of dead sheep were stunning, but the photos and Shelldrake's allegations were insufficient for a wire service story. I needed more.

Chinatown in Soho was only a block away and I knew there were any number of immigrants from Hong Kong there, but it was nearly impossible to find anyone who would talk to me about the Hong Kong riots of the previous couple of years. The proprietors of the establishments tended to live at fashionable city addresses and keep a tight rein on their employees. The owners did not want to be seen as criticizing the British government. Their employees, however, mainly immigrants, tended to live in the East End in a less-than-fashionable area called Limestone, just north of the Thames.

London's first Chinese settlers had been sailors who decided that staying in the city was preferable to returning to the Middle Kingdom. More recently, the enclave's arrivals tended to be intellectuals and others fleeing Mao's regime.

I sought the help of Salvation Army major Ivory Chen-Jones, who served as the unofficial vicar of the informal Limestone church community, operating from a soot-caked church called God's Fine Light Mission.

The major preferred to be addressed as vicar and I was happy to oblige him.

Chen-Jones spoke very fast, choppy English. "Victim?" he said when I explained my interest. "Who say victim here?"

"It's a surmise," I said. "There are many people from Hong Kong in Limestone and I thought there might be someone who had witnessed the riots."

"Her Majesty within rights!" Chen-Jones shouted. "Devil Mao and Red Guard make civil disobedience! Cannot allow Reds this!"

I explained patiently, "I'm not interested in the reasons for the situations, only what happened during them."

"No help!" Chen-Jones said. "You must go now!" He pumped his hand at the door, trying to encourage me along.

In the vestibule of the church a man stared at me and followed me outside.

"I hear," he said, shaking his head in distaste. "Chen-Jones only care about reputation. Tonight you come number fourteen Eatery Lane. You come alone, okay? Nine?"

I agreed, not because I thought it would bear fruit, but from desperation.

That evening I met my mysterious benefactor, who introduced me to a nervous man named Li, who in turn took me through dark and odiferous streets to a dank flat to meet a woman called Jen Chia Yi Yi. She was twenty-six, a diminutive woman with long black hair and a disfigured face that defied description. Her cheekbones had been crushed, her nose mashed to a lump that barely protruded from the plane of her face; both of her eyes hung to the outside of their orbits. She could see, but without depth perception. Li said she had to be led everywhere.

Li served as translator.

"What do I call you?" I asked.

Li translated and the woman answered in halting English. "I am Joy, please. Jen Chia Yi Yi has gone to Father Christ's Heaven."

"You were in the riots."

She nodded once.

"I waiting for boat to Kowloon for work," she said. She switched to Chinese with Li and he continued the story.

"She say angry crowds come running and they are very loud; these people followed by police firing crying gas and shooting wooden bullets."

"You were struck by a wooden bullet?"

The woman nodded.

"Did you seen who shot you?" I asked her.

"Yes, very close," she said softly.

"What distance, twenty feet, thirty?"

She had a quick discussion in Chinese with Li.

Li explained. "She say, arm length.'"

I reached toward Li to approximate the distance. "Like this?"

The woman nodded.

"What did you say to him?"

"Please, I want go work. No trouble."

"And he said?"

They conferred quietly and Li looked befuddled as he tried to sort it out.

"Not exact translation," he said apologetically. "Miss Joy say policeman say no more yellow Blackamoors make baby with God's white people."

"Blackamoor?" I repeated.

"Negroes," Li said.

She nodded solemnly.

I had a pretty strong suspicion she had been targeted by the Hong Kong constabulary for racist reasons. Never mind Mao and Red politics.

I explained as delicately as I could that the baton round that had injured her might be used in England. Did she want others to suffer what she had gone through? It took a great deal of convincing, but in the end Jen Chia Yi Yi agreed to pose for photographs. Charlie and I went to see her a couple of days later and she posed for nearly an hour.

I assembled photos of the sheep carcasses and interviews with Shelldrake and Jen Chia Yi Yi, and from these wrote the first draft of my story, which I showed to Joe Daly. He read the draft without comment, gave it back, and went through the photographs, grimacing as he studied the woman's disfigured face. When he was done, he carefully stacked them on the edge of my desk.

"Okay, these bullets are shitty things. But will the government use them, and if so, where and against whom? Right now all we have are allegations and we can't really grade the validity of our sources." I liked his choice of pronouns. What a change from Del Puffit. "I think we need to confront the government," Daly continued. "Let's see what sort of reaction we get."

I told him I had an appointment with Gerow Hedge, deputy commissioner of the London Metropolitan Police.

"Why Hedge?"

"He's responsible for special actions and technical support."

Daly nodded. "You think he's responsible for the development pro-gram?"

"That's one of the things I want to find out." I had also asked Dolly about Hedge and she told me that he was new to London, having been brought in from Hong Kong—a fact that irritated a great number of senior London police, who felt they deserved the job. I wondered if this included Shelldrake, who remained a shadow.

"If we're on to a government plan, they aren't going to take kindly to us," Daly said.

"Are you saying drop it?"

"Nope. Go get 'em but get it right. That's our job."

Two years before I got to London, the city's Metropolitan Police had relocated to the Westminster district in old Victorian buildings next to the Thames. The new offices were referred to as New Scotland Yard. Gerow Hedge initially asked me to meet him at his offices in the Yard, but at the last minute switched the venue to a building called the Sanctuary, which was not far from Scotland Yard and kitty-corner to Westminster Abbey.

Hedge was a short man with a wrestler's neck, dark eyes, and a pugna-cious countenance. He wore a black cashmere overcoat, a white silk muf-fler, and a black bowler hat pushed down so far that it bent his ears. He puffed on a brier pipe with audible sucking sounds. Three large and fore-boding men loitered nearby trying to look like they weren't with him. Bodyguards.

"Commissioner," I greeted him.

"Rhodes," he said in an almost estrogenic voice. He did not offer to shake hands. "Shall we get to the point?"

"Mister Hedge, it's being said that Scotland Yard is developing baton rounds made of new substances, that tests show these substances equal to teak in their lethality, and that these weapons will be employed by the British government to quell civil disorders."

Hedge didn't bat an eye. "Ah, we English so love rumors," he said. "We adore conspiracies. Psychology of a monarchy, I think. Could make a smashing academic inquiry. There are no such rounds in development, sir."

"But the British did employ teak baton rounds in Hong Kong."

"The Hong Kong constabulary utilized them."

It was standard political tactics to shift blame, to shed responsibility on a technicality.

"Mister Hedge, Hong Kong is a British colony. The governor is appointed by the queen. The vast majority of senior positions go to Brits. The cops in Hong Kong report to Brits."

Hedge showed no emotion and I knew he wasn't going to budge from his position.

"Let me get this right. You insist there are no such rounds under development? That is, no such things as the Relative Incapacitation Index and sheep being slaughtered by government scientists?"

Hedge remained impassive. "You say 'government scientists,' which takes in a great deal of territory. I can speak only for the Metropolitan Police and in that context I can assure you that we are absolutely not developing such weapons."

"But another government agency could be doing the development on your behest."

"I repeat," he said, "Scotland Yard is not involved in such research and development."

This angle wasn't going anywhere. "Mister Hedge, you worked in Hong Kong before moving to London. Were you involved in the riots there?"

"My position was entirely advisory and observational. The riots there were nationalistic, stimulated by mainland China."

"But baton rounds were employed?"

"Yes."

"Have you personally witnessed injuries incurred by such rounds?"

"I have," he said.

"Closely?"

"Yes, sir."

"You endorse the use of such weapons?"

"It was not my decision. You must remember that Hong Kong is a different culture with different values. Officials faced with civil disruption must weigh many factors: the magnitude of the threat, the estimated size of the force needed to restore peace or prevent the problem from escalating. Such decisions are invariably agonizing."

"You agreed with the decision to use teak rounds?"

"I did not say that, sir. Such decisions are not taken fatuously. There are established rules of engagement."

"Such as?" He was starting to talk.

"The rounds must be used only to break up a congregation, aimed only at the lower halves of targets, never discharged from more than twenty meters, and not discharged at all unless lives are threatened."

"Were all these guidelines adhered to in Hong Kong?"

"I cannot say they were."

"Would such rounds be used here?"

"Teak would never be used in England," he said. "Not against English-men."

"By that you mean *white* Englishmen?" I said.

"English is not a color," he said with the slightest hint of irritation.

I had spent a great deal of time reading the clippings given to me by Shelldrake at our first meeting.

"Press reports claim high rates of head injuries, extensive firing when lives were clearly not in jeopardy, and the targeting of people who were not involved in the disorders."

"I pay no attention to press reports," he said sanctimoniously.

He would soon, I hoped.

"You're quite new in London," Hedge said. "Do you know this building?"

"No."

"It was at one time a place where criminals could hide to escape justice."

"Convicted criminals or *alleged* criminals?"

Hedge smiled maliciously. "Anyone who hides must be guilty. There are no more sanctuaries, Rhodes. Not in England."

"Is that a message?"

"Think of it as a history lesson."

I was tired of warnings disguised as history lessons.

"You say no rubber or plastic bullets are being developed by the government."

"I am saying that Scotland Yard is not involved in such a thing," Hedge answered as he sauntered away. His muscular companions walked to his sides with one in front, like a small squadron of aircraft.

I called Joe Daly from a pay phone. "I just talked to Hedge."

"He give you anything?"

"He denies that Scotland Yard is involved in developing the weapons. He doesn't deny that the government is involved."

"He can't speak for the entire government."

"Joe, I can keep talking to politicians and officials and getting denials or we can run the story and see what happens. We have the photos."

"Write it," Daly said after a pause.

The story went on the wire two days later and the next afternoon I found a bleeding sheep carcass on the landing outside my flat. There was no note; there didn't need to be.

One week later Jen Chia Yi Yi was found dead in an alley in Limestone.

I went to see her companion, Mr. Li, who said he had left her alone for two hours to conduct some business and found her gone when he returned. He said she never went out without him.

An autopsy concluded that she died of a blow to the neck from a blunt object.

I went to see Deputy Commissioner Hedge, but his assistants and supernumeraries blocked my way into his office.

I also went to see the medical examiner who'd performed the autopsy. She was in her sixties, squarely built, the sort of person who made direct eye contact.

I presented my credentials and launched right into my questions. "Reports say you've concluded that the cause of death was a blow from a blunt instrument."

"Yes, that's correct," she said.

"Was the damage significant?"

"Quite," the doctor said.

"Anything odd about the injury?"

She looked hard at me. "There were some oddities, yes."

"Did you consider the possibility that the blunt instrument in question was in fact a teak baton round fired at close range?"

Dr. Haley Patrickson didn't respond right away. "We never considered that," she answered pensively.

I said, "You might want to take another look."

When I got back to my office, I called Hedge's office and told them I had asked the medical examiner to look into the possibility of a baton round having killed Jen Chia Yi Yi.

That night I got a call at home. It was Shelldrake. "Well done, Rhodes."

"It cost a woman her life," I said.

"War entails costs," Shelldrake said.

"There is no war," I countered.

"Says you, boyo."

I drank the better part of a bottle of Scotch that night to try to rid myself of the terrible feeling that I had been used in some way I could not yet comprehend.

Sheep continued to be dumped weekly on my landing for the next month.

My work over the next few months was not the least bit taxing. The row over baton rounds continued quietly as I tried again and again to meet with the medical examiner, but she continually refused. I suspected the government had gotten to her under the subterfuge of national security. I was haunted by my sense that I had been the cause of Jen Chia Yi Yi's death. Meanwhile, I learned the haunts of England's up-and-coming musicians, went to art and style shows, met artists and eccentrics and architects and anarchists, hung out with Charlie, and essentially enjoyed myself. Daly said he liked my work and I was happy enough. Whenever I needed something for work, Dolly Aster got it for me.

I got copies made of the Vijver-Key article and sent the journal back to Danny. She wrote a letter back saying that her search for further information was leading nowhere, but that she would keep digging and wished me well.

In mid-May Charlie showed up at my office one morning, his smile even more intense and animated than normal. "Mayflies are risin', chum. Time we headed southwest, eh?"

We left on Thursday evening, to avoid the "Friday Jam," taking a train across the southern part of the country. We got a direct from London to Exeter, and then a branch line from there to Penzance, a name I had always thought was fictional. It took us many hours to cover a distance we might have done in half the time in an automobile. I didn't ask why we were using the train. Charlie always had a reason for the things he did and I knew that in time all would be revealed.

The station in Penzance was small and old but brightly painted. We unloaded our bags and a woman came across the platform and presented her cheek to Charlie for a ceremonial kiss. She bent over and Charlie had to stand on tiptoes to reach her. She was dark skinned, Indian I guessed, and wearing Wellies and faded bell-bottom blue jeans. She was six-three, reed thin, with cascading black hair, intelligent eyes, and an enchanting smile.

"Anji," Charlie said, pronouncing it *Angie*. "Meet Mister Bowie Rhodes. He's American."

We shook hands and I felt her eyes appraising me.

"Anjali Toddywalla," she said. "Welcome to Cornwall."

We drove in her old dust-covered Land Rover for about thirty minutes along narrow lanes, first through forests and then into more barren land, and stopped at a two-track to lift an unadorned gate. Anjali drove through,

THE SNOWFLY ❖ 137

Charlie shut the gate behind us, and we headed down into a valley, which I didn't see until we were in it. It was dark and I couldn't make out the land-scape, but I saw lights ahead, some small ones in a cluster below and, high above them and beyond, a brightly lit sprawling house that dominated the side of the hill.

We parked in front of a thatched cottage stuck in a grove. The head-lights shone on thick clusters of huge rhododendrons.

The cottage was that in name only. The interior was expansive, with a large foyer opening to a massive room decorated with paintings, bronze and porcelain statues, and framed photographs, mostly black and white. There were fly rods in a rack along one wall and a fly-tying bench cluttered with feathers and fur patches. The floors were dark green slate but covered with thick carpets. The furniture was soft and looked well used. No television in sight. No stereo. Built-in shelves overflowed with books.

Anjali brought us tea and a platter of cucumber sandwiches, which Charlie and I consumed ravenously.

"So," she said, "what makes you mad for trout, Mister Rhodes? Charlie's always been that way."

"I don't know," I said. I had never really thought about my motivation for fishing.

"Pity," she said.

"Don't mind her," Charlie said with his mouth stuffed with tiny sand-wiches. "She's got her own madness."

"Piss off," she said in a polite tone and Charlie laughed his laugh.

I wondered what their relationship was. They obviously knew each other well, but there were no physical signs of affection. Many Brits I had met were this way, but Charlie wasn't one of them. One night in a cab he undressed a woman he'd met in a bar and had her right there beside me. He was forever pawing and kissing women we met at various functions I cov-ered. His attentions were rarely rebuffed.

"I feel like a bloody matador ready for the first bull of the season," Charlie announced. "Shall we organize our gear for the morning?"

It took us about an hour. I noticed that he had an eight-foot rod like mine, what the Brits called a one-hander (as opposed to the much longer two-handed spey rods often used for salmon). Charlie had box after box filled with thousands of flies.

"Bit of a collector," he said, grinning.

This was like calling John Paul Getty a little rich. "Got a snowfly?" I asked casually.

Charlie gave me a quizzical look. "Never heard of it."

I briefly outlined the legend as I knew it and Charlie listened attentively. "Bleedin' hell," he said. "Thought I'd heard everything. Got any Adamses?"

"Pretty good supply."

"May I?" he asked. "Yanks tie them so much better."

"We're going to use an Adams?"

"And Callibaetis, but I'm flush in those and my dressings are top of the line, what?"

Charlie and I were awake early the next morning and settled for coffee and dry toast before climbing into our waders.

"I thought Brits fished from the banks."

"Only the rigid fools. I like to mix with the fish, but mind you, we've got to be bleedin' cautious, stay to the sides and remain low. These fish don't grow large, but they're born smart."

The river was called the Drake.

"After the insect?" I asked.

Charlie laughed out loud. "Right, Sir Francis, he was certainly a right bleedin' pest to the Spaniards, eh?"

We were on the river a few moments before sunrise. Charlie said, "I release most of my fish." I told him I did too. There was a hazy overcast and a forecast of showers later in the day. I tied on a small Adams and hit a fish immediately. It was a brown, a healthy ten inches, bright silver with dark markings and not a lot of yellow.

"Give us a look," Anjali Toddywalla said from the bank behind me, startling me. She had two cameras around her neck and was carrying a small tripod.

I showed her the fish, careful to not take it out of the water.

"Lovely," she said, "but the light's not quite right. Mind if I follow along?"

"Of course not."

The river flowed down a slope, forming a series of terraced drops. We were in a narrow gorge with growling water and some pools under the shadows of large gray boulders. There were undercut banks in places and man-made stone walls on some bends. There wasn't an abundance of aquatic vegetation, but enough to provide cover for fish and insects. Ancient oaks towered above us. The water wasn't deep, but it had a firm and steady flow. The rocks were a combination of sandstone and granite, the latter covered with multicolored lichens. It was a lovely setting for trout fishing.

The fish weren't as spooky as Charlie had made them out to be. They were mostly small, but fought valiantly and stubbornly.

At midmorning I came around a bend and, out of the corner of my eye, caught a silver flash to my right. It was a trailer, what the Brits called a caravan, set back from the bank, built up on a wooden platform. A porch with a railing of barkless wood had been built along the side facing the river.

Anjali, who had followed me in silence, announced it was time for tea; I got out of the river and followed her into the place. The furnishings were spartan: a table and chairs, stove, small refrigerator, and stone fireplace built into one side, where the metal had been cut away. There were three small shadow boxes on one wall, filled with displays of flies, mostly naturals. Several spare drawings of trout looked almost alive.

Charlie came in as Anjali began to brew tea.

"My dears are skittish wee things, aren't they?"

I said, "Not bad."

"Howjado?"

"A few," I said. In fact, I had not been counting. I had been concentrating too hard on figuring out where they were.

"Twenty-six," Anjali announced from the stove.

Charlie's mouth hung open. "Kiss my glorious goolies," he said.

"Truly," Anjali said. "I counted them all. And you, Charles?"

"Four," he said, "and I can tell you I was bleedin' well pleased with that. Thought I'd have to console Bowie. You're a cheeky bastard, Rhodes! Catchin' my brownies so easily."

"He casts beautifully," Anjali said. "Pinpoint radar in his arm. He might give you a lesson or two, Charles."

"Might he?" Charlie said, laughing.

I wished Anjali would stop needling him. "Lucky morning," I said.

"Yes," our water boiler said, "the sort of luck you have with birds, Charles."

Charlie reddened and grinned with embarrassment. "Rather have the bleedin' browns," he muttered.

The three of us drank tea and ate fresh honey-oat muffins, which Anjali pulled from her rucksack.

"I didn't see another fisherman all morning," I told Charlie.

"And shan't," Charlie said. "This is mine."

"His aunt's," Anjali said, interrupting. "To be accurate."

Charlie ignored her. "Auntie bought this back in the nineteen-forties, right after the war. Nobody fished the river back then. Too small, not enough flow, fish too small. But she bought it and had some chaps down from Wales and they did this and did that. Never planted a fish; the natives prospered."

"Your aunt fishes?"

"Whole bloody family," he said. "What's left of us."

"She's quite famous," Anjali said.

"*Infamous* would be more to the point," Charlie said.

"Women's rights," Anjali said.

"You name it," Charlie added. "My mother's sister. My father and mother were killed in 1948, in India, soon after independence."

I wondered if this was his connection to Anjali.

"Auntie took me in," Charlie continued. "Of course, she was gone knockabout most of the time, shedding her knickers for peers and pals. When I showed promise at football at public school she had them remove me from the team. Wouldn't tolerate her nephew playin' a 'gutter' sport. Naturally, I told her to piss off, left school, joined Arsenal, and you know the rest."

"They didn't speak for years," Anjali said in a scolding tone. "Charles refused to apologize and she insisted *she* had been right. It was a frightful contest of misdirected wills."

"She *was* wrong!" Charlie said, his face flashing anger. "Why would I apologize?"

"For being a cheeky, self-absorbed wowser," she said.

He lowered his eyebrows. "Besides that?"

They both laughed. It was obviously an old joke.

"They've only recently reconciled," Anjali said to me.

"Who finally surrendered?" I asked.

Charlie rolled his eyes. "I did. The old girl wasn't gettin' any younger and maybe I'd grown up a bit."

"Not all that much," Anjali Toddywalla said dryly.

"Ever hear of Sir Thomas Oxley?" I asked.

Charlie rolled his eyes. "*Heard* of him? I should think so. The man was a *giant*. Not that the other Lordships appreciated his single-minded dedication to spreadin' trout. They felt he ought to concentrate on bleedin' old England and bugger the rest of the world. His offspring did not inherit his love for fish, which is somewhat of a tragedy."

"Trust went under," Anjali announced.

Charlie gaped at her in disbelief. "You must be joking."

"It's true," I added. "A very recent event."

"How do you know that?" Anjali asked. "It's not been publicized."

"I had business with St. John Wonbrow, the Trust's former managing director."

"Dreadful man," Anjali said.

"You know him?"

"His reputation," Anji said.

"My dear Bowie," Charlie said, "in certain social circles in England everyone knows everybody. It can get quite tiresome. I simply can't believe the Oxley Trust has gone under."

"It was Ozzie's fault," Anji said.

She seemed quite well informed and I decided to listen rather than talk.

"Ozzie!" Charlie said. "Complete bleedin' idiot." He looked over at me. "Oswald Oxley, the great man's great-great-grandson or some such thing. Couldn't manage a half quid. The Oxley fortune has been pissed away for generations. The truth is that it's a miracle the patriarch himself ever accumulated anything. The old boy reputedly had a terrible head for business."

Anjali interrupted. "The National Trust tried like the dickens to get hold of the Oxley properties, but the trustees felt they could make more on the open market."

"Nothing remains?" I asked.

"Dribs and drabs," Charlie said. "What's the name of that awful place in Hampshire?" he asked Anjali.

"Greavy House," she said.

Greavy! The word startled me. In his article on cryptography M. J. Key had talked about Irish monks at a place called Greavy. And now I was finding that Oxley had a place called Greavy House? A connection between Key and Oxley? This was not only a weird coincidence, it was scary. I couldn't speak.

"Right you are. That's the place. Ozzie's now," Charlie said, "if he's alive. Last I heard he was into the psychedelic scene and taking constant trips to Morocco, hash-with-trash and all that." Charlie suddenly stopped talking and stared at me. "What business would you have with the Oxley Trust?"

"Sir Thomas collected fishing books. I was at his Trout House on the River of Trout on the Vietnam border with Cambodia."

"Bugger off!" Charlie said incredulously. "His *what?*"

"The name of his place in Vietnam. Seriously, there were trout in Vietnam, planted by Oxley. And some of his books. I saw a manuscript called *The Legend of the Snowfly* but never got to read it."

Charlie was grinning in disbelief. "And why's that, old chum?"

"It got blown up and burned."

Anjali said, "My God."

"While you held it?" Charlie asked, still not believing me.

"No, a few seconds after I put it down." I told the two of them about the North Vietnamese attack and Tet and Gillian and the books and what had happened and how the place had been destroyed and they listened politely until I was done.

When I finished, they were silent and exchanged glances until Anjali said, "How absolutely dreadful."

Charlie poured us more tea and stared out the caravan at the river. "Who was the author of the manuscript?"

"M. J. Key."

Charlie looked at me. "The snowfly bloke you mentioned last night?"

"The same."

"You said he wrote other books?"

I provided dates and brief descriptions.

Charlie nodded. "Long interval, eh?"

"Fifty-one years," I said.

Charlie asked, "Manuscript dated?"

I shook my head. "Estimated late nineteen-thirties to mid-nineteen-forties, but I'm only guessing."

"Only the one copy?"

"Again, I don't really know."

"Snowfly, eh?" He looked at Anjali Toddywalla. "Something, eh?"

"Worth a look," she said with an even voice. "We could drop in on Ozzie sometime."

"I should say! Smashing idea for an expedition, Anj. Be rather like visitin' a zoo run by the mentally infirm," Charlie said, slapping his hands on the table. "But now it's troutin' time and we'll deal with Mister Key later." He lowered his chin and glared. "This time we'll see who the Angler of the Beat is." He flashed a mock-fierce face. "I shall thump your colonial arse this afternoon, Rhodes."

But the outcome was the same and at dinner Charlie was as pleased as if he had done all the catching. "Bleedin' spectacular!" he proclaimed over port and Cuban cigars.

The next day we got into Anjali's Land Rover and drove up to the huge house on the hill. *Palace* was more like it, a castle that had been tamed with sculpted gardens in front and back. The flowers were multihued and fragrant, their scent wafting down into the gorge. I had smelled them on the river.

We were met at the front door by a butler who looked surprised to see Charlie.

"Auntie in?" Charlie asked.

"Mister Charles?"

Charlie glared comically at the servant, "No, I'm his bleedin' doppelgänger. Where is she, Lewis?"

The unsmiling servant pointed down the hall.

We walked into a hall that was close to fifty yards long. The walls were festooned with oil portraits. Hair and clothing styles suggested that the paintings stretched back hundreds of years. A lot of the subjects wore military uniforms or armor.

An old woman in a wheelcair sat by a large window, which had been cracked open. She had binoculars in hand and a novel open in her lap. *Slaughterhouse Five,* by Kurt Vonnegut, newly released and already a best seller. A gray sweater was wrapped around her shoulders like a shawl. A small multicolored dog was squeezed into the chair beside her. It looked like a small cocker spaniel.

"Auntie?" Charlie said, stepping between her chair and her window. He knelt down on one knee in front of her. "You are looking ravishing today, darling."

"Indeed," she said after an extended silence. The dog's ears perked up, but the old lady's hand stroked the dog's head and it relaxed. "You are looking quite fetching yourself, nephew." She gazed fondly at Charlie and asked, "How are Arsenal these days?"

"Barely competent," Charlie said.

"You should be managing the side."

Charlie laughed. "I thought you didn't want me in that gutter sport."

"I'd purchase the side, of course. It would be perfectly acceptable for a peer to be the executive in such an undertaking."

I wasn't processing all this. Was she suggesting that she buy Arsenal for Charlie? What peer? I kept my mouth shut.

"Got that out of my system," Charlie said.

"Trout," she said. "And sporting in the kip."

He laughed happily. "You'd know."

"Don't be impertinent."

"It's accurate."

She granted a little smile. "Perhaps. What brings you to your knees in front of me?"

Charlie grabbed my elbow and pushed me in front of his aunt. "This is Bowie Rhodes. American journalist, former Vietnam war correspondent."

"Godawful little war," she said. "A legacy of the French."

"He's a top-shelf trout man. Caught yesterday . . . how many, Anji?"

"Twenty-six in the morning, twenty-one in the afternoon."

The old lady looked astonished. "In *our* river?"

"Impressive, what?"

"Unthinkable," the old woman said. "Forty-seven? Are you sure?"

"Yes, ma'am." I figured it was my turn to talk.

"On what?"

"Size twenty Adams."

"American dressing?"

"Yes."

She seemed relieved. "Well, that explains it. They are not used to it. You simply surprised the poor dears, I should think. Ambushed them."

Her tone of voice suggested something less than approval.

"Sir Thomas Oxley," Charlie said.

"Fine man," Auntie said. "His grandson Harold asked me to hold his glove and promptly shoved his ungloved hand up my dress at Ascot one year."

"Shocking," Charlie said, grinning affably.

"Yes, and when he had finished I told him to remove it and never put it there again. My horse won."

Charlie laughed so hard he nearly cried. Anjali looked at me and rolled her eyes. "Two of a kind," she said, forming the words but not saying them out loud. "Both pots."

"What about Oxley?" Auntie asked her nephew. She seemed physically feeble, but her mind was keen, her tone and manner indicating that she was accustomed to giving orders and having them obeyed without question.

"I believe he had books."

She nodded. "He did indeed, but I should think they've all been sold off by the idiots running the Trust. Incompetent sods, the lot of them. I should think all the intelligence in that family settled in one and never moved on."

"Enthusiastic collector, was he?"

"Quite. Saw the books once. At the Hampshire place."

"Greavy House. Belongs to Ozzie now."

She looked surprised. "That one's not dead yet? Will be soon, I expect. Worthless as Chamberlain."

"Did you know M. J. Key, Auntie?" Charlie asked. "Another beau of yours, perhaps?"

"Charles Jowett," Anjali said in a low, scolding tone.

"Bugger off, Anji. She doesn't mind, do you, Auntie?"

"Miss Toddywalla is a lady, Charles dear, and you are a *scalawag*, but no, I don't mind. Yes, I knew Mister Key. He was a man who followed his own path. Excellent mind, you see, but premature on some matters. Appalling style as a writer, but his ideas carried the day. Content over style, which in my experience is unusual in this world. Key was not at all prolific with the pen. The man traveled to angle and nobody can say they really knew him. I most certainly did not." There was a sudden misting in her eyes and her voice dropped. "Not that I would have objected, mind you. Handsome fellow, strapping and rugged."

Charlie's hand went to her shoulder and rubbed affectionately. "He leave family?"

"Not likely," Auntie said. "Had the bachelor disease with no time for women or men, just fish and his sciences."

"Biology," I said, butting in. And maybe cryptography, I thought, but left this unsaid.

The old woman looked askance at me. "Mathematics," she said emphatically.

"He taught in America," I said, trying to recover.

"Balderdash," she said. "Never! Ghastly thought. Why should you think such a thing, Mister Rhodes?"

I was really confused. If there was an M. J. Key of England, who was the M. J. Key who taught in East Lansing?

"I must be mistaken," I mumbled.

"I should think so," Auntie said, but it was said sympathetically. "He died in 1939. I attended the funeral." Her eyes went to Charlie to see if he was supporting me.

Key died in 1939? Then who wrote the book in 1943? Or the manuscript? The farther I got into this, the more muddled it got. Could her Key be the same man who had taught in East Lansing?

"Ever hear of the snowfly?" Charlie asked his aunt, whose back stiffened. She sat rigidly in her wheelcair.

"In what context?" she asked tentatively.

"How many contexts does a trout dressing have, Auntie?" Charlie asked with a dismissive chuckle.

"Ah, yes, the dressing. I've heard of it. The hatch is supposed to be something that occurs rarely but, when it does, brings monstrous fish to feed. Timing and location are not predictable. Pure rot, I always thought."

It did not escape my attention that she had asked in what context Charlie wanted to know about the snowfly. What did she mean?

"May I ask a question?" I asked.

"This is not an interrogation," Anjali said, her voice conveying concern for the old woman.

"You may," Auntie said. "Anjali dear, I am more than able to take care of myself."

"You asked Charlie in what context he wanted to know about the fly."

"I did, didn't I?"

"What did you mean by 'context'?" I asked.

Her eyes avoided me. "I'm an old woman and can't account for every word I utter. I dare say no human being can."

She was being evasive and somehow I wasn't surprised. Every time the subject of the snowfly surfaced, conversations took odd and unexpected twists. Still, she had at least recited the outline of the myth as I'd first heard it so long ago in Idaho. Having opened this line of inquiry, I decided to keep pushing her.

"Some in America maintain that Key was a spy, a Nazi sympathizer."

"Nonsense," Auntie said. "Worse, it's scandalous! Key was an English patriot."

"He spoke German."

She harrumphed loudly. "He was a mathematician. If an American historian spoke Italian in those days, did that make him a Mussolini supporter?"

"It has been suggested that Key was involved in espionage during the war."

The old woman crooked her head and stared at me. "Intelligence is not espionage," she said, "though espionage is indeed one facet of intelligence. And Key was deceased, you must remember. *Before* the war."

Interesting distinction, which I interpreted as confirmation that Key had been in intelligence. "Are you telling me he was not involved in intelligence?"

"I'm not telling you anything, Mister Rhodes." Her voice was rock hard. She turned to Charlie. "I'm tired and I'm old, Charles, and need my siesta. Do you and your guest mind?"

" 'Course not, Auntie." He leaned over and kissed the top of her head and nodded for Anjali and I to leave.

We got reserved bows and quizzical looks from servants as the three of us departed to drive back down to the cottage in the valley below.

Until now Anjali had done all the cooking, but today it was Charlie in the kitchen.

"He can cook?" I asked her.

"Charles can do anything except go in one direction." It was not a compliment.

"His aunt said something about a peer."

Toddywalla looked over at me. "Lady Hoe is his aunt," she said. "Hereditary. When she passes, Charlie will become Lord Hoe. Auntie is a direct descendent of Sir Francis Drake. Hoe was the name of the ground where he was bowling when the Spanish Armada was sighted. He finished his game before taking to his ship. Showed no fear. He was rewarded for his bravery and service."

Charlie Jowett a peer of the realm? It was almost comical. "Will Charlie take it?"

Anjali smiled gently. "He has no choice."

"Why do you call Lady Hoe 'Auntie'?"

The tall woman sat silent for a moment. "Because it would be awkward to call her Mum."

My mouth must have hung open as I tried to process this revelation. She was the daughter and he was the nephew, which made Anjali his first cousin. I was surprised at how relieved I was by this knowledge.

"She was on in years when she had me. It was scandalous, of course. My father was a soldier in the Indian army, a colonel. He was married to another woman. Lady Hoe returned to England and I was born here."

Something puzzled me. "But if you're her daughter, shouldn't you assume the peerage when she is gone?"

"This is England and Charlie is the family's eldest male heir. If he wasn't around, it would go to me."

"That doesn't seem fair," I said.

Anjali smiled. "Charlie gets the title and hereditary lands, but I get the rest." Her tone made it clear that the rest amounted to a lot. "Auntie's cause is women's rights, after all."

Dinner was traditional, very English, and delicious. Roast beef (cooked longer than I liked), potatoes roasted in garlic and rosemary, peas with onions, a thin but savory gravy, a thick and powerful horseradish sauce, and Yorkshire pudding. We polished off three bottles of a very dry claret.

Afterward we stoked the fire and sipped brandy. Cornwall's adjacency to the sea gave it a mild climate, neither hot nor cold, and allowed for the cultivation of a wide array of certain fruits and flowers. I had noticed palm trees in the back garden of Drake Hall, the huge house on the hill. But the nights were damp and cool, even in summer, and a fire was much welcomed.

"Up to tacklin' the Drake again tomorrow?" Charlie asked as we listened to the fire crackle.

"That's what we came for."

"Is it?" Charlie asked, his tone shifting to serious.

"What's that supposed to mean?"

"All this business about Oxley and Key and the snowfly. Not on one of your journalistic forays, are you?"

I laughed. "The snowfly is strictly personal."

"Well, old chum, it being personal, I shall ring up Ozzie Oxley when we get back to London and see if a visit can be arranged."

"Thank you very much. Do you mind me asking what your aunt did during the war? She was rather tight lipped about this subject."

Charlie sighed. "Bletchley Park, Enigma, all that."

Now I guessed why she was evasive about Key. "She was a code-breaker?"

"No idea, old boy. I know only that she was at Bletchley, but precisely what she did will go to her grave with her. That whole generation is like that, you see? Swore to queen and country to never reveal the work."

I had a hunch she had known Key at Bletchley, but if she had it was unlikely she would ever confirm it. But if Key was dead, how could she have known him there? There was some connection she was holding back. Could there have been more than one M. J. Key? Joe Daly had told me he knew somebody who knew all there was to know about codebreaking during the war. I would have to follow that lead when I got back.

Charlie retired first, leaving Anjali and me seated by the fire.

"You're cousins," I said.

"Did you think we were lovers?"

I ignored the remark. "You followed me around with a camera."

"Fish," she said. "Trout. My strain of the family disease."

"You didn't fish with us."

"My symptoms are a bit different," she said. "Care to see?"

We each took another glass of brandy and I followed her to one end of the house where she had a large room. All around it hung color photographs of fish. Not exactly fish, but the colors and patterns of fish. I had never seen anything like them and they were beautiful.

"Charlie's a photographer, but you're an artist," I said.

"Good God, don't tell him that! He thinks he's Ansel Adams!"

We both laughed.

"Tomorrow I will do my best to get you a beautiful trout to work with," I said, raising my glass in salute.

"Try for the little ones," she said. "They're the gaudiest."

When we said good night, she hugged me and presented her cheek for me to kiss, the way polite and civilized Brits did, but when my lips neared her cheek I kissed her on the mouth.

She did not immediately pull away and when she did she declared, "Very, very nice."

Charlie was gone when I got into the kitchen in the morning. Anjali was brewing tea. "Bugger ran down to the best holes to get the edge on you. He's very competitive," she said, with the sort of tone reserved for incorrigible children. "Always has been. Simply cannot help himself."

"Must've been a hell of a soccer player."

"Had he not been injured, Charlie would have been the best to ever play for England," she said proudly.

But his head start that morning didn't help him. I caught many more fish than he did, largely because I focused on small ones for Anjali. I held each one so that she could work her camera magic, releasing them carefully when she was done.

"You are," she said, "not at all what I would expect in an American journo."

I also caught two browns that both were longer than twenty inches. When Charlie heard this he threw his rod on the ground and cursed for five minutes.

Tantrum done, he extended his hand. "I hate to lose, but when it's to a better man, it's an honor."

I doubted that I was a better man in any sense.

Charlie cooked mussels that night, serving them in a huge vat of seawater, and we ate them with hard rolls and drank white wine until we were all stuffed.

We retired after dinner to brandies in front of the fireplace and again Charlie went to bed first, not to get a head start in the morning but because we had to return to London. After he had been gone several minutes, Anjali set her glass down, stood up, stretched, and reached her hand out to me.

"The fish today were up to your standards?" I said, standing up.

"Yes, perfect, and you were so helpful."

I wanted very much to kiss her again but was hesitant. There was an aloofness to her that was daunting.

I lay alone in my room and thought of her in hers and took a long time falling asleep.

Anjali drove us to the station in Penzance early the next morning and kissed me on both cheeks in a very proper way before we boarded our train. Charlie grinned, but said nothing and I slept most of the trip.

As the train swayed and clattered east through outskirts of London, Charlie said, "I'll hunt up Ozzie, but be forewarned, it may take a while."

"Thanks," I said.

Charlie looked nervous and flashed his toothiest smile. "Anji has had a rough go on the roads of love, old boy. Wouldn't do to get your hopes up."

I couldn't think of a clever or sensible rejoinder and as soon as we alit in the station, he was on his frenetic way.

I went to see Daly the next morning. Dolly smiled when I walked in. "Good angling?"

"Not bad," I said.

Daly seemed distracted. "Problem?" I asked.

"My daughter," he said. "She's disappeared into the north. Nobody knows where she went or when."

"Probably just following a story," I said.

"The shit is starting to fly between Catholics and Protestants," he explained, before looking up at me. "What do you want?"

"You told me you knew somebody who knows about codebreaking during the war."

"I did?"

"When I first got here."

"Right. General Centre. Gotta be mideighties now, and crusty as week-old bread, but he was still sharp last time we talked."

"Can you call him for me?"

"Sure, no problem. What's this about?"

"I'm not sure," I said.

"Working a story?"

"Not exactly. Don't worry, Joe, your daughter will show up. You know how reporters are."

"Shit," he grumbled. "Don't remind me."

It was a couple of weeks before I met the general. We met at the Inner Temple of the Middle Temple Inn. The property once belonged to the Knights Templar and the Inn now was akin to a bar association. The complex was a maze of courtyards with old offices and people wandering about in black robes and misshapen white wigs perched on their heads.

Lieutenant General Sir Edington Centre arranged for us to have a private dining room. He was dressed in a pinstripe suit. One of his supernumeraries met me on the street and escorted me to the dining room.

The general pulled out a black pipe and asked, "Mind?" I said no and took out my cigarettes. He scowled at them, but I lit up anyway.

"How's Joe?" the general asked, popping smoke puffs from his pipe like a steam locomotive trying to get started.

"He's well," I said. There was still no word on his daughter and he was beside himself, but I didn't share this with General Centre.

"Interested in the war?" he asked.

He had a soft voice and deliberate way of speaking.

"Yes, sir."

"Something to do with that business in Vietnam?"

I said, "Not exactly." He waited for me to explain. "There's a man called M. J. Key," I said. "Or was. Author and expert on trout." I told him about Michigan Agricultural College, Key's leaving, the rumors, his article on codes with Vijver, all of it except that my only real interest was the snowfly and what Key's work might tell me about it. The general listened attentively and silently, asking no questions, betraying no emotion. "I visited with Lady Hoe a few weeks back," I said.

"Did you?" he asked, his eyes subtly wary. He set his pipe on the table.

"She told me Key was a mathematician and though she did not say this, I have been told that Key was part of Bletchley Park during the war." I had no evidence of this but wanted to see how it played with the general, knowing he'd correct me if I was wrong. "Your Key may or may not be my Key. They may be different people."

"How'd-she-look?" the general asked, speaking all the words so quickly they nearly blended into one. He leaned slightly forward over the table.

"She's in a wheelcair, but her mind is keen."

"Always was," he said. "Always was. Hard as diamond." I saw in his eyes that he wasn't with me anymore.

"I'm not trying to pry into state secrets," I said. Then, taking a chance, I told him about Key's manuscript and the Trout House and the North Vietnamese attack. Having finished my tale, I again asked if he knew M. J. Key; I wanted to confirm that there were two men with the same name. Was the Key who wrote the snowfly manuscript the Bletchley Key?

As before, the general listened without comment and, once again, took his time answering. "It would seem to me, young man, that if the alleged manuscript is gone, there is no point wasting your time chasing it, eh? It would be like seeking Camelot."

Why had he immediately focused on the manuscript? "I have a reliable source that indicates that Key was writing a manuscript for publication in the early to mid-nineteen-forties. Not the book that was published in 1943, but something different, probably the manuscript I saw in Vietnam. It occurs to me that with manuscripts, there's often more than one copy."

"Curiosity and cats," he said.

Was he threatening me?

"I'm an angler," I said, trying to explain.

"All Fleet Street types may fairly be said to be anglers," he told me.

It was not intended as a joke.

"As are intelligence types," I countered.

"Shall we dine?" the general asked, snipping off the exchange.

We ate in heavy silence. Dover sole fillets and creamed potatoes. The general picked at his food like a bird, chewing thoroughly before swallowing.

After lunch we went into a sitting room and had tea. The room's walls were covered with photographs of people in robes and wigs.

"The German code was broken at Bletchley Park," I said.

"Yes," he said, after considering his response.

"M. J. Key was involved."

The general leaned over to me. "Do you know Shakespeare?"

After a momentary pause, he said, " 'For Jesu's sake forebear to dig the dust enclosed here. Blest be the man that spares these stones, and curst be he that moves my bones.' "

"His epitaph?" I said, guessing.

"And Bletchley Park's," the general said somberly. "Good day, Mister Rhodes. My regards to Joe, if you please. I must go."

I sat there alone, watching him stride from the room, his jaw stuck out.

After the fishing trip, I had written to Anji to thank her for her hospitality. She'd responded briefly and with a perfect decorum that left me no clue to her feelings. For my part, she was often on my mind, but I could not bring myself to call her.

Northern Ireland was suddenly in the news. Protestants were brutalizing Catholics in Londonderry and other parts of the north and Parliament was discussing sending paratroops to lend a hand to Royal Ulster Constabulary. Joe Daly's daughter was still unaccounted for. People were being killed.

It was August and Charlie and I had finished an assignment in Liverpool, where I had interviewed young musicians trying to follow in the footsteps of the Beatles. They were hard-edged and desperate. Living conditions in Liverpool were appalling and pent-up anger among young people was palpable. I smelled bad times ahead and saw racist graffiti worse than anything I had ever seen in the States.

We took the train back to London. It was a Sunday night and I was tired when the train pulled into Victoria Station. As we waded into the herds of humanity returning to the city, we saw Anjali Toddywalla standing beside a black limousine, her arms crossed tightly and a shocked look on her face, the same look I had seen on soldiers emerging from a bloody fight. She looked like she had been crying.

"It's Auntie," she announced with a quivering voice.

"Gone?" Charlie asked.

She nodded and they moved silently to hold each other and I heard Charlie weeping. When they separated and he got into the limo, I held out my arms; Anji turned and put her head softly on my chest. I slid my arms around her and held her.

"I'm very sorry about your mother," I told her.

"I'm so glad she and Charlie reconciled before she went. They loved each other, you see, but they both were so bloody stubborn. She went quietly in her chair, looking out on her river. It was a cerebral hemorrhage."

"When is the funeral?"

"In a few days, I should think. We shall bury her in Cornwall, beside the Drake. She wanted a private ceremony, invited guests only. There's so much to prepare for and we simply must pay attention to the lists or push some blue nose out of place," she said with a weary smile. "I'm taking Charlie home now. Can we drop you somewhere?"

I was disappointed not to be invited to the funeral, though I knew I had no reason to be there. I turned down the offer of a ride. They were family and I wasn't.

To my surprise, Charlie called the next morning from Cornwall and said he and Anji both wanted me there and would I mind catching a train to Penzance?

I was met by a chauffeur in another limo and rode in silence out to Drake Hall.

Charlie met me on the back steps of the manor house. "This will be an event to remember," he said. He said it with a less-than-enthusiastic tone and I wondered where Anjali was.

There was no ceremony in a church and no clergyman to officiate. We met instead in the rear garden of the giant house as people arrived in chauffeured Bentleys and Rolls-Royces. The affair was by invitation only and I expected a small crowd, but it was anything but. Most of the mourners were elderly people, many of them in wheelchairs or propped up on canes.

Anjali came in wearing a black dress and a hat with a veil. She took my arm and I sat with her and Charlie in front of the guests.

"She believed in God," Charlie whispered to me, "but not in churches. She'd boff a vicar quick as lightnin', but not take his spiritual advice." Charlie got to his feet, smoothed his hair, and opened the ceremony very simply. "Good to see you all, thank you for coming. Auntie, you will be pleased to know, went peacefully and without pain. Most of you know that she and I were at odds for a long time, but we made our peace only recently." The mourners applauded politely. "She left no instructions for how this should go, so I suggest that if you wish to say a few words, please step forward and do so."

Charlie sat down beside Anjali, who was beside me, and whispered, "You're her daughter, Anji. Bloody ridiculous for me to be up there."

She patted Charlie's arm in sympathy.

At least one hundred people offered some words, memories, condolences, and nearly all of them shed tears. The vast majority were males of the upper class, sirs-this and lords-and-ladies-that, all the titles meaningless to me.

As the parade went on, I saw General Centre, sitting alone, his hands atop a cane, his face long and sad.

I slipped out of my row to approach him. "Hello, General."

"You," he said, not looking up. "Saw you up there." His tone suggested he did not like seeing me with Anjali and Charlie.

"You knew Lady Hoe," I said.

He nodded almost imperceptibly.

"She died without pain," I said.

"Death is the enemy of life," he said. "At any age, with pain or without."

He was in a very bad humor and I decided to leave him alone.

After everyone had an opportunity to speak, I watched Charlie and a contingent of elderly pallbearers carry the unadorned casket down to a grave that had been dug at a small outcrop overlooking the River Drake. It looked down on the cottage as well.

"Her favorite place," Charlie announced, his voice fading.

General Centre made his way over to me, his eyes red, chewing his bottom lip. To everyone else he looked like a dutiful mourner, but the voice I heard conveyed a very different impression. "Leave this Key business alone, Rhodes. You're rubbing against the Official Secrets Act and I assure you the powers of *this* state to protect itself are vast and unforgiving."

With that he shuffled away, not waiting for Lady Hoe to be lowered into the ground.

There followed an informal dinner in Drake Hall and the crowd ate but did not linger. Charlie surprised us by announcing that he was going to bed shortly after nine P.M.

"So early, Charles?" Anjali asked.

He answered with a nod and shuffled away, leaving us alone.

Anjali and I sat together in the room where I had met Lady Hoe. Rain danced off the windows and we talked about things that seemed to flow out of her. Anjali was not bitter about being unable to be publicly recognized as Lady Hoe's daughter.

"I'm glad you came," she said.

"I'm pleased to be invited," I said. "I'm glad to be here for you, Anji."

She gave me a quizzical look and I thought we were on the verge of a very personal conversation, but she only smiled and said, "In her later years, I was with her nearly every day. She was a wonderful woman. I won't say she was a great mother; she was more like my closest friend."

"What will happen now?"

"Ah, the loot question," she said.

"I didn't mean it that way," I said.

"Of course you didn't, and if you had I wouldn't give you a drop of sweat. I have my mother's infallible instincts about people. The estate will be settled in due course. Charlie will ascend to the title of Lord, loathe it, and move himself into Drake Hall. He will, of course, have a seat in the House of Lords. It shall all be very civilized."

"Where is your father?" I asked, not wanting to pry, but curious nevertheless.

"Dead in the struggle for Indian independence. Gandhi preached peace but my father was trained in war. He died violently, killed by Muslims opposed to Gandhi. I was still an infant and have no recollections of him."

I felt bad for her. "Did Charles tell you that Ozzie Oxley was supposed to be here today?" she asked. "But he never appeared, and I cannot say I'm the least surprised. Pitiful human, that one. Did Charlie arrange for you to see him yet?"

"He said he's working on it." That had been after our first trip to the Drake.

"Then it will happen. Our Charlie's good for his word."

I told her about meeting General Centre and his refusal to answer my questions and how he had approached me at graveside and warned me away from prying into Key's past.

"The general wanted desperately to marry my mother," he said. "Smitten by her all his life. So many men were."

"The general?"

"She refused, of course. She told me he was nice enough, but boring and far too mired in his career. Spent his life in military intelligence, you see. Very hush. I believe that's how they met. During the war."

"She told you that?"

"Not exactly; it's the sort of thing a daughter knows without benefit of words. She did tell me he was very boring in bed," Anjali added with a giggle. "Can you imagine a mother telling her daughter such an intimate thing? I am so glad that we were close." She cocked an eyebrow. "Like to know what my mother thought of you?"

I nodded anxiously.

"She said it was a bloody good thing that she wasn't closer to your age."

I felt a blush creep up my neck. "Is it?"

"Extremely leading question," she said. "It's lucky for me you're a gentleman." She smiled, brushed a butterfly kiss on my cheek, and left me wallowing in disappointment.

The next day Anjali, Charlie, and I visited the Drake. It was slow but we managed to coax a few fish to dry flies, Anji got a couple of rolls of film exposed, and the three of us had a lengthy cold lunch at the caravan by the river. Servants had set an elegant table and brought the food. We sat down and unfolded our napkins. Charlie rubbed his hands together and declared, "Ah, vittles!"

I thought about Anjali constantly after that.

Within two days of my return from the funeral the British government announced that paratroopers were being sent to Northern Ireland to protect Catholics. I stepped out of my building one morning soon thereafter to find myself face to face with Shelldrake.

"Following the news, boyo?"

He looked angry. "I've seen it."

"They'll soon be shooting Catholics with their plastic bullets."

"Catholics?"

His face turned hard. "Catholics have been England's niggers for a long, long time. Mark my words, they're going up there under the rubric of protecting Catholics, but soon enough it'll be the Catholics being killed by Brit troops."

"This is what you feared all along?"

Shelldrake turned and stalked away.

Within a matter of weeks his predictions had proved accurate. The protectors soon turned on the protectees and it was to go on for a long time. Though debates would sometimes address the issue of plastic and rubber bullets, these would be used for the duration.

The bullets were used by the local constabularies, but even more so by English troops. Assistant Police Commissioner Gerow Hedge had not lied to me, but I was certain he knew all along where and how the weapons would be employed.

One Sunday morning in early October Charlie bounded into my flat to roust me from bed. I thought I had locked the door, but there he was at the foot of the bed. I was clawing for covers as Anjali stood behind him, radiant and grinning, her hair tied in a French braid.

" 'We few, we happy few!' " Charlie declared brightly.

"Bugger off," I said, "and save the Shakeschirps"—his term for Shakespearean quotes. I struggled up onto my elbows and tried to rub the sleep out of my eyes. "What do you want, Charlie? Are you pissed?"

"You bruise my feelings," Charlie said. "Ozzie will see us!"

I leapt up out of bed, the sheets falling away.

" 'We burn daylight!' " Charlie shouted, raising an arm as if he held a sword. " 'We must to horse, to horse!' "

Anjali passed Charlie and made direct eye contact with me. "If I go to horse, Charles," she said, "I should choose to do so in privacy."

Charlie suddenly stopped and looked down at me. "Good God, Rhodes! Be a decent fellow and cover your alleged asset." He began laughing, and Anjali and I also laughed as I grabbed the covers to wrap around my waist.

"What about Ozzie?" I asked, trying to pretend composure.

"I told him I had a potential buyer for the Oxley angling books."

"You don't know if there *are* books left in his possession," Anjali said. "Or, for that matter, if books were *ever* in his possession."

"They were, dear, they most certainly were. And I figured these would be the last things that Ozzie's chemically laden brain would let go of. Quite clever of me, actually."

"Was he sober when you talked to him?" I asked.

"Sounded lucid enough," Charlie said. "For Ozzie."

It was a warm autumn afternoon by the time we departed. The trees and fields along the way were in full color and the drive to Greavy House in Hampshire was pleasant. Charlie, Anji, and I sat in the back of the Rolls, Anjali beside me and Charlie in the jump seat facing us. I felt warmth where Anji and I brushed against each other and each time we did, I felt her pull away. Her presence intoxicated me, but I had no idea how she felt. It was mildly rolling country and the house was set back on a dark river thick with cress and other aquatic vegetation.

"The venerable Test," Charlie said when the river hove into view. "Planted fish and more rules than a men's club," he said disgustedly.

The house was not as impressive as Drake Hall, but it was large. It was also in need of repair, and the gardens around it were going wild.

"Shameful," Charlie said, his eyes sweeping the poorly maintained grounds.

"Thus spake Lord Green Thumb," Anjali said playfully.

We were greeted at the door by a young woman with wild orange-dyed hair, no makeup, and sunken eyes. She was barefoot, wearing a bra but no underpants, and a little unsteady on her feet.

"Good mornin', dearie," Charlie said, brushing past her. "Is Himself about?"

The woman looked at where Charlie had been then pivoted awkwardly to see where he had gone.

"Oo're *yew?*" she asked in a sharp accent.

The walls in the house were bare and there was little furniture. Dust covered everything; spiderwebs gleamed in the corners. I saw two hypodermic needles on the floor.

"Bleedin' dungeon," Charlie said.

We found Oswald Oxley sitting in boxer shorts on the floor with his legs drawn up and crossed. He was holding a cigarette in a long ivory holder.

"Charlie old boy! You see my bird?"

The woman with the orange hair said, "I ain't yer bird, guv."

Ozzie nodded his head as if it were filled with mercury. "Righto. Everybody's bird. For a price, what?"

"It's a livin', ain't it?" the woman said.

"Honorable profession," Ozzie said.

"Yew wanker," she said, bringing a crooked smile to his face.

Ozzie looked up at us with glazed eyes. "Charlie, so sorry I didn't get to the doings for Lady Hoe. She was a grand lady. I think she boffed my grandfather, or perhaps my father, or both. I never could keep such things straight. Got any aspirin?"

"Sorry, old man."

"Gretch, old girl, please be so kind as to find old Ozzie some aspies, what?"

"Oy'm not yer bleedin' servant," she said defiantly.

"The customer is always right," he said. "You want to be paid, or not?"

She skulked away to find aspirin.

"I'd get up, but my legs won't cooperate," Ozzie said. He was a tall man with a gaunt face and long hair with white streaks. "Lord Hoe now, eh? We'll have to get together with the Parlies, give 'em something to titillate."

"Right, Ozzie. I called about the book collection."

"Books, old chum?"

"Angling."

"Ah, angling," he said in a sorrowful tone. "Money is money, I suppose. Hated to part with the dears, but life is life and one has no bloody choice but to live it."

"You've sold them all?"

"Course I did. The dealer finally found an eager buyer, didn't he? Positively drooling for the lot."

"Who?"

"It's bad form for a gentleman to sell and tell," Ozzie said.

Charlie reached down suddenly, grabbed Ozzie's shirt, and hoisted him roughly to his feet. "Stupid sod, we've come all the way down from London!" He shook Ozzie hard enough to snap off his head. I stepped over and separated his hands and Ozzie fell forward to the floor, emitting a grunt of misery when he hit the uncarpeted stone.

Orange-haired Gretchen came back with aspirin, saw Ozzie sprawled on the floor, and threw them at him. "Pathetic sod." She had repaired her face with makeup, run something through her hair, and donned trousers and a blouse with billowing sleeves. She sidled up to me.

"Yew're a right huge bloke."

Anjali surprised me by slipping her hand into mine. "He has no need of paying for it," she said with undiluted disgust.

I tried to put my arm around her shoulder, but Anjali subtly stepped away as if I had just wedged open her bedroom door.

Gretchen cackled. "They all pays for it, love. Indeed they does. Only question is method of payment, eh?"

I felt like Alice down the rabbit hole.

"Oy 'eard talk ov books, did oy?" Gretchen asked.

Ozzie began to belch and the belch soon faded into an uneven snore.

"His angling books," Anji said.

"He sold 'em through a broker, see. Consignment, they calls it."

"Do you have the name?"

" 'Course," she said. "What's it worth?"

Anjali stepped threateningly toward the woman, who held up her hands. "Just a joke, eh? Mister Brogger is the name. One of me most regular clients."

I could not believe my good fortune.

"Why him?"

"Because oy'm better in the kip than his wife."

"I mean the books," Anjali said. I thought she was on the verge of punching the woman.

"Ozzie's near-bust, eh? Wants me service, but not enough quid. Oy set Ozzie up wid Brogger, oy did. The books sell, oy gets a piece, which is me just due, and so does Ozzie, if yew know what oy mean?" She leered at Anjali, who turned away in contempt.

"Do you have a telephone number for Mister Brogger?" I asked, to see if she was telling the truth. I had been unable to get the information from St. John Wonbrow, and now it seemed as though I might have the leverage I'd need to get it from Brogger.

"Sure, love." She fetched a huge purse and pawed around in it until she found a card. "Here he is." She handed me a second card and in a low voice said, "That's mine, eh love? Give me a call and oy promise oy won't disappoint you."

We departed with Ozzie snoring away.

Anjali spent the weekend at Charlie's place in London. I wanted very much to spend time alone with her, but I couldn't bring myself to call. It was as though there was a wall between us that could never be broken down.

Joe Daly held a rare staff meeting on Monday morning and told us that UPI was having severe financial difficulties and all of us needed to "mind" our expenses. After the meeting I asked about his daughter and he said that she had still not surfaced, but news about her disappearance was about to break and he was unhappy about it. I told him about my encounter with Shelldrake. Joe looked tortured, hurt, and angry. I felt terrible for him, but his daughter had been missing for a considerable length of time and it was a miracle the news had not leaked before this.

I was working at the flat that evening, trying to write a story about fishing the River Drake—not naming it, of course. The phone rang and I answered.

"Bowie Rhodes?"

"Speaking."

"This is Danny, from New York."

"How are you?"

"I'm calling on a pay phone," she said hurriedly, "so *please* listen." Her voice was shaky and bordered on shrill. "I found a way to get information about emigrants. Your Key is listed as going to Switzerland in 1938. I also found an FBI bulletin with him on the list of wanteds. Same year. The funny thing is that he was only on the list one week. We got weekly bulletins from the FBI for about twenty years and archived them all so I could look down the road to see if there were further listings and there weren't." She was talking fast.

"I called the State Department about Key and the next thing I know I was visited by two fascists who said they were with one of the alphabet agencies of the federal government. They had credentials, but I couldn't find any reference to the agency later when I looked in our government index. I'm sorry to unload like this, but these jerks told me that M. J. Key was a national security matter and that I should, and I quote, 'cease and desist' from my search. They gave me a lecture about how private citizens should not be disturbing things they knew nothing about and they made it clear that if I continue, I'm gonna have some serious problems, including getting admitted to the bar. I'm probably paranoid, but after they left I went to check the card file on Key and his listings had all been removed. I checked around. Nobody here will own up to doing it and nobody knows why. Now

I'm wondering if the fascists have my phones bugged at home and work so I came over here to Staten Island to use a pay phone. Bowie, I can't help you anymore. I'm a coward."

"I'm amazed you've gotten as far as you have. You are *not* a coward, Danny." In her shoes, I'd feel paranoia too. References removed from the New York City Public Library? What the hell was going on? And, more important, why?

"I'm afraid," she said. "I'm real sorry about this, okay? Take care of yourself and maybe you ought to forget about Key too?"

After I hung up, I poured a glass of Scotch and sat down. General Centre was warning me away from Key in England and now some government jerks were doing the same to Danny in New York. If I had possessed good sense, I would have quit. But I was convinced that solving the mystery of Key was the way to solve the snowfly, and I refused to be deflected.

Several days later, the news finally broke on Daly's daughter. She had been missing for weeks and was believed taken by one of the warring factions in Northern Ireland, but no group had claimed credit and nobody knew where she was.

Meanwhile, I began to pursue Anjali to no avail. I asked her to dinner, but she was busy. I asked her to breakfast; same answer.

One afternoon I went to Brogger's office and caught him on the way out.

"Brogger," I said. "Congratulations are in order. You've finally sold the Oxley books."

"That's a private matter," he said, backing away.

"I spoke with Gretchen."

I saw signs of confusion. Then fright. His face flushed, the red deepening to crimson. He would not fare well in a poker game.

"I know nobody by that name," he said, his eyes darting around anxiously.

"Well, she knows you. Says you pay handsomely for her personal services. Or should I say intimate? I'm thinking your wife might like to know."

"I will not be intimidated," he said weakly.

"This isn't intimidation," I said. "I'd like to know the name of the buyer and I'd like it to check out. Otherwise I go to your wife. You can use whatever word you like to describe this transaction. I call it a promise. It's the books I'm interested in," I added, "not your personal business." He looked a little relieved, but still skeptical.

"I'm sorry," he said, "but I simply cannot help you."

I countered in a reasonable tone, "Then help yourself."

Brogger stared daggers at me, but took a pen out of his coat, scribbled a note on a small piece of paper, and handed it to me. There was a name written in a crooked hand.

"Mikhail Peshkov," I said out loud. "Who is he?"

"Peshkov bought the entire collection. He's in the Soviet embassy here in London."

"Why would a Russian want the collection?"

"The Russians *do* read," he said sharply.

"I know. But why Peshkov?"

"Like it or not, Rhodes, the books are out of reach." Brogger looked miserable. "I can tell you that Mister Peshkov is exceedingly well known to Her Majesty's government. He acquires various items from time to time. As a representative of certain personages in Moscow, if you take my meaning."

Meaning Kremlin big shots? "For whom, exactly?"

Brogger gave me a malevolent smile. "You'll have to take that up with Comrade Peshkov."

"The books are in the Soviet Union now?"

"This has been most unpleasant, Rhodes. Now you really must excuse me, and I hope we never meet again."

I left feeling dirty. I had not intended to play dirty, but sometimes you had no choice.

Joe Daly's daughter was discovered dead in early December in a hotel room in southern Spain. The death was attributed to an overdose of drugs.

Daly handled the news better than I would have. "She didn't use drugs," he said. "The fucking lunatics got her is what happened."

She would be buried in Massachusetts. There was a lot of news coverage and speculation about her disappearance from Northern Ireland. Joe Daly announced he would take a month off.

Dolly handed me a memo as I left the office that night. "Miss Anjali Toddywalla telephoned you today."

When I called, Anjali seemed pleased to hear from me. She wondered if I would escort her while she did some Christmas shopping. I readily agreed and took a few days off to trail around with her. She was a careful shopper with expensive tastes. She bought a fly reel for Charlie that cost the equivalent of three thousand dollars American. It was called a Carlysle and she told me that the maker produced only about twenty of them a year.

I had Christmas dinner with Anjali and Charlie at Nolan's. They were very gracious about the food. Anjali gave me one of the same reels she gave Charlie, explaining that she didn't want him to have an unfair advantage, him being so competitive and such. I gave her a painting I had chanced upon in a London shop. It was of a brace of trout, finning in green water that flowed languidly over them carrying flies. It had cost me nearly two weeks' salary, but it was worth it and she made a great fuss over it.

"A Victor," she said after scrutinizing it silently for the longest time. "Not signed that I can see, but this is his work."

"Victor?"

"Don't pretend you don't know," she said in a scolding tone.

"I found it in a secondhand shop and liked it."

She stared at me, aghast. "Found it? How much?"

"It's a gift. You're not supposed to ask that question."

"Bollocks. How much?"

I told her. She started laughing and covered her face.

"Share the joke?"

"Good God, Rhodes. Alistair Victor is one of the country's greatest painters of fish and pastoral scenes. Ranks with Turner. I should think this is worth twenty thousand."

"Dollars?" I asked faintly.

"Pounds sterling."

I did the mental calculation and redid it.

"We must get it appraised," she said.

"Why?"

"Doesn't hurt to know what one has. Sure you want to give it as a gift?"

"That hurts."

She kissed me chastely on the cheek. "Feel better now?"

"Almost," I said. She only smiled in response.

As fate would have it, the painting indeed turned out to be an unknown Alistair Victor and was worth an estimated forty thousand pounds as an auction starting price. But Anjali hung it in her bedroom in the cottage and said she would admire it at the start of every day for the rest of her life.

On New Year's Eve I was invited to join them at Charlie's town house for a party he was throwing. The gathering featured a real assortment of characters: footballers, professors, cops, peers, several men in kilts, sailors in uniform. And, of course, more women than men.

It got very drunk out that night and we brought 1970 in through a thick haze and lots of laughter and singing. As the other partygoers collapsed in various parts of the house, with arms and legs intertwined and snores buzzing like a summer thunderstorm in the offing, Anji and I found ourselves alone and staring at each other.

"I'd like very much to see where you live," she said.

We took a cab to my flat and she methodically look over my belongings, especially the strange painting of five women making love.

"Amazons," she announced.

"What?"

"No right breasts. The Amazons had them removed so as not to interfere with shooting their bows. Very practical women, I must say."

I didn't know whether to believe her.

What happened after this was less sequential than simultaneous. It began with Anji asking if I was familiar with the "wants," and transferred directly and expeditiously to bed where we let loose with such intensity that during a momentary lull, Anji clung close and asked in a whisper, "Know why lovers feel so good?"

I had an idea, but said, "Tell me."

She said, "Because you never know when you will lose it all. This is what makes every second precious. Time is the essence of love, Bowie."

As was normal, my flat was devoid of food. We decided to go out to a place I knew that served early risers.

"Perhaps we can even catch the sunrise?" I suggested.

Anji laughed out loud. "You mean purple smog?"

As we slowly descended the stairs arm in arm, Anji asked, "What took us so long to get together? Is it my imagination or have you been avoiding me?"

"I could say the same thing about you."

"Hmm," she said. "We are compatible, are we not?"

"You have to ask that after what we just experienced?"

She smiled and squeezed my arm. "Point well taken. What then has held us back?" adding quickly, "I will readily admit that I share culpability. As you have just seen, I have entertained certain prurient thoughts, but simply couldn't muster the courage to talk about them, much less act on them."

"You don't lack courage," I said.

She stepped to the stair below me, stopped, and leaned her head back for a kiss.

"I love your tallness," she said.

"And I love yours," I replied.

"I am more the timid rabbit than you can imagine, Bowie dear," she said.

"Perhaps you fear attaching to a nomadic journalist?"

"I can't picture me chasing you around battlefields like some sort of common camp follower," she said. "Can you?"

"I doubt you could be a common anything," I said.

She rolled her eyes. "Please, we are attempting to have a serious conversation. Could you see yourself settling down in England, perhaps writing a book or two?"

"I can't see that," I said, and immediately wondered if I was too selfish for another person.

"Oh dear," Anjali Toddywalla said. "We seem to be at an impasse. Now what?"

I didn't know. "Make every second precious?" I ventured.

"Such a lovely thing to say," Anjali said.

I wanted to spend the day with her, but I had a story waiting for me at the office. It wasn't earth shattering, but I thought of myself as a pro, so we took a cab to Charlie's, had a passionate leave-taking in one of his bedrooms, and I headed for work.

The next night, a Thursday, the phone rang. When I finally answered it, I heard Anjali's muffled voice; she sounded scared out of her wits. "What's wrong?"

"I'm alone at Charlie's," she whispered. "There's an intruder!"

"Where are the servants?"

"Off tonight."

"I'll call the police," I said.

"Oh my God," she said. I heard a clunk and we were cut off. My heart was racing, my adrenaline pumping. I called Dolly Aster at home and asked her to call the police while I caught a cab to Charlie Jowett's place. The lights were off in the house and the front door was standing open. I was shaking badly as I approached the front door and eased my way in.

I called softly to Anjali but got no answer and proceeded up into the house until I heard noise on the third level. A loud thump and a muffled squeal. I pushed through a door and saw a man with a black truncheon. Anjali was on the floor, her hair glistening with fresh blood. I charged the man, who deftly stepped out of my way and whacked me in the side of the head not once but several times as I fell.

Once I was down, the man drove kicks into my ribs and I rolled around trying to avoid further punishment; as I lay there in a defensive curl I realized that I recognized my assailant. It was the man named Thigpen, the enforcer for the gang Charlie had told me about.

" 'Ere it is, guv," the man said. "You been givin' a lot of good people a pain in the arse. I'm to tell you that you back off now or the woman 'ere will be the one to pie the price. *Capice?*"

He ended his speech by kicking me in the small of the back.

The police entered with whistles shrilling seconds after he left.

Anjali was taken by ambulance to a private hospital. I spent the night at Scotland Yard with the police. I did not identify Thigpen. I knew that if I did, someone else would hurt Anjali. I was sick that she was hurt and more than a little confused. Why had this happened? Simple revenge for Thigpen, or had Hedge sent him? Or was it Brogger or Wonbrow or General Centre? Shelldrake? I had no idea and every direction I turned, I saw enemies. Anjali was seriously injured and had to have her spleen removed. I had a cracked rib and some nasty contusions.

Daly retired and never returned to England. In taking his leave, he informed only Dolly, who was quite distressed. As far as the rest of us on staff knew, Joe was on vacation and would return any day. Then, the day after the beating, his office was cleaned out.

Grady Yetter arrived a few days after we learned about Joe Daly and took me out to dinner. Over drinks he looked at my battered face. "Something I should know about?"

"Nope." Yetter smartly changed subjects. "I guess Joe couldn't deal with the loss of his kid," he told me. "Good thing you didn't go over there. That could have been you."

"Bullshit. You can't project like that. Different people, different styles. Besides, I'm an orphan now."

He shook his head. "You'd stick your nose up the devil's ass if there was a story in it."

The comment struck too close to home and I let it pass.

"There's a new chief coming in," Yetter said, looking very unhappy.

"Who?" I asked.

"Puffit," he said.

Del Puffit, my asshole superior from Manila. "You're putting me on, right?"

"I wish I was, but I'm not that cruel."

"He's an incompetent slab of shit."

Yetter's head bobbed. "Politics."

"Politics! That's your fucking explanation for everything!"

"Politics are always behind shit," he said weakly.

"Puffit will can my ass," I said.

"There's a whole world to work in."

"Yeah? What about Moscow?" It was out before I could think about it.

"Moscow?" he said. "I was thinking New York."

"New York's not in the wide world. It's its own little one. What about Moscow?" I repeated.

"I can't," Yetter said.

"Then fuck it," I said. "I quit."

He looked surprised but remained calm. "Think it over. I'll get you something sweet. I don't know what's got your crank turned, but stick with me."

"A job without politics?"

"I can't promise that," he said.

"Then forget it."

I parachuted my napkin onto the table, pushed my chair back, and stalked out of the room. I was done with UPI and writing stories that resulted in the death and injury of innocent people.

I went to see Anji in the hospital every day that I was able. She was sore and silent and I sat beside her bed and we did not talk. After nearly ten days, she was released. I went to visit her at Charlie's, bringing flowers for her and Scotch for him, my meager offerings for forgiveness. Charlie had changed toward me. He blamed me for Anjali's injuries and told me that I needed to curb my ambition. The words stung, but there was no discussion. I was guilty of her getting hurt; I didn't know how, but I knew it was true and I made no attempt to defend myself. Not only had Anji been beaten, my friendship with Charlie had been damaged. Everything seemed to be imploding on me.

Yetter called me just before he left London and announced, "Puffit won't have you, so I've arranged for you to have a slot in New York. Think of it as temporary duty until we find something more suitable for you."

"Shove it, Grady. It's Moscow or nothing." Moscow. I had nothing to lose.

"You can't leave this business. You can't fool me."

"Watch me," I said.

I was scheduled to leave the day Del Puffit arrived and out of spite I called Ozzie Oxley's hooker friend, Gretchen, and asked her to go up to Puffit's office. I paid her and told her not to take no for an answer. She thought this was quite funny. I had no idea how it would turn out, but I suspected and hoped Dolly would appreciate the scene. I also suspected that sooner or later she would force Puffit out.

I had hoped to go to Heathrow with Charlie and Anjali, but Charlie was still angry and not talking to me. I went to Charlie's to see Anjali; she came downstairs alone to meet me in the foyer. She kissed me with the utmost tenderness but held me away, squeezing both of my arms firmly. "I'll note you in my book of memory, my sweet Bowie. 'Of all base passions, fear is most accurs'd. Remember, wisely and slow; they stumble that run fast.' " Like Raina Chickerman, she liked to spout Shakespeare.

She put her cheek against my neck. She felt warm.

"I shall miss your tallness," she said. "What happened was not your fault, Bowie. We were simply not meant to be. I will content myself with life as it develops and you, my sweet man, my fearless hunter, ever brave and resolute, you must do the same. You have a volcano for a heart, and much as she may dream, no woman may tame a volcano."

So it was that I left London, Charlie Jowett/Lord Hoe, and Anjali Toddywalla.

It was time for me to get my life in order.

8

T HE weather any place in Michigan in January can be bad, but my part of Michigan was often the worst. I flew to New York from London and on to Detroit and then up to Pellston, where I called Lilly. She complained about not hearing enough from me, about my not warning her I was coming, and about having to drive in a snowstorm, but she came to fetch me and when we saw each other she threw her arms around me and held me tight.

"Problem?" she asked. My sister had always been able to read me.

"I quit. Decided I needed a break."

"Quit your job?" she asked incredulously.

"I'm no longer employed."

"What will you do for money?" She was always practical.

"I don't know yet."

"And you came *here* for a break?" She laughed for a long time. "My dumb little brother."

I had known Fred Ciz at Michigan State. He was mild mannered and nearly forty when I first met him. He had saved for close to twenty years for an education and had trekked down to State to get his degree in journalism so he could return to Grand Marais to take over the town's weekly newspaper. Journalism students did not much run together. Most of us were loners with oversized egos. But Fred and I had gotten along. He was gentle and thoughtful with a sharp, wry wit and utterly devoid of cynicism. He had worked for his uncle's weekly since high school and knew more about putting together a paper, top to bottom, than most of our faculty.

I asked him why he would bother with school so late in his career.

"The paper belongs to the town," he told me. "It's not the *New York Times,* but we do serve our people. You can barely make a living, but what a way to live. I figure four years down here will make me better. I serve a public trust and I want to serve it the best I can."

It was pure hokum, I thought, but over time I learned that Fred Ciz was just what he claimed to be and I admired him for it and maybe even envied him.

Living with Lilly and her family wasn't an option. She and Roger Ranger were stretched and their house cramped. After two days of camping out on their living room sofa, I took a bus into the Upper Peninsula to New-berry and called Fred from there. It was thirty miles on bad roads and the weather was terrible, but an hour later I was in his old Ford headed north to the south shore of Lake Superior. We had not seen each other since college, but he didn't ask any questions and I didn't volunteer any information.

Fred lived alone in the village in a small house two blocks from the paper.

"If it was closer, I'd be at work all the time," he explained. "Almost am as it is." There had been a fiancée in his distant past, but the relationship had fouled. If he had regrets, he did not let on. He was a slow-talking, painfully deliberate man and so homely that MSU students used to ask him how he had gotten so ugly; he would say it was God's gift, and he meant it. Grand Marais was not the place for such a man to easily find a mate. Most young people fled when they finished high school. Those who stayed tended to pair up for life or remain unmarried. I figured Fred had to be lonely, but if he was it never showed. His family was his readers and the affection and attention he showered on them was returned with equal ardor.

I had been there two days when he declared one morning, "You didn't come all this way for the scenery or the company. Things go sour?"

"I got a little confused," I said.

"It happens to all of us."

"I quit UPI."

There was a slightly raised eyebrow. "Do you have plans?"

"Not a thing," I said.

We stared at our coffees. "If you want to keep your hand in, I could use some help here, but I can't pay. You ever tend bar?"

I told him I hadn't.

"No matter. Up here it's beer and whiskey neat. I can get you on at the Light. Belongs to a friend. The room here is yours for as long as you want, but you could share chow costs. If you make it through winter, you might have a new appreciation for everything. Cold always helps focus the mind."

I accepted and it turned out to be one of the best decisions of my life.

The Light was a tavern that dated back to the logging heyday, before the turn of the nineteenth century. It had high ceilings and a carved wooden bar imported from Baltimore. The owner was an octogenarian named Staley who still worked behind the bar and cooked short orders when the mood hit him. Staley had been the local rake and had tried marriage several times with no permanent takes. His interests in life were fishing, shooting big deer, bingo, and the misfortunes of the Detroit Red Wings. Staley had bought the bar when he was sixty. Before that he had done just about anything you could do for money in a small town and seemed to be one of the few locals to lift himself above the level of mere survival. Having achieved that, he seemed to be continually giving back to the community.

My bar training took about ten minutes and consisted mostly of learning to tap and untap metal barrels of beer.

On Sundays Fred went to early mass at Our Lady of Saviors Catholic Church (which everyone called OLS) and after that it was out by snowmobile to Lake 50 to fish through two feet of ice for yellow perch and the occasional walleye. Below the Mackinac Bridge, ice fishing tended to be a communal activity. Down there, on legendary Houghton and Higgins Lakes, pickup trucks with studded snow tires dragged fancy, heated prefab huts on skids out onto the ice and assembled shantytowns with shelters numbering in the hundreds. But up here there were no shanties and no shantytowns. If you went to a lake and somebody was there, you went elsewhere. You could be invited by a friend who had spudded some holes, but without an invite you were expected to move on. In the U.P. people respected privacy more than in any place I have ever been. And at the same time they looked out for each other.

I often went ice fishing with Fred. We dressed in layers and stayed warm by stamping our boots. Fred had fished Lake 50 most of his life and knew its moods and wrinkles the way a husband knows a wife. Some Sundays we went to the same spot, but other times we'd traipse across the snow-covered lake to a new position. Wherever we went there were fat perch, ten inches usually, but once in a while we'd hoist up a fourteen-inch, two-pound monster. The fish did not fight. If you found them, you could catch them. They were deep in holes, sixty to eighty feet down, and bit on spikes, a form of maggot. If you hoisted the perch fast, they came up bent like apostrophes and froze as soon as they were clear of the hole. We caught only enough for three meals a week and when we had our self-imposed poundage, we packed up and returned to town.

Vietnam's heat and England's wet winters had ruined my constitution for subzero weather, but as the U.P. winter wore on I began to adapt. In March we got three feet of fresh snow in twenty hours. The state news wire chattered with bad-weather stories, but the denizens of Grand Marais kept their rhythm. We had six to eight weeks of serious winter remaining and frosts until after Memorial Day. If we were lucky, summer would give us a half-dozen days over eighty. The previous summer hadn't seen a day over seventy-six and there had been only ten over seventy from Memorial Day to Labor Day. But weather didn't seem to matter in Grand Marais. People did what they had to do or wanted to do, and to hell with the elements.

I settled in and was almost content. At the paper I got serious about writing obituaries. A person's life was important here; every loss was deeply felt and mourned by all. I liked talking to people about the deceased and wrote details that had folks nodding. I was still an outsider, but Fred vouched for me and villagers suspended their disbelief and I tried not to do anything to alienate them. The local taverns served as social clubs except on Thursday nights, when the Catholic church hosted bingo. Because Staley was a bingoholic we closed the bar on Thursday nights. People came from fifty miles around and through the worst winter storms to play. Sometimes, in particularly heavy snows that turned to whiteouts, the bingo game would go all night and out-of-towners would sleep on church pews and floors.

OLS was about as interesting a Catholic church as could be imagined. The main building was formerly a state highway department garage. The chapel was built in one corner. The town's library was in another part and held a distinctly unsecular collection.

The local priest was called Buzz. Not Father Buzz, just Buzz. He was a corpulent man with the baby-faced countenance of Fatty Arbuckle. His acne-scarred chins were covered with gobs of Clearasil and this made his face look like it was one color from the nose up and another color below. He wore civilian clothes and battered, unlaced leather hunting boots. He drank Jack Daniels in copious amounts and would sometimes play his electric guitar at the Light when he was in his cups. The Grand Marais Elementary School had few teachers. When one was sick, Buzz filled in. He drove an ancient Ford Woody station wagon whose fenders had rusted off and been replaced with sheet metal riveted into place. A steel-frame luggage carrier had been installed on the roof. The priest carried a loaded 30-30 at all times. It was a lever-action Model 90 and if edible game wandered across his path, he shot it and distributed the meat to parishioners. The local conservation officer looked the other way.

Bingo in Grand Marais was much more than a mere game. In some ways it was more a religion for the locals than the Catholic church that sponsored it. Over the years three babies had been born during the games. Several elderly people had died. Once a black bear got into the building on

Thursday night and Buzz had gotten his rifle and shot the animal and the game never stopped. One of Staley's ex-wives had started an affair at bingo. Several times each year the area lost electrical power; bingo went on with lanterns and candles and, if it was winter, all the participants decked out in parkas and white air-force-surplus Mickey Mouse boots. In deer season hunters came directly from their blinds and stacked their rifles in the corner. Once Staley accidentally shot himself in the foot and came to bingo limping and bleeding. He played six cards all night before driving himself to Newberry for repairs.

While bingo was a social event, there wasn't much socializing while the games went on. A pall of smoke hung over the tables and the games were played in tight-jawed silence. Chips whick-whacked against tabletops. Winners announced themselves matter-of-factly. It was fine to win, but you didn't rub your good luck in the faces of those with lesser fortune. First-time protocol violators were taken aside and set straight. Second-timers were dismissed for the night by Buzz with a lecture on good sportsmanship. There were no third-time offenders.

In March Buzz asked me to spend a day making rounds with him and I agreed. We started at the Red Owl, our local grocery, where we loaded his ancient Ford Woody with supplies for shut-ins. Then we stopped to see the deputy sheriff, who was stationed in Grand Marais but reported to a supervisor in Newberry.

The deputy's name was Amp. He had been a Marine in Vietnam and did not talk about it. He was polite, short, and stout with a neatly trimmed beard. I remembered how Fistrip wanted to be a cop only to die in Vietnam. Deputy Amp was the antithesis of Rick.

"The Aho boy is at his uncle's," Buzz told the deputy. "He won't be a problem. The old man was pounding hell out of the boy's mother and he stepped in to protect her."

"I'll take care of it," the deputy said.

"Billy Aho's sixteen," Buzz explained to me outside. "His father came in last week with a snootful, said the boy beat him up and ran off. He swore charges. Truth is that Billy was defending his mom."

"How do you know?"

"The boy came to see me in the confessional."

I was shocked. "I thought the confessional was secret—a sacred trust."

"Well, it is, but this is a good boy and his father's a crumb. A priest has to use judgment."

"I thought you were bound by Church law."

Buzz grinned. "Well, the Pope and his crowd are in Rome and that's a helluva long way from these parts." He glanced at me. "You always follow the rules?"

"No."

"And right you are. Life is just not simple. Like it or not."

We visited several houses. Most were shacks hacked out of isolated sites in the woods. At one we met Janey, a young woman obviously fallen on hard times. Her face was lined with stress. She had five children, all young.

"Janey," Buzz said. "How's little Robert?"

"Better," she said. "Arguing with everyone. The medicine worked."

The priest gave her several cartons of food, a grocery bag with history books, and a piece of paper. "Loretta Hinchley's gonna drive out to see you."

"I don't know about this," Janey said.

The priest smiled. "Nature is nature," he said.

"What about the Church?" she asked.

"Let me worry about the Church."

In the Woody Buzz told me Janey had never been married. "When she meets a fella, she thinks she's in love, gets pregnant, and he disappears. Some people seem destined to pick the wrong partners. Janey's an intelligent girl, a helluva smart kid, first in her high school class over to Marquette, this despite missing a year while she had her first baby. Sometimes I think God is a mean bastard, giving a kid so much beauty and brains, but we all have parts of ourselves we can't control. Despite her smarts, her hormones got the upper hand. And she's a good mom if you ignore her sleeping with strangers. She's stretched bad. Some of us look after her, but she's gotta stop making babies. Loretta Hinchley's a nurse over in Newberry. She's going to get Janey on the contraceptive pill." He looked over at me. "What good's a Church ruling against contraception if the kids are born into hopelessness? Janey's got five. God and Rome should be happy with that. Now we need to help her do the best she can to raise the ones she has."

This was a priest who didn't fit any definition I knew except that he lived the way I thought any person, priest or not, ought to. Fred Ciz had told me Buzz was a remarkable man and I had to agree.

We distributed groceries all day. Our last stop was at a cabin several miles west of town. Buzz said I should stay in the car for this one and I agreed, though his request made me curious and I rolled my window down. I watched him pull his American Flyer sled up to the front stairs. The house was made of huge logs. I smelled smoke from a wood fire. There were snowshoes leaning against the trunk of a white pine and a woodpile with layers of sawdust mixed with snow. Buzz did not go to the door and knock. Instead he kept back from the front porch and yelled.

Even from the car I recognized her immediately. I wasn't thirty yards away. Her hair was cut severely short now and she was gaunt but it was, without question, Raina Chickerman and she was carrying a shotgun. She did not look toward the car and I sat in silence, stunned.

I heard Buzz talk to her. "Sorry to intrude, Miss."

"I told you before, Father. I don't need help. I am just fine and I will continue to be just fine." Her self-confidence permeated the air.

"We're a community up here," Buzz said, trying to open a dialogue, but she cut him off.

"I'm my own community. I'm here to work and I will not tolerate disturbances, well intentioned or otherwise."

Buzz left the boxes at the foot of her steps.

In the wagon Buzz was sullen. He was unaccustomed to failure. I didn't mind the silence, but I was more than a little curious. "Who is she?" I asked. I could barely contain myself.

"Smith," he said, gripping the huge steering wheel. "A pseudonym, no doubt. I heard she was out here and alone. I've tried several times to establish contact. Same outcome every time. She's a hard case, that one."

Hard case: That fit Raina Chickerman. I could still see her at the creek after the old man's funeral. I tried to think how she could possibly have come to live here as a recluse. As a child she had had no social life, joined nothing, did nothing with other kids, a true loner. I had been her only friend and now I felt like I had never really known her. She had shown up after I burned the homestead and promptly disappeared. And now she was here and it seemed too bizarre a coincidence to reconcile.

It was three days later before I got up the courage to go back out to her place. I had sweaty palms and a rolling stomach, but the effort went for naught. The place was empty and she was gone.

When I got back to the newspaper office, I found Grady Yetter arguing loudly with Fred Ciz about the layout of a page.

"Wire service guys," Fred said playfully. "Know-it-alls."

Yetter grinned at me. He was wearing a shiny new fire-engine red parka with a mad bomber hat whose flaps stuck out like wrinkled wings. A price tag still dangled from the hat. "Geez, kid. Five miles from here you can drive off the edge of the earth."

"How'd you find me?"

Yetter held out his hands. "Hey, I'm a reporter. Or used to be."

"Go home, Grady. Crawl back under your company rock."

He held up several issues of the paper. "These obits are good, kid. Obits are an art and writing is a gift. You don't wanna waste talent cause it don't last forever." He rattled the papers.

I lit a cigarette and sat down.

"You wanted Moscow," Yetter said. "I got it for you. Center of the Cold War, a real plum."

"I quit, remember?" Since arriving in Grand Marais my desire to go to Moscow to hunt the Key manuscript had ebbed. My search for the snowfly had too often brought injury and misery to others. I just wanted to get on with my life and to live normally.

"Yeah, yeah. Only you're still on the UPI payroll."

"I'm still on the payroll?" I was astounded.

"Yeah, we banked your dough. I figured you'd surface sooner or later. I gotta beg?"

"Do what you want, Grady. I'm not interested."

Yetter shrugged and pointed at Fred. "You've got a great little paper, pal. Thanks for the coffee." He then turned to me. "You know where to find me. Take some time to think about it."

After I returned to the newspaper office, I placed a call to Gus Chickerman.

"Bowie Rhodes?" he said, when I announced who it was.

"Yes, sir. I'm up in Grand Marias and I think I saw Raina up here, but we never got to talk. Can you tell me how to reach her?"

"It couldn't have been our Raina," he said. "She works in Washington now."

"D.C.?"

"No, Washington State."

"Doing what?"

"We're not really sure," Gus Chickerman said with palpable sadness. "We're worried about her, Bowie. She has changed."

Her own parents worried? That added to my concern, but what could I do? I asked him for her number and address, but he seemed so reluctant to give them to me that I found myself apologizing and hung up.

Though I sometimes thought about Raina that summer, I was content in Grand Marais.

In July, after the blackflies finally died off or went wherever blackflies go after they torture humans, I found a river that dumped into Lake Superior. It was twelve miles west of town on rutted dirt roads and difficult to reach; at the big lake it spread out into a swampy lowland before it reached a beach delta of gravel sprinkled with a rainbow of agates.

Upriver from the mouth at Lake Superior it was fast and wide, but at the mouth there was a flat trickle of gentle clear water. There were no fishermen's trails along the banks, no discarded worm cartons or rusting beer cans, no coils and bird's nests of monofilament. It was pure wilderness with clouds of mosquitoes.

Buzz didn't know much about the river. "It's called the No Trout because there's no fish in it."

"Baloney! I caught dozens of brook trout on a size sixteen female Adams. The fish were short, but some of them went a pound or more." The priest acted disinterested, which was entirely out of character; Buzz loved trout fishing and my finding a hot spot, especially in a place he thought was dead, should have lit him up. It always had before. I knew Staley would open up, but he was in Marquette for a few days. He had long since sworn off marriage but was reputed to have lady "friends" all over the U.P. He spent time on the road making what he called "visitations."

Over the course of the summer I went back to the river every day I could, staying longer and longer each time, exploring, making my own mental maps. By the end of September when the trout season legally closed, I had worked my way about ten miles upriver and found trout all along the way. The farther I got from Lake Superior, the more the river was stained dark orange by tannin, which made the bottom inky and wading dicey. The week before the season ended I camped for a week on an oxbow carpeted with bright green moss. It was a hot and sunny fall and shade was afforded by tilted white cedars that had somehow escaped the eyes of timber cruisers decades before.

Just about any fly I threw out seemed to raise a fish, which suggested they were natives and not hatchery plants.

I dug a shallow fire pit and lined it with stones and each afternoon I got my fire set for a fast start when I got back from my evening fish.

I had just awakened on my last morning and rolled out of my sleeping bag when I sensed movement to my left. I had no weapon other than a small knife. "Who is it?"

A deep, gutteral growl issued from the underbrush and I imagined I heard words that sounded like, "*Our* land" or something like that.

It wasn't a dog or a bobcat or a lynx. No bear made such a sound and, whatever it was, man or beast, I had no desire to find out. As I hastily packed my equipment I thought I heard the sounds of human footsteps crunching the brush nearby. I stood up abruptly and the sound stopped. Or I never heard them at all. The woods can do funny things to a man's mind. They had never spooked me before, but this was different. Something or someone was out there and I felt an eerie pall settle around me.

I returned to Grand Marais and checked in with Fred Ciz. "Catch any fish in your river?" he asked.

"No," I lied. I didn't know why I was holding back information.

"Told you," Fred said with a smile. "Place is fish-dead. Logging killed it a long time ago and it never came back."

I went to Newberry to check land records. I was sure I had been on state land, which turned out to be true, but I also learned something else that stopped me in my tracks. The river and most of the land along it had once belonged to the American Oxley Foundation, "a subsidiary of the Oxley Trust of London." The AOF had sold a huge land parcel to the state in the 1950s for one dollar, with the stipulation that it "forever remain wild and undeveloped." Why would Oxley have wanted to own this land in the first place? What the hell was this?

Most trout strike because they are hungry for a particular food and in this condition they tend to be finicky about what they eat and when. But sometimes a trout will strike out of anger to protect its own territory or out of sheer annoyance. I wasn't a trout and I wasn't protecting my turf, but I was plenty annoyed and confused. This damn snowfly thing was like a mirage. There, not there. Things seemed to lead forward and go nowhere. I wanted to know how Oxley fit, why the Russian bought the collection and manuscript, who Key was, and what the hell was going on. I made a decision on the spot.

I called Grady Yetter. "Okay on the Moscow assignment, but under my conditions."

"Which would be?"

"First, where's my money?"

"In the bank."

I told him to send me some of it.

"It's on the way." I intended to repay Fred and Buzz and the others for their kindnesses. I also wanted to leave extra cash with Buzz, specifically for Janey and her children.

"Next, I'll need tutoring in Russian when I get there." I knew better than to think my college Russian would carry me.

"No problem. When can you leave?"

"Don't I need a visa?"

"Hell, the Soviet consulate is practically next door. We have an arrangement with the bastards. I bribe the comradeskis and they expedite. All devout Reds like making a buck on the side."

"Next week, then. And I want a layover in London on the way."

"I'll mail you everything you need."

The bribe must've been inadequate. It took nearly a month to get the visa, which didn't let me head for Moscow until November. While I waited, I tried several times to call Anjali Toddywalla, but never connected. I wanted to see her while I was in London and understood that maybe she wouldn't be so eager to see me. Father Buzz had a parishioner called Hutamaki who searched the forest for old, wormy maples and used the wood to make bird's-eye maple decorations. I bought a brace of candlesticks and a set of boxes, peace offerings to Anjali.

When the details were finally set, Fred Ciz and Buzz took me to Newberry to catch the bus to Pellston. "You'll always have a place with us," Fred said. I did not have the words to thank them for their friendship and many kindnesses.

I spent a couple of days with Lilly, who had gotten pregnant again but miscarried.

"Use the Pill," I said.

"The Church forbids it," she said.

"You're not Catholic."

"Don't quibble," she said. "Russia's our enemy," she said at the Pellston Airport.

"So was England, but that changed."

"This is different," she said. "Can't you work in Tahiti or somewhere nice?"

It was November and London was gray, perpetually damp, and stinking of gasoline and mildew. The streets glistened in the constant drizzle and the chill ate into bones and nobody complained because the English were inured to it, bred not only to endure but also to overcome, carry on, and rarely brag about it.

I had a ten-hour layover to await my connecting flight so I took a chance and grabbed a cab to Charlie Jowett's place. Anjali came to the door, shoeless, wearing a baggy sweatshirt and jeans. She looked at me and the packages under my arm and laughed delightfully.

I felt bad for having not been in contact, but seeing her in front of me sent my heart racing. I blurted out, " 'Bid me discourse, I will enchant thine ear. Having nothing, nothing can he lose.' "

Her left eyebrow arched approvingly. " 'I am not in the giving vein today,' " she countered.

" 'Harp not on that string.' " I hoped this didn't go on too long or my quote account would be overdrawn.

She cracked a slight smile. " 'O! what a war of looks was then between them.' "

I stammered. "Er, uh . . . 'the heavenly rhetoric of thine eye.' "

" 'Your wit's too hot, it speaks too fast, 'twill tire,' " she said.

I had hit the end of my Shakespeare. "You look wonderful."

"I look like a hag," she said, opening her arms and inviting me inside.

When I told her I was headed for Moscow, she did not welcome the news.

"That horrid place and those horrid people?" She sounded like my sister.

"The manuscript is in Moscow and I intend to find it."

"You've been honing your ruthless side," she added. "Why is this snowfly thing so bloody important to you?"

"I don't know." This was the truth.

"You are a frighteningly intense man, Bowie Rhodes."

"Intensity gets things done."

"It certainly seemed to fail your General Custer."

I knew better than to keep on. "Can we drop this subject?"

She said, "Can *you?*" She had to get the last word in.

Charlie was in Egypt on a freelance job for *National Geographic*.

"He's still working?"

"Hasn't even been to the House of Lords yet. Charlie will always be Charlie."

"Will I always be me?" I asked, half joking.

"It's too early to tell," Anjali said ponderously.

When I left Heathrow for Moscow, I was alone. Anjali and I had said our final farewells without actually saying the words and I was sad, but also excited to be moving forward. The manuscript was in the Soviet Union and I was determined to find it.

9

THE UPI office in Moscow was not a one-man show. There were three correspondents. Our chief was Susanna Ovett, the daughter of Russian parents who had fled the Soviet Union before the war. She was a graduate of NYU and Columbia and fluent in the language. She was a colorless woman, hardworking, deliberate, and calculating, her Russian blood giving her the perfect temperament for dealing with the obfuscatory Soviets. She was also single, but we never socialized. The other member of our triumvirate was Charles "Beany" Anderson, a redhead from Boise, Idaho, who had a Ph.D. in Russian studies from Stanford. Beany was our main bird dog at the defense ministry. Susanna covered the political events at the Kremlin. My beat was what we called Soviet life, the everyday life of simple comrades.

I met my Russian tutor the morning after I reached Moscow. Lydia Yonirovna was sixtyish, trim, well dressed, and all business. She gave me a copy of *Izvestia* to read out loud and after a while proclaimed that my comprehension was adequate but my pronunciation and accent were "atrocious and unlikely to be corrected in a lifetime." She then set about to correct my deficiencies. Her standards and goals were somewhat higher than mine, but I worked hard and was satisfied with my own progress. The more I used the language, the easier it became. It had been a hindrance not to know the language in Vietnam. I was determined not to have to operate with this disadvantage again and in the Soviet Union I knew I needed to know what people were saying, even if I never let on that I could understand.

It was difficult making contact with the sort of people I was most interested in. There were plenty of allegedly rebellious young people eager to talk, but I didn't trust their motives and wanted to meet and understand people who lived simple lives and had no visions of grandeur. I learned to troll: the farmer's market, sporting events, museums, trolleys, and buses. Day after day I returned to write stories about cab drivers and bus jockeys and grave diggers and street sweepers. I did not compare their lives to counterparts in the West and I did not use last names. I simply told their stories, the facts of how they lived, their hopes and dreams. It was the approach I'd learned in Vietnam and refined in Britain.

I had been in the Soviet capital less than a month when I made a formal request for an interview with the officials in the Kremlin responsible for purchasing antiquities in the West. My request was ignored, which was pretty standard. A few weeks later I requested an audience with Brezhnev and this was refused before being processed. He was far too busy for journalists. All during this time I refrained from making inquiries specifically about Mikhail Peshkov. As driven as I was to solve the mystery of the snowfly, it was apparent to me, even before I arrived, that I needed to tread lightly in the USSR, at least until I understood how things worked and figured out how much leeway I really had.

In summer the Moscow River was a magnet for people. I had arrived in November and struggled through the slashing winter. By May, with the barest hint of sunshine, the grassy banks filled with the fish-belly white bodies of Muscovites in scanty bathing garb. Fishermen, swimmers, picnickers, bird-watchers, strollers, and sunbathers all shared space, a practice in peaceful coexistence. The kiosks along the river sold inexpensive *kvas* and ice cream and loaves of sweet black bread.

In a nation as spacious as the Soviet Union, it was hard to comprehend its overcrowding, but people could not move freely and were constrained by laws overlapping, interconnected, and almost always conflicting. Moscow was crammed beyond its holding capacity with five or six people shoehorned into space designed for two. When the weather warmed, people spilled into the city's parks and green areas. When the sun began to sink, the wooded areas filled with lovers and, though the uniformed militia were ubiquitous, there seemed to be an unspoken rule that summer belonged to the people and the police left them alone. Summer gave people the chance to depressurize from the frustrations of a seemingly endless winter. Those in power or with connections escaped to their dacha communities in the birch forests outside the city, but most citizens had to find their retreats within the city limits.

It had been a particularly long winter and a dismal, rainy, and muddy spring. With spring came a lengthening of days and I felt the familiar urge to find moving water and fish. I was partially successful. There were fishermen all along the banks of the river in the city; where they got their equipment remained a mystery. There weren't many stores in the city and none had sporting goods. Most of the gear I saw looked homemade.

During my first forays along the Moscow River I was given the cold shoulder, a default for Russians with outsiders. My clothes, especially my shoes, immediately marked me as a foreigner, and contact with foreigners was risky business. After the war, Stalin had sent tens of thousands of Red Army soldiers into the gulags simply because they had seen the West and were therefore assumed to be contaminated. Stalin was dead, but his lessons and far-reaching paranoia lived on.

Once summer turned serious, I visited the river regularly and began to observe a group of five fishermen. I had no idea what they did for a living, but they seemed to have time to come to the river every day. Eventually mutual curiosity took hold and we struck up a dialogue in mixed pidgin English-Russian. There was no ideology on the river and interest in catching fish transcended cultures. They were bait-and-bobber fishermen and we talked of fish caught and to be caught, of food and drink, of weather, and of women. We came to call ourselves the Anglo-Soviet Piscatorial Society. Nicolai, Pavel, Ivan, Georgi, Misha, and me. They were all veterans of the Great Patriotic War, men who had proven themselves against terrible odds and, having done so, felt no need to relive the doing. We fished for lethargic mirror carp, which were greenish brown in the Moscow River. I got hold of canned corn, marshmallows, and Vienna sausages and showed them American baits and ways. I never talked about fly fishing, which seemed light-years beyond what they were interested in. Somewhere in the Soviet vastness I knew there had to be trout, but I was pretty much stuck in Moscow and there were no trout there.

Then one day we fished just outside the city at Sabrony Bar, made a fire, and cooked the fish we caught. Two militiamen came to sternly lecture us on the rule against open fires. We offered them food and vodka, they accepted, shed their gray tunics, and joined us. We all got so drunk that we had to sleep it off on the side of the river that night.

Though Russians tended to be standoffish with strangers, once their suspicious natures were satisfied they embraced friends as few people I had known.

I wrote about many things in those early months after I forged friendships with my fellow anglers by the river, but I never wrote about the Anglo-Soviet Piscatorial Society. My fishing friends were mine alone.

In August we were fishing off a barge on the southern fringe of the city. I had no idea how this had been arranged, but it had. Russians learned the art of personal networking before it became a buzzword in American business schools. It was a hot and humid night and my Russian friends had small torches burning along the gunwales. The captain of a river tug joined us, as did several Russian women. I had a small Japanese-made, portable eight-track player that we used to listen to the Beatles and

Fats Domino as we drank and fished off the vessel. Georgi brought a balalaika and strummed and picked while we danced the *gopak*. One of the Russian women and I went skinny-dipping, then crawled onto a platform at the rear of the barge and made love frantically while the Piscatores jounced boisterously above us. I did not even know her name. She had bleached hair and brown eyes and a come-hither smile. When it suddenly went silent on the barge, I had a sense of foreboding. I climbed up to see what was going on and a powerful set of hands clamped onto my shoulders and hoisted me aboard, scraping me over the railing and dumping me unceremoniously onto the filthy wooden deck. The woman was nowhere to be seen.

A heavy, rough blanket was was pulled over my head and I was handcuffed and taken stumbling to an automobile and driven away. I could see nothing. I did not want to think about what lay ahead, but I had heard legions of stories about Westerners grabbed without warning by the security services; usually such events were intended only to harass or show official displeasure, but some such events ended badly with a foreigner's expulsion or worse, an untimely and lethal accident, complete with witnesses and corroborating evidence.

The car came to an abrupt halt. I was dragged from it into a building, shoved into a room, and left in the dark. I managed to get the blanket off. I felt the splinters from my slide along the deck of the barge. Pitch black. My heart pounded. Still naked. Jesus. It was common knowledge among Westerners that the KGB often stripped prisoners for interrogations. Why was this happening to me?

Eventually the door opened. I was given trousers. The cuffs made it nearly impossible for me to use my hands. I stumbled around trying to put the pants on, then lay down. I was hauled into another room and shoved unceremoniously onto a chair.

The man before me was immense. Most Russians I had met were short, but this man was tall and powerfully built. His hair was blond and cut close; a thick reddish brown mustache drooped over the corners of his mouth. He had gray eyes and dense eyebrows.

"You have committed a crime against the Soviet people," he said. His voice was deep and menacing, his English flawless, hinting of England rather than America.

I thought of the willing flesh of the Russian woman and went cold. Had I been set up? The Soviet security services were famous for entrapments using women—enticements that spooks called honey traps.

"I have nothing to say," I told him. "I've done nothing illegal. I want to talk to my embassy."

He leaned close to my face. "You have violated a Soviet woman. This is not allowed."

"I didn't violate anyone!"

His voice modulated. "It will be to your advantage to cooperate."

"I *am* cooperating. I *am* telling the truth."

"Truth is determined by the state."

I countered. "Truth is determined by facts."

My interrogator said, "Facts, like numbers, can be assembled to support many conclusions."

I had just enough vodka lingering in my bloodstream to be combative. "I have nothing more to say, asshole."

"In our system silence is an admission of guilt," my interrogator replied, glaring at me and holding up a beefy fist. His knuckles were streaked with scars, some of them looking very recent. I tried not to flinch.

"Do you deny congress with a Soviet citizen?"

"I've only slept with Brezhnev's wife," I said, lashing out. "I think he watched."

The giant looked appalled and stepped back. "That is a *truly* disgusting image," he said, allowing a smile to creep onto his wide face.

The doors to the room burst open and the members of the Anglo-Soviet Piscatorial Society tumbled in, smiling and jabbering, carrying bottles of vodka. The women were with them, including my swimming partner. A setup indeed.

My interrogator poked me in the center of the chest with a finger as thick as a broomstick. "You are not afraid," he bellowed. "You have *balls!*" He turned and said something to the others about courage. They nodded drunkenly and began to applaud in the peculiar rhythmic way Russians clapped.

"What the hell is going on?" I was no longer afraid; I was embarrassed and more than a little infuriated by their practical joke.

Misha unlocked my handcuffs. Ivan gave me a tumbler of vodka.

The big man cocked his head to the side, crossed his arms, then grabbed my arms. "I am Viktor Andreyevich Valoretev." He kissed me on both cheeks and gave me a playful shove that knocked me backward.

"Our comrade," Misha said happily.

"A joke? You think this is a fucking joke?" I felt my temper flaring but before it could gain real intensity, I found myself laughing with the others.

"You are all assholes," I told them in Russian, which only made them laugh all the harder.

We stayed at the cabin for two days. There was a lily-pad-choked lake a hundred yards away, but we were having too good a time to bother with fishing.

My female companion was named Talia and she was a pediatrician. In fact, my colleagues were not simple working folk, but professionals and academics, and the dacha belonged to Misha's family.

The mysterious Valoretev and I talked nonstop about fishing. He said he wanted only to catch trout and that carp were the serfs of the fish world, bottom feeders like politicians and beneath his dignity.

When I asked him if there were trout near Moscow, he shook his head and said, "Not close." Then he asked, "Do you use a fly rod?"

"Yes. Do you?"

He did not answer and I had no chance to follow up because Misha appeared and pulled me away.

"Only here are we truly free," Misha confided. "The forest has no ears and Viktor Andreyevich is our sword and shield."

It would be some time before I came to understand that Viktor, who was in his midthirties, was in the KGB and that our lives would be inexorably linked. The KGB called itself the "sword and shield" of Mother Russia. The only thing it shielded was the truth and that from the Russian people more than from the outside world.

There was no official Christmas in Russia, but the Russian people sidestepped this technicality and put up trees and decorated them for New Year's. The happy days of fishing on the river had given way to crushing cold and blowing snow. The expatriate community felt isolated in the Soviet capital and tended to pounce on the slightest excuse to throw a party. These were not elegant affairs, but more like impromptu college dorm bashes with guests bringing whatever they had hoarded or brought back from the outside world during their most recent trip. I did not like such gatherings and avoided them to the extent I could. Ignoring them completely would have been unwise because there was always information and speculations to be had off the record. In the figurative sense Westerners in Moscow were all fishing for one thing or another and, like good anglers everywhere, we would trade and share some of our recent finds.

Once summer fishing ended, I did not see much of my pals from the river. I was not invited to their homes. To invite a foreigner home was to invite the suspicion of the state—and worse. The government had informers everywhere. The Russians also nursed a curious national inferiority complex and I was sure they would not want me in their homes because they felt these would not measure up to the West.

Moscow was a gray city filled with gray people. In winter the morning sun came late and left early, if it showed at all. People worked from dark to dark and in early evening the slushy streets were filled with people walking shoulder to shoulder, all dressed in heavy, dark overcoats, shuffling forward to keep from falling on the ice, all moving in the same direction, nobody speaking. The only sounds were coughing, from smoke or bugs, and in the street there were few vehicles. There was no life in the crowds, just motion. The city was only marginally lit, as if it were at war and keeping light low to not attract enemy attention. It was a sprawling, silent city filled with silent people and to walk among them as they went home from work was to feel their sullenness move into your flesh like a virus.

In Stalin's day the Soviets knew little about the West, but Khrushchev had opened the window and though Brezhnev was anything but liberal, information came in sporadically on contraband and homemade shortwave radios from Radio Free Europe and the BBC. Soviets lucky enough to travel outside the country on state business returned with wondrous tales. What they learned was turning them defensive. Paradise was showing its age and its incompetencies.

I was alone on New Year's Eve. I would've liked to have called Dr. Talia but she had made it clear that our dacha dalliance had to remain a one-time affair—for her protection. I couldn't fault her for self-preservation. To understand freedom required you to lose it. The Soviet Union had given me new appreciation for the things I had taken for granted. I could find company among expatriates, but I was in no mood for their ritualistic whining about the difficulties of life in the gray and ominous Soviet capital.

I wanted to surprise Lilly and the gang in Grand Marais with a phone call. Before my arrival, reporters had been required to go to Moscow's Central Telegraph Office in order to wire stories to the outside, but now we had telephones and I stopped by our office, which was connected to Susanna's flat, but the phone service was down. The Soviets tried to disrupt us with planned technical interruptions and interminable red tape, but they underestimated our resolve. I could hear a loud party under way on the floor below Susanna's and, to avoid the crowd, I took the back stairs down and went outside.

I was barely out of the building when a black Pobeda swerved toward me and slid over to the curb through the slush. The passenger door swung open. I peeked in.

"Get in," Valoretev said in an anxious growl.

As soon as I settled into the seat, Valoretev flashed a conspiratorial grin and handed me a bottle of vodka. "Tonight we celebrate."

I accepted the bottle willingly. "You have rescued me from the slag heap of boredom. Where are we going?"

"State secret," my huge companion declared, touching a finger to his lips. "Shhh."

Once out of the center of Moscow, it was virtually impossible for most Westerners to identify landmarks, and I was as incompetent as others. There was block upon block of housing tracts, all dark, all the same. We had driven more or less north, which was about the best I could place us.

Eventually we pulled up to a garage. Valoretev blinked his lights twice and the door abruptly opened to admit us. Two bearded men with shotguns closed the door behind us and watched as Valoretev led us down a darkened stairwell to a steel door, which he hammered with a fist.

There were six men inside, most of them in their thirties, like Valoretev. They were seated at a table that nearly sagged under the weight of food, bottles of vodka, and wine. There was cabbage soup and *pelmeni,* ravioli that looked like ears, cabbage leaves stuffed with diced meat, a huge salad of pink rice, gobs of butter, wheels of black bread, *kasha,* wooden bowls of pickled vegetables, and mushrooms. It had taken some effort to accumulate so much food, which was always in short supply in the city.

"This is my friend Bowie Rhodes," Valoretev announced. "He is a heartless capitalist pig."

One the men tore off a hunk of bread, held it out to me, and said brightly, "Welcome, capitalist pig."

Another of the men filled tall, thin glasses with vodka and distributed them.

Valoretev said to me, "Make a toast to peace and friendship between our countries."

"To peace and friendship between our countries," I said. We drained our glasses. Refills all around.

Valoretev said, "May rivers never run out of fish." Drained all around, more refills.

I saw the others grab for food between toasts, especially the heavy bread, and I did the same. With Russians you had to learn the art of defensive drinking.

One of the men said something in Russian I couldn't quite decipher. "He toasts to vodka that will make you blind," Valoretev said. The drill.

And yet another, each speaking in Russian, Valoretev translating, though I could follow most of it.

"This man wishes to have carnal knowledge of your sister," Valoretev said. Then a whispered aside, "The green snake has him," meaning he was crocked.

"My sister accepts in the spirit of Soviet-American friendship," I said. The men hooted and drained their glasses.

The last man's toast was short. "He says, 'Drink to Robin Hood,' " Valoretev said. My head was spinning. A succession of shots of vodka Russian style was a fast and unforgiving high.

"What the hell does that mean?" I asked, then added, "Robin Hood was English."

Valoretev growled and chucked my shoulder. "You are wrong! He was nobleman who joined the Party to take from royalty for serfs. Robinevich of Locksky . . . a true Russian hero."

I laughed out loud.

"Eat!" Valoretev commanded and we all obeyed, piling our plates high with the abundant food.

The toasts stopped, but the alcohol flow didn't. We had sweet Georgian champagne and Armenian red wine and more vodka. Empty bottles were tossed over our shoulders. Some shattered. I was yelling in English and Russian. Valoretev was roaring in Russian and English. The rest were just roaring. I knew none of them. I was having a great time.

At some point Valoretev got up and clapped his hands on the table. "Okay, now we fish."

To the extent that I could think at all, I thought he was crazy and wondered if I was hallucinating. We went into another room that stank of gasoline and oil. The men picked up brocaded valises and knelt down to open them.

I was weaving. What the hell were they doing?

"You must judge now," Valoretev said. One of the men handed him what I thought was an antenna. Valoretev held it out to me. I squinted. Not an aerial. A fly rod, made of wood, light and well balanced, about seven and a half feet long.

"Good?" Valoretev asked.

"It's fantastic. Where did you get it?"

Valoretev thumped his chest. "We each made our own. They are Russian!" I noted that he did not say Soviet. "We got plans from books. Tonkin cane is from our socialist brothers in China." The big Russian then lowered his voice and grinned. *"Na lyevo, da?"* The black market.

Each of the rods was a work of art.

Valoretev gave me a reel. It was crude, but sturdy. We pulled the line through. I whipped it back and forth with false casts. "Perfect," I said. "Have you used these?"

"You will *teach* us!" Valoretev thundered gleefully.

"Now?"

"Da! Tonight. *Now!"*

I spent nearly five hours with them, teaching them a roll cast and a reach cast and what I called a sidearm curl. Most of my students were a little clumsy. All but Valoretev, who picked it up almost naturally, grinning the whole time. We had no real fly lines, which was a problem, but they had heavy braided line and for the distances they were working it served well enough to approximate the action of a weighted fly line.

When the beautiful rods were put away, we returned to eating and drinking and I talked about fly lines and leaders and fly sizes and nymphs and dry flies and streamers. I wanted to share everything I knew with them and talked like a machine gun until we were all too tired and too filled with booze. The men left one by one, each bidding me farewell with wet kisses on my cheeks.

Valoretev and I were the last to leave. We could barely get up the stairs.

"What the hell was that about?" I asked him.

He grabbed my shirt, nearly lifting me off the ground. "All America is private?"

"No."

"Fish belong to the regime?"

"No, to the people." In a manner of speaking.

"We are communist," he said. "We own everything equally. And we own nothing." He sounded forlorn. "Bastards," he added. "The czar owned all. Now the Kremlin owns all." He stared at me. "Where do you fish?"

"Rivers."

"The people own them?"

"The water and the fish in the water. Some of the land is private, some is public."

"The owners can forbid you to fish?"

"No. We have laws. All citizens may fish in navigable water. But you can't get out on private land. You have to stay in the water and wade."

He grinned. "You have balls."

His tone suggested trouble.

"I don't fish with them."

He grinned maniacally. "Here you *must!*"

No more was said. I was delivered to my flat and I slept all that day and the next night.

I had gone my own way the first time I asked for an interview with Brezhnev. This time I enlisted Susanna's help.

"I want to interview Brezhnev," I announced.

"Why?" she asked, stifling a laugh.

"He's a sportsman. People say he hunts and fishes. Our readers would like to know about this. It's a human angle. Nobody's done it."

"He rarely gives interviews."

"I still want to give it a try."

The simple act of making such a request was complex, requiring interviews, phone calls, continuous prodding and cajoling and voluminous paperwork, all of which had to go through layers, across departments and ministries. I got two turndowns. In the third request I noted that I had sources indicating that the General Secretary's agent had purchased rare fishing books for him in London and that I would like to talk to him about fishing and his collection. I didn't know who the Oxley books were for except someone in the Kremlin and since Brezhnev was the boss, I figured I would allege they were his. What was the harm?

Still no answer by mid-May. Instead, Valoretev picked me up on the street one night. He was driving a boxy green vehicle that looked part jeep and part VW. He looked grim, glanced my way, and growled, "Get in quickly." It was an order, not a request.

When I was in he said, "*You* are insane!"

"Is that a diagnosis or an opinion?"

"Do not make jokes."

We raced south and left the city. His credentials got us through security checkpoints. In the morning we dumped the strange vehicle in a woodlot and stood in the bushes beside the road. A green truck came along, stopped, and we clambered into the back and closed the canvas. We drove all day and all night. The truck dropped us in a forest and we slept in a ramshackle barn.

A motorcycle was waiting there. At sunrise we were on the motorcycle and aiming west. I kept asking what we were doing, but Valoretev was stone-faced and refused to talk. I was unnerved by his behavior.

We stayed on dirt roads, deeply rutted, and followed spine-juddering trails through dark forests. Eventually we reached a poor excuse for a shack. It was unpainted, leaned to the left, and looked like a light gust of wind would flatten it. Valoretev stashed the bike. We went into a cellar through a trapdoor. The cellar was well equipped. Kerosene lamps lit the area. There was canned food. This was a cache. I realized that whatever was happening was neither practical joke nor spontaneous event. Valoretev had planned this and I wanted to know why.

"What the fuck is the deal?" I asked angrily.

He poked me in the chest with a powerful finger. "*You* are deal!"

"I could use just a touch more detail."

He opened a can of beets. German label. "Okay, facts. You requested audience with Brezhnev and accused him of crimes against the people."

"I didn't accuse him of anything." Was he serious? I had to stifle a laugh.

"Rare books," Valoretev said. "The regime is corrupt, Bowie. We know and pretend not to know. They know we know and pretend we don't know."

"That's twisted."

"*Da,*" Valoretev said. "This is the Soviet way. You said an agent of the General Secretary bought books. The agent's name was Mikhail Peshkov."

I was shocked. I had not identified Peshkov in my requests. "That's right." I initially missed the tense distinction.

"Comrade Peshkov was recalled to Moscow and transferred to a more distant place."

"How distant?"

"Eternally," Valoretev said.

I felt sick. "He's *dead?* Just because I wanted to get an interview?"

"Yes, he is dead, and you are in trouble. They are trying to decide what to do about you."

"Expel me?"

"At the least take you into custody and trade you for a comrade traveler. They already have a warrant with your name on it. They have been trying to determine how to proceed next. They talk and talk and flit around dark offices debating your fate."

I couldn't comprehend this. I was a fugitive? In the Soviet Union? This couldn't be.

Valoretev nodded. "I think they are inclined toward a permanent solution. They don't know how much you know. They do not want you writing in the West that Brezhnev is using the people's funds for his personal benefit."

"This can't be real." I was nauseous. Dizzy. They killed Peshkov? "How do you know these things?"

He answered my question with a question, spreading his hands and looking around us. "Is *this* not real?"

It was, in an unreal way. Surreal. "What are we doing?"

Valoretev grinned and narrowed his eyes. "We are on lam, *da?*"

I said, "Oh shit."

He dismissed my words with a wave of his hand. "We are going out."

"Out where?"

"Through the Iron Curtain, as you put it. To the West."

"How? Can't we go back? I can explain this. Really, I can," I implored him.

"If they arrest you, you are guilty. That is the system."

I was so focused on myself that I had not thought about him. "What about you?"

"I will go to America and fish for trout."

"And you think *I'm* insane?"

Valoretev laughed. "Don't worry, Comrade Bowie. I have the situation under control."

"Why are you doing this for me?"

"For you?" he said with a laugh. "I do this for me. I have been planning for a long time. You will be my insurance, my ticket, my passport into the West."

"Insurance with whom?"

"We shall see," Valoretev said. "Paranoia is the heart of the Russian soul."

"It ain't paranoia when people are really after you."

Valoretev smiled, took a piece of paper out of his jacket, and handed it to me. It was typed in Cyrillic, a carbon copy, not an original. It was the itemized contents of Oxley's collection. Near the bottom of the page was the snowfly manuscript.

"The books were bought for Brezhnev?"

"Yes."

"He fly fishes for trout?"

"No, he invests. He likes the rare and beautiful. He has fleets of automobiles, even an American Cadillac. It is red, which he claims as patriotism."

A red Caddy. Ironic. "How do you know these things?"

Valoretev looked at me. "I am colonel, Komitet Gosudarstvennoy Bezopasnosti."

"Fuck me," I said. KGB. "You're too young to be a colonel."

He smiled. "Competence is rewarded in the Soviet system. I have achieved a position of high trust, which in our system is also a position of high risk. My job is to oversee people who make acquisitions from the West for members of the Politburo."

I was dumbfounded and speechless. "Peshkov worked for you?"

"No one works for me. I assure security. I was aware of him."

I wanted to crawl into a hole and pull the dirt on top of me.

The next night we began walking. We walked for five nights. Each day we stopped and each place we stopped there was a cabin or shack, well pro-visioned. My escort had painstakingly planned this, and though such knowledge did not calm me, it boosted my confidence in Valoretev. I did not let myself dwell on the consequences of being caught.

On the sixth day we continued to walk. We were in a tangled forest, but Valoretev seemed to know his way. Eventually we came to a river. It was narrow, with glissading clear water and yellow boulders stacked neatly in retaining walls along the sides. There were long riffles down the center. Val-oretev dumped his pack and began rummaging through it. In minutes he had his homemade fly rod assembled and was attaching a gut leader and a bushy brown fly. Somehow he had gotten hold of a fly line.

I was stupefied. He stepped onto the rocks and cast into a dark green slick. But casting skill in this river was nothing like on the Drake in Corn-wall. The take was immediate. He played the fish to shore. It was twenty inches and fat, yellow with green and orange spots.

"Brown trout?"

"Yes. Join me?"

He carefully took a second case out of the pack and handed it to me with a bow. "A remembrance of your Russian comrades."

I found a newly made four-piece fly rod in the case and I was moved beyond words by the gift. The fly line on the reel was not in good shape, but it would do. Valoretev gave me a leader and one of his flies and I rigged up and joined him.

We didn't fish long and put all but two fish back. Val cleaned and cooked the two large trout over a small fire made on the gravel bar under an overhanging cedar tree. He cooked the fish quickly. When we ate, the pale white meat fell off the bones, and Val dug in his pack and brought out black bread and vodka and we each had a couple of shots and grinned at each other like schoolboys playing hooky. Self-delusion is a close companion of obsession and errant judgment.

When we were done eating, we disassembled the rods, put on our packs, and headed into the forest. Mosquitoes came at dark. They were large and carnivorous. At one point Valoretev said, "I just saw a mosquito carrying a hare." I couldn't help but laugh.

We walked all night. From time to time we rubbed mud on our exposed skin. I felt like I was being bled to death.

In the morning we came to a road. "Remain here," Valoretev said. He bathed in a puddle beside the road, left his pack with me, and, when a truck came along, stepped in front of it and held something up. Then he got in and was gone and I was overwhelmed by fear.

Two hours later I heard a small plane. It circled once at treetop level, dipped down to the road, bounced, and taxied to a stop, scattering gravel. Valoretev motioned for me from the cockpit. I grabbed our packs, ran, and crawled in. The plane had a single engine that ran rough. There was a metal barrel lashed on its side to the floor behind me. I was cramped in my seat, but no more so than Valoretev, who looked like he had no room to move.

"You can fly?"

"Better all the time," he said solemnly.

"Where are we?"

"Eastern Poland," he said. "On Soviet border."

It would be my fate to know a number of pilots who might've spent their time and effort more productively on other endeavors. Val was not smooth, but the bird stayed aloft and I took what comfort I could in this. In a tight spot a few small facts are often enough to hold us together, this the definition of a false sense of security.

"We'll be shot down."

"No. It's easy from here on!"

We flew at treetop level. It was a rough ride and gave me the dry heaves. "Where are we going?"

"Sweden," he said.

When we reached water, the weather got worse and the ride turned violent. I prayed we would crash but we didn't and eventually we landed on a road on a rocky island. Valoretev jumped down to the road and held the door open for me and I stumbled out, fell to my knees, and puked my guts out.

The Swedes detained us for several days until an American came down from Stockholm. He was short, fat, graying. "I expect you fellas have a story."

He talked to us separately and I told the man as close to the truth as I was able. I did not tell him anything about the snowfly or Key's manuscript. I told them I knew that the Kremlin had arranged to buy a book collection, that Brezhnev was a sportsman, and that I was following that angle and apparently rubbed people wrong. I had no way to know what Valoretev told them.

We were taken by boat to Malmö after the initial interviews. There Valoretev and I were again separated.

Three men interrogated me. They were always polite. They asked me to tell my story and I did. They rarely interrupted, but they were anal about details. I would tell the story, they would ask questions, and I would tell the story again. It was the same routine every day.

"Do you know the man you traveled with?"

I tried to explain our relationship.

"Do you know who he is?"

"Not precisely. He is a KGB colonel who has something to do with imports. That's all I know."

"Good," one of the men said. "Let's maintain the status quo. It's safer for him."

I never liked half an equation.

This is how the interrogations went: "What color was the house?"

"It had no paint."

"What color was it when it had paint?"

"I'm not that old."

"Was there a tinge?"

"No."

"Do you think of a color when you picture it in your mind?"

"No."

"We need your cooperation."

"You have it."

"Would you agree to hypnosis?"

"I'd rather not."

"What color was the house?"

Ad infinitum, ad nauseum. For three weeks, sometimes days only, sometimes day and night, sometimes nights only. They were trying to wear me out, looking for inconsistencies. They would have been great reporters.

I endured. They were CIA and presumably on my side.

Sometime in the fourth week Valoretev and I were given five minutes outside together, in full view of several sets of watchful eyes. I was exhausted. He looked fresh and happy.

"My friend Bowie, I am going to America," he said in a whisper.

"When?"

He shrugged. "When they unravel their red tape. I will come to see you."

"You won't know where to find me."

He smiled. "I can find a track before it's made."

I suspected this was not an idle boast.

The next day I was given a new suit, which fit perfectly, and driven to an airport outside Stockholm. I was kept in a room in a drafty hangar and taken out to an SAS flight just before other passengers boarded.

"You've been on vacation," my minder said. "Your Soviet companion is a clever man. He sent a confederate to Vienna, traveling with your passport and suitcase. The confederate has disappeared, and you are clean and clear. But you will not write your story."

I was tired of mandatory obedience school. "It's a free press out here."

My minder gave me a copy of the *Times of London*. A story had been checked with ink. The headline read, RARE ANGLING BOOKS SOLD TO CANADIAN MINE DEVELOPER.

"You can read on the plane," my escort said. "Here's the between-the-lines: You got their attention. The Kremlin bosses were scared shitless you were going to blow the whistle on them. Everybody knows they are dirty, but they don't like seeing it in print. They pulled their man back from London, arranged a resale through the original broker, and made sure Fleet Street got the word. You've got no story. The broker will say he's had the collection in his possession all along."

"That's baloney." How did the CIA know what books I was looking for? Had it been the CIA who threatened Danny in New York? So many questions, but I wasn't anxious to ask them.

"It's bullshit, but airtight. No paper trail."

"They killed their man from London," I said. "Peshkov."

My minder shrugged as if to say that was not his business.

He walked me to the steps up to the plane and gave me my old passport. "One other thing."

"You people always have one more thing."

"You are to have no further contact with your former traveling companion. This is a matter of national security."

A term that could mean anything and often changed meaning.

"He rescued me."

"He used you for his own purposes," my minder said.

"I don't even know where he's going."

"We're going to keep it that way."

I got on the SAS flight and ordered a vodka straight. The seat was in first class. That was something. I folded the *Times* and stuck it in my jacket. I had entered the Soviet Union as a journalist and exited as something else. Precisely what was still up in the air.

10

I found Grady Yetter waiting for me outside customs and immigration at Kennedy Airport. "I was on vacation," I said, following the script I had been ordered to follow by my debriefers in Sweden.

"I heard." He looked weary, his eyes puffy, the creases in his face deeper than when we had last seen each other.

"You want to hear the details?" I asked.

"Is there a story in them?"

"That depends on who you ask."

He raised an eyebrow. "Then it can wait. The Soviets officially expelled your ass after you *officially* got to Vienna."

I had never been anywhere near Vienna. The way he said it suggested that he knew what was going on. "On what grounds?"

"Probably because you're an obnoxious sonuvabitch."

"That's against the law there?"

He grinned and stuck out his hand. "You wrote some great stuff over there."

"Yeah," I said. "I did."

"Suppose you're gonna tell me you want the summer off to fish."

"I accept the offer. Then where?"

"Let's worry about where when then becomes now. Want a hot dog?"

"Those things'll kill you."

"Everybody dies from something, kid."

"Don't call me kid."

"Okay, asshole."

According to the edition of the *Times* I had been given in Sweden, the new owner of the Oxley collection was Lockwood Bolt of Elliot Lake, Ontario. Bolt had made a fortune in uranium in the 1950s and early 1960s and had parlayed his money into a conglomerate called Canadian Forest Products. According to the article, the book collection had cost him in excess of a quarter million dollars, an amount that made me dizzy. That much for books?

I flew to Detroit, rented a car, visited my sister and her family in Alpena, and stopped briefly to see Buzz and Fred and my other friends in Grand Marais.

I felt a powerful urge to remain in my adopted town, but I knew I had to move on. I had asked the right questions in the wrong country and now that I was out and free and knew where the books were, I was determined to find them and get this mystery solved. Buzz and Fred complained about my leaving so soon and Staley just growled at me.

I saw Janey in town with two of her kids.

"You here for a while?" She did not look haggard anymore. Her eyes were lit with unexpected intensity and brightness.

"Just for a few days."

"Too bad," she said. "You left money for my children."

"You've been misinformed."

Her lips narrowed. "Buzz told me and priests never lie."

Damn him, I thought. I hadn't wanted her to know. It was purely a gift for someone down on her luck.

"You got thrown out by the Russians," she said. "Did they hurt you?"

I didn't understand why, but the Soviets had announced that I had been expelled for national security reasons, which was abject bullshit. It had been in papers all around the U.S. and I had been called by too damn many reporters wanting to talk about the situation. Following my instructions, I had refused all interviews and kept my mouth shut. It made me very uncomfortable to be a news target. And I was paranoid enough to feel pretty certain that the CIA and Soviets had made some sort of a deal. I was kicked out; no specifics would be discussed on either side. All the U.S. government had said was that the expulsion was "unjustified."

"Don't believe everything you see on TV. Nothing is the way it seems."

Janey cocked her head. "Is it anywhere? You be careful wherever it is you're running off to this time."

I had never really had a real conversation with her before. Usually it was hi and how are you. As I watched her walk away with her kids, I wondered why I had never noticed she was pretty and felt an unexpected surge of interest in her. That's the last thing she needs, I thought. It was just as well that I had decided to go to Canada.

I drove my rental car east and crossed into Canada on the ferry at the Soo, then continued east along the north shore of Lake Huron, eventually turning north on the serpentine concrete of Highway 108, rising into the craggy granite of the Canadian shield, and suddenly there was the town on the hill, lit by the sun, a beacon, foreboding in its austerity and unexpectedness.

Along the way I gased up in Blind River. The station attendant had long black hair and yellow teeth. "What do people around here think about uranium?" I asked.

The man grinned. "It's like sex, eh? You let her, she'll bake your balls?" Uranium as insatiable female. I wondered if bomber pilots called their nukes *she*.

"I say let's cook the sand niggers," the attendant added.

In the recent Arab oil crisis everywhere you went, somebody was someone's scapegoat-of-the-moment. In Russia they had Georgians and Chechens. And American reporters.

"Think about the nice profit you're making." Gas prices were three times their usual in the U.S. and even higher here.

"I look like I own the bloody place?" the man replied.

Rough edges on the edge of rough territory. Cause and effect? Complementary, to be certain.

Elliot Lake did not fit my mental picture of a boom town. I had seen mining towns in Montana and Minnesota and they were gray, cluttered, and haphazard, last-leggers even at launch, born to perish, a future married to a capricious body of ore and world economics. Elliot Lake looked like the centerfold for *City Planning Illustrated*, its houses built in neat neighborhoods on spokes off the neat town center and all of it thoughtfully built above Elliot and Horne Lakes so that most of the inhabitants had a view of both. The sight made me laugh. How many times as a journalist had reality shattered my preconceptions? This is why correspondents corresponded, there being no substitute for being there. In the distance, to the northeast, I saw the head frame and surrounding metal buildings of one of the mines, the whole complex rising out of the gray-green forest like a medieval castle, an impregnable keep anchored in hot rock. I wondered how dangerous it was to live on top of uranium.

I took a room at the Algoden Hotel. The sleeping rooms were above a long hall, advertised as the Biggest Beer Parlor in the World but smaller than the average Russian nightspot. I shared the long bar with a wrinkled man with all his fingers gone at the first joints. He held a beer bottle the way Satchmo lifted his horn.

Just over a decade had passed since the confluence of the discovery of uranium in the town and the U.S. government's massive need for ore to process into nuclear weapons. But fortuitous events have a way of disconnecting. In 1955 Elliot Lake was formed into a political unit and a mining camp appeared. It was a trailer town at first with mud roads and nonexistent sanitation. Double-digit dysentery swept the miners two years later and there was no hospital until a year after that, but the boom was on; there was ore to be dug and money to be made and workers and opportunists flowed in. Trailers were replaced by simple bungalows. Churches were built. Per capita liquor sales were the highest in Canada. Income, too. Whores arrived on buses via Toronto from Cleveland, Buffalo, Detroit, and Chicago. The government sent agency workers.

Ontario's political parties sent in their hacks to organize and unions battled each other for the right to represent the miners. The Mine Mill Smelter Workers had been shown to be communist sympathizers and were booted from the CIO and CCL; the Reds battled the United Steel Workers of America. Both unions hauled prospective brothers to Sudbury, which was the closest town of any real size, for food, whiskey, and union-paid prostitutes. Mine Mill had four organizers, the Steel Workers eight. Numbers and Cold War sentiments won out. The rise of Elliot Lake to economic prominence was a familiar story in the Canadian bush and had a predictable ending. With more than twenty-five thousand people packed into an area where there had been only a few hundred Ojibwa Indians before, the U.S. government suddenly canceled orders and, in the perpetual search for security, transferred its needs to uranium producers on American soil. In six years the population of Elliot Lake plummeted to six thousand hardy souls. Most of the mines had closed. A few remained open. But the boom was bust and miners and opportunists moved on. Those who remained were not gregarious. The fingerless man stared into the neck of his bottle.

A woman came into the bar and sat two stools away. She had smooth, tanned skin that shone like brass in the bar's light. She wore a sleeveless red blouse with the collar turned up. Her dark hair was cut short and straight and she had long legs and small feet tucked into red sandals with short heels.

"You're definitely not a glowworm," she said in my direction.

"Pardon me?"

"You're not a miner."

"Afraid not," I said.

"You lack the eyes," she said.

"How's that?"

"Yours aren't desperate enough. You have more the look of a salesman. What's your line?"

"Words," I said.

She gave me a half grin and called an order at the barkeep, a short matron with sparse white hair.

"No sass, lass, or I'll trim your sails before you're outta port," the bartender snapped back.

"Is there job security in peddling words?" she asked.

"Until they run out."

"Like the mines," she said, raising her glass. "There's not a lot of call for words out here. Actions count."

"I'm looking for a man."

She shot me a quick questioning glance. "For business, not pleasure, one hopes."

"It's strictly business. His name's Lockwood Bolt. Do you know him? He's supposed to live in Elliot Lake."

She stared into her libation, cogitating. "Green flint," she said.

"Come again?"

"Bolt loves his rocks and the rarer the rock, the more he loves it. There's green flint out near Flack Lake. He's got himself a whole hill of it, maybe all there is in northern Ontario. You want Bolt, you should try out that way." She sipped her drink, calculating. "You have business with Bolt?"

"Words," I reminded her.

"Not with the Bolt this town knows."

"How far is it to Flack Lake?"

She sighed. "Twenty miles by crow flight, more in reality. The road's a twister."

"Bolt's not popular?"

"He's a killer," she said.

"Figuratively speaking?"

"Not if you live among us." She looked at me, put money on the bar, and slid off the bar stool. "My name is Pierrette," she said. "If you want to talk, I'm available."

"Where?" She wrote her address and phone number inside a matchbook cover and left it in front of me.

I was up early and sought the library. Every planned town had one.

The keeper of the town's books was middle aged with chemical red hair piled high on her head and bright red nail polish. "Morning," she said, more a statement of fact than a salutation.

"You wouldn't happen to have any of the works of M. J. Key, would you?"

"Key? Who would Key be?"

I gave her a very short version.

She tilted her head sharply left and locked her eyes on me. "I should imagine you might ask that question and receive the same answer in every library in the province."

"You don't have Key?"

"This institution, such as it is, serves to enlighten, but true erudition is beyond our scope. There is nothing so hopeless as a bibliophile among *barbarians* and I would hasten to underline that final word. For work such as your Mr. Key's, one would need to forage the rare-book emporia of New York or San Francisco. There's no Key here, nor will there ever be."

"Except in the private collection of Lockwood Bolt."

Her head snapped to the other side. "Mister Bolt is among us, but no longer *of* us, if you take my meaning."

That made two for two. Bolt was definitely not a popular guy in Elliot Lake.

"You know about the Oxley collection?" I offered her the clipping from the *Times,* but she only glanced at it and let it sit.

"Civilization is thin and population sparse this far north, but not absent. We subscribe to the belief that *rural* and *isolated* need not mean 'ignorant.' I read the *Times* from both sides of the Atlantic. And the *Globe and Mail.* Of course, the post is slow, so I view these more as history than current events."

"Is Bolt well known as a book collector?"

Her face remained impassive. "Lockwood Bolt is a pure capitalist. His focus is pecuniary to the exclusion of all else and I have no time to waste discussing the likes of that one. If your interest is Bolt, you should pursue your business directly with the man and good luck to you on that count. Good day, sir," she added, abruptly ending our little conversation.

North of Elliot Lake was what Canadians referred to as the bush, meaning where the tracks ended and, near as I could tell, so did everything else. The roads went from paved to stone dust along a rocky spine. There were no houses. Some lakes were marked with crude signs. Flack Lake was one of them. I found two roads to the water's edge, one curving down to a boat launch, and the other one leading to a black steel gate guarded by a large man in a yellow rain slicker standing in a gatehouse behind a red iron barricade. A forested hill lay behind the gate, off to the side of the lake. Green flint, I guessed.

"I'd like to see Mr. Bolt."

"It's a long queue," the man in yellow said. "Got an appointment?"

"It's serendipitous that I'm here. I think he'll be glad I stopped by."

There were blackflies crawling on the man's face. A trickle of blood ran down his cheek. He did not react.

"Well, that'd be a first," he said. "Get an appointment."

"How do you suggest I go about doing that?"

"Do I gotta tell ya everything?"

Elliot Lake was quiet at night. Perhaps radium in the bedrock sapped rambunctiousness. I dined on a soggy beef Wellington at a café, had several beers, and went to bed early.

Early the next day I went to find Pierrette Rouleau. Her directions took me south on 108, then east on a crushed-stone road to a small white house with no grass around it. Visqueen was taped over the windows to keep out winter breezes. She came to the door red eyed and squinting.

"You," she said, her face deadpan. "The word seller. Are you still looking for Bolt?" The door was cracked open and her face peering out. An invitation to come inside was conspicuously absent. She was far less welcoming than she had been in the bar. Perhaps a morning visit wasn't what she had in mind.

"I found him."

"But?"

"I didn't have an appointment and he won't see anyone without one."

"He's like that," she said. "He's not exactly what you'd call social."

"You know him?"

She shook her head. "No and I don't really care to. What's your interest in Bolt?"

"Books," I said.

Raised her eyebrows. "Are you some kind of investigator?" I heard bemusement in her voice.

"No, not those kinds of books. Books about a certain subject."

"I never thought of Bolt as the reading type."

"I need to get in touch with him."

"He doesn't let strangers in. In fact, he doesn't let many people get near him."

I fished a twenty-dollar bill out of my pocket and held it up. "So who do you know that he knows?"

"Are you one of those Americans who thinks money's the answer to everything?"

"That depends."

"On what?"

"If you take it."

She smiled at me with flashing eyes and started to swing the door shut, but I got my foot wedged in.

"I'm sorry," I said, stuffing the twenty back into my pocket. "Can we start over?" I saw her tongue press against the inside of her cheek. "I'm a reporter and I have been following something for a long time. Bolt bought some books that could unlock some answers for me, but I need to get to him and I need help."

"I suppose you'd better step inside," she said after a long hesitation.

She wore a heavy red flannel robe and floppy blue slippers. The house was furnished but not decorated. She poured coffee for me, disappeared for a while, and came back dressed in jeans and a gray sweatshirt with a fresh face and light makeup.

"You don't live here," I said.

"No?" Bit of a smile, which I read as encouragement. "Now you're a detective."

"No homey touches, no eau de personality."

She eyed me with suspicion. "You're sure you're not a cop, eh?"

"Words," I reminded her. "I'm a reporter for a wire service."

"After Bolt."

"Interested in his books."

"You know his story?" she asked.

"The barest outline. He made a wad on uranium."

"That's true as far as it goes." She warmed my coffee and poured her own. Her skin seemed even darker than in the bar. Long fingernails, well cared for.

"How far does it go?"

"To the root," she said. "He's made his money, the bloody magic bundle, and now he'd like to ruin it for the rest of us."

There was no need to prompt her; she had a story to tell. "Bolt originally drifted up from Sarnia," she said. "Which makes him barely Canadian. He fled to the bush. There are men like him everywhere up here. Misfits, dreamers, drunks."

"Women too?"

She raised a brow and granted an almost imperceptible nod of assent. "Chapleau, Timmins, Porcupine, all the places where there were mineral strikes; he seemed drawn to ore like a deer to salt. He learned a bit along the way, enough to look, but not quite enough to find on his own."

"But here he did find."

"Yes and no. In the late nineteen-forties a couple of mineral cruisers from the Soo found radioactive rock down by Quirke. A few years later a geologist from Toronto got interested. It was a puzzle. The rock was radioactive, but there was no uranium in the samples. Eventually the geologist figured out that the weather or something made the ore sink deep. This was all kept very hush-hush. They decided there had to be uranium, and a lot of it, so they organized a secret operation. They flew a hundred men into the area from the north, even had lawyers with them, and for a month they staked claims and almost nobody knew a thing was going on until the claims were filed. By then they had tens of thousands of acres all to themselves."

"You said '*almost* nobody.' "

She smiled. "Wordman. You listen carefully. There was an American banker with a cabin on Quirke Lake. I think he was from Ohio and he came up every summer on floatplanes to fish, enjoy the outdoors. Turns out that the cabin was smack in the middle of some of the richest ore deposits and, of course, there was no way for the secret stakers to avoid the American's place. The banker was a good man. He fed the stakers and became their friend. He knew something was up but didn't press them. The day before the claims were filed the stakers told him their story. He went out and did some of his own quick staking and put together his own investment group and they all made a bundle."

"How does Bolt fit in?"

She smiled again. "Bolt had no real money of his own back then. But he was a bit of the phantom of the backwoods. He turned up at various places and times, often unexpectedly. The American banker used to bring his family to the lake. The banker's wife made friends with an Ojibwa woman who lived up the Serpent River in a cabin with her prospector-trapper boyfriend." Pierrette Rouleau looked at me. "When her boyfriend was out, Bolt would stop by."

"Hanky-panky."

"Exactly. The woman liked a bit of variety in her bed. She told Bolt about the strangers. Bolt knew rock, and he knew something was up and started watching them. He figured it out and did some staking of his own right in the middle of where all the action was. It could've turned out to be worthless, but it didn't. He had nine claims, all prime. Talk about lucky."

"And sold his claims."

"First he staked his claims. Then he tipped another group, chums of sorts, who sent in their own stakers. He wanted major competition against the first group. After claims became public, speculators poured in, trying to buy property all over the area. That shot the prices up."

"Then Bolt sold."

"For a bloody fortune. You saw the emblem on his gate?"

I had. A black cat with a dollar sign.

"Pussy money," she said, disgustedly.

"A true romantic," I said and she smiled in response. From her description Bolt did not seem the type to be interested in rare and arcane books.

"He's an opportunist," she said. "And a pure predator."

"And this makes him unpopular?" Ordinarily such people were folk heroes.

"No, people don't much mind how he made his money, but now that he's got his, he's found religion," she said.

"A godhead."

"No, it's not like that. It's got nothing to do with churches and such. He says the uranium makes people sick. There are mine tailings in the water system. He says there's poison everywhere."

"Is he right?"

"That's not the point."

A curious response. "What is?"

"Uranium's what's here. It's *all* that's here. One of the papers in Ottawa called us nuclear whores, which is about the truth of it." She fell silent.

"The town looks pretty empty," I said.

"It still has life. Maybe a lot of life. People here say 'Thank you, A-rabs.' That oil embargo business helped us. Now Ottawa says Canada's got to become self-reliant for power. No more Arab oil."

"A conversion to nuclear?"

"That seems to be the consensus."

"The phoenix could rise again."

"It would be a new boom. The Japs have already been here. The French too. Fuel's an even worse problem for them."

"Which makes Bolt's position a threat to Ottawa and the local powers."

"There you have it in a nutshell."

"What's your own position in all this?"

The lifted brow again. "A girl has to work."

"Where?"

"I have a job at the mine, the only one still open, but not underground. They pay well and they'll pay even better if demand goes up."

"Supply and demand."

"Right you are." There was a catch in her voice.

"What if Bolt's right about the effects of the mines?"

"It's a dilemma," she said sadly. "I have a kid, a nice kid. She thinks I sell real estate."

"She's here?" There was no sign of a child in the house.

"No, she lives down in Espanola with my sister and her brood. I go back and forth. I can't risk her living here."

I could see Espanola on my mental map. It was south and farther east of Elliot Lake. And not close at all. "Are there mines there?"

"No, but Bolt says there's radiation in the water there too. He says it starts here and goes elsewhere. How far is far enough away to be safe?"

I had no idea. "What will you do?"

She propped her left foot on her right knee and rubbed her toes. "My church has always been the path of least resistance. You get accustomed to a certain standard of living. A few more years and I will have socked away plenty for my kid and me. Then I'll get her and we'll move somewhere we don't have to worry about all this."

It was a sickening gamble.

"So," she said. "You still want to see Bolt?"

"Yes."

"Why?"

I'm still not sure why, but I told her everything I knew about M. J. Key and the snowfly, leaving out only the cryptography history and the fact that I had been thrown out of the Soviet Union and warned by the Brits to steer clear of Key.

When I was done, she cracked a smile and shook her head. "This is about *fish?* I'll never understand men."

"I'm not sure what it's about," I confessed. All I knew was that I could not let go.

"Chances of seeing him aren't good. He stays to himself."

"I have to try."

"Effort always matters, even for fish," she said. "It may take a while."

"I'm rich in time."

"Let me make some calls," she said, getting up. "Make yourself comfortable."

I put my feet up on her coffee table and sank into her couch. I heard her voice on the phone, then the shower running. When she came out of the bedroom a while later she was wrapping a towel around her wet hair. "We'll have to drive down to Cutler," she said. "There may be a way for you."

It was late afternoon before we headed for Cutler in two cars. Pierrette had a half sister, June, who had a half brother, Luc Brokendog. June had some sort of job in Iron Bridge and Luc lived north of Cutler on the Serpent River. We had to cross a wooden bridge with a sign that said DANGER: UNSAFE. Pierrette didn't even slow down and I inched my way across behind her with an iron grip on my steering wheel. Once across, we climbed a hill covered with thick stands of yellow and paper birches and skinny poplars. We left the vehicles on the hill and walked up a trail to a clearing on top of a granite outcrop. Below was the dark, clear water of the Serpent and, to our left, a smaller stream that tumbled down the steep hillside to form thick yellow foam in the main river. Blackflies hovered overhead in carnivorous clouds. A pile of wood was stacked to the eaves beside a house, which was covered with weathered tar paper. Several dogs bayed from an area back in the woods. A small raccoon was on the front porch and clacked its jaws as a warning. It bared its teeth at me, but retreated after the show, its self-respect intact.

We did not mount the porch. We stayed back and Pierrette called out and after a time a woman came out. She was short with black hair and brown skin and an oblong face. Behind her stood a man, shirtless, short, thin, with a too-delicate face. His black hair was loose and long, down to his shoulders, and he had hard lumps of muscle that pushed against skin the color of burnished oak. He examined me with dark, neutral eyes.

"You're the one wants to see Bolt?" the Indian woman asked.

"June," Pierrette said, looking over at me.

I nodded.

The man stepped forward. "Could take a week, two weeks, maybe more, eh? Everybody rags on Indi'n time, but Bolt time is worse."

"But you have a rough idea of how long?"

"None a-tall. That one's crazy for fish. That's all he cares about. His place is on good spec water, but there's a lot of beavers, eh? Coupla times a year he calls me in to take out the beaver works. I call some of the boys and off we go. He'll call anytime now."

Bolt was crazy for fish! So Bolt's acquisition of the Oxley collection might be more than an investment. I was mildly encouraged. Maybe I was getting somewhere after all.

"I thought he could stay with you," Pierrette told Luc, who shrugged.

"Can you pay?" he asked me.

"How much?" I sensed a little game.

Luc considered for a moment. "Twenty a week."

A bargain was struck. There was no handshake. I walked Pierrette back to her car.

"I hope it works out," she said.

"Time will tell. Thank you."

She shook my hand before she got into her car. "This isn't good-bye," she said. "I'll be seeing you."

I had a lot of time on my hands. I visited several area towns and went through their newspaper morgues, looking for more information about Bolt. I also talked to UPI and Reuters reporters in Toronto, but Bolt was a secretive man and I could see that there was no point in further research. I tried calling him on a private number Luc gave me, but got no response.

I went to his place several times, but each time the guards refused me entry. The only choices were to try to sneak in or go in with Luc and his crew, and I decided the latter was the more sensible course of action. Luc didn't ask me to share the chores around the cabin, but I did and my life soon settled into a routine built on hard work. Like a lot of bush folks, Luc Brokendog survived by being able to do many things well. He reminded me of Staley. We cut wood every day. Sometimes we drove up to the mines close to Elliot Lake and hauled barrels of trash marked CAUSTIC to a dumping area northwest of town. Some days we went to Spanish or Blind River to buy bits and pieces of hardware, or groceries.

A week turned into two. Blisters began to harden to calluses, a workingman's scales. We saw neither Pierrette nor June, who slipped away that first day. Just Luc and me, monks on a work farm among deciduous trees and flying carnivores.

Once a week we drove across the TransCan highway to the Ojibwa reserve and got into a sweat lodge built of willow and covered with dark plastic and tarps. Outside the lodge, which was shaped like a turtle's back, there was a wall of stones, waist-high, built in a circle. The fire was in the ring. Hot stones were brought into the dark lodge and dropped into a tub of water, raising plumes of steam.

One evening I bought lamb chops and fixings in town and cooked them in a black skillet over an open fire outdoors. Luc ate an entire jar of mint jelly.

"No need for you to pay from now on," he announced after our dinner. "You're a help."

Like virtually all the Indians I had met, Luc lived on the edge, acquiring most of what he got by work and barter.

"You think Bolt will call?" I asked.

"He will or he won't."

"What's on tomorrow?"

"Had enough work," he said. "You'll see."

Early the next morning we drove north then west, parked his truck, and walked a couple of miles through the woods. We eventually reached a river with raucous white water where a dozen Indians were setting up camp. We smelled wood fires long before we found the camp. "What's all this?" I asked.

"Indi'n fishin'," Luc said.

It was done with nets. Eventually there were nearly a hundred people strung out along the river. The nets were weighted, cast out, retrieved by hand. There was no distinction for species. Only size counted. I saw two brook trout that would go ten pounds, true greenbacks with vermiculated markings on their backs.

"They're huge," I told Luc.

"There's bigger hereabouts," he said.

June came to camp the second night. We had numerous fires and a lot of smoke rising and hanging over the camp like fog. Insects everywhere: blackflies, mosquitoes, chiggers, deerflies, all bloodsuckers and meat eaters. The Indians talked and laughed and laughed more, social beings freed of conventions and stereotypical expectations. The fish were gutted, split, and laid across makeshift sawhorses over smoking fires, like sooty bats in repose.

Whiskey arrived in brown crock jugs and clear Mason jars and was passed around. Children ran around shouting, giddy with freedom. Dogs skulked. A black bear approached the smoking fish at sundown and was driven off with stones.

A cow moose was found upriver from the encampment, shot, butchered, and shared with the group. Everything we were doing was illegal.

On the third night June and I sat by the river. I looked for Pierrette but didn't see her.

"Luc says you work hard," she said.

"Your people work hard all the time."

"It's that or we don't make it," she said.

"What about the mines?"

"When there was work in Elliot Lake, they mostly brought in outsiders. The owners don't want to waste the money on training. They brought in all the skills they needed. Economics, they said. Indians are used to this."

"Pierrette works for the mine."

"Most of us don't look like her," June said.

There was no rancor in her voice. It was a simple statement of fact.

It was a Sunday. Luc had been out and when he came back, he told me Bolt wanted his crew.

"Will we see Bolt?"

He nodded. "He'll come out with us, show us what he wants us to do, and come back at the end to check how we done. If we don't do it right, we won't get paid."

The crew consisted of three Indians, Luc, and me. We drove Luc's truck north and were ushered through the gate with the cat and dollar-sign emblem before sunrise the next morning. From there we drove several miles on a smooth, narrow road bedded with reddish green gravel before stopping at the shell of an A-frame built on the tip of a peninsula that split a fast river in half. We ate moose jerky and drank lukewarm coffee from thermoses.

Bolt arrived in a pickup truck. It had once been dark green but was now patched with Bondo and various splashes of dull gray primer. Lockwood Bolt was not what I expected. He wore leather hunting boots up to his knees, heavy trousers, and a faded red-and-black-checked Mackinaw over a stained T-shirt. He was balding, but wisps of white hair stuck out to the side. He had a huge belly that protruded and pushed his belt down. His eyes were bloodshot and his nose and cheeks red, showing a lattice of blue veins.

There were no greetings. Two of the other men began to unload boxes from the back of the pickup. Cans of hash. A sack of potatoes. Canned vegetables. Supplies. Bolt walked slowly to the edge over the river. "Beevs been busy," he announced. "Upstream they've got four solid dams and five more in the works. I figure a week." He stood there for a while, breathing laboriously, then shuffled back to his truck. "Week tomorrow. I'm gonna be down to Tarana for a few days. Draw gear from Butch."

Luc stepped up to me as Bolt got into his truck and drove slowly away.

"How you pictured him?" Luc asked.

"Not at all."

Luc grinned. "Hard to believe he's got all that dough, but he's smart enough and mean enough to get whatever he wants. Truth is, he didn't find anything. What he did was nose around and find out what other fellas had discovered, then he quick-like filed claims in the middle of them. Called a doughnut and he was the center. See, Bolt never had an original thought, but he knows a good thing. Ping over there has a nose for moose." He nodded toward one of the Indians in our crew. "When nobody can find 'em at all, Ping can. And if others can find 'em, Ping goes right to the biggest bull every time. Bolt's the same way with money."

"You sound like you admire him."

"I know he's good for his word. He's just a bush bastard like the rest of us, but he seen him an angle and played it. And I think he knows now what all this done to us."

"So he wants to close down what's left?"

"It won't happen."

"Pierrette says he has evidence."

"She's a woman with a good job and she doesn't want to lose it. She's trying to balance her purse and her heart, eh?"

"Do you think this place is poisoned?" If they knew the water and land were dangerous, why didn't they move? Or raise a ruckus in Ottawa? I didn't understand their complacency.

Luc grunted. "We'll see."

I had seen beaver dams around home, but had never really examined one. From a distance they looked sloppily made, walls barely holding water back; up close they were engineering marvels, veritable fortresses made by creatures with brains the size of pecans. There were five of us and it took endless hours to break the dams and free the water. Luc's companions worked the way we had worked at the fish camp, silently, without complaining. At night we repaired to the A-frame, ate, and slept. I had never worked so hard in my life and I understood that, while I would eventually move on, this was their life. It was summer and we worked the week straight through, sixteen-hour days. My hands were raw, my muscles and joints numb. The river water was in the midforties and for three straight days there was a relentless cold rain. We were in the water and wet and frigid, but we worked on, troubled by insects beyond description.

It seemed a miracle when we finished midday on Monday. We all collapsed where we were.

"Where's Bolt's house?" I asked.

Luc looked at me for a long time. "Back down the road we come in on. Three miles, then left."

"Security?"

"Only what you seen at the front gates."

He gripped my arm when I started to get up. "It's your business," he said. "But I brought you in here."

His message was clear. If I caused a problem, Luc and the others would lose work. I realized that, as much as I wanted to find M. J. Key's works, I could not jeopardize the people who had unexpectedly become my friends. I was not that much of a jerk.

Bolt arrived at sunrise on Tuesday. A warm front had ridden up the jet stream from the southern U.S. and collided with the cool Canadian air. The air was warming and wispy blue fog clung by tendrils to the dark river valley below. Luc and Bolt went down to the river and disappeared into the fog. They did not come back until noon. The sun was up by then, the fog burned off, the air still, mosquitoes sailing around us.

"Fair work, fair wages," Bolt announced as he walked over to us. To me he said, "You the one looking for books?"

I glanced toward Luc, who remained impassive. "Yes, sir," I told Bolt.

He shook hands with Luc. "See you next year."

Luc nodded.

"You ride with me," Bolt said. It was not a request.

I watched the others disappear down the gravel road in Luc's truck, raising a lingering rooster tail of stone dust.

Bolt's house was made of logs creosoted black. It was a simple house made to look larger by an open verandah around three sides. It was in the woods at the base of the hill. There was no view.

"Were you expectin' the house of a country squire?" Bolt asked.

I didn't answer. Like Bolt himself, it was nothing like I had expected.

"I built a log shack here in 1946. It's the kitchen now. I wandered to hell and back through these hills. No geology to speak of, but I got hold of a Geiger counter, which was rarer than a virgin in those days. I had a boat with a little outboard and I used to run her up the Serpent from the big lake, all the way up to the Elliot area. I settled up this way, but eventually I found the ore down along the river. An Ojibwa trapper I knew told me of a place where deer and moose bred monsters. Two, three heads, eight legs. I asked him if it was holy ground. He said it was more like the devil's. Exposed ore, right in the open. I staked claim and the rest is history. Who the hell told the likes of you about my books?"

It was a different story than Pierrette had told but not surprising. We all revise our own histories, some more than others.

"It was in a newspaper in London."

"The only reason I got fences is to keep the likes of you out. Dig into a body's life. None-a your bloody business. You didn't answer my question."

"*Times of London.*"

He grunted. "Why the interest? I may not be book educated, but I didn't get where I am by being stupid."

"M. J. Key," I said.

"Whiskey?" he asked. He went to a cabinet, took out a bottle and two tin cups with handles, and poured a dollop of Bell's in each. "What's so special about this Key fellow?"

How to explain it? "He's to fishing what you are to mining."

Bolt handed me a cup. He looked amused. "Son, I don't know the first damn thing about mining. I know how to find rocks. It's up to somebody else to claw it out of the ground." He sampled his drink and smacked his lips. "You still haven't said what your interest is. You looking to buy? Excuse me, but you don't look like you can afford your next squeeze, son."

"I just want to read."

He was caught off guard. "The hell you say?"

"That's the truth."

He took another slug of whiskey. "If I had the books by this fellow Key, you'd be welcome to them, but I don't have 'em."

"But you did buy them."

"I did. It was just an investment. I have business representatives in London and Toronto. When there's a chance to make money, they let me know. I didn't have the collection a month and somebody wanted something by this Key fellow you mentioned. I sold it and made one hell of a profit. It was good business."

I felt weary and looked for a chair. "You have the collection, but not Key's books?"

"Are you okay, son?"

"I'm just tired."

He chuckled. "Don't surprise me. Bustin' beaver dams'll pop a strong man's balls, Luc says you work like an Indian."

I couldn't believe this. Key had been sold again, like some potentate's crown jewels.

"Can you tell me who bought the Key books?"

"Hell, I've got no idea. I didn't sell them all. Just one. The price was too good to refuse. It was all done through some Jew in New York."

"I'd sure like to talk to the buyer and know which one was bought."

"I can do that for you. Luc says you're crashin' at his place. I'll get word to you there."

I nodded dumbly.

When he finished his drink, he plunked the cup down. "Got work to do," he said. "You can find your way out, I assume. The books that weren't sold are all in New York and I can fix it for you to see them, if you want."

"Thanks." I had a strong hunch that it was the manuscript that had been removed. There was nothing else in the collection I wanted to see.

I walked and hitchhiked and didn't reach Luc's until the next morning just after daybreak. Luc was already at the woodpile. He didn't ask how things had gone and I didn't volunteer. I went into the cabin and straight to bed.

When I awoke, I wasn't sure if the sun was coming up or going down, but it turned out to be morning and June was sitting across from the bed patching one of her brother's shirts.

"Where's Luc?"

"He said to fetch you when you woke up."

"Another job?"

"He just said to bring you."

We drove across the bottom of the reserve to Whalesback Channel, which divided the Serpent Peninsula from John Island, and watched a red floatplane flitting around as if the pilot was getting up the nerve to let down. He finally did on relatively calm water, bouncing and bucking several times before the small plane settled and pushed a wave up in front of it. When it taxied to the pebbly beach, June said, "Go with him."

I waded tentatively into the water then stepped up onto a pontoon and into the flimsy door that swung open. The man in the pilot's seat had thick curly black hair, a large head, a flat pug nose, a thick neck, huge scarred hands. His hands reminded me of Valoretev's.

"No belt, so hang on," he said.

I settled in and looked out to see June's hand cupped over her mouth, as if she were holding her breath.

"I'm Turk," the pilot said. "If we go down, stick with the plane. If the plane don't make it, you're on your own."

Talk of crashes before takeoff has always bothered me. We made three long runs and got airborne a few feet several times during each attempt, but we always eventually pancaked hard back onto the surface, drenching the windscreen with our own splash. Turk looked at me before the fourth attempt and said, "Gordie Howe had a lotta no-goal games."

No doubt this was intended to comfort me. "Maybe we should wait for the wind to let up." Or when elephants were born with wings. I did not want to take off in this plane with this pilot.

"And make a night landing? Are you crazy?"

Getting there, I thought.

We got airborne on our fourth try, but Turk had to veer sharply to avoid a small island covered with stunted balsams. He cursed as we rounded the obstacle nearly on our wingtip. "All this water and there's always some bloody thing in my way," he shouted.

I gulped. It was as if he had not noticed the island until we were nearly part of it.

We rocked and yawed our way north through rocky air, though I had the distinct impression that my pilot's technique made for most of the roughness.

"Nice view, eh?" he said as we bucked along.

We were barely above the trees. I did not look down. "A little altitude might give us smoother air."

"One," he said, "everybody else also flies up there. I got enough problems, I don't need nothing else to clutter my mind. Two, none-a my instruments work worth shit. This way I can keep her level."

Some explanations provide relief. This one didn't. "How long to where we're going?" I asked.

"Hour-fifteen, depending."

I didn't ask the obvious follow-up. I just wanted it over. Safely over. The sooner the better.

At about an hour the engine began to cough and sputter and Turk mumbled, "Fuck," and we dipped down toward a small lake, a finger of water that the setting sun turned red-orange like a narrow tongue of flame, and suddenly we were down, but not down, skipping along like a well-chucked flat rock until we finally lurched hard, the windscreen filling with green, followed by more hard bounces until we were at the water's end and Turk's powerful arm snaked out across my chest and there was a horrific crunch and the tail came up as the nose jerked down sharply and dirt, bark bits, and gas spewed.

Then there was silence and a hissing sound. We were sore but not seriously hurt and crawled stiffly out of the wreckage.

The shoreline was littered with fallen trees, their bark stripped away over time by wind and ice. We sat on a fir snag blown over by wind. The aircraft was a few yards away, perched vertically, tail up, vertical stabilizer a tattered aluminum pennant, here marks the spot.

"Wrong lake," Turk said. "A bit short, eh?"

"You bent your prop." It looked like a wilted lily. My head throbbed but I felt a peculiar serenity, the comfort of earth under foot.

"Short is not lost," Turk said. "One bad shift isn't a period. A bad period isn't a game. We'll have to walk from here."

"How far?" He was an idiot and I had come with him willingly.

He scratched his whiskers. "Fifteen, twenty minutes by air." He went to the plane, fetched a pack and a rifle with clothesline rope for a sling and hobbled back to me.

"How far by foot?" I asked. "Timewise?"

"We'll just have to see."

"How fast were we flying?"

Turk grinned. "Dunno. No instruments, remember?"

The walk lasted fifteen minutes and covered what I guessed to be less than a mile, eventually emerging from a rocky spine through low, wet muskeg at the boulder-strewn shore of a large gray lake. The surface prickled like gooseflesh. Two loons paddled around offshore, diving now and then.

"This is it?"

Turk dropped his pack and began to gather driftwood.

"This is here."

"Meaning?"

"You ask a lot of questions," he said.

"It's my job," I said.

"It's not mine to answer," he said.

We built a large fire and kept it hot and smoky, which kept some of the insects at bay and, presumably, provided a marker of our position. I had no idea where we were and Turk turned silent and snoozed, then snored, with his back against a log.

A boat came just before dark. Luc Brokendog hopped over the bow while Pierrette Rouleau lifted the small outboard at the stern.

Turk slept through the rescue.

"What happened?" Luc asked.

"We went down," I said. "Back that way." I pointed in the approximate direction.

Luc gave Turk a disgusted look and kicked the bottom of one of his boots.

"What?" the muscular man asked. "I'm awake."

"Why were you flyin'?"

"I'm not," Turk said. "Now."

Luc kicked his boots again and glared at him.

"There was nobody else to bring him," Turk said defensively.

Luc tried to kick the pilot again, but Turk pulled his feet out of the way and scuttled backward. "Get in the boat," Luc ordered.

I sat beside Pierrette on a hard bench in the middle of the aluminum boat. Luc handled the motor. Turk pouted up front with his arms crossed, staring straight ahead.

"All right?" Pierrette asked.

"What's *with* that guy?" I asked her, stabbing a finger in Turk's direction.

"Later," she said, taking my arm with both her hands and squeezing gently. "I'm glad you're okay."

We were on the water a long time. Sometime during the journey I realized I had lost my watch. The stars came out for a while, but clouds slid over us and the night got darker and the bow continued to pop-pop-pop and wobble against low rollers as we wallowed forward.

When we finally beached the boat, my body was still vibrating and I stumbled into the trees led by Pierrette. Luc followed, but Turk was suddenly gone. Luc made a small fire and Pierrette unrolled sleeping bags. I was surprised that there were no insects. I expected we would eat, but Luc took his sleeping bag and went away into the darkness and Pierrette laid her bag beside mine. I was too tired and sore to talk and got into my bag and she got into hers, smiled at me, and then I was asleep.

In the cool dawn, the beginning of a morning twilight, faint and wispy lavender feathers of clouds glowed in the east. The fire was out. I tried to move but my muscles had hardened to cement.

"Good morning," Pierrette said from the dawn.

"I'm wrecked."

"That's the only good thing about Turk's piloting. He goes down a lot, but everybody seems to more or less walk away."

"I don't think that guy has all his marbles."

She chuckled softly. "You don't know who he is?"

"Obviously not."

"Practically everybody in Canada knows Turk Moon. He was a hockey player with the Leafs. Their warrior, their fighter. Hands like granite."

"It shows in his flying," I said.

Pierrette laughed out loud. Her hand touched my shoulder. "When he left hockey, he bought a bush pilot business. He has five planes and people working for him. He loves to fly. Has no fear."

"And no skill."

Another laugh. "That's it. He just can't do it."

"So you sent me up with a disaster."

"No. He's not allowed to fly and Luc is really angry, but sometimes the desire in Turk gets so big he can't help himself. I think it would be terrible to love something so much and be bad at it."

"How did you and Luc get here?"

"By the long route. We thought a plane would be faster for you."

"For what?"

"You'll soon know," she said.

I was famished, but there was no food. Luc and Turk showed just after we got the sleeping bags rolled. Turk was sullen and looked like a chastised adolescent.

Luc said, "Ready to walk?"

"Where?"

"This fella asks a lot of questions," Turk said to Pierrette.

Luc was wearing his pack. "Let's do 'er," he said and headed into the forest at a brisk pace.

Pierrette gave me a gentle shove in the back. "Go ahead," she said. "Follow Luc."

"What about you?"

"Just go," she said.

We immediately climbed up a hill and followed a ridgeline. The sun popped in and out of mustard-colored clouds. Luc kept a punishing pace and I struggled to keep up. The terrain was steep and severe and there were small lakes and streams everywhere, but there was no game to be seen, not even birds, as we passed through stands of white and black spruce, hemlocks and balsams and white cedars, sugar maples, birches, various pines and poplars. All the trees had a lean to them and many of the trunks were twisted as if they had been under extreme stress. Rocks were gray and blue and some of them rusty and everywhere, trickles of water sweated from the rocks. It was early for ferns so the ground was relatively clear, but curled shoots covered the earth. They looked like tiny green question marks. Soon the forest would be lush green with a carpet of ferns.

Eventually Luc stopped and, when I caught up to him, we stared out at a lake whose water had been replaced by grayish yellow sludge. All the trees and vegetation along the shores and on a couple of small islands were dead and black, lifeless and leafless.

"Mines," Luc said and then we headed away up a stone razorback. After a half hour we cut down into a narrow canyon with steep rock walls and a clear stream falling over gray-blue rocks. When the canyon split, we took the left branch. The sun was hot and I wondered if the rocks served as reflectors. I was sweating and my stomach growled and I had questions that were more emotions than words and all I could do was walk heavy-legged and stare at the ground so that I didn't trip.

The canyon dead-ended and widened some and we were left staring up at sheer rock walls, which seemed to hover overhead. At our feet there was a hole, five or six feet across at the opening. I approached it cautiously and saw that it was lined with stones.

"Man-made?"

Luc removed his packboard but didn't say anything. The hole was dark, its bottom, if there was one, unseen.

"Some sort of mine?" I asked again. "Or a well?"

"The people say you need a name," Luc Brokendog said.

I blinked. "What's wrong with the one I've got?"

"Nishnawbe name." Anishnabe, pronouned *Nishnawbe,* was what the Ojibwa called themselves. "This is an honor," Luc added.

I was too tired to argue.

Luc pointed at the hole. "You go down there."

"No fucking way," I protested.

"You don't have to worry about snakes."

I stared at him and grimaced. "I wasn't worried about them until you mentioned them. Is this really necessary?"

"I'll help you down."

Luc gripped my hand and I hung on and dropped, bumping my knee on the way down. The ground at the bottom was packed hard. The stones that lined the sides fit tightly. The hole was ten feet or so deep, shallower than I had anticipated, but deep enough to leave me feeling isolated.

"Not much of a view," I said up to him.

He smiled down at me.

"What am I supposed to do down here?"

"Stay put."

I looked at my bleak surroundings. "How long?"

"You'll know."

It was ridiculous. "What about food?"

"Feed on your spirit," he said, and then he was gone.

There was enough room to sit if I crossed my legs, but there was no way to stretch out. The hole was five or six feet across at the top, wider in the middle, but it narrowed to three feet or so at the bottom. The sun was over the top and lit the opening, but I was in shadow and soon chilled by my own cooling sweat. I had on only a light jacket. It wasn't long until my legs ached. I tried to crawl out by bracing my back and shoulders against one side and using my legs to inch my way up, but I kept falling back at the place where the hole widened.

"Goddammit, Luc!" And Pierrette, too. She was in on this. They all were. Another practical joke, like my Russian friends had played on me. Did I come across as an easy mark to everyone?

No answer came from above. I was sore. Pissed. Uncomfortable. Hungry. Fed up.

Trapped.

Rain came in the night and it was a frog strangler, leaving me drenched, cold, and shivering. I curled my legs sideways and tried to sleep sitting in standing water, which eventually bled away. I slept in fits. I dreamed of food, a roast turkey with stuffing. I screamed at and for Luc. Begged Pierrette to get me out.

Night passed to day. I went from cold to sweltering. At midday the sun was overhead and I couldn't escape it. More sleep. Confusion. I tried to jump out, smacked my face on the wall, bled from the nose, got giddy. Then night finally came. Then day. Then something else. I imagined sin, drowning in every one ever committed. I fought for air, imagined sin could raise me up, but the sin was heavy and had no buoyancy. Snakes came, black shapes with heads shaped like trowels. They had bright red, yellow, and green stripes and dropped heavily, thudding on me. Not real, I told myself. Then they struck and I screamed. I went from fire to ice. The flames did not heat and the ice did not cool. My flesh became loose, like a robe, and sluffed off my bones. A raven came and took my eyes and told me they were only dressings for humans who were born and lived blind and since I was in darkness and had no need to see, he had hunger and he apologized for taking my eyes and when he had flown away I could feel the sockets where my eyes had been. There was no pain. If this was death, it was soothing. Life had never been so serene. My body was gone. I levitated, then passed into a sweet void, awakening only when my heart caught fire and blue flames leapt from my chest and there was an aura of light around me and I was burning hot and felt unafraid and powerful and voices were around me and in me, my voices, then different ones, all talking gibberish, all the parts convened from their secret places inside me.

I awoke beside the lip of the hole with no idea how I had gotten out.

I saw Polaris above and, below it, the glow of a fire. I crawled toward it and tried to touch the fire to be sure it was real, but my wrist was grabbed firmly and kept away.

Pierrette gave me a cup of cold water. "I welcome you home," she said.

"Fireheart," I said.

She looked concerned.

"Fireheart," I repeated. Long ago Raina said we both had fire in our hearts. I hoped hers was taking her to better places than mine. I kept this to myself.

"Eat," Pierrette said, handing me a bowl of warm mush.

When I had eaten, she helped me onto a thick bed of spruce branches and draped a blanket over me and I slept.

I awoke with her in my arms. We were undressed, our hair damp, our bodies slick with perspiration.

"Am I still hallucinating?" I asked in a whisper.

She giggled softly. "If so, I think we're sharing the same dream."

We made love again, slowly, deliberately, neither of us hurrying, and I felt her arms loose around my neck and our hips undulating with short slow thrusts and the sun throwing yellow-white shafts across us and time did not exist and I could not tell where my body ended and hers began because it was all one thing, sweet and unending.

Afterward, we slept.

Later we gathered the blankets and rolled them and tied them to her packboard and started back out of the canyon and when we got to the stream, we drank with our hands. In the distance I heard a raven sounding his alarm and the sky turned blue as sapphire and everything around me seemed beautiful, every detail crisp and I knew I could see, not as before, but truly see and I did not want to leave where we were or let go of the moment.

But let go we did. I took her pack and we resumed our walk. We made the long climb out of the canyon and reached the yellow-gray lake. We smelled smoke. Then we saw a camp ahead and Luc was there smiling, surrounded by others. His people touched me and rubbed my back and I was guided to a campfire and invited to sit down with several old men who gave me food. Behind us a drum began and the sound blended with smoke and voices chanted a high-pitched song with no words.

"Fireheart," one of the old men said. "The woman told us. This is a powerful name. It is the name of a man who must know himself or burn up. Gitchee Manitou gives us our names and there is great glory in yours and great peril. We will each go to the spirit world to join our ancestors when it is our time, but you must mind the fire inside you, my son. It could take you into danger."

We shared a cigar that was passed around. And then there was a feast. I felt as if I belonged, and Pierrette sat close to me and smiled.

Later I saw Turk. "Ready to fly back?" he asked.

"Fuck off," I told him. We both laughed and he gave me an affectionate shove that sent me sprawling.

Luc and Pierrette led me down to the dead lake that afternoon. We followed a rocky trail to a cave and Luc turned on a flashlight and we went inside and there on the ground was the skeleton of a small bear. It had three heads and a spine shaped like a Y and at least six legs. All the bones were laid out in proper order and the skeleton surrounded by red-painted rocks and several sticks with partridge feathers.

There was no need for an explanation. The uranium mines had caused this. The sight sickened me.

"This is also happening to your people?"

"It's not so dramatic for people," Luc said, "but the effect is the same. The land gave us life and sustained us. Now it gives death."

"You should fight the mines," I said.

"The poison is in the ground," Luc said. "How do we fight an enemy that is everywhere and invisible?"

I had no answer. People asked the same question in Vietnam.

Pierrette and I went by boat across a huge lake to where her car was waiting. She told me I had been in the spirit hole for five days and that this was a long time and had worried the people and that there had been discussions about my safety. An argument ensued. The elders thought I was too strong and would die before I gave in to a vision, but Luc had intervened.

Pierrette drove us to Luc's place. He did not return and we spent the night together. I asked her to tell me her spirit name and she whispered, "Slippery Beaver."

I laughed so hard that she pushed me out of bed, which made me laugh all the harder until it got her too, and we laughed together and I got back into bed and we slept the sleep of satisfied lovers and friends.

Luc came back in the morning as we were brewing coffee. He sat at the table in his small kitchen and put an envelope on the table and yawned and said he needed sleep. "Bolt," he said with a nod at the envelope. "He said you'd want this." I opened the envelope. There was a piece of paper inside, folded once.

I opened it.

"What's wrong?" Pierrette asked. She took the paper. "I don't understand," she said.

Written on the paper was: "M. J. Key. *The Legend of the Snowfly.*"

The imbecile had given me the name of the author whose books I sought! Did he think he could yank my chain? I was pissed.

Pierrette and I drove into Cutler to a bar called the Kettle. I used a pay phone to call Lockwood Bolt. This time I was put through to him.

"This is Rhodes."

"Yeah, you got that name? I sent it myself."

"It's wrong," I said. "I don't need to know who wrote the damn thing."

"Son, you wanted the name of the person I sold to and the name of the book and now you've got both."

"But you sent me the name of the author," I said.

"It's also the name of the buyer," he said, snapping back.

"But they're the same."

"Bloody phone books are filled with same names," Bolt said, hanging up.

11

I couldn't explain it then, and I still can't explain it, but I felt different when I left Canada. I had gotten my car from Luc's and followed Pierrette back to her place, where I lingered for several days. There was a creek in the valley below her place. It was wide in places, narrow in others, and cut its way through willows where I saw frequent signs of moose. I took out my Russian fly rod and put one of my fly lines on it; while Pierrette worked I explored the creek. The area might be contaminated with radiation, but it did not seem to affect the trout. There were lots of them and quite a few with good size for brookies. They took nearly any fly I tossed their way. I might have stayed with Pierrette a long time, but I awoke one morning feeling an overpowering urge to move on. The next morning she dressed for work and walked out to my car with me and we held each other for a long time.

"Fireheart," she said.

"Slippery Beaver," I said.

When we separated she said slowly. "Fire can make your heart burn pure or it can consume you. *Manka pikkisi*," she added.

"What's that mean?"

"You must grow larger." She tapped my chest. "In there."

"The snowfly," I said.

She nodded solemnly. "You must conquer it."

"How?" I had hit a stone wall and saw no clear route to moving ahead. She pressed both hands to my chest. "When it is time, you'll know."

I left Elliot Lake and drove toward the Soo still buoyed with a sense of calm from my experience in the spirit hole. I was also still perplexed by Bolt's message, but decided that as crazy as it seemed, he was telling me the truth. An M. J. Key could be the buyer of M. J. Key's books. The questions were who and how. There were more switchbacks in my life than an Idaho logging road.

It had been months since my unceremonious exit from the Soviet Union and I still had a bit of the summer left to fish. I took the ferry across the St. Mary's River and telephoned New York from a restaurant in the Soo called the Antlers. The elder had never said it, but I knew the fire in my heart had something to do with the snowfly.

The phone sat on the bar beside a stuffed anaconda with an open, garish pink mouth. The snake was looped around a steel post to make it look like it was descending and the pose must've worked on drunks because the carcass had been abused; pimples of sawdust showed where fork tines had punctured it. I thought immediately of the reptilian rain that had deluged me during my vision and turned my back on the thing. I asked Yetter to wire money to a bank in Newberry, where I picked it up later in the day.

I reached Grand Marais in the evening and Fred Ciz wasn't home, so I dropped my suitcase and drove west toward the No Trout with growing excitement. There was no time to hike inland or upriver so I contented myself with the holes and tight runs near the spot where the river dumped into Lake Superior.

No fish came to the surface, but I wasn't discouraged. Insect hatches on most rivers range from sporadic to nonexistent, but deep in the rivers where there are trout, they are almost always eating. Crawdads, worms, beetles, other fish, even their own spawn. As finicky as trout writers make them out to be, the truth is that a trout will eat virtually anything it can find in water, but it won't come far to food. The trick is to get the mountain to Mohammed. I rigged a gray leech with two split shot and began striking brookies and some browns every few casts. I preferred the effortless cast of a dry fly on a long leader, but at least I was catching and for the moment results outweighed style. It had been too long since I had been on this river, which I had come to think of as my own.

Fred Ciz was at home when I returned. We embraced like brothers.

"How was life among the moose humpers?"

I didn't even know where to begin, and I didn't try. Something was bothering Fred.

"What's wrong?" I asked.

"Staley died," he said. "We didn't know how to find you," he said apologetically. "Cancer filled him up. His doc said he shoulda died ten years ago, but Buzz says God wasn't ready for him. You staying for a while this time?"

Staley's death deeply saddened me. I had not known him as well as Fred and Buzz, but I respected the kind of man he was. He lived hard, but he gave back.

"At least through September, if you don't mind."

"You and your fish," he said with a sympathetic smile. "I'm glad for the company."

This is how it always would be with Fred. I would slide in and out of his life and the town's and over the years they would think of me as theirs and they as mine. Home is an elusive concept. My sister and I still owned the folks' land but no longer thought of it as home. Grand Marais had become my home, the place I ventured forth from and always returned to, not an accident of birth and providence, but chosen. My center.

We visited Staley's grave as the sun went down. There was a simple gravestone with STALEY engraved on it. The grave itself was covered with fresh flowers and there was a piece of construction paper attached to a stick like a flag. There was a child's drawing on the paper, a crude hockey player in a red uniform.

"One of Janey's kids," Fred said and I teared up.

"I think I'd like to buy a house here," I announced over dinner, the news surprising me nearly as much as Fred.

"Karla Capo's the one to talk to," he said.

"Capo? Is she new?"

"Just talk to her. She's good people."

"What'll happen to Staley's place?"

"It'll be sold. He's got no kin. It'll go in an estate auction. Why?"

"Just wondering." Thoughts and ideas often start as feelings without logic.

I went to see Karla Capo in the morning. She was forty-two, divorced, the mother of three girls, and new to town. She had moved in since I left. Her ex was a Ford dealer in Traverse City. They'd had a camp in the woods on Pike Lake and she'd gotten it as part of her settlement. Her kids were in T.C. for the summer with their dad and she was trying to build a real estate business and make a new life for herself. She was a tall, muscular woman a long jaw and a liquid smile. Her house overlooked the harbor. It was small with a freshly painted white picket fence around it. There were books and clothes and boxes strewn around. We took to each other right off.

"Pardon my mess," she said, "but I was never much of a housekeeper and now that my former is my ex I don't have to feel guilty about it. The man was anal about clutter. What sort of a property intrigues you?" She wore baggy denim shorts, a T-shirt, and sandals.

"I want to know about Staley's."

She seemed to study me. "Are you a breakfast eater?"

The kitchen, unlike the other parts of the house I saw, was spotless. We fried bacon and eggs and toasted slices of rye bread. She ate twice as much as I did. I was still not back to a normal appetite after my time in the spirit hole. It would be a long time before I could eat a full meal in a sitting.

"Why Staley's?" she asked.

"I worked for him and I liked him and I don't like the idea that it might go under. It's more than just a business for people around here."

"Somebody will snap it up," she said. "Downstate's filled with little men with cash-register minds and the hots for the backwoods. I guess they figure the north country will put some lead back in their pencils. I've seen this trend coming. People are gonna escape north in big numbers. At least I've convinced myself of that enough to take a flier on real estate. The thing is that Staley's margins weren't all that great if it's an investment you're looking for."

"But it was in the black."

"You could do a lot better playing the stock market poorly."

"What if it was reorganized as a nonprofit? Like a club or something."

She screwed up her mouth. "Why would anybody want to do that?"

"To keep it alive. I wouldn't need profit, and this would help keep costs down. Might even draw in more people. Maybe we could spruce up the food. There's a chef's school over in Madison. We could invite students up for six months or a year as an internship." As I thought out loud, I could see that she was listening.

"Fred Ciz says you're a foreign correspondent, which means you'll be an absentee owner. Who'll run the place?"

"Let me worry about that." Fred had told her about my job. I wondered what else he had said.

She poured coffee. "Well, it's a pretty, uh . . . creative notion."

"Do you have a lawyer who can set it up?"

She nodded. "You haven't mentioned price."

"Whatever it takes," I said, big-timing it. I had been saving most of my salary for years and I could think of no better way to invest it.

Buzz joined me fishing the next night. We drove out to the Blind Sucker River east of town in his antique Ford and he tramped upstream with a cloth sack of worms hooked to his belt, a canvas creel over his shoulder, and a pack on his back filled with ice and beer; he fished back toward me and I slid into the river and worked up slowly, looking for rising fish. We met at a bend at dusk. The river was an ugly rubicund-and-cream color, with moderate current and finicky fish, but Buzz had seven brown trout in his creel. We popped two cans of beer and saluted each other.

He said, "Jesus ate of fish and I mean only to emulate my Savior."

Father Buzz was a singular man, collar or not. I asked him, "How's Janey?"

He peered over his beer and belched. "Not pregnant," he said, eyeing me suspiciously.

Janey Pelkinnen stared at me through the screen door. Two kids eyed me from behind her. She had the sort of face that invited rubbernecking. It was the face of an angel who had lived hard.

"Hi," I said by way of a greeting. I was inexplicably nervous.

"You came back."

"Like a boomerang. Can I come in?"

She didn't answer right away, but she was shaking her head. "I don't think it's good to let strange men into the house. No offense, but I've got kids to think about."

I wondered if there was a difference between strange men and male strangers. "How'd you like a job?"

One of the kids, a boy about twelve with long hair said, "What's he mean, Ma?"

"Hush," she said, gently pushing the boy away. "I have a job," she said to me. "I work nights as a cashier at the Red Owl and I take phone calls for people."

It took some talking, but Janey finally invited me in and tentatively accepted the job as manager of the Light. Her house was neat, orderly, and homey.

While Karla and her lawyer took care of the sale and closing, I spent the remainder of the season hunting fish, exploring, and working out the details of the Grand Marais Food & Beverage Society. In the end Fred Ciz, Father Buzz, and even Karla Capo bought in, and Karla was elected honcho. The building turned out to be more than a century old and Karla said she thought we could get it and other town buildings off the tax rolls by having the state declare the Grand Marais Bay area a state historical preservation district. Three hundred years before, French voyageurs had pulled their canoes into the bay to camp and escape Superior's nasty and quixotic moods. All the details of business planning were trivia to me. My money was in and it was up to our little board to make the thing work, which they did.

In early September we had a board meeting in Staley's apartment above the bar. I was going to move my stuff out of Fred's, but I realized that when I moved on the space would be wasted, so I arranged for Janey and her kids

234 ❖ JOSEPH HEYWOOD

to have the place as part of her job. When I came to town I could stay with Fred or Buzz. Anticipating that Janey would be reticent about moving in, I left it to Karla to tell her.

After the meeting Karla and I had a drink. "Fred says you'll be leaving soon."

The television was on and the Tigers were playing the Indians in the season wind-down.

"That's the general plan."

"Where to this time?"

"I don't exactly know yet."

She smiled. "I'd go crazy if I didn't know."

"It goes with the job."

She laughed. "I envy you in some ways, but don't you get nervous going to faraway places?"

"Not really. If you have no expectations, there're no letdowns."

"Or highs," she said. "Fred said you were in Vietnam."

"Two years."

"Bad?"

"I had it easy. Bad was being a grunt living in the dirt."

"You divorced?"

"Never married."

She grinned. "I guess that makes you the local prize."

"Yeah," I said. "Booby prize."

She looked at me seductively. "I meant *bedroom* prize."

The last week of September I decided to hike up my river. I figured I'd take three days up, make camp, and finish the season there. I'd hike out when I was done. Fred warned me to be careful of bears.

I told him they were like dogs.

He said, "Right. Four-hundred-pound dogs."

Buzz said that he'd like to go to keep me company, but I told him I needed time alone. Karla thought I was crazy and told me to let her know as soon as I was back. In the weeks since we had met Karla had been giving off less and less subtle signals of an interest in taking the relationship to a more personal level and I was anything but sanguine. Karla was a handsome woman, filled with life and energy, and I was tempted. One night I had walked over to her place at two in the morning, but I lost my nerve when I got there.

Buzz, Fred, Karla, and Janey all stood outside Staley's to see me off. It was early morning. The men shook my hand. The women hugged me.

Karla whispered, "Goddammit, be careful."

Janey shook her head and said, "Going alone isn't too smart."

I had gotten topographical maps from the DNR and plotted a course. The first day I wanted to get as far upriver as possible, so I parked east of the river and followed the ridgelines west and south, looking for an intercept.

It was a glorious day. There were no insects, the ferns were browning under shortening days, the sumac was flaming orange, and bright yellow birch and popple leaves quaked frenetically in a soft breeze. I figured it would take four to five hours to strike the river, but my ridges quickly dissolved into a gloomy cedar swamp intertwined with tag alder and it was late afternoon before I stumbled onto the river. As anticipated, it was substantial, with racing clear water. There was a lot of timber down and long boulder fields, nice pocket water. I even saw trout rising in a small pool next to the bank.

I got into the river and worked my way along the shallows, zigzagging to the inside turns across from where the river cut the banks and the water dug out the deep holes. Eventually I found the tip of an extreme oxbow where a cluster of huge white cedars provided shelter. I took off my pack. I had no energy left for fishing. I ate my food cold, hung my food bag fifty yards away in a tree, crawled into my sleeping bag, and passed out.

Loud splashes awoke me. There was a sliver moon, emitting pale blue light. Two bears the color of ink were moving around in shallow water only yards away. I was too surprised to be afraid, but caution is best around anything wild. I unzipped my bag quietly and slid out onto the wet grass; when I got to my knees and tried to stand I was knocked forward.

"Do you think he's dead?"

"Shush."

"But he's hangin' up there. Why's he doin' *that?*"

I could see light. The voice was a child's and I wanted to see what she was looking at, but my eyes didn't seem to work and when I tried to touch my face my arms wouldn't move. Then the pain switched on.

"Mommy, he's screaming!"

Somewhere in my brain it registered that he was me.

I was in a bed. When I tried to move, my chest felt like it would explode. A hand immediately touched my shoulder.

"Don't move, Bowie."

Some instructions are easier to follow than others. It was Karla's voice and if she didn't want me to move I would become a statue.

"I can't see."

"Your eyes are swollen shut," Karla said.

"What happened to me?" I remembered the splashing bears and the moon and getting out of my sleeping bag. I remembered a little girl's voice. Now Karla. There were some serious gaps between events, assuming any of them were real.

"Listen to me, son. You've taken a real beating."

"Who're you?"

"This is Doc Miwanteyo, Bowie." Karla's voice.

"You've got bruised kidneys, a couple of broken ribs, and your shoulder has been dislocated," the doctor said.

"Did I get bit?"

"No, sir. Looks more like somebody beat the applesauce out of you."

"What happened?" Another voice.

"It's Amp," Karla said. The deputy.

I asked, "Where're Fred and Buzz?"

Fred Ciz said, "I'm right here. Buzz'll be here soon. He had something he had to do. He was real upset when they brought you in. He'll be here soon," Fred repeated. It would be some time before I understood the significance of Buzz's absence.

"I'm here, too," Janey said.

I felt queasy. "I don't know what happened. Am I dying?"

"No, but there's a lot of damage. You're going to have to give it time." The doctor's voice. What kind of name was Miwanteyo? I wished I could see.

I told them what I knew, which wasn't much.

Amp said, "No friggin' bear did this. How'd you get out to where you were found?"

"Where was I found?" I got no answer. "Where am I now?"

"Karla's house," Fred said.

The doctor butted in. "But we may have to move you to the hospital in Marquette."

I thought of the USS *Snow*. "No hospital."

"He's hardheaded," Fred Ciz said. I took it as a compliment.

"Thank God." This from Karla, who draped a warm cloth across my forehead.

It was just over a month later and we already had eight inches of snow and another early-winter storm bearing down on us. I could see again and my ribs were pretty much healed, but my shoulder and back still hurt, and I had recurring headaches. I slept in a ground-floor bedroom at Karla's place and had to be awakened by her every morning. We ate meals together every day and between calls with clients she stopped in to check on me, hovering around, encouraging me. When Karla couldn't be there, Janey stopped in. I had no idea why, but Janey's presence made me nervous.

The wind roared outside and wet snow pelted the north face of the house. There was a fire in the fireplace. My shoulder ached when I got cold so I wrapped in a blanket and sat in front of the fire with my feet propped on a stool. The wood popped and the smoke perfumed the house.

Karla came in with cups of hot chocolate. She wore a heavy red robe and thick, heavy white socks. "How do you feel?"

"Beat." I still didn't understand what had happened to me. Deputy Sheriff Amp had hiked in to my campsite, but my gear was gone and it had rained, so there was nothing along the lines of tracks or other evidence. Some asshole, was Amp's unofficial ruling.

"Doc Miwanteyo says your body's healed," Karla said. "It's time you got yourself back to normal. Your boss in New York calls Fred every day to find out how you're doing. You have to get up and out."

"Are you trying to get rid of me?"

She rolled her eyes and shook her head. "Lord, no. I just want you well again." Her hand rested on my arm.

We drank our hot chocolate in silence. We both dozed in our chairs and when I awoke, she was adding wood to the fire. When she bent over her robe pulled tight across her hips and I felt a stirring. She glanced back at me and smiled.

"Nice nap?"

I nodded. "Weren't your girls supposed to be back this week?"

She turned around and crossed her arms. "Yeah, but the ex refuses to let them go. He's got his legal beagles throwing curveballs. He says they can't get a proper education up here. His lawyers are involved."

Karla's voice was sad. "*My* lawyer says we'll win. I asked her, 'Who's *we?*' Do the kids win when their parents fight over them like they were a Lincoln? Why does such crap happen to essentially good people? I should write a book about it, but I don't have the discipline to sit down every day. Do you think my husband's right?"

"I doubt that education is the issue."

She half smiled. "You don't want to talk about my troubles."

"I think education isn't a product of big schools."

"That's what I think, too." She sat down on the footstool and rubbed my foot. "What do you think of me?"

"I can't believe how you took me in. I don't know how to thank you."

"Maybe I had an ulterior motive," she said. "Men are supposed to fall in love with their nurses, right?"

I chuckled.

"You hold everything pretty close, don't you? Tell me the truth, Bowie. When you look at me, what do you see?"

We were headed into something, but I wasn't sure I was ready for it. "Intelligence," I said. "Thoughtfulness. Energy. Enthusiasm. You like people and they like you. Organized. Courageous. I think it took nerve to move up here and start from scratch."

"That's it?"

"I see a friend."

She ran her hand up my leg, sending a shiver up my spine. "I'm glad you didn't say sweet. When I was a girl I loved church, Christmas, Easter, the choir, the Latin. My folks thought I might become a nun, but I didn't really take any of the church stuff to heart. Church was peaceful and uplifting, like fine entertainment, a sophisticated circus, and that's all. I was expected to be a good girl and I was, even at college, and for a while after. I took a job at J. Walter Thompson in Chicago. But nature is nature and my buildup lasted nearly twenty-four years, so when I finally indulged my libido I took to screwing like Amelia Earhart took to flying. It is one of life's truths that women are at least as sexually inclined as men, though not many men ever recognize this. Having finally taken the big step, I continued to indulge and offer no apologies."

Her hand was higher now, feathering me, and I was in full response. She pulled the blanket away and looked down at me. "My goodness," she said. "I think you're cured."

"That wasn't my problem."

She looked me in the eyes. "Couldn't tell that by me."

I closed my eyes.

Later, in bed, she told me more about herself.

"I moved from Chicago to New York and then to Detroit," she said. "One of my college girlfriends had inherited some money. She was in Traverse City and bought a small ad agency up there, so I quit the big time and moved. Katherine, my friend, was a lot like me. We were nearly thirty, our business got going, and we both exercised our rights as adults. We had taken on an account with a new Ford dealership. The owner said he believed trucks would be hot, so we developed a series of ads to attract accountants and doctors and lawyers to trucks. 'You don't need a blue collar to live a man's life.' Sounds infantile now, but it worked back then. The owner's name was Roman and he and I got involved. He had a wife but no kids. His wife, Laurie, was mixed up with a prosecutor named Carvelly. That's how T.C. was in those days. And still is," she added.

She had her arm over me and her head next to mine on my pillow.

"Well," she said, "the truth is, I pursued Roman. I threw the full-court press on him, and you know how it is, when you're young and lusting, you come in a snap. Fourteen years later he was still Mr. Sudden and I'm talking Wyatt Earp fast. I took to watching the clock: ninety seconds max. I told him we had a problem. He told me his other women had never complained. I was badly frustrated. I stopped getting off less than two months after we started dating and faked it from then on. Well, hell," she said. "I knew it was a mistake, but I couldn't talk to him about it, so I just accepted it. After thirteen years I let myself get involved with another guy. It lasted a few weeks, but I knew I couldn't go back to Roman, so I got a lawyer and the rest is history. *Then* it got ugly. I told a friend about his problem and it got back to him and he went berserk. His play for the kids is a way of striking back at me. I'm sorry it's a mess," she whispered, "but I'm not sorry I left him."

I was always surprised by the intimate details of the lives of others and that they shared them so freely both to reporters and in bed. When I awoke in the morning Karla's side of the bed was cold, but I could smell food so I got up and showered and shaved and dressed for the first time in weeks and went into the kitchen.

After breakfast, I walked over to Staley's and checked in with Janey, who gave me a warm smile before I went into the back office to telephone Yetter. I felt weak and a little lightheaded, but I also knew I needed to get some semblance of order back into my life.

Yetter was in but had to be tracked down, and I was sitting there waiting for him to return my call when Janey came through the door with a fresh cinnamon roll and coffee and sat down across from me. She wore a tight purple sweater and black ski pants. Her blue eyes were dark and searching. I couldn't read the emotion.

"Are you and Karla getting serious?"

I didn't know what to say. "Pardon me?"

"She's my friend and I don't want her hurt," Janey said.

"She's my friend, too."

"Look, you gave me a job and I'm thankful for that, but I won't have my friends hurt. Men always move on." Her nostrils flared. She had real fight in her and I was impressed.

"I offered you the job because I thought you'd do a good job. That's all there was. What's between Karla and me is between us."

"Men always want something," she said, growling. "What're you up to?"

"Nothing," I said, which was true.

"Don't break Karla's heart," she said as she got up from the table.

When she was gone, I felt like I'd just run a hundred miles. I called Yetter again and got put on hold.

"Is this Lazarus?" he asked when he finally answered.

"Good as new, my doc says."

"What is he, a vet?"

"I'm ready to go back to work."

"Well, that might not be so easy. We've got financial trouble, kid."

My gut tightened. "I'm still on the payroll, right?"

"For now, but we're going to cut back. Hell, I may not survive."

I felt panic building. "What do you want me to do?"

"Just sit tight and keep your pants on until I see how this thing shakes out. And don't worry, if UPI goes in the toilet, there's plenty more fish to fry. I'm not hanging you out to dry, kid. Sometimes the best thing you can do is hunker down and wait."

It was disconcerting. Karla had asked me if I got excited about new assignments and until now I hadn't, but now I began to understand that maybe the work was more important than I had realized. If I got cut loose, what would happen to the Light? To me?

Karla was already at the house when I got there. "You went out?"

"To Staley's."

She rubbed her hands together. "Feel good to get out?"

We took a nap together. She had an evening meeting in Newberry. "I'll be back late," she said, "the weather and all." We kissed like old marrieds when she left and I tried to read but couldn't concentrate. I finally walked over to the Light and had dinner. Janey smiled and waved when I walked in but stayed away, which suited me. She still had on the purple sweater.

Buzz came in as I was finishing my fish dinner and had a tuna sandwich and a shot of peppermint schnapps, issuing several loud belches. "Janey looks great," he said. "Healthy. I think she looks younger every time I see her."

"You helped her a lot," I said. "Not many people would have."

He frowned. "Priests are the worst, enamored with hopeless causes."

I said, "But Janey wasn't a lost cause."

The priest nodded solemnly. "I have plenty who are. Do you look better or is that a mirage?"

"I'm getting there."

"That's good," he said, pushing back. "I feel terrible about what happened to you."

It was a strange statement. "It wasn't your fault."

"I should've been out there with you."

"So we both could've gotten the crap kicked out of us?"

Janey smiled and waved on her way out. A woman named Mona would close.

I got increasingly antsy as each day passed. Yetter remained silent. Snow blew down from Alberta. Hunters went out and killed their bucks. On Thanksgiving we hosted most of the village at the Light and ate several geese and venison brought in by Buzz. On December 1 Deputy Amp stopped to examine an abandoned pickup during a snow squall and was hit by a seventy-two-year-old man in a hand-painted Studebaker. The man was legally blind without his eyeglasses on, and of course he wasn't wearing them. Not that it mattered: He was drunk, his heater fan broken, and his windshield iced over. Amp was in the hospital for more than a month and Buzz was sworn in as a deputy while Amp was on the mend. There seemed no limit to what Buzz would do for the town.

December 10 Karla got her kids back and told me we would have to be more discreet. I took this as a burden lifted. I cared about Karla, but we were more close friends than lovers, two ships opting for the port at hand. We were both lonely and made good company.

On Christmas Eve day several of us went to see Janey and her kids. I had gone to Marquette the day before and loaded the car with presents. Janey hugged me tight and I hugged back. Janey's kids swarmed over me and I relished their attention.

That night I headed for Lilly's. Snow fell straight down, rendering the world black or white in my headlights. I encountered few vehicles on the snowy roads. The villages and collections of crossroads houses that served as informal communities were decorated with Christmas lights muted by snow that left them with a warm glow in contrast to the frigid air. My life, such as it was, had taken many strange turns, which I accepted as fate, but my sojourn in Grand Marais was beginning to complicate my life in unexpected ways. Staley, who was gone, Buzz, Fred Ciz, Amp, Karla, and Janey represented my first set of enduring friends; I had always walked and stalked my own path and oriented myself primarily or exclusively to my needs, but friendships altered this formula.

I worried about my effect on the community. At its worst this was pure arrogance on my part, because the community had no expectations of me; nor had it anointed me. Yet I understood that my circle of friends and I did affect other lives. Fred Ciz was their link to the outside world and he was the thread that sewed the community together in a secular way while Father Buzz tended the spiritual needs of the flock and served as a one-man social service agency, artfully flitting in and out of lives at opportune moments. Staley's contribution had been more commercial than the others, but the Light also served an important social function as the gathering house. Karla's place was not yet certain, but her personal commitment to launch a business in a most unlikely place could, with success, have profound effects on the community.

And Janey, how did she fit? She was elusive and brooding, always on the defensive, yet she was courageous and passionate. Intelligent and beautiful, Janey was like the town itself, a hidden jewel, both strong and weak. *Love* was not a word I attached to myself, yet I did love my friends. With Karla the love was overlaid with intimacy, now dissipated. For Karla lovemaking was a social activity—sex as a natural expression of an emotional tie. Sometimes when I was with Karla I would think of Janey and I didn't know what to make of this except that it was not healthy. It was time for me to get away for a while.

I wished Yetter would call.

My job was in jeopardy and in my mind the Light's future in part rode on my ability to continue to provide for the mortgage. This weighed heavily on me. Passing through the western fringe of St. Ignace, I noticed more and more houses and laughed out loud when I realized that in some ways I was now as staked to the ground as they were.

My sister, Lilly, and her family had left Alpena to live in a house trailer on a two-acre lot in the pine flats east of Vanderbilt, a town settled after the Civil War on property that had been part of the vast holdings of the commodore. She and Roger planned to build their dream home on the site and I envied them their shared dreams.

It fascinated me that some of the country's oldest families had vast tracts of land in the state and that by and large such ownership, forged long ago, should now lead to huge areas available to the public. The contemporary rich were adept at mouthing the conventions of stewardship and noblesse oblige, but the old guys like Vanderbilt and McCormick and even the Nazi-loving Hank Ford himself had taken stewardship seriously and because of it, woods and streams were the public's to use and enjoy. When they died, they gave their lands back to the state.

Lilly and I had always been close when we were kids. As the elder Lilly naturally took to the role of assistant mother, and there were times when her demands made Queen Anna's look paltry. Lilly tried to rule with an iron hand, but when Queen Anna was on a tirade, as she often was, it was Lilly who intervened or shielded me. Nowadays I did not see Lilly often, but on those occasions when we were together I was grateful that she was my sister. She was Queen Anna without the sharp edges.

I arrived in early morning, making a grand and loud entrance with bags of presents. It didn't take long for her three children to be awake and ripping wrappings off gifts. Lilly stood close to me, smiling and clinging to my arm, patting the top of my head like I was seven. I sensed that she was upset about something and I knew her well enough to not pry. If she decided to share, she would.

It was midmorning before the children finally settled down. Lilly and I sat in her small kitchen and drank coffee.

"Where's Roger, on road patrol?"

Lilly's lips quivered. "I'm worried, Bowie. He was supposed to be home at midnight. Delays are part of being a cop, but Roger always calls if he's going to be late."

"Did you try calling him?"

She made a sour face. "He'd hate that. Cops are too macho to have the little wifey worrying and checking up on them."

"He'll be along," I said, trying to soothe her.

Lilly wanted to be distracted.

"The gifts are wonderful, but they're too much," she said. "You can't afford all this. You're living up there in the middle of nowhere and you're not working."

"Living here is the middle of somewhere?"

"You always gave everything away," she said. "Queen Anna would carp that you were empty headed and that Punky Chickerman was using you and that women would always use you."

My sis. I could only smile. "UPI is still paying me."

"They pay you *not* to work?" She was shocked.

I shrugged. "It's a pretty strange world out there."

"I'm so glad you're here," my sister said, squeezing my hand.

Just after we cleared the lunch dishes off the table, a blue state police cruiser pulled up beside the trailer. Two troopers got out and moved as if they had artificial legs. Lilly sagged when she saw them. Then she sank into a chair and asked me to open the door.

The trooper with sergeant's stripes looked into my sister's face. He had red eyes. The other trooper stared at the floor.

"Lil," the sergeant said, "I'm so sorry, but Roger's dead."

Lilly let loose a loud and violent sob. A lump rose in my throat and I knelt beside her chair.

"He was shot, Lil," the sergeant said, his voice catching. He looked at me with hard eyes. "Who're you?"

"Her brother."

"I'm sorry for your loss," he said.

Lilly cried quietly. The kids stood watching us from a doorway. The oldest, a boy of eight named for his father, asked, "What's wrong, Mom?"

Lilly said, "Can you take the girls in the other room, Roger?"

My nephew did as he was asked.

When the children were out of earshot, Lilly sucked in a deep breath, exhaled, and looked the sergeant in the eye. "What happened, Al?"

"You don't want the details right now, Lil."

"Tell her," I said.

The sergeant nodded.

"He never came in after his shift. Dispatch tried to get him on the horn, but he was silent."

"I never got a call," Lilly said.

"We were all supposed to check in at the post. We didn't want to worry you when he didn't show. Roger's a good cop. He'd been off his horn for three hours. The lieutenant sent us out to look and started calling extra people in. His vehicle was found off Calcut Road, west of Flanders. He wasn't in the car." The sergeant paused. "A trapper found him this morning in the park at Ocqueoc Falls."

Lilly looked up.

"Thirty miles away," the sergeant said, nodding.

"Tell me the rest," Lilly said quietly. I was amazed at her composure.

"His hands and feet were tied. He was shot once in the back of the head."

"Execution," I said, the word slipping out before I could think.

"You a cop?" the trooper asked.

"No," I said.

"We don't know any more, Lil. We've got people going over the car and where Rog was found."

"It was an execution," I repeated.

"It looks that way," the sergeant said.

Lilly held it together until the troopers were gone, then she broke down. I held her in my arms while she sobbed and in a quiet moment I asked if she wanted me to tell the children, but she only patted my cheek and wiped at my tears.

When we looked up, Roger Junior was standing there. "Dad's dead, isn't he, Mom?"

"Yes, honey. I'm so sorry," Lilly said.

It was a week before we could hold the funeral. The killing has never been solved. Rural areas are no less susceptible to unexplained mayhem than cities. More than two hundred uniforms attended the ceremony. The ground was too frozen for a burial in winter and bodies were collected in a warehouse in town to await the thaw.

Lilly and her children were surrounded by friends at the funeral home in Vanderbilt and as I stood there I saw two men I recognized and went over to them. The white man wore a conservation officer's dark green uniform and the black man was in the navy blue of a Detroit cop.

"You guys remember me? Bowie Rhodes."

"You still fishing in minefields?" Treebone asked with an infectious smile.

"No, and the photo you gave me, it's a species unknown to eggheads."

"Told you," Conservation Officer Grady Service said. "You here to write a dead-cop story?"

"The dead cop is my brother-in-law."

"We're sorry," Service said. "We both knew him. Rog was a good cop." Cops and COs often worked together and in northern Michigan they all seemed to know each other.

"I'm glad you guys made it out alive."

Service pressed his lips together. "Sometimes Tree and me wonder which is real life, this shit or that?"

I understood. After Vietnam they had both become COs with the DNR. But Treebone hated being a "fish cop" and moved to a job in Detroit. He was in vice. A natural talent, Service said. Service was a CO near Escanaba. I was pleased to see them and had a feeling we would meet again.

Fred Ciz, Buzz, Karla, and Janey came to the funeral service and back to Lilly's afterward. Janey wanted to know if I was okay and when I would be back. I didn't know.

Later in the day Lilly and I sat on her couch together, the room crowded with people in uniforms, all talking softly with each other, the way people do at reunions, which is what funerals always are. "I could kick myself," she said. "I never said good-bye to him. It's not fair."

I kept my mouth shut.

"The first time I saw him, I fell in love and I never lost that. How do you live when the center of your life has been cut away?"

I envied Lilly her love, but not her pain.

She rested her head against my shoulder. "You loved Punky, didn't you?"

"I think so."

"Well, you'll love again and when you do, you'll understand that part of the power of love is knowing you can lose the other one. It makes every moment precious. You know the worst thing? I don't know if I can sleep alone."

Rose Yelton's words came back to me, her prediction that I'd never be comfortable without a woman beside me. I wanted to tell Lilly that the pain would pass, but that would have demeaned her grief. Besides, I couldn't imagine then what it would be like to lose someone so close to you.

I drove down to the old homestead a few days later. What remained of the house was buried under a blanket of crusted snow, but the stone dams were still in the creek as well as memories that resided there. The old man and Queen Anna had always seemed content with the life they had made. By contrast, my life was chaotic and unfocused and if I had a purpose, it had not yet revealed itself.

Chickerman's General Store had not changed, though there were houses at the four corners now, including an Arctic Cat snowmobile dealer and a place called Muggs' Cones, which was closed now and apparently catered solely to seasonal tourists. The idea of my home as stomping grounds for tourists made me shake my head.

Gus Chickerman was seated on his barrel. He stared out at me through thick glasses but did not seem to recognize me. My hair was much longer now and I had grown a beard since my trouble in the woods.

"How ya doin', Mister C.?"

He squinted, then smiled. "Bowie Rhodes?"

"Yes, sir."

He thundered toward the back. "Ruby, Bowie Rhodes is here."

Mrs. Chickerman came out behind a walker. She looked frail, her skin jaundiced. But she smiled warmly when she saw me.

"Roger Ranger died," I told them.

"It was in the paper," Mrs. C. said. "A terrible thing, all the violence in the world. We couldn't get up there. Are Lilly and her children all right?"

"They're trying to cope."

"We thought you were off over some ocean," Mr. C. said. "Pokin' your nose into other people's business. Your ma was like that, too," he added. "You get that from her."

"The place looks good," I said.

"It looks like what it is," Mr. C. said. "Old."

"We have tourists now," Mrs. C. said. "In the summer."

"We're quaint," Mr. C. said sarcastically. "A fella told us we were like a time capsule." He looked at me. "What's that mean, a time capsule?"

"Your hair's long," Mrs. C. said.

"They all got it long nowadays," Mr. C. said. "You come out from the back more often, you'd know that."

She made a face of disapproval. It reminded me of the faces Queen Anna fired at my old man.

"You still a newspaperman?" Mrs. C. asked.

"Between assignments," I said. "How's Raina?"

"Fine," Mrs. C. said. "Fine." Her tone suggested something different.

"It's funny, but a few years ago I though I saw her in the U.P. I called you about it. Remember?"

"She's a city woman now," Mr. C. said, looking past me.

I saw them exchange glances. "She moves around," Raina's father said evasively.

"We don't see her much," Mrs. C. said. "Because she's in the city." It had the ring of a rehearsed line.

I thought of the woman I saw that day with Buzz. I had no doubt it was Raina. I felt sad for the Chickermans. They seemed to have lost Raina too.

I had been staying with Lilly for nearly a month since the funeral. She needed a break and was invited by friends to a party. I volunteered to look after the kids. I built a fire outside and we bundled up and had s'mores and later I made popcorn inside and Roger Junior and the girls and I watched television and we all cuddled on the couch and fell asleep. I awakened to a soft tug on the shoulder and a test pattern on the TV. Lilly and I moved the kids to their beds. I was ready to turn in, but Lilly had been drinking and was feeling loquacious. I made coffee and told her about my visit with the Chickermans.

"I heard Raina went to some bluenose college out east," she said. "The Chickermans are funny people, Bowie. They're generous and friendly, but only so far. The store is their public face. I doubt anybody really knows anything about their private lives. I heard Daddy tell Queen Anna that Gus traveled a lot and would be gone not just for days, but sometimes for weeks, even months. Gus would just go off alone and if people asked where he was, Ruby would say it was just business and that would be the end of that."

This was news to me. As a kid it seemed that the Chickermans were always there and never even went on vacations, not even to see relatives. Raina never said anything about her father traveling.

"Were you ever in their house?" Lilly asked.

The house was attached to the store by a breezeway. There was also an apartment above the store.

"Sure," I said.

"Then you're the only one."

When I thought back, though, I couldn't actually remember being *in* the house. I had been on the porch and I thought in the kitchen, but the rest was a blank.

"The Chickermans were so friendly that you never noticed," Lilly said. "Roger told me he'd see Gus come out of Whirling Creek, way above our place, carrying his fishing gear. He was upstream where Daddy told us never to go. Once Roger and Bill Roquette set up for poachers." Roquette had been the local game warden when we were kids. "It was in the fall and after dark and they saw a light and waited. It was Gus. They scared the hell out of him and he swore at them in a language neither of them recognized. Then he said they should keep this quiet because Ruby didn't like him to be out in the river. Roger thought it was funny."

"I used to watch you and Roger," I told Lilly. "In his car."

She began to laugh. "I was a hot one," she said. "I miss being hot with Roger."

12

THERE was still no word from Yetter by early March and I was still living with Lilly and her kids. She was in pain but trying to hide it. She and the kids went off to see friends or had company in on a regular basis and I was pretty sure she was avoiding being alone.

I saw an AP piece in the *Detroit News* saying that UPI was having another bout of its periodic fiscal problems and that there were rumors and indications from "reliable sources" that we were up for sale. UPI's reputation for satisfying the public hunger for news was equaled by its peripatetic financial history. It irritated me that Yetter hadn't called, and whenever I called him he was "in a meeting." I called my bank to see if my February check had been deposited and it was there, easing my anxiety slightly.

Lilly came home from the grocery store with unexpected news.

"Raina's parents are dead." She seemed numb.

"What?"

"It's on the radio. They were killed in a fire at their store this morning."

I called down to the sheriff's department and asked for details.

"We don't give out that sort of information over the phone," a woman said brusquely. Bureaucratic indifference was endemic.

I drove down to Pinkville to check it out. A fire truck was still at the scene. A deputy stopped me up the road and I showed him my press card.

He was overweight, his face bluish red from exertion in the cold. "That ain't from here," he said.

"I'm Bowie Rhodes. My sister was married to Roger Ranger."

"No shit?" he said. "We were all sorry about Roger."

"The Chickermans are old friends."

"More like were," he said. "Sorry." He waved me on.

Some of the building still stood. Water was frozen in strange shapes on the ruins. The ground was thickly iced and slippery. Steam hissed. Water from high-pressure hoses hung in the air, an icy mist. It looked like an insane sculptor had been at work.

There was a state police panel truck parked near the ruins. It had MOBILE LAB painted in blue on the sides.

"Press," I told a fireman as I flashed my UPI ID. "What happened?"

"You'll have to talk to the chief," he said. His face was black with soot and there were icicles on his black helmet. His lips were blue.

The fire chief was Vince Vilardo, the brother of one of my father's friends. "Vince?" He stared at me through bloodshot eyes. "I'm Bowie Rhodes."

Vilardo nodded wearily.

"What happened?"

"The hell it looks like," the chief mumbled. "Goddamn fire. It was going like a sonuvábitch when we got here, but my boys did good. We almost strangled her, but the wind popped up and off she went and that was that. Ten, twenty minutes more and we'd-a had her flat on her back."

The ruins were still warm, the sun sinking. The mist darkened. Artificial spotlights were turned on. Only a few firemen remained and they wore black, shadows casting shadows in the eerie light. Cold crept into my legs. The Chickermans had always treated me well. I had seen a lot of carnage in my life and had learned how to turn off my emotions, but this was personal. My parents were gone, then Roger Ranger, now the Chickermans and their place. Piece by piece my past was being erased. I wondered how Raina would learn of this and knew I should call her, but all I knew was that she was in the "city." I felt guilty that I had let her slip so far away.

I asked Vilardo and some others about Raina, but nobody knew how to contact her. Vince told me that a Traverse City lawyer had called even before the news of the fire broke, saying he'd contact the survivor.

"What was his name?"

"Eubanks, I think."

"You know him?"

"Nope, and I never heard of him. You might want to call Maria Idly in T.C. She's my second cousin and works for the county prosecutor. If there's anything to be known about a local mouthpiece, she'd be the one to know it. She's in the book."

I drove up to Traverse City that evening, checked a phone book, and placed a call to Maria Idly from a pay phone. I apologized for calling outside business hours, told her I had talked to Vince and explained who I was and what I wanted. I asked her about Eubanks. She uttered a few noncommittal *uh-huhs* and asked me to meet her at ten the next morning at a Big Boy on the south edge of town. I got a room at a sleep-cheap, called Lilly, and arrived at the restaurant the next morning.

Maria Idly was short and a little on the hefty side, dressed in a dark suit and high heels. We both ordered coffee.

"I called my cousin last night," she said. "Vince described you pretty well."

"Did you think I was up to something?"

She laughed. "Hell, in my business I think *everybody's* up to something. Besides, I deal with reporters all the time. It never hurts to verify who you're talking to. In my line we trust nothing."

"You work for the prosecutor?"

She nodded. "His name's Carvelly and I'm his chief deputy, at least in title. If he ever retires, I'll try for his job, but people here may not be ready for a female prosecutor." She rolled her eyes. "Besides, Carvelly won't give me the nod unless I give him an incentive. We girls are just so soft."

I laughed. She didn't strike me as soft. "I've heard of Carvelly."

"You have?"

I said, "Karla Capo."

Idly looked surprised. "Karla? Hell of a gal. How do you know her?"

"I live in Grand Marais part of the time."

"I guess she finally got Roman to let go of her kids."

"Just."

"Old Quick Shot was really frosted. Damn shame—a man with all those natural attributes and none of it amounting to anything. He's good at making money and that's about it."

"Karla told me." This earned me a raised eyebrow and a sly smile.

"I won't bore you with tales of Michigan's Peyton Place. Most of it's meaningless," she said. "What do you want to know about Eubanks?"

"Who he is, what sort of practice he has. I grew up with the Chickermans' daughter, and Vince told me Eubanks called before the fire was public knowledge and said he'd notify their daughter. I guess that means he's the family's lawyer."

Maria Idly cocked her head. "If so, they'd be his first clients. Eubanks is a member of the state bar, but he doesn't belong to any local groups and I've never heard of him appearing in court."

"What're you trying to say?"

She raised her hands. "I'm not really sure. I just find it a tad curious that a lawyer who doesn't practice suddenly has a rural grocer for a client."

"Do you know Eubanks?"

"Only of him. Carvelly claims he's met him, but Carvelly was pretty closemouthed when I pushed him for details early this morning."

"Does anybody else around town know him?"

"Could be, but nobody I know. He has an office," she added. She took out a notepad and read me the number.

Here I go again, I thought.

I used the pay phone at the Big Boy to call Eubanks, but there was no answer. I checked the phone book, but there was no residential listing.

"Nobody there," I said, when I returned to the table. "And no home phone listing."

"This guy has a smell to him," she said.

"Meaning?"

"I don't know. Intuition, I guess, a nagging feeling that he isn't entirely what he seems to be. Carvelly doesn't much want to talk about him, which usually indicates the other person has clout and Carvelly thinks he's cultivating power. Usually he gossips about everyone. What will you do now?"

"Call him later today."

"If that doesn't work?"

"I'll visit his office."

"I like determination," she said. "If you need help, call. And say hi to Karla for me. That woman is a barrel of laughs."

I promised I would.

I went back to my room at the motel along the lakeshore and tried Eubanks again. No answer. Raina's folks were gone. I was going to make sure she knew what happened and find out what the hell she had been doing in the U.P. I was tired of her now-you-see-me, now-you-don't routine. I napped briefly, but awoke with an idea.

After another fruitless call to Eubanks, I called Father Buzz.

"What can I do you for?" he answered brightly.

"It's Bowie. You remember that woman who was alone in the cabin west of town? I was with you delivering groceries. She wasn't friendly."

"Bowie? Where are you?"

"BTB," I said. Yooperese for Below the Bridge. "Do you remember her?"

"Not really."

"You have to. It was a log house. The woman had a shotgun. Dark hair."

"*Shotguns.* I remember," he said.

"I need to know who she is."

Silence. "Are you on a toot?"

I wished I was. "This is important, Buzz."

"I never knew her name."

"You said she was renting."

"You have a helluva memory."

"Who owns the place? Who did they rent it to?"

"This will take a while," the priest said.

"I'll call you back in the morning. Eight?"

"Make it noon," he said. "I think the people who own the place live downstate. The assessor will have the owner's name."

"I need this, Buzz. It's important."

"Why?" he asked.

"I thought then she was somebody I knew. A girl I grew up with. Her parents just passed away and nobody seems to know where she is. It's important that I find her now. I know it's a long shot."

"Long shots are a priest's specialty," he said. "Be patient, my son."

I tried several more calls to Eubanks, had baked walleye at a place called the Cream Log and Five Eatery, and turned in for the night.

Buzz called the next morning at eight.

"Get it?"

"God seems to be smiling on us."

"Well?"

"The house is owned by an Ovid Merchant of Southfield, but he's never seen it. He bought it as an investment. He owns a lot of properties in the U.P., but he's an absentee landlord. A management company in Marquette handles the rentals, maintenance, the whole shebang. They're the people I talked to."

"I don't need a history of shipbuilding to recognize a white whale."

Buzz chuckled. "Melville did tend to run off at the mouth. The company says the place was rented to somebody named M. J. Key."

I stared at the phone. "What did you say?"

"M. J. Key. K-E-Y."

"I heard. Male or female?"

"Just M. J. The records don't show."

"Address?"

"None. Paid ahead, in cash. Are you in trouble?"

A shrink might have an opinion on that, I thought. M. J. Key? I couldn't believe it. Buzz thought God was smiling. It seemed more like a Bronx cheer to me. "I'm fine." Raina had used the name M. J. Key, or somebody by that name had rented the place for her. And someone named M. J. Key had bought Key's manuscript from Lockwood Bolt. Everything about Key was like a huge whirlpool.

"Are you sure?" I asked.

"You sound distinctly perturbed."

"Supremely confused is more to the point."

"The eternal human condition," Buzz said. "God will show you the way."

To a rubber room, I thought. "Can you have the company in Marquette mail a copy of the rental agreement to me?"

"At your sister's place?"

"Please." I gave him the address.

"Anything else?"

"That'll take care of it."

"Count on me," the priest said. "How's your sister?"

"She's doing as well as can be expected."

"Mourning and grief take time. Any word from UPI on your job?"

"They've gone mute."

"Don't worry," he said.

"I know, God will provide."

"Not for journalists," he said with a malicious chuckle. "I don't think he likes what scribes did to the Bible. Journalists are on their own. Frankly," he admitted, "we all are."

"I'll remember that."

"I'll tell everyone you called."

I called Eubanks after I talked to Buzz and got through. I told him I was a close friend of Raina's and wanted to talk to her.

"She's been informed," the lawyer said. He had a sandpaper voice and paused between words. He also had a faint accent but I couldn't place the nationality.

"Could I get her number? We're old friends. I'd like to help if I can."

"Everything has been taken care of," Eubanks said. "If, as you say, you are a friend, you would already have her number, wouldn't you? Good day, sir."

"How about you pass along my number and she can call me?"

My answer was a dial tone.

The Chickermans' obituary was in the *Traverse City Record-Eagle*. The obit traced their lives only from the time they arrived in the area. Just Raina was listed as kin. No address was given for her. There would be no services, no flowers or donations, end of write-up. I wasn't about to give up.

The lawyer had an office above a T-shirt shop with a special on shirts that read CHERRY FESTIVAL. I went up unannounced. It was a small, musty suite with high ceilings and distressed furniture. There was a decrepit receptionist with hair the color of tin. It was stacked in a beehive. A couple of curls had worked themselves loose.

"I need to see Eubanks."

She wore half glasses and stared over them. "For that, you'll need an appointment."

I walked past her into his office and stopped, my mouth agape. There was fly-fishing regalia everywhere. One wall held dozens of split-bamboo rods with sumac handpieces that shone. There were several sizes of willow creels in various shapes. Shadow boxes filled with flies. A wall of books. On a table there was a bullet-shaped glass minnow trap with C. F. ORVIS MAKER etched into the side. Everywhere I looked there were treasures, and the more I looked, the more I saw, until my eyes came to rest on a rectangular frame covered with glass. Inside it were three rows of three huge flies each, all white, each different, all of them pristine. The box looked very much like the one I had found and lost in the Natural Sciences Collection Room many years before. I wanted desperately to look at the back of the frame.

"Chase the trout?" a voice asked.

Eubanks was an old man with a bent back and a face spattered with liver spots.

"Now and then," I said.

"You would be Rhodes."

I did not apologize for barging in. "I want to talk to Raina Chickerman."

Eubanks studied me with a tight squint. "The thing about trout," he said, "is that some just aren't meant to be caught and chasing won't make it different. There are some people just like that as well."

"I need to talk to her."

He joined his hands in front of him. "Need's granite. Want's sand. Need stays put, centered and insistent. Want blows in and out, drifts between your toes. It takes a whole life to understand the difference. Most never do," he added. "You'd best leave Raina Chickerman alone, Mister Rhodes. Infatuation is a long road from commitment and granite's not sand."

"I saw her a while back in the U.P. near Grand Marais. She rented a house under the name of M. J. Key. Is that name familiar?"

"The trout writer."

"Why would she use that name?"

He said, "Don't chase what can't be caught, son."

I turned to the white fly displays and stared at them. "It's a fine room," I said.

Eubanks nodded.

"Are those snowflies?"

The old lawyer looked at the case for a long time before he spoke. "If you're meant to know, you'll know. Good day, Mister Rhodes. Please don't intrude again."

"Is that a threat?"

"I would never make a threat," he said, turning his back on me.

"I understand you called the fire department about handling the Chickermans' affairs *before* the fire was in the news. How could that happen?"

"Get out," he said, not bothering to look back at me.

Eubanks was a hard old man, raised in a generation that put great value on hard jaws and duty, and I knew there could be no argument, no wedge of logic that would move him off his course. I had been dismissed many times before and would be many times again, but Eubanks had cut me loose with the sure-handedness of a bomb maker. I mumbled an apology to the receptionist on my way out and walked numbly down to the street. I had but one image in my mind, the snowfly.

When I got outside, I lit a cigarette and tried to think. M. J. Key bought M. J. Key's manuscript from Bolt. Raina rented a house under the name of M. J. Key. Eubanks knew who the writer Key was and had a shadow box of snowflies. There was not enough to figure it all out, but it was all connected and eventually, I was going to put it all together.

I called Maria Idly at the prosecutor's office. "I met with Eubanks."

"And?"

"He basically told me to take a hike."

"Will you?"

"Not exactly."

She laughed abruptly. "What can I do to help?"

"I'd like to get a copy of the autopsy reports."

"I'm not sure I can do that."

"Can you read them and tell me what they say?"

"That I can do."

"There's something else. Vince told me that Eubanks called about taking care of the Chickermans' affairs before the fire was on the news. I'd like to know who tipped him off."

"You want to meet later for a drink?"

"Name the place."

"The Gander. Take M-22 north. You'll see it on the bay side. Nine okay?"

"Thanks, see you there."

Maria Idly was an hour late and looked exhausted. She ordered a double martini and drank it down in one long pull. "I couldn't get the reports.

The coroner said that the FBI came and took them. I called down to the federal prosecutor in Grand Rapids and he doesn't know anything about it. We went to law school together. He said it sounds to him like a witness protection deal of some kind. He said he'd nose around, but can't promise anything."

Now I was really disconcerted.

She said, "I called the cops. There's a detective there that I see sometimes." She looked to me for a reaction, but my mind was lost. "He said the chief announced that no foul play was suspected, but that the FBI would take care of the case."

"What the hell is going on?"

"I don't know," she said. "I'm getting another double. You want a hit?" I most certainly did. "My friend said that the cops in one county don't get called on fires in another county unless there is some sort of possibility of a spread. This time of year a fire isn't going anywhere. My friend thinks the chief got a call, but he doesn't know why."

"From Eubanks?"

"Yes, and very quickly thereafter from the FBI," she said. "It all seems connected."

We had another round of doubles and my head was reeling.

"I don't understand this," I confessed.

"Me neither," she said. "And my friend in Grand Rapids didn't sound too happy. I'm going to see if he can get anything on Eubanks. Somebody has to know something about the asshole."

I must've raised my eyebrows. She grunted "I guess I've got the bug now too. The thing is, I work for the government, but we have a lot of lawyers in this country and they all have secrets, especially the feds. I don't like all these games. If there's something to be learned about Eubanks, or his clients, I'm going to nail it down."

I decided Maria Idly would make a terrific prosecutor. I thanked her for her help and gave her Lilly's phone number.

"You headed back?"

"My sister lost her husband on Christmas morning. He was a cop. I've been gone long enough."

"The state trooper, Roger Ranger?"

I nodded.

"Good cop. How the hell does a cop get hit up here?"

There was no answer.

"I'll be in touch," she said.

13

YETTER finally called at the end of the month. There had been no word from Maria Idly. Yetter said, "It's a thirty, kid, the last take, end of chapter."

"I'm out?" Yetter's silence only served to fuel my suspicions. Although for months I had tried to imagine it, the reality of being jobless came as a shock. I didn't take it personally when companies laid off thousands, which was news, but this was me and although not news, it wasn't fair.

"Hold on to your trousers," he said. "This place is bloody. The personnel pukes say we're 'adjusting to optimum workforce parameters.' What the fuck does that *mean*? When the corporate suits take their flensing knives to the language, you know it's bad news. We had a personnel veep here once who kept confusing T. S. Eliot and Eliott Ness. I don't think these guys have birth certificates. They hatch from eggs in sewer scum."

"*My* job?" I said, trying to refocus him. Once Yetter got up his bile, he was tough to turn.

"Well, your days as a foreign correspondent are over, at least with this sorry outfit."

Before I could reply, he added, "Take a deep breath, kid. With apologies to aka Twain, the rumors of your professional death are greatly exaggerated. The main thing is to keep writing."

I had to sit down. "What the hell are you telling me? I'm canned?"

"Geez," he said. "Not yet. Not if I can help it."

I imagined my hands crushing his windpipe.

"You think I'd leave my star high and dry? You're my discovery, kid. I've got sweat equity in you. Have faith, for Chrissakes."

I had no words. I felt my body temperature rise, then plummet.

"You still throwing those silly-ass feathers at fish?"

Another U-turn on the boulevard of Yetter. "Wrong time of year." Where was he headed now?

"Bullshit. Gotta be the right time of year somewhere, am I right? You know, the equator flip-flop thing."

"Jesus Christ, get to the point."

"Here's the deal. There's this guy, Angus Wren. Heard of him?"

I had. Angus Wren was the Ernie Pyle of fishing writers. He wrote about factory workers and shoe salesmen and went with them to fish in the little places people without means always seem to find. He was the master of an invisible style. When he finished writing about someone, you knew the guy, and he did it with a vocabulary the average newspaper reader could understand. I had read Angus Wren's work since I was ten.

"You like all that feather-and-hook shit, right?"

I didn't answer.

"You've been picked to replace a legend, kid. You ought to be wetting your pants."

My mind was racing. Who had replaced Lou Gehrig on the Yankees? Legends were by definition irreplaceable. I tried to remain calm.

"Picked by whom?"

"Who do you think? *Me.*"

I started laughing. "You?"

"Well," he added, "there is one little detail."

I had tears in my eyes. Every place I turned, the legend of M. J. Key cropped up, and now Yetter wanted me to replace Angus Wren. One of us had rounded the bend and at the moment I was in no condition to say which one of us it was.

"What detail?" I couldn't stop laughing.

"A technicality," he said. "No big deal."

His shift in tone suggested otherwise. "What is it, Grady?"

"He wants to meet you," Yetter said.

"Angus Wren?"

"He wants to go fishing with you."

It sounded like Yetter was walking barefoot through broken blue Mason jars.

"Is the job mine or not?"

"Sure it's yours," he said. "I told you that, didn't I? He just wants to meet you and fish with you. You *do* know how to fish, right? You spent enough time dicking around with it."

He was talking fast now and suddenly I understood. "I have to pass muster, is that it?"

"It's a technicality," Yetter said. "Not to worry. It's a *t* to cross, an *i* to dot."

"You bastard."

"You want the job or not?"

"I want it," I admitted.

I thought I heard him exhale.

"Tucson, April first."

"You'll be there?"

He growled. "They got gila monstrosities out there."

"Gila *monsters.*"

"Don't split reptiles," he said. "And don't let me down."

"I thought the job was mine."

"Figure of speech," he said and hung up.

Replace Angus Wren? It was preposterous. When Lilly came in, I was laughing.

"Want to share the joke?"

I laughed even harder.

I called Maria Idly from Lilly's before I left for Tucson.

"Are you going to be at this number for a while?" she asked.

"Yep."

"Stay put. Give me ten minutes."

She called back from a pay phone. "Listen carefully. I am under orders to not inform you of the following, but you called me and in my book informing is reaching out, not just responding, so I am not breaking orders."

"You're walking a fine line."

"That's the law for you. Eubanks is a lawyer and a former fed, agency unknown. Chickerman was in some sort of new-identity program, details not specified. Eubanks was his keeper, is how it was put to me."

"A new identity for a criminal or a witness?"

"I don't know the answer, but my guess is that it's something else. Spooks, maybe. That intuition thing again. That's all I could get. My curiosity is buzzing like a cat's back in a lightning storm, but there's no way I can chase it as long as the county pays me. I need to tell you that I called Karla and she said you are one hell of a man. Until then I'd followed orders, but at that point I decided that if you called I'd lay out what I knew. Karla's a great judge of men."

"You mean their characters?"

She chuckled softly. "That too," she said.

I thanked her for her time.

"One other thing," she said. "Eubanks is gone."

"Dead?"

"No, he moved. It's like he split town. His office has been sold and he cleared out. I managed to find out where he lived using the phone company, and his house is empty too. I think that whatever this is all about, you spooked him."

Either that, I thought, or his work was done.

PART II

If the fool would persist in his folly, he would become wise.
—William Blake

14

THERE was no laughter and no talk as I walked through the terminal at Tucson. The air conditioning wasn't working and heat seemed to suck the life out of everyone, dry heat or not. I had never seen a photograph of Angus Wren. He had been old when I began reading him. And now? I had no idea and stood outside sweating in the sweltering spring heat, waiting for my ride.

An ancient Ford pickup rolled slowly past. When the brakes squeaked, I turned to look. A man about my age got out. He wore a dusty black cowboy hat and his jeans tucked into boots up to the bottom of his knees.

"Rhodes?"

"That's me."

He jerked a thumb toward the truck bed. "Gear goes there. You go up front with me."

As we drove away he said, "Bailey Wren."

"Son?"

"Nephew. My uncle didn't shoot boy bullets. My daddy's his brother. You puke in pickups?"

"Not so far."

He grinned. "There's a first time for everything."

We drove northwest for three hours across high desert and into some barren hills along what amounted to the suggestion of a trail. The Ford swayed and rocked and bounced and I bounced with it, banging my elbow, my knee, and my head. When we finally began a steep descent into a canyon, I saw the glint of water below and was relieved.

There were several houses in the narrow valley. They had tin roofs, no paint, and no grass. The dirt around them looked like it had been raked smooth. Bailey Wren dropped me at a small house. There was an old man seated on the stoop. He had white hair, cracked skin, a prominent Adam's apple, scrawny legs, feet pushed into faded black high-top sneakers, and no socks.

"Rhodes?" he said by way of greeting.

"Mister Wren?"

He smiled. "Call me Angus. Could you use a beer?"

I thanked him.

"Your friend Yetter sent me your stuff to read," he said. "Do you have to work hard at your writing?"

"No harder than most."

"Kidder," he said. "Let's talk straight, son. I don't expect anybody to replace me. Bully pulpit, Teddy Roosevelt said. This is like that. There are a lot of dudes and scam flashers in fishing. Flies attract money. Outside America it's a rich man's game, but here I always thought it should be a game for anybody who wants to try. I'm eighty-eight and I still fish nearly every day. This job's not about the Test or Patagonia, it's about right here. Some guy turns screws all day, goes home, does his chores, maybe gets a couple of hours a week to run off to his fishing hole. It's nothing fancy, nothing expensive. He works within his means and his limits. He loves his crick; takes care of it and follows the rules, just an everyday Joe who likes being outside and thinks an eight-inch brown is about the most beautiful thing in God's creation, even if it came from a hatchery. There's a heap of power in what we write. It draws people, but the ones we want aren't looking for fame. They just want to fish. Are you following me?"

"Yes, sir."

"That feller Yetter. He talks a lot."

I smiled and nodded.

"He's a city feller, but he thinks you're about the best thing since sliced bread. Says you head for rivers every chance you get. How many fish you catch last season?"

I had no idea.

"Biggest you ever caught?"

I showed him with my hands. "About like so."

"You kill fish?"

"When I'm hungry."

"You aren't real talkative," he said.

"You seem to fill up most of the space."

He grinned. "That I do, sonny. Are you a big eater?"

"I get by."

"I eat like a buzzard," he said. "Anytime, any place, any food. I've got all my functions and most of my teeth. I like my liquor the color of water, two packs of smokes a day, and a woman that squirms. You're not married."

"No, sir."

"That's a plus, if you ain't light in your boots. Not that I got a problem with that, but are you?"

"No."

He nodded and continued talking. "I always liked women," he said. "But most women can't stomach the trout bug or trout biz. I had four wives and they all tried, tried like the dickens, but they just couldn't deal with it. I've got me nine daughters and they all fish. Women're starting to do all the things men do. I think that's probably a good thing, but I'm also glad I grew up when I did. This job'll fill up your life if you let it. Take it from me, find a woman who wants the same things you want. Maybe you'll be luckier than me."

A woman came across the dust toward us. Her scuffed red boots kicked up little puffs. "All set," she said.

Angus said, "Hannah, meet Mister Rhodes. He can write like Shakespeare, but now we're gonna find out if he can fish like . . ."

"M. J. Key," I said.

Wren's head snapped sharply in my direction. I had the distinct impression I had just lost points. "Key don't set well with me," he said. "Damn headhunter."

The old man got up from the stoop. I heard his knees crack, but he took off at a fast clip and I had to hurry to keep up. Hannah fell in beside me.

"Trophy fishermen," she said to me. "Headhunters."

"New term," I said.

"Angus hates Key and glory hunters like him."

"I'll try to remember that." Key a trophy hunter? This had never occurred to me. Was Angus wrong, or was I mistaken?

The river that flowed beside the ranch was fast, its shores strewn with flat boulders with pastel tints. The rubber raft was yellow with a green board bottom and a huge orange hand rudder.

Hannah steered us through several bends and beached the raft on a gravel bar with fast green runs on either side. The old man walked down the left run and began casting. I had expected some conversation about the idiosyncrasies of the river and its fish, but he ignored me and after a couple of minutes of watching him, I tied on a green nymph called a Patrickson and flicked it into the tail of the green pool on the opposite side of the gravel bar. As the fly started to swing back to me, I lifted and was rewarded with a sharp strike. I pulled the line and lifted the rod to set it and the rainbow came out of the water and skidded away and sounded, but I knew it was caught. When I knelt to release the fish, I saw that Angus Wren was watching me.

It was one of those days when luck lived in my rod. I took three fish out of the first run, one from the second, another from the third, and three more from the fourth and the old man had none I had seen. He looked increasingly morose as Hannah took us to the next bend, which she declared his favorite. When we landed, he scrambled out and headed straight to the head of the pool, leaving me the tail—a breach of etiquette, but I didn't object. When I hit a large fish on my second cast the old man angrily threw his rod into the raft, got in, and yelped, "Get me the hell out of here." Off they went past me, Hannah giving me an apologetic look as she leaned on the rudder. What the hell, I thought, and started wading back upstream, taking fish steadily, wondering what Angus Wren's problem was.

It was well after dark when I got back to the ranch and there was no sign of the old man or Hannah or anybody else until I got to the cabin. Bailey Wren was sitting on the stoop and said, "I guess you'll be on your way." I had no idea what he'd heard, or how, but I gathered I had failed my audition.

Minutes later we were headed out of the valley and I didn't know whether to get angry or laugh so I stared into the darkness and tried to keep from breaking my teeth as we bottomed out.

Bailey let me off at a generic motel near a town with no sign. I threw my gear in the room and went looking for a drink. What I found was a bottle of tequila and I drank until it was gone and some part of my brain with it. Facing rejection is idiosyncratic.

I awoke to a room flooded with narrow shafts of red-orange light and Angus Wren sitting in a rickety chair beside my head, smoking a cigarette in an ivory holder.

"You always catch like that?"

"No." What day was this?

"Damn good thing. Half-dozen fellers like you could empty the world's rivers. Didja have yourself a dandy bender?"

My brain felt the size of a watermelon. "Tequila."

"Get the worm?"

"I think."

He grinned. "Gives me the shits."

I tried to sit up, but couldn't move. "What do you want and how did you get in?"

"I just walked on in. Your door was as open as a whore's legs. I came to apologize, which don't come easy. Nobody outfishes me on *my* water. What you did knocked me back. I couldn't fish for squat when I first started out. And the writing came even harder, and still does, but I worked like a dog at both of 'em. Then you come along, better at both than I'll ever be, and just a whippersnapper. I guess I threw myself a tantrum like when I was three. Didn't really understand till today, but my day's done and now it's your time. The job's yours, Rhodes, on one condition. We work together till next spring. Don't get this wrong, it's not a test, not that at all. I just thought I'd show you my ropes and we'll have us some fun. You'll do the job your way, but I'd like to be along one final season."

I did not expect an apology, much less to get the job. "Guess I went off half cocked, too."

Angus Wren grinned. "Hot fish in a cold river can make any man crazy. You want a lift out to the ranch?"

"I think I'd best stay here and heal."

He nodded solemnly. "There's no substitute for common sense. Hannah will fetch you in the morning."

He got up slowly and ambled to the door. "Want some advice?"

I tried to nod.

"In bed and on the river, eight inches is all that counts, son. Any more is pure wastage."

I awoke the next morning tired and without a headache, but my limbs were heavy. The bathtub had rough-textured turquoise and pink plastic footprints glued on the bottom. The water was rusty and came out in a trickle; it left my skin slippery even before I used soap, which was mostly pumice and peeled off a layer of skin. The towels were tiny and threadbare and did not wrap all the way around. When I walked into the bedroom, the door was open again and Hannah Wren was sitting where her father had sat twenty-four hours before.

"Um," she said.

"Don't they teach people around here to knock?"

"And miss the sights?" she said.

"Enjoy," I said, removing the towel. I was in no mood for modesty.

"I surely am, cowboy," Hannah said with a hoked-up twang. "Glad to hear you got the job. I've never seen my father the way he was on the river the other night."

"He's been Angus Wren a long time," I said as I pulled on my jeans.

She smiled and nodded. "He dearly loves his work."

"Who wouldn't?"

"Guess you'll get the opportunity to know. What fly were you using? I saw green."

"It's called a Patrickson."

"Does it make a buzz sound or do you drag it over the top of the water?"

"You put it in the right spot and let it do the job."

Hannah grunted. "You tie it yourself?"

"Got it in England."

"But you do tie?"

"No. I buy them where I am. I'd rather spend my time on the water."

"Just like Angus," she said. "Do you collect?"

"Nope."

"Angus has a thing for whites."

I perked up. "White flies?"

"He's got a room full of them. Big fluffy things, in double-oughts and ones. I used to sneak in to look. I asked him once what they were for. He said, 'Fools.' He put extra locks on after that."

I remained silent. White flies. Again.

"My jeep's outside," she said. "Ready when you are."

She watched me finish dressing, and when I had gathered my stuff we drove out to the ranch. She was thirty-four, Wren's youngest child by his fourth wife. Hannah had an ex-husband, no children, a degree in fish biology from Arizona State, and a daughter's unswerving admiration for a legendary father.

"Angus showed me your writing," she said as we drove along. "Don't you think fishing stuff will be a little tame for you?"

"We'll see," I told her.

"Are you always so frank?"

"It tends to be situational."

She smiled. "I doubt that."

Lunch was all business. Technically I would be an employee of Angus Wren Enterprises (AWE), not UPI, which only contracted for the column. Yet another Yetter prevarication. AWE included a print and publishing business, a video production company, two lines of trout-fishing tackle, including a famous red spoon called the Wren Wobbler, a half-dozen fly-shop franchises in Colorado, Utah, New Mexico, and Arizona, and a small ad agency in Phoenix. AWE had twenty employees, all of them Wren's relatives and offspring. The other businesses employed about a hundred more. I would be employed by Angus Wren Adventures, a new unit.

I could write under my own name or another, if I wanted it that way, but until Angus actually retired the column would be called "Angus Wren with . . ." Line drawings of both of us would appear on the column's header. The salary was more than I was making at UPI, and the operating budget to cover our travel expenses was generous. Income was based on the number of subscribing papers. Angus would not allow himself to be bought by the big fishing enterprises. His focus, our focus, was the little guy, which meant we covered our own expenses and the little guys' too when that was necessary.

After lunch, we spent the afternoon going through his files. He had several Rolodexes and card files, all full. Story ideas were kept on three-by-five cards tacked to a cork wall. Our contract called for forty-two columns a year. What we wrote about was our business. The contract was renewable annually. All we had to do was to keep our readership, which UPI tracked with more interest than its own fiscal house. One-off assignments were negotiated separately. My AWE contract did not preclude me from taking freelance assignments from magazines and newspapers. I liked the setup.

In the late afternoon we went out to the verandah and had cold beer. Angus said, "You know Ray Kroc?"

"Of him." He had invented McDonald's.

"Ol' Ray says, 'Feed the rich and die poor. Feed the poor and die rich.' "

I understood. Angus was talking about our audience.

"You can live where you want," Angus said. "The job will take you all over hell and back and we can meet on location. We can put you up right here for as long as you want, or go on your own. It's your choice. Shall we wet a line tonight?"

"You bet."

I was even hotter this night than our first time, but now Angus was smiling and full of questions. "Why'd you put the fly over there?"

"Felt like a fish," I said.

He cackled happily. "You *do* have the gift."

The next morning I worked my way though story ideas and made some telephone calls and roughed out a schedule.

Yetter called just before lunch. "So?"

"I got the job."

"Told you."

"It's not with UPI."

"What's your beef? I hear he's a quirky old coot."

"He doesn't bullshit people."

"That hurts."

"I guess I should say thanks."

"Damn right you should. Stay in touch, kid."

I remained at the ranch for three weeks, fishing every evening with Angus and Hannah and other members of the clan until one cool afternoon it was just Hannah and me.

"Just us today?"

"Dad's on his way to Denver. We don't have to fish," she added.

"We're here," I said.

She said, "Great. Want to see some new water?"

Few trout chasers could pass up such an offer. "You're the captain."

We floated several miles to where another stream dumped into the river, and we dragged the raft onto the stony shore. The feeder came down a canyon with sheer sandstone walls, leaving only a crack of sky above. The water was as clear as crystal. The current moved but not all that fast. A quarter mile up the canyon there was a one-room shack. Inside were stacked bunks, a wood-stove, kerosene lanterns, shelves with cans, some fishing gear, and a two-way radio with a small gas-powered generator, which Hannah cranked up.

"Base, this is Hannah."

"Base here." The base was the ranch.

"Bowie and I are at Rathead's. We'll take the raft down to Carlysle's Bridge tomorrow afternoon. Can you fetch us there?"

"Three o'clock?" the voice at the base asked.

"That should work," Hannah said.

"Seen Rathead?" the voice asked.

"Not yet," Hannah said.

"Who's Rathead?" I asked when she had finished.

"You'll see," she said mischievously. "Let's lasso us some trouts, cowboy," she added with a grin.

We did not have to go far. A short walk above the shack, the stream cut along the base of the cliff. There was a run close to two hundred yards long.

"Nice," I said.

"And how," she said, stripping line and loading her rod for her first cast.

We fished for nearly three hours, into the darkness. The fish were small, ten to twelve inches, but thick bodied and strong. They were bright gold with orange and black spots and fought hard and long.

"Gilas," she said when she caught the first one. "Pure strain. Left in only three or four places. And here, which even the Fisheries people don't know about."

The fish weren't finicky, but neither did they come easily to the net. They seemed hungry for anything and everything, but our casts had to land on top of them or they let the flies pass. There was no vegetation along our shore or in the water. In Michigan such fish would never have been caught. Too little cover. They would've come out only at night.

"Beautiful," Hannah said, releasing a perky twelve-incher.

"It looks barren," I said.

"Looks can be deceivin', cowboy."

I laughed.

"It has good temp, steady year-round inflow from lots of springs, the right pH, enough food, and there's great cover under the ledge so the birds can't get at them. Fish are where you find them," she said.

"Thank you, Professor."

"You're quoit welcome, I'm shu-ah," she said with a mock accent and a laugh.

I liked watching her. She handled the rod with a minimum of effort and had lightning reflexes and soft hands. She also filled out her waders in a memorable fashion and her long brown hair hung loose and free.

We were both tired when we decided to call it quits after nightfall. We did not talk during our walk back up to the shack. It was clear that we both enjoyed being ourselves together and we were content. There was no need for conversation. It felt like a friendship in the making.

But when we neared the shack she said, "You'd better wait out here."

I heard her open the door. A shriek shattered the silence and I ran for the shack and found her in the doorway with a flashlight.

She was mumbling. "God dang you, Rathead. You sneaky little *bitch*."

"What was *that?*"

"Wait," she said, blocking my way with her arm. "Rat, it's me, Hannah."

I tried to see past her.

"There," she said, steadying the light.

I saw two tiny green eyes. A throaty growl sent a chill up my spine.

"She's mostly show," Hannah said. "Let me get a light on."

Hannah went inside, lit two lanterns, and wicked them up. The room glowed yellow. The eyes were gone.

"What was it?"

Hannah held her hand out to me. "Come on." She took my hand firmly and said, "Be still and don't move."

Something brushed firmly against the back of my leg.

"Steady," Hannah whispered.

The thing pressed against me again, growled low, and sidled between us.

The animal was a foot high and two feet long, not counting a two-foot-long tail. It had a tiny conical head with triangular ears on a long neck. The body was thick with short fur marked with spots and smudges of stripes.

"What is it?"

"Rathead, meet Bowie."

"Jesus," I said.

"She's something, isn't she?"

"Is 'something' a species?"

Hannah laughed and Rathead hissed menacingly and leapt effortlessly to the top bunk where she stood staring down at me, ready to pounce.

"Cat?" I asked.

"Mostly," Hannah said. "The Apache called them devil cats. Officially they don't exist."

"Extinct?"

"Rumored, but unproven. She fits with the gilas, I think, things that cling to life where they aren't supposed to be and science says isn't possible."

The creature extended a paw and flashed her long claws.

"Strangers make her edgy," Hannah said.

"The feeling's mutual," I said.

"Be glad she's here. When she's around, there're no snakes, no scorpions, no mice, no rats, and no gila monsters."

The animal growled and stared.

"She's fine now. She thinks this is her place. She's territorial and typically female," Hannah added.

"It's hers, if she wants my vote."

"Let's rustle up some grub," she said.

"I love cowgirl talk."

"You'd better hope that between you and me, you can cook. Angus didn't push us anywhere except toward rivers."

"We'll make out," I said.

She laughed. "We just might, cowboy. We just might."

But we didn't. Instead we talked almost all night about everything and anything. Her marriage, she said, had been a "dumb-ass" mistake. She had married a "pretty boy," but beauty was only skin deep and there wasn't much inside him and what was inside was only interested in his needs and money.

"Figured I'd better divorce him before I killed him."

We didn't sleep much. Rathead growled and purred contentedly from the top mattress on the bunk bed across the room. I imagined her saying, "Anything is possible." My Lurp pals from Vietnam would understand that.

It was a memorable start to a new phase of my life. Lessons had been learned as they are always learned, and observations made as they are always made, all of it sinking quietly into that primordial swamp called the subconsciousness, there to meld and perhaps to rise as something new.

15

MUNCHHAUSEN Sink was less than a hundred yards across, a hole filled with black water inside the Cincinnati city limits, a curious wet spot in the center of Floating Rose Salvage, a twenty-acre compound piled with two-foot rust cubes that had once been Volkswagens and Pintos. Our host was Parley Finger, who operated the compactors that rendered discarded automotive produce into dense steel blocks. There was a trail through the mounds, but only our intrepid guide could see the way. It was Independence Day and Mr. Finger promised we'd have the best junk-yard trout fishing we'd ever known. We went in before sundown because after dark, we'd risk breaking a leg on the trail, our host said.

On the water's edge cubes of steel had been assembled into benches and draped with army-surplus tarps. Finger put long-necked beers into a metal milk basket and lowered the basket into the dark water. He built a small fire in a trash barrel with a grate on top, filled a huge pot with water, which he set to boil, and threw some other ingredients into another cast-iron black pot.

"Sun's gotta get below the mounds," he said, taking a seat.

Angus and I unsheathed and assembled our eight-foot four-weights and slid the reels into place.

"These are sorta like them English rules," Parley Finger said. "Dry flies to rising fish and no damn priests. I run a sustainable fishery here."

Priests were wooden clubs used to kill large fish, a form of last rites.

The sun hung on for a long time. Angus dozed and snored evenly in the lingering heat.

Parley Finger watched his pots and when the water boiled, he dumped in spaghetti. "Cincinnati specialty," he explained. "Spaghetti and chili. Ain't he kinda old?" our host asked with a nod toward Angus.

"He gets younger when the fish rise."

Parley Finger nodded. "Ain't that the truth. Johnny Bench come here once, him and that Pete Rose, but Ol' Charlie Hustle, he can't sit long. Never caught a thing and the next day Pete went oh-fers and swore off fishin' for-ever. There was a city councilman come over once, diddled his administrative assistant over there." He pointed. "It was night and dark, could see the stars on the water, and she squealed all the time he was pokin' her. No fish that night, neither."

There were lessons in the stories, I assumed, but they weren't immediately apparent.

When the sun was low enough, Parley Finger turned his grimy baseball cap backward and picked up his own fly rod. "Twelve-foot leaders, fine as hair. My trout are partial to teensy skeeters."

I tied a size twenty mosquito on my line and nudged Angus, whose eyes fluttered. "What'd I get?"

I laughed at him. "Forty winks. Put on a mosquito." At age eighty-eight he could tie on a small fly in near-darkness and do it in a wink.

We were ready, but no fish rose. The sky went from blue to lavender to pale blue to gray to black.

"Watch for rings," Parley Finger said. "They come up quieter than daydreams."

Two hours passed. No rises. I dug a thermos out of my day pack and poured coffee for Angus. "Nothing," I said.

"Patience," Angus said. "Man like this wouldn't bring us if there wasn't something. Learn to trust people, son. Enjoy the stars."

Silence virtually in the middle of the city. The steel rubble blocked sound or absorbed it.

Parley Finger made his way around the pool of stars at our feet. "Soon," he whispered when he passed us.

Then it began.

Soft rises.

Whisper sips.

Rings expanding, crossing others. Stars jumped on the mirror, changing shapes, moving inward, shimmering, retreating, dancing.

Parley Finger squatted and patted his hat. "Every man for hisself," he called over to us.

I watched him make a short roll cast. There was a small splash. His pole bent and stayed that way. I heard the drag clicking like an angry cicada, watched him strip it in, heard him crank, heard the line go out again. Five minutes turned to twenty. Angus poked me. "What's taking him so long?"

"Big fish maybe?"

"In this spitwad?"

After another fifteen minutes Parley knelt at the water's edge, dipped his hand into the stars, and stood up.

"What was it?" Angus called across.

"What we come here for, a fish," our host said. He sat down. "Your turn."

Fish were still rising.

"Age before youth," I told Angus.

"Can you swim, sonny?"

We both laughed, but he stepped up, stripped out some line, and threw a short cast. The fly landed without a trace. Then a plop. Angus set the hook. The little rod arched.

"Jesus H.," he said. His reel clacked and screeched. "Jesus H.," he said again.

I sat down and lit a cigarette. Thirty minutes passed. "My arm may fall plumb off," Angus said through gritted teeth. I had fished with him enough by then to know he wouldn't quit. It was more than forty minutes before the fish gave in. We both knelt. I had a penlight in my shirt pocket and aimed the beam into the water.

"Horse," Angus said.

It was more than two feet long with shoulders as wide as the back of my fist. I caught the fish's tail and turned it on its side. "Brown."

"Female," Angus said. "Look at her belly. Weight?"

"Seven, eight, maybe more."

"Jesus H. This magnificent creature, from a spitwad in an Ohio dump."

When the fish swam away, Angus sank heavily beside me. There were more ripples on the surface.

"Thick with them," Angus said. "Horses."

My fish wasn't quite as large as his, but it hit just as various fireworks exploded around the city, splashing our pond with reflected color.

We stayed at it into the morning and when the stars went away and the eastern sky showed milky gray, the fish stopped and the water glassed over and we trekked stiff-legged back through the rust hills to Parley's truck.

We had coffee in his filthy workshop. "Whaddya think?" our host asked.

"We can't write it," I said.

"I thought that was the idea."

"If we write it, somebody will figure it out, and pretty soon you'll have people all over the place."

"Probably right," Parley Finger said. "At least you fellas had some good fishin'."

"Where'd these fish come from?" Angus asked.

"Brood stock come down from Wisconsin. They was to close a hatchery up there. I had this pal and he got me some. I studied up, got the temperature just right, alkalinity, you name it. Perfect."

"How old?" This from Angus.

"Some big mamas pushing twenty," Parley Finger said.

Angus blinked. "Are you sure?"

"I oughtta be. I put 'em here myself."

On the way to the airport Angus was uncommunicative. We flew coach, and each had a beer.

"Twenty years," he said, fumbling with a pack of beer nuts. "Twice the age what most books and science say."

"Controlled conditions. No stress."

"Still," he said. "That's one of the things about trout. About the time you think you know it all and have seen it all, you see something else and the whole damn shebang gets discombobulated. Trout aren't supposed to live that long, junkyard nirvana or not."

"You've seen."

"Sometimes seeing ain't enough for believing. What's the biggest brown you've ever seen?"

"Twenty-eight pounds. Hanging on the wall of a fish market in northern Michigan."

"Lake Michigan fish?"

"Yep."

"Not twenty years old, though. Ten max. Big lake, unlimited chow. Big water grows big fish. Small water, lives and fish are shorter. Nature's way, son."

"They've taken bigger in the White River."

"Big, deep water. Rule holds. Eight, ten years. Odd one might go a bit older. Genes and habitat set the limits. Hard ceilings."

We were silent for a moment.

"Rathead," I said.

Angus stared at me.

"Hannah showed me. We only know what we know. We don't know what we don't know."

"I were you," he said, "I'd stay off the road of what we don't know."

"Snowflies?" I asked.

"Think I'll grab some shut-eye," he said, abruptly ending the conversation.

We flew to Minneapolis, where we took a boat up the Mississippi and caught small rainbows in a deep river hole using canned corn kernels.

From Minneapolis it was on to South Dakota, where we fished with a mother and daughter using nymphs made of old pantyhose.

In Elko, Nevada, we visited a sporting ranch where hookers had built a trout pond and fished between johns. Some customers were there only to fish.

In Merced, California, we caught small cutthroats from a large ditch that ran through fields of produce. A man named Jesus was our guide. His wife and five kids wintered in Texas and summered in California and he made fly rods out of small willows glued together and taught his kids about hatches. They lived in a trailer and worked migrant camps. Jesus made flies out of those materials he could get, cheap and easy stuff from ducks, chicks, songbirds, yarns, threads. They were works of art. The column I wrote about him helped him launch a mail-order business, which is now run by his sons.

I called Grand Marais from Fresno and talked to Fred Ciz. The club was going well. Karla Capo was seeing a dentist from Munising. Father Buzz had made his way through a bout of pneumonia, but was out and about again. Janey Pelkinnen was doing a "bang-up" job managing the club. Fred said they all wanted to know when I was coming home, but the best I could say was not soon. *Home:* I was taken by surprise by the emotions the word provoked.

Hannah met Angus and me in Tucson. It was hot beyond words and she was wearing a halter top, gauze skirt, and gold sandals.

"You go out in public like that?" Angus asked her.

"Daddy, I went butt-naked on a beach down the Baja one time," she said. "I like being looked at."

"I didn't hear that," he said, opening the tailgate of the jeep to stash his gear.

"You heard." She planted a kiss on my cheek and patted my left buttock. "How was the trip?"

"Exhausting," I said. "I don't know how he does it and I'm not even half his age."

"It's because he can sleep between two thoughts," she said.

Which Angus promptly did before we were out of short-term parking. "I rest my case," she said. "How long are you back?"

"A week, give or take."

I spent the first three days catching up, writing columns. Yetter called. "Great stuff, migrant making flies outta horsefeathers."

I laughed.

"See, I told you this would work out."

"You never said that."

"But I knew it. You okay?"

"Terrific."

"That's what I like to hear."

Angus read the stories and was a solid editor. Hannah was gone, guiding. The days were unbearably hot, the nights cool.

Hannah returned on Thursday. We ate steaks with Angus, then the two of us retired to the porch with gin and tonics.

"Got a lake I'd like to show you," she said. "Spend the night?"

"Fish?"

"That too," she said with a come-hither grin. She liked to flirt and I liked it too.

Ten-Glass Lake was four hours northeast of the ranch, deep into a small mountain range. We parked at a forest service line shack in a saddle at seven thousand feet and hiked a thousand feet or more down to the lake. It was horseshoe shaped and small, bent around a huge, gently tapered black rock outcrop. There were small, gnarled Ponderosas around the shore and a lot of timber under the clear water.

"Should've brought tubes," I said.

"Don't need them."

We had nine-foot six-weight rods.

"Dries?" I asked.

"I've never seen a hatch here," she said. "Try streamers and short leaders. Two or three feet long, and no longer. Work the outer edge of the timber."

"For what?"

"You'll see."

On new water it made sense to first watch somebody else. I sat down, but Hannah shook a finger. "No way, cowboy. This is just for you."

I made several casts and stripped in the retrieve. Nothing moved. "Are you sure there's fish in here?"

"There's fish, all right. The question is, can *you* catch them?"

"What is this, a competition?"

"Not between us," she said, smiling.

I went back to work but still got no strikes, not even a follow. I walked back to Hannah to change flies.

"Your fly is fine. They'll hit any streamer."

"Ghost trout?" I said.

"They're all ghosts if you can't figure them out."

"You're a fountain of information."

"You're supposed to be the expert."

After two more hours, I still did not have a hit. I had tried several places. "I surrender," I said.

Hannah grinned. "Varying your retrieve?"

I had done everything I could think of. "Yep."

"Do something you've never done before."

"You mean with the fish?"

She shook her head. "Maybe you gotta earn your way, cowboy."

"This isn't a lot of laughs."

" 'Course not. It's work."

Do something I had never done before? I cast out, let the line carry the fly to the bottom, and let it lie. After a few seconds, I gave the tiniest twitch on the line, just enough to make the fly move a fraction forward and up. I did this every few seconds with no results. Then I stood and retrieved the fly with a series of bounces, like a bass jig. Still no takes. I let the line sink to different depths on the next few casts and pulled the fly back quickly. Still nothing.

"You're getting there," Hannah said from behind me. I ignored her. She had said streamers, meaning we wanted to mimic minnows. She had said to work the outer edge of the timber. I studied the water. The lake became dark where it dropped off at the edge of the sunken trees. The fish, if there were any—and at that point I had no reason to believe there were—had shown no interest at any depth or retrieve speed. I walked along the edge of the lake, turning over stones, lifting drowned timber and rocks. Nothing. No insects, no crustaceans. I waded in the shallows looking for minnows. None in sight. From the other side of the lake I saw Hannah put down a large towel and lie down.

"Got one," I called over to her.

"Liar," she answered.

By the time I got to her she had cream on her nose to keep the sun off.

"Frustrated?" she asked. "The fish are there, Bowie. I promise. What haven't you tried?"

"Dynamite."

She stuck her tongue out at me. "Spoilsport."

I tried to think. Most fish struck for food and out of anger or aggressiveness. Bass fishermen sometimes pulled their lures quickly across the surface, what they called buzzing. You could do this with a caddisfly to make it look like an emerger with a problem as well. But bass lures were mostly downsized to look like minnows and other small fish and would no way look like an insect. Why a small fish would skitter across the surface was beyond me. I knew that bluefish would circle baits and drive them in schools onto sandy beaches to escape. But here in a mountain lake? A trout wasn't a bluefish. Could I buzz a streamer? More important, why would I?

I loaded the rod and shot the line no more than twenty feet out and started hauling almost before the streamer landed, and the water almost immediately turned into a boil. I felt several bumps and raw flashes of bright red, but nothing took.

"Damn," I said.

Hannah was beside me, talking calmly. "Make a longer cast," she said. "They need time to track it and line it up."

I made the cast and after the fly traveled ten feet I had a fish, an arm-long slab of muscle that came out of the water and skipped along on its tail, angrily and desperately shaking its head before it sounded. It was a big fish and when it went airborne I lowered the tip to provide slack, and when I felt the weight again I pulled the tip sideways and buried the hook deeper and the fish began to take line, but I knew I had it, and if the leader and my knots held, it was only a matter of time.

When the fish was finally in the net, I could only stare at it. The head was dark green, the body scarlet. No markings. There was little doubt it was a trout, but what kind?

"It's a red," Hannah said.

I let it go and we sat on her towel.

"Weird," I said.

"A fisheries guy showed Dad this place a long time ago. They have no idea where these trout came from, or even what they are. There's a small team at Arizona State studying them. There may be more lakes with them, but they only hit streamers the way you fished them. The biologists can't explain any of it."

"But they *are* here."

"Exactly, and you figured it out first time. Dad came here twenty times before he solved it."

"I had help," I said. "Why did you bring me here?"

"Because I wanted you to see this. There are a lot of places with fish that nobody can catch. There are a lot of fish living in small, delicate habitats that nobody knows about. Freaks of nature, maybe. Evolutionary left-overs. Dad says any fish can be caught if the time is right and you know what you're doing. Dad says you have the gift. I guess I wanted to see that for myself."

"There's no gift, just luck."

"Real cowboys make their own luck," Hannah said. "You thought your way through the problem, step by step. Dad's job let him see a lot of remarkable things. It will do the same for you. Dad told me about Cincinnati. He was real proud of you. He says you understand how precious all this is. He says you understand the responsibility. I think he can retire now and be happy."

"What're you trying to say, Hannah?"

"There's more of this kind of thing than most people can imagine. For the few that know, it can become a disease."

"M. J. Key," I said.

She poked my chest. "You're purty quick, cowboy. Key had the gift, but he couldn't control it."

I thought of Fireheart.

"How do you know this?"

"Dad told me about Key."

"He knew Key?"

"I don't know."

"Key was a headhunter."

"Exactly. He made sure people knew what he was after and what he got."

"But he also made a lot of important contributions to the sport."

"Early on, yes, he did."

"Did Angus know Key?" I asked again.

"I honestly don't know, Bowie," she said. "Logically, I'd say no. Key must've been dead before Dad could've known him."

"But you're not sure."

She shook her head. "Maybe there never was an M. J. Key," she said.

"And maybe he's immortal," I said, making a joke.

She smiled, but her tone was serious. "Some people believe that. They say he gave his soul to the devil, that he would live until he got whatever it was that he was after. Lotta hogwash, I'd say, but there's no doubt there's an aura around his name. I guess people need their gods," she added. "Large and small, real and imagined, and they always get the gods they deserve."

Darkness fell as we climbed back to the line shack. We spent the night while wolves barked and howled outside and I wondered if their voices were intended for me.

16

ANGUS had a stroke in late August. He was at the ranch and had gotten up in the middle of the night to take a leak and, instead of going into the bathroom, had wandered onto the front porch. A niece found him the next morning at the foot of the steps, still clutching his penis. Hannah called me in Crow Loop, Nebraska, where I was interviewing an alfalfa farmer who had built an eight-foot-deep trout pond in his tavern. I drove to Omaha to catch a flight, but there were thunderstorms all across the Great Plains and air traffic control centers were holding all flights. The terminal was overrun with angry passengers and surly airline employees and I did not get out until the next morning.

Hannah met me at the airport in Tucson. "How is he?" I asked.

"In a coma," she said. Her eyes were red and puffy.

The doctor looked younger than me. "This is normal," he said. It struck me that experts of the abnormal always lost perspective. "These things tend to resolve themselves in forty-eight to seventy-two hours," he added.

"Resolve *themselves?*" If so, why did we need a doctor?

He nodded. "One way or the other. Our options are limited. His body and God will decide the outcome." He checked his watch. I wondered if he had a tee time. If the doctor required the help of God, Angus was doomed.

Angus came out of his coma at four-seventeen the next morning. He tore away his tubes and sat up on the side of the bed. A nurse's aide was in the room. The rest of us were asleep in the lounge.

"Sir," the aide said.

Angus pulled up his dressing gown and fumbled with his testicles. "You wanna see a big one?"

The aide was thirty and single, a Jehovah's Witness from Lubbock. All she could do was stare and begin quaking.

"Dammit, I mean trout!" Angus said. "*Big* goddamn trout."

"I'm calling the doctor."

"Snowfly!" Angus shouted, raising a fist. "The devil's, the devil's . . ."

By the time we saw him he was under a sheet. The aide's account was relayed through an intermediary.

His fourth ex-wife, Hannah's mother, was with us. "Fish," she said disgustedly after hearing the account. "At the end, on the threshold of God and eternity, he was still thinking about those damn *fish!*" Disgust (or disappointment?) aside, she cried hard. I remembered the same anger in the red-haired woman in her Cadillac many years before.

Angus was cremated and the crowd at his funeral was immense, despite the difficulty of getting to the place. There were notables from every walk of life, but more impressive were the hundreds of regular people from all over America, many of them paying tribute to Angus by wearing fishing vests and waders. I wrote his obituary. The lead went this way. "Angus Wren spent his life chasing trout in unlikely places and taught us that fishing was about people, not fish. At his funeral, former Supreme Court justice Brennan said that if God was not a trout fisherman, he soon will be."

Schmaltz, but I cried when I wrote it.

That night Hannah and I sat by the river and drank a six-pack of her father's favorite beer. The rest of the family had decided to build a memorial on that spot.

"That isn't what he'd want," Hannah said.

"I'm with you," I told her.

She asked, "All the way?"

"Press on."

We went through the main house into a little annex. The door had six locks on it. Hannah went and got a crowbar and snapped the locks off like they were paper and glue.

When we stepped inside, she flicked on the light and my jaw dropped. There were hundreds of immense white flies, in shadow boxes, hanging from nails on beams, in jars, in boxes. It looked like it had snowed in the room.

"This is unbelievable," I said.

"He hated all Key stood for and I think this was his way of trying to keep people from following his big-fish ways."

I didn't follow.

"If Dad saw white flies in a shop or found somebody who tied 'em, he bought every last one of 'em, and put 'em here. I'm sure he tied a lot of these on his own. He locked them up to remove temptation."

"He told you this?"

"No, I sort of figured it out. I think he'd want us to get rid of them all."

"Are you sure?"

She put her arms around my neck and rested her head on my chest. "I'm not sure of anything." She cried quietly.

We ended up stuffing the flies into boxes and paper bags, took the urn with his ashes, loaded the raft in silence, and ran downriver. The sun was rising as we walked up the canyon. I made several trips to get all the flies, then dug a hole behind the shack and dumped them all in, covered them with dirt, and burned the boxes and bags in the potbelly stove in the cabin. I felt like I had finally buried something that had given me nothing but frustration for so much of my life.

When the disposal was done, Hannah put the urn beside the river. We sat together and watched the water.

"We'll wait till the gilas rise," Hannah said.

I saw Rathead come down from the shadows of the rock. She advanced cautiously to the urn, sniffed at it, and lay down, curling herself around it.

When the first fish rose, Hannah took the urn and poured the ashes into the clear green creek. Rathead stood beside her. When it was empty, Hannah threw the urn into the water. It hardly made a splash. Rathead waded into the river and slapped her head against the water several times. I put my arms around Hannah and we stood there like that for a long time and that night we slept in the same bunk, with our clothes on, entwined with each other, friends, not lovers.

I had a schedule to keep and convinced myself Angus would want it that way.

At the airport in Tucson I found three snowflies stuffed in my briefcase. They were in waxed paper with a note taped to the package. "Just in case!" the note said. I laughed out loud and wondered if she'd kept a few for herself.

While I was in Bend, Oregon, a few weeks later, I read in the paper that a strange catlike animal had been shot by a prospector in Arizona, but the corpse had disappeared and he could not prove his claim.

Two weeks later I was in Five Jills, Colorado, and got a telegram from a lawyer informing me that my contract was terminated. I called Hannah from a town called Star Range.

"What's going on?"

"Coup," she said. "I tried to call you. The whole family's fighting over Dad's little empire. The will's being contested. We have several camps. I can't deal with this bullshit."

"What will you do?"

"I have my memories. I don't need his stuff and I can't stay here. I *won't* stay here. I have a friend in Albuquerque. He needs a guide."

"That's it?"

"Not with a bang," she said with a pained laugh, "but a whimper. What will you do, cowboy? Wanna try Albuquerque?"

"To guide?"

"Sure, and we can hang out."

Me a guide? I laughed. "You're wonderful, Hannah. But I don't think guiding's the thing for me. I guess I need time to think. I read about Rat-head."

"Rat and Dad are both beyond trouble now," she said, adding, "I'm sure they're together. I'm so sorry this didn't work out for you. Angus was fond of you, Bowie. And proud, as well. Use your gifts wisely, Bowie. And if you pass through Albuquerque, I know where you can find an enthusiastic guide. Free of charge."

I went into the hotel coffee shop and ordered breakfast. The waitress had round red cheeks and thinning gray hair tied in a bun.

"You look like somebody just run their Chevy over your best bluetick," she said.

It was true that I'd been taken by a case of the long face. Angus Wren's death had hit me hard; the loss of the job was secondary. I believe Angus had anticipated the turmoil that followed his death because my contract had a clause providing a year's pay in the event of termination, regardless of reason or cause. Ordinarily contracts were voided by death, but Angus had written the document so that I would not have to file a claim in probate. I didn't know when the money would come, but I knew it would and, because of it, money would not be a concern for a while. Angus hated Key and shunned the temptation of big fish. I told myself I should follow Angus's example and be done with that foolishness forever. As often happened in my life, fate had other plans for me.

17

I was jobless, disconnected, and felt adrift. I wanted to see Lilly and her kids and the gang in Grand Marais, but I wasn't up to either. I had no plans and no prospects and after Angus Wren's death I had heard nothing from Yetter, which surprised and bothered me. Maybe I expected Yetter to be my safety net, as he had been in the past, sitting in the wings, watching out for me. Or claiming to. This was the first time since joining UPI that I felt totally alone and it was taking time to get adjusted to the feeling.

I drove northeast from Durango to Estes Park to fish the Big Thompson and from there headed over into the Snowy Range in Wyoming to fish nameless creeks and float the North Platte in a green johnboat I rented from a man named Slim. I caught fish everywhere I stopped and thought about nothing else. And despite the insatiable hunger for catching trout, I did not once think about the snowfly. Sometimes I went two or three days without eating. After Wyoming it was the Black Hills, and from there to some rivers I didn't know the names of, or care. After meandering, I felt the undeniable pull of Michigan. I didn't think about it then, and only realized much later in my life that Michigan was a magnet for me.

I was driving away from the fight over Wren's empire, not toward anything, violating a cardinal principle of life—that you should always advance toward, not regress. The pathologically brave said, "Charge, don't retreat." I wasn't brave. We can sometimes dictate directions, but rarely actual destinations. I was moving, I found fish, I was alive, and this was enough for now.

North, I knew down deep, was where I belonged, north being as much a philosophy as a direction or destination. You knew when you were there, or you didn't. Those who couldn't feel it and embrace it generally only tried it once. You fit or you didn't. The basic law of nature was the law of the unexpected. In the woods, or on a fast river, you were attuned to this; at home, in a job, in relationships, you were not, yet nature pertained in all settings to all species in one way or another. North was the home of the unexpected. North spawned chilled chaos, yet warmed my heart.

I tried to sort through my past, but all that registered were lessons learned long ago—that no matter how docile life seemed, it was a temporary game and a cruel one at that, the ultimate contest that everybody lost. It seemed to me that God had set the universe in motion for reasons we are not likely to ever know and promptly packed off to a cosmic bowling tournament. If there were a holding tank for sinners on the mend, it was life itself. I had been to wars, hot and cold, rickety as their moral underpinnings might have been, and found no meaning. War was death, and life just a form of war slowed down.

I had seen death in many forms and came to understand that some people were destined for the bag early. Others, like Angus, were lucky enough to live long, full lives. And yet I mourned the passing of Angus Wren as I couldn't mourn the deaths of my own parents. I was happy working with Angus and now understand that my mourning then was as much for what I had lost as for his actual death. We humans tend to be self-centered, this another genetic default, our genes ever pushing us to actions we think we have chosen when we are merely flesh-and-blood marionettes.

The worst part of being unemployed was lack of purpose. In the war and during my sojourn in Russia I had been adrift, but this was different. What it was that work defined was not clear, except that it provided context in one scheme or another.

I was weary and knew I needed change, but not continuous change. Nature abhors a vacuum. Emptiness is destined to be replaced eventually by something with only the appearance of choice.

I found myself late one afternoon standing on a riverbank in northern Michigan, a spray of fine rain peppering my face, and needing a piss. The river was red, colored by tannin and who knows what else. The water was high and fast. To my surprise, there came a wooden driftboat with a fat fellow standing in the bow and a red-haired man standing amidships, the rower feathering his oars as they rounded the bend to my right and shot over toward me.

Proximity on a river entails certain courtesies.

"Looking for big ones," Redhair announced, somewhat disconsolately. "Maybe too cold today, though."

At this juncture they were no more than thirty feet away. The oarsman suddenly stiffened his back. "Jeepers!" he said with a squawk as the driftboat veered sharply to starboard, popped over a partially submerged sweeper, and pitched on its side, dumping both men with hardly a splash into an ominous dark hole.

I had no memory of events from then until I awoke wet and shivering. I knew I had been in the water, but this might have been the steady rain falling on me. Redhair was on his back on the ground nearby, breathing shallowly. The fat man had also developed a red head—it had struck something that peeled back his scalp. Twins. Lights flashed more red. People stepped around the men, pawed at them, poked at them. Medical instruments clinked and backboards rattled. A radio crackled.

"You got breathers out there?" a voice inquired. I smelled hot brakes, cigarette breath, wet wool.

"Three breathing," a voice reported. "So far."

"Good thing you were here," another voice reported. "Willis had himself a dandy coronary. Client's head got stoved in. You pull both of 'em out?"

Was this voice directed to me? "I cannot tell a lie," I announced, the only fact to which I could testify. I felt fire in my chest and clogging in my throat and began coughing and retching and someone rolled me onto my side and held my head while I vomited.

The same voice. "He's clear. Move him out."

And another voice. "Fucking lucky you don't got three floaters." A kibbitzer, I decided, my last thought for a while. I remember closed space and molecules of air pressed together. A gun barrel pointed at my head. Rose squeezed in tight against me, wrapping her arms around me. Gillian hissing "godfather" when she came, her lips pressed away from her teeth like an animal in pain. Hallucinogenic non sequiturs. Rathead keening as Angus's ashes floated downstream to eternity.

The doctor was bald and had clumps of copious port-wine stains spotting his scalp like schooling smelt. The light was too bright for me to fully open my eyes. I listened instead of looked. "You hear me, Mister?"

"I hear somebody," I reported.

"I can't find anything wrong with you. Other than you swallowed half the river and dang near drowned."

Chest pains told me he was obviously looking in the wrong places. "I need sleep." Medical science still had no generally accepted treatment for an injured soul.

"How about a night with us?"

"I can pay cash."

"Your money's no good here, friend. Not for a man who saves two lives."

"Two lives?" I recalled nothing.

"Had to be you. Client says it was you, and there were the three of you up there on the bank, wet as laundry. They went over and you went in after them. People here are impressed."

I suspected that they were erroneously adding two and two. "Where is here?"

"Wolverine Emergency Room. We call it the Meat Shack."

The room reeked of antiseptic. The sheets were slippery. Somebody taped a call button to my left wrist and coughed.

"Any allergies?"

Did life qualify? "No."

"This will make you a new man."

"Must be great medicine," I mumbled. I felt the prick of a needle. All in all, it was unexpected good news, the first in a long while.

The mayor was short, legless, and strapped to a wheelchair. He rolled in just as my breakfast was served in a tray that straddled my lap. "People appreciate what you done," he said.

"I'm afraid I remember nothing," I said.

"That don't matter. It was you. Nobody else was around. There's no other explanation and one of the saved remembers you tugging him ashore. You plunged yourself into the spate and saved two souls from perdition. You've earned yourself an official Well Done."

Life rendered us all well done eventually. I plucked a strip of crisp bacon off my tray and pondered it. Nitrates. Fats to close my arteries. Bacon was odd hospital fare. The flavor was excellent. And the aroma. "Is there more where this came from?"

"We towed your vehicle over to Sturdivant's."

"Where's that?"

"Two miles south of town, where the river shoots under the highway."

What town? A woman in a plaid shirt and bright pink lipstick brought me more bacon. I laid a slice over my tongue to let it swell with saliva, and studied the eggs, imagining cholesterol, blood sacs, and random embryos lurking inside the golden aureoles. Wheat toast, brushed with pure butter. I liberally peppered my eggs, ignoring salt.

"He's a hungry one," Plaid said.

"What were you doing down by the river?" the mayor asked.

"Passing by."

"Good thing you stopped. Must've been God's doing. Headed where?"

"Undecided." The eggs oozed sun-yellow under the edge of my fork. I toyed with answering no preference, but that would be misleading.

"What sort of work do you do, drive around looking for lives to save?"

It was more like driving around waiting to be saved. "Consult," I said, making it as ambiguous as I could. I was in no mood for explanations and would not admit to unemployment.

"Consulting on what?"

"Whatever needs consulting on."

"Sounds soft as unchilled pudding."

I sluiced my eggs down with orange juice, freshly squeezed and filled with pulp that stuck between my teeth. "Not once you get the hang of it," I told the mayor. The best way to defeat an interview is to reverse roles, meet questions with questions. "What about you?" Most people couldn't resist talking about themselves.

"Insurance game and politics."

"Tricky?"

The mayor smiled knowingly. "Not once you get the hang of it. You fish?"

"From time to time."

"The Dog?"

I looked at him blankly.

"Dog River, the one you had your swim in yesterday."

The Dog? The Dog River was one of fly fishing's great meccas, a destination of fantasy. One did not simply drive to the Dog River and fish it. I had always believed that one had to earn a place there. "Just swimming."

"It's a sweet life," the mayor said. "For some."

Ah, a clan hinted at. Life was filled with clans, mostly unnamed and untitled. Time to move the conversation on. "How do I get down to this . . . what's it called?"

"Sturdivant's."

"Right."

"You could walk it, but we sure won't allow that. You're gonna ride in style, Mister. Get yourself dressed and you'll find our police cruiser out front."

The mayor departed on squeaky wheels. I finished my coffee and couldn't remember enjoying a breakfast so much.

"You the hero?" The deputy had mirror sunglasses, thick brown hair, no jewelry, no makeup, full lips, high cheekbones. I looked past her into the cruiser. Her cap was on the passenger seat, a shotgun was standing upright between the seats, the usual radio gear, a frayed clipboard. The shotgun was a Remington with a short barrel. The deputy's brass name tag said CASHDOLLAR.

"I'm Rhodes."

"Good for you. Hop in," she added, stuffing some of the gear under her seat. "You see Hizzonor?"

"He stopped in."

"The man gives me the creeps," she said, wheeling the car in a tight U. "Not the chair, *him*." Then, "*Both*, truth be known."

The village was called Dog River. She gave me a tour. I knew about the river, but I'd never known there was a town of the same name. How was this possible? Not that it merited knowing. It consisted of two dilapidated churches, four well-lit taverns, a small municipal building, an outdoor basketball court with netless, rusted rims, and two huge fly shops directly across the street from each other.

"Owned by the same guy," Cashdollar said. "If it's got to do with money up here, you can bet it's got to do with fish. People come from all over the world, pay cash, a big bill a day for top guides, not including tips. River's open year-round, most of it no-kill and always that at Sturdivant's."

I was glad to let her talk.

"A few people make a wad, but most up here don't have a pot to pee in. It's probably that way everywhere," she added.

She talked a lot for a cop.

"Here we are, a county on a shoestring and tourists paying a fortune a day to chase fish."

I nodded and remembered that wars had been fought for this, the freedom to maintain economic disparities.

There was an edge to her voice and something told me to steer the conversation to new ground. "Been a cop long?"

"College, five with the state, five here. I'm thirty-three and unattached, if that's where you're headed."

"I never hit on a woman better armed than me."

"Being a woman and a cop," she said with a pause, "one doesn't automatically cancel out the other."

Eventually we pulled into a gravel lot in front of a pale log lodge with a huge red-and-gold sign, STURDIVANT'S. I looked for my car, but it was nowhere in sight.

"It's not here," I said.

"I'll be go to hell," Cashdollar said.

Her tires skidded on loose gravel and the emergency brake made a rasping sound when she engaged it. When I got out I saw that her cruiser's tires were nearly bald.

"Sturdivant's people probably stuck it somewhere," she said.

As plausible an explanation as any. "Thanks," I told the deputy, who touched two fingers to her forehead as a farewell.

The back entrance of the silver cedar log lodge opened into a towering great room with a cathedral ceiling and circular skylights. There was a field-stone fireplace, three stories tall. The walls were paneled, not with the usual faux boards from Handy Andy but varnished cedar halves that stopped me in my tracks. The floor was hardwood, covered with an acrylic polish to make it shine. There were huge fish mounted on the walls. One of the specimens drew my attention. It was a brown trout, a great fat sow with orange spots as big as my thumbnails and teeth like a bone saw, a great hooked jawbone, eyes like silver dollars. A brass plaque underneath. DOG RIVER, SALMO TRUTTA. L: 47.25 G: 29.75 WT: 54.6. No date, no name. The monster looked vicious. The reality of the mount aside, I knew there were no such things as fifty-pound-plus brown trout, definitely not in Michigan and probably not in the world.

World-record brown trout had come out of the White River in Arkansas and Lake Michigan, both of them considerably smaller than this ridiculous thing. I decided that the mount had to be a joke, a grand put-on, no doubt to twitterpate cash-laden clients.

The front wall held original oils and watercolors. The oils showed a steady but heavy brush; the watercolors were diaphanous, well planned, rich in white space, brilliant executions. I was impressed.

There was a reception desk in the main room, manned by a scrawny teenager.

"My name's Rhodes. I'm looking for my car."

The boy gave me the once-over. "Sturdivant's in the shop," he said in a voice that suggested it hadn't quite settled on its final timbre. He pointed to a door to the left.

The shop was paneled in glossed white cedar and ringed with felt-lined, glass-topped cases filled with multicolored flies. An enormous man sat in the center of the square formed by the cases. Rolls of fat pressed against his shirt and draped irregularly over a belt, which itself had turned mostly inside out under sheer pressure. The man had a topknot of fine white hair on the top of his head; the sides were shaved clean. There was a wispy tuft of white hair between his lower lip and first chin. He wore over-sized sunglasses and was so still that for a moment I thought he was a mannequin.

"Mister Sturdivant?"

"The gods willing," the old man said with a rheumy croak.

"My name is Rhodes. The mayor said my car was hauled here."

The old man chuckled softly. "You'd be the hero."

I didn't like his tone of voice. "Is it here?"

"Was," Sturdivant said. "I am almost certain it was."

I was in no mood for games. "Where is it now?"

"Gone. This is not a public parking lot."

"But it was brought here?"

"I heard it said, but cannot attest." Fat fingers adjusted the military-style sunglasses. He did not look at me.

I leaned over and saw a white cane with a red tip. He was blind?

"Where's the car now?"

Sturdivant grimaced. "Things come and go. I can't keep track of everything."

"Who can tell me?" I asked, exasperated.

"Whoever moved it."

I was confused. "Are you trying to tell me somebody stole it?"

"I have no insight into motives. It was here and now it's gone. I can only attest to facts. I leave conclusions to others."

"When was it taken?"

"After it was here."

"What the hell am I supposed to do? I need that vehicle."

Sturdivant spread out his hands and grinned. "Make do, adapt, persevere."

What a weird bird. "Can I use your phone?"

The old man pointed toward a corner of the shop where there was another door. "For a mere dime anyone may use the house phone."

I went to the phone, dialed the operator, and asked for the police.

"Dog River Police. Officer Cashdollar."

"This is Rhodes. My car is gone."

"What's that mean, gone?"

"Not here."

"You talk to Sturdivant?"

"I talked *at* him."

"He is a tad odd," she said.

Up here odd was beginning to look like the norm. "No kidding. What do I do now?"

"I'll be there in a few."

A time unit was not specified, and this bothered me. People hereabouts seemed pretty loose with what I had previously taken to be fairly mundane social interactions. It was like being whisked off to Oz and finding it populated by lawyers.

"Thanks."

"It's my job," she said and hung up.

"I'll pay you back," I said when I went back into the shop.

"There's no hurry," said Sturdivant.

I started to go outside to wait for Cashdollar, but stopped. "That big brown in the other room. Is that for real?"

Sturdivant smiled. "Some say yea, some say nay. I leave it to each to make his own determination. We are, after all, a democracy."

"It would be a world record. I've never heard of browns that size."

"One man can't hear everything. Big fish are everywhere if a body knows how to see them."

The man was talking gibberish. "What was it taken on?"

"Certainty, imagination, luck," Sturdivant said. "And a snowfly," he added after a long pause.

My gut tightened. "Never heard of that. Is it a local pattern?"

"In a manner of speaking."

"Got any on hand?" I glanced at the glass-topped cases.

"Each must tie his own."

"Are there pictures, guides, recipes?"

"They vary," Sturdivant said. "Mine and yours would no doubt be different."

I started to reply, but stopped myself. I glanced up at the fireplace on my way out for another look at the fish and decided my initial conclusion had to be correct; it was an elaborate put-on. *Un truite faux,* the French might say. A fake.

Cashdollar had pulled up behind the lodge and was waiting for me.

"I put the word out on your wheels. I'll talk to Sturdivant and his people later."

"Meaning?"

"Meaning you should probably find something to do with your time until it shows up."

"That's it?"

"You want me to drive aimlessly around the county looking for it?"

I leaned against her fender. "I don't need this."

"There's not much you can do," she said sympathetically. "Have you got money?"

"Not without the vehicle. My wallet was in it."

"Relax," she said. "It'll turn up. They always do up here. It's probably just kids wanting a joy ride. You being a hero and all, Sturdivant might put you up until we locate your wheels. I'll have a word with him. He's got fancy cabins with nice views of the river. You'll at least be comfortable."

"You do real estate on the side?" I asked.

"What I do on my side is my business," she said sharply. "Anybody ever tell you you've got a chip on your shoulder?"

"You're the first."

"Then I won't be the last," she said. "You want me to ask Sturdivant or are you one of those big, strong macho men?"

I felt foolish. "I'd be obliged."

She adjusted her gunbelt, clomped up the wooden steps, and disappeared inside.

I sat down on the steps and watched a man knocking dents out of an aluminum driftboat with a rubber mallet. I wished I could knock the dents out of my own life that easily, push the clock back and let me have another go at everything, but I had no idea what I could do differently to change the outcome. I had stopped to take a leak and gotten caught by circumstances. There was no logic. I had known men killed in Vietnam who had done nothing more than use a different shaving cream; that had been sufficient to turn the tide of luck. Why not, then, a cause as simple and inexplicable as stopping to micturate at the wrong place? There were scholars dedicated to finding rationality. They might as well try to find hair on a snake.

The boy from the reception desk led me to a cabin beside the Dog River and presented me with two sets of keys while Cashdollar looked on.

"Sturdivant says everything's on the house long's you need it. Guides and drifts eat at oh-six-hunert and twinny-one-thirty. That's military time. Dining hall's thataway," he concluded, with a jerk of his thumb.

"Drifts?" I asked.

"Clients," the boy said, enunciating carefully. Satisfied that I had no further questions, he pointed crisply. "Follow the trail through the white pines. All lunches are at rest stations on the river, prearranged, which means those back at the lodge gotta fend for themselves. Sturdivant runs a tight ship. Clean up after yourself. You wanna fish, Sturdivant says he can fix it. We got browns legal all year, but it's all no-kill."

I couldn't resist an opportunity. "What's the story with the snowfly in the lodge?"

"Snowfly, snowball, what do I know?" the boy said. "I'm joining the army in September. Gonna be an Airborne Ranger. You know the Rangers?"

I did. Dead ones mostly.

"They're the best," the kid said wistfully. "Rangers don't do fish, man. They do people."

When the boy was gone, I looked at Cashdollar and said, "Misdirection is better than no direction?"

She grinned.

"It's good to see patriotism alive," I said.

"He's a decent kid," she said. "He just wants out."

"Is that a common theme around these parts?"

"Not as common as you'd think."

I was ashamed by my earlier surliness. "I was out of line earlier."

"You were just upset," she said. "If you get seriously out of line, I'll make sure you know."

A statement of fact, absent animus. I had little doubt she could back it up.

"How long do you think it will be?" I asked.

"To locate your ride? A day, maybe two. Not much goes unobserved in these parts. Folks around here see abandoned wheels and we hear. If you need anything, give a call."

I thanked her and watched her walk back toward the lodge.

I was in no mood to go inside yet. The air was heavy. I made my way over to the river and worked my way downstream, staying back from the bank to avoid slipping. The river was nearly black under the gray sky. The water was up and fast and every turn had its own series of notes. I was amazed at the density of cover. Everywhere there seemed to be logjams and boulders and sharp turns that pushed the flow downward to chop deep beneath the obstacles and create holes. Every object pushed water aside, which in turn changed the course of the river. Natural power at its finest.

Obviously God was still bowling.

Deputy Cashdollar called ahead and stopped by my cabin early the next afternoon, her hat pulled down tight, her jaw set.

"Better have a seat," she said. Cashdollar was a small, compactly built woman with an appealing face, which was now angled deeply into intense fury. "We found your vehicle. It's been stripped."

"My wallet?"

"Gone. Everything."

All I could think was that I had been wearing the same clothes for days.

I trudged sullenly over to Sturdivant's lodge. I was out of work and had neither money nor wheels. The lodge was full. Two dozen people were drinking, broken into smaller groups, talking, laughing, like any cocktail party anywhere, only here the sole subject seemed to be fish. Sturdivant was camped on a stool in the corner, his dark glasses on, his white cane in hand like a scepter.

I noticed that people gave him a lot of space.

"Mister Rhodes," Sturdivant said as I approached.

"How did you know it was me?"

"The eyes are gone, but the ears remain sound and other senses enhanced. Nature compensates. I hear you've had more bad luck."

"How far to a town where I can rent wheels?"

"Forty miles, but why encumber yourself? You're quite welcome to remain here."

"I couldn't do that."

"We all make our own choices," Sturdivant said. "You can stay or go. Either choice does not inconvenience me or my staff."

"I appreciate that, but as soon as I can get in touch with my bank, I can pay."

Sturdivant smiled. "There are many ways to pay. The rate here is two hundred and fifty dollars a night, meals included."

I blinked. "I didn't know." More to the point, it was *way* out of my league.

"I've embarrassed you," Sturdivant said. "I repeat, be my guest. I insist."

"I don't understand."

"As I said, we do things for our own reasons and these suffice."

"Maybe for a few days," I said, relenting. "Until I can make other arrangements." The image of the trout over the fireplace flashed through my mind. I had finally seen the Dog River, had lived with its reputation all my life, and knew that its trout were calling my name. I'd accept his generosity, maybe do a little fishing, and then move on.

Sturdivant nodded approvingly.

I started to turn away, but turned back. "The kid who took me to the cabin said you'd set me up to fish."

Sturdivant nodded lugubriously. "Talk to Mister Medawar down in the guide house."

I walked down to the guide house before sunrise. Del Medawar was an older man with swept-back silver hair and bright blue eyes. I had slept uneasily, trying to push my mind away from my predicament. The rain had finally stopped; thermal plumes rose from everything.

"I'm Rhodes," I said. "Sturdivant told me to see you about getting set up."

"That's my job," Del said. "Hard to raise them right now, the water being this high."

"I don't mind working for my fish," I said.

Del nodded. "The natural order. Where do you want launch and pick up?"

"I thought I'd just wade some."

"Be better if you took a boat."

I accepted the offer. "Thought I'd spend all day. Want to give me a good idea of where to get in and out?"

Medawar took a crude river map out of a drawer and spread it out. "We'll put you in above the Spook Pool and you can run down to Little Red Bridge." He marked the place with a pencil. "That'll be a good day's float. Just work the holes or it'll be a heckuva lot longer. We'll be there to meet you tonight, nine sharp. That too long for you?"

"No, that's fine."

"Good, you'll see a lot of water. Sure you'll be okay? We could send somebody with you and you ought to have a lunch."

"I'll be fine. Don't bother with lunch."

It took about thirty minutes to get my gear and load it. Medawar outfitted me with two rods, then trekked back to the fly shop and bought some tippet spools, a box of flies, a bag of sandwiches, and a six-pack of pop. I was going to have a lunch, period. I would learn that at Sturdivant's, rules were rules.

I was on the river and afloat by seven-twenty A.M. and it was light, but I took it easy and played with the driftboat and practiced turning and stopping with the heavy drag-chain anchor until I felt a modicum of control.

The first major hole was a surprise, a horseshoe to the right, but in the back of the bend there was shallower flat water and sinewy ropes of foam. The hole was more in the middle of the river than against the bank, and the current rocketed quietly around the section. I beached the boat and dropped my chain anchor onto the bank. The chain was as big around as my forearms.

I did not fish immediately. I found a spot up high, sat down on a stump to smoke, and watched. A surface feed this time of year and day wasn't likely, but every river had its own rhythms and ways, and I wanted to be sure. One of the tricks in fishing is to deal with the reality of the situation, not your perception of it.

No fish were rising. When the light was better I climbed back down to the river, unlimbered a nine-foot rod, and started working the front of the hole. I tied on a dark fly called a Deep Side-to-Side and affixed it to a short four-foot leader. I used a pinch of weight a foot or so above the fly and cast and retrieved and added weight a little at a time until the fly started ticking bottom. This is the thing about rivers. They are always dynamic. You have to read and adjust constantly, which is what makes time go so quickly. Like life.

On my tenth serious cast I had a hard strike and set the hook. The fish played up quickly and I brought it into the shallows to release. It was a handsome creature, all muscle and dark, sixteen inches. I cupped a hand under its belly in the water and floated it while I worked the fly loose. I held the fish by the tail for a moment before it pulled loose and slid back into the current.

The day passed swiftly and I lost sense of anything except the river and the fish. By midafternoon I had gotten a dozen strikes, but only three fish in. One of these was twenty-six inches, a wonderful, bright-colored fish that left me smiling.

I had only a rough idea of how far the Little Red Bridge was in float time, but it was getting to be time to start thinking about the rendezvous instead of fish and I decided I would fish only those holes that looked exceptionally promising. River time and river distances are different than time and distances on hard ground and easy to underestimate. I had already put in a long day and been so busy that I hadn't touched my lunch.

At six o'clock I found myself sliding along a slate wall and decided that the base of the wall would hold big fish, this a matter of intuition as much as experience. Sometimes you look at a place on the water and you just know.

I had to slide downstream of the wall to find a place for the boat, then work my way back up the shoreline shadows on foot to where I wanted to be. I was almost there when I thought I saw something move in the woods. I watched for a while, saw nothing, and decided it was a trick of evening light. Maybe a deer walking by.

I took no fish from the hole, but it was beautiful, deep water and I felt good. I got back in the boat and fished other holes quickly and when I finally saw the bridge, Medawar was on shore, waving me in.

"Any luck?"

"A few."

He eyed me. "You're the first one I heard that even saw a fish today."

"Probably some are just being tight lipped."

Medawar laughed. "Around here, people *always* talk about their fish. Fish are money and talk attracts customers."

I met Sturdivant in his office. "Mister Medawar informs me that you got on the fish today. How many?" He leaned forward.

"A dozen or so strikes, and some follows, but only four fish in."

"Size?"

"Biggest was twenty-six inches."

He was very still. "Where and on what?"

I explained.

"Why a Side-to-Side?"

I shrugged. "Good motion, sort of circular, a little different from what the fish usually see."

"Do you always catch fish?"

"Nobody always catches fish."

"I do," Sturdivant said. "A few do, the special ones, but then I'm certain you already know that."

"I was lucky."

"Maybe," Sturdivant said. "Who *are* you?"

"You know who I am."

"A stranger comes to the Dog, risks his life saving two strangers, then takes fish when the best guides in the world can't? Half my people didn't even go out, the water as high and murky as it is. Why did you?"

"I fish when I can, not when conditions are just right."

The cabin had a common room between two small bedrooms, a large bath with a small tub, a kitchen and dining nook, an aged silver cedar deck covered with gold lichen, and a wooden platform that looked out on the river. I heard the muffled sounds of people moving toward the morning feed, but pulled a pillow over my head and tried to sleep on.

At noon I went out onto the deck and found fishing gear on the table. There was a nine-foot six-weight glass rod, reels with floating and sinking lines, tippet spools, a new vest stuffed with boxes of flies, soft and pliable waders, a wide-brimmed hat, everything I could want, even a map showing the river and the names of its holes and runs: Shrovetide, Maridly's Rock, Silverfish, Gordon's Whirlpool, Yoni's Triangle, Walter's Log Slide. There was a card with the gear, and a scribbled message, "Tools for a master artisan. S." Why was Sturdivant being so generous?

A bluebird sky overhead told me that the trout would spook at their own shadows and the big fish would stay deep, under the food tube. Like men, trout had a hierarchy of needs: Food and refuge were at the top. I had no idea where reproduction ranked for a trout, which was equally true for me. Sex was high, but not reproduction. The drive, not the practice. It had been quite a while since I had enjoyed that pleasure and I thought of Karla. There had been the chance with Hannah along these lines, but we had not taken that step and in some ways I was glad. River days sated something in me and gave rise to other needs. I fought off the introspective mood and turned my attention back to the river.

No insects were hatching. I tied on a tiny beetle, squeezed on a dollop of flotant, and rubbed it in gently and thoroughly. No rises either, but this wasn't unusual at midday. I waded zigzag downstream, casting forty-five degrees upwater, reach-casting to eliminate belly and drag as the fly bobbed through intersecting currents along the far bank. Every cast had purpose. The rod was a bit stiff, but manageable. I took two nine-inch browns on successive casts into an eddy near the bank, at the base of a decaying sweeper. They were healthy fish with thick sides and brilliant colors, with less yellow tint than browns elsewhere.

In the head of the next hole the beetle brought out a thirteen-inch fish that had been holding in the cutout of a sunken stump. I made it a short fight and released the creature without taking it out of the water, working with one hand, as deft as a surgeon.

In an hour I had landed and released fifteen fish, all legal, including a lethargic seventeen-incher. The farther I waded downstream, the bigger the fish seemed to get. I kept fighting off thoughts of the fifty-six-pounder on the fieldstone fireplace in the main lodge.

I sat on the bank and smoked. There were large bright green hoppers in the brown grass, but I saw none floating in the water and heard no telltale slurps announcing that hoppers were on the trout menu. When I reentered the river, I reversed course. I was glad I was wading and not tied to a boat. Now that I had seen the stretch and created a mental map, I could work upstream with intent. Most water in any lake or stream is fish-dead and there is no sense wasting time on it; this is where most fishermen, including trouters with a fortune in equipment, go astray. Hundreds or thousands of dollars of gear all aimed at giving you precision is washed out when you put your fly over unproductive water.

At the first bend I saw faint smudges of dark patches of insects fluttering around the tag alders at the water's edge. I paused against the bank and watched. The cloud of insects descended, plopped on the surface, and were carried downstream, spewing eggs. For the first two or three minutes there were no takers, but then I heard the rises begin. I selected a small Adams and watched for white mouths winking open to inhale the flies. Most fish stayed near a single position and fed in a rhythm. Watching, I picked up the timing and, when I saw a wink several times in the same place, roll-cast to within inches. The fish struck hard, diving deep for cover, bending my rod momentarily, but it was small and the physics of the rod too much for it to overcome with pure instinct. The feeding frenzy lasted less than twenty minutes. When it was over, I cupped my hand and splashed water onto my face. I had landed eleven more fish, all small, but it had been a glorious hatch.

I was full of myself, drunk on freedom. I continued wading upstream.

There was a sip against the bank in black water under a brushpile. In front of the brush there was a narrow chute of fast water that struck a boulder, splitting the flow and turning it upstream, a curling whirlpool that pushed food gently under the branches. The fish in there was protected, confident, focused on food, certain of its invincibility.

I circled the brushpile from a distance, finally spotting an opening. It would be a one-chance thing; the slightest intrusion would put the fish down. Only a large fish could hold such a sweet spot. Nature's laws were immutable: The strongest ruled. Genetically all species were accidents. Man included.

I considered changing flies but decided that if the fish felt secure enough, it would take anything that drifted into its zone. I backed up, began false-casting, concentrated on nothing but the channel to the fish, focusing everything not on the nearly weightless feathers at the end of the tippet but on the target, the fish. For a moment I thought I had missed and wrapped a branch, but when I lifted the rod tip I felt resistance and faint movement and with a firm twist of my wrist I lifted the rod tip.

The water behind the brushpile exploded and I stripped line hard as I waded through thigh-deep water toward the disturbance. The fish would try to swim into the pile and break me off, but I had the rod tip high and the rod was bent severely. I tore at the pile with my free hand, trying to clear a path, kicking at it, breaking it apart piece by piece, until I had an avenue in.

The fish's dark back was visible just below the surface, but there was no time for admiration. I saw that it had wrapped me once and I found the branch, slid the line loose, and pulled firmly to encourage the fish to run, which it did, stripping more line. My drag muttered under the strain.

I chased the trout up a series of riffles, splashing and slipping, trying to maintain tension, but the fish reversed and charged downstream; instinctively I scrambled up the embankment to get a high position, braced my foot against a dirt hump, and eased the fish into a small pool. No horsing: I knew the light tippet was probably abraded by the brush and I was on luck's clock.

We were frozen in space and time, my chest heaving, the fish holding. After what seemed a prelude to eternity I felt the fish turn and give way to the tension of the line, exhausted.

I sat in the water with the brown trout between my legs, her huge head pointed upstream, my hands guiding her side to side, trying to keep her gills working, supporting her until she recovered.

When she went, she slid quietly downstream past her demolished hiding place and dropped slowly like a submarine into a deep pool below, there, then not, gone, in search of a new place.

I stared at where the creature had been; head to tail she had stretched from my boot laces to well above my knee, twenty-nine inches, thirty. I had never caught anything like her. I laughed when I realized I was shaking. Fifteen pounds, maybe more, I had no idea. The river there was no more than thirty feet across. Where had such a monster come from? How had she survived? I lay back in the cold water and let it run into my waders. Had she been real? Sometimes it was hard to tell, and this was part of the attraction.

"Ascending the embankment was sheer genius."

The stentorian voice startled me. I turned to find the sightless white eyes of Sturdivant staring down at me.

"There was nowhere else to go."

"You didn't think it," the old man said. "You felt it. The good ones never think. When they connect, it's alive. You felt it and it felt you. You were linked in your minds."

"I did what I had to."

"Like yesterday."

I shrugged.

Sturdivant grinned. "If you want work, Mister Rhodes, I could use a competent guide."

"Me?" Hannah had made a similar offer and I had turned her down.

"It pays handsomely."

"I don't know the river and I've never guided anyone. Why me?"

"You know more important things. A river can be learned. What you know, can't. You'll be replacing the man you saved. I relish the irony. In any event, he's lost his sap for river work. He considered his accident a warning from God."

"I was just lucky."

"That too. Even Christ needed some luck. There's always big fish under brush. Most of them break off and never move."

"I caught her shallow. She didn't have enough time to get tricky."

"You knew to go to her and get her into open water. I'm certain she had never faced an opponent like you."

I studied the old man and it suddenly struck me. He was supposed to be blind. "You can *see?*"

"Seeing incorporates a plethora of physiological possibilities."

"How big was the fish?" I asked him.

"Twenty-plus pounds. She'll go thirty later in the fall. What about that job, Mister Rhodes? I'll pay four hundred a week. You'll get room and board on top and I assure you, the food here is the finest. Days without clients are yours. You get paid no matter what and all tips are yours. If it makes you more comfortable, we'll call it a trial period."

"Tell me about the snowfly."

He grinned and nodded his head. "You stay and maybe I'll do that. You can take one of the boats for the next few days, run the river, learn the holes, the get-ins and get-outs. Talk to Mister Medawar and he will explain all procedures. When you're comfortable, you let me know."

"How about you hold the salary until I take my first client?"

"Suit yourself."

I had always tried to do just that.

18

M Y first day as a guide was scheduled to be the first day of the official season for hard drifts—Sturdivant's term for his most favored and best-heeled clients, who paid double and triple the usual fees and were treated like family. The night before the season began Sturdivant called together his twelve guides for a group dinner. We were seated at one long table, all looking out on the river. Sturdivant was in the center, Christlike, with me to his immediate right and a woman to his left. I tried to recall which was the Judas seat but couldn't.

There were six men and five women, all wearing navy blue polo shirts. I was surprised to see so many women working as fishing guides. Sturdivant tapped his water glass with a spoon. "Miss Allen, will you please introduce your colleagues to our newest member?" he asked. I had seen most of them around and talked to a few of them, but until now there had been no formal introductions.

The woman to Sturdivant's left pushed her chair back and stood up. She had short silver hair and purple glasses on an orange string. "Phaedra Allen," she said. "Trax, Arizona. From my far left: Armand LaRue, Paradise Valley, Labrador; Selwyn Berlin, our rabbi, Sloveridge, New York; to his right, Van Dunlop, Circle Tree, Michigan, an almost-homey; Dusty Whipkey, she worked Tierra del Fuego and spent last season in England; Angus Macquoid, from the wee hamlet of Clahdon-Spey, Scotland; and King Sturdivant, himself.

"At the far end: Laird Bennett, Electric Oak, Maine; Hessian 'Eddie' Edmann, Missoula, Montana; Badger Barney Turner, Ashland, Wisconsin; Magdalen Cyrilia Deleven, Sulac Camp, Michigan, she goes by Maggie; and Carl Collister of Jeannie-Gone Key, Florida, here for his first season. Carl holds two dozen bonefishing records, which is what got him to this dance. And you, sir, what are *your* credentials?"

"I'm Bowie Rhodes, sometimes of Grand Marais, and I was offered the job," I said. "All other things being equal, that would seem to be the qualification that carries the most weight." The remark drew cool stares.

I expected conversation, but the group ate in silence and afterward went their own ways. I went out front and could hear Sturdivant roaring about something in the kitchen.

Carl Collister was seated on a bench beside the trail to his cabin. I saw the ember of his cigarette before I saw him. "About what you expected?" he asked.

"Pretty subdued," I said. "Last Supper–ish."

"Have a sit," he said. "They're all good," he went on, in a low voice. "Arguably the best in the world."

"Including you?"

"It's my first season in sweetwater," he admitted, "but it shouldn't be a problem. I can see the fish. The rest is detail. You're the mystery man, you know? They're all trying to figure out what your game is. You have no background—from their perspective. That makes you an unknown."

None of it made any sense to me either. "Right time, right place."

He laughed softly. "Bullshit. Nobody ever heard of you, Rhodes, and Sturdivant *never* employs unknowns. To get here you have to prove yourself elsewhere first. You need a reputation. Sturdivant is *very* selective."

"They can't expect to know every guide in the world."

"They wouldn't want to," he said. "Just the best ones and your name ain't on that list. That's the rub."

"With good reason," I said. "I've never guided before."

"Never?" His voice betrayed his surprise.

"Tomorrow's the first day of the rest of my life."

"Sturdivant explain the game?"

"I know the procedures."

"You don't show them the big fish," Collister said.

I had not been told this. "What if they see them on their own?"

"That qualifies as an act of God. Help them, but don't put them on gorillas and don't tell them anything. You say, 'Tie on the Muddler, pulse it through there.' If they want a reason, you tell them, 'That's just how it is.' "

"That's cheating them."

"You've got it backward," he said. "Putting them on big fish is cheating because it makes them think they're something they aren't. Anybody teach you the ropes?"

"No." It had been trial and error mostly and a lot more days without fish than with until I began to learn from my mistakes.

"There it is. The drifts give us a chance to plan. You help them stay out of trouble, let them catch a few fish, they pay big, go home happy, and the world is in harmony."

"Everybody operates this way?" A chance to plan what?

"This isn't about romance. It's about making a living. Tomorrow we start with the hard drifts, those with big money. Everything changes. So far it's just been soft drifts, the wannabes, wrench twisters and firemen who've saved up, housewives trying to see what it is that keeps pulling hubby away on weekends, people looking to get started. They have plenty of time for learning. Not a lot of expectations from such people, but now it gets serious. You mind my asking how much you're getting from Sturdivant?"

"With all due respect, I don't think that's any of your business," I said.

"He starts most of us at two hundred a week. Don't worry, he'll bump you up when the drifts pick up."

I was surprised. I was starting at double the normal salary. I decided to keep this to myself. "I have to make the drifts happy in order to move up the pay scale, but I can't put them on to big fish? It's a catch-twenty-two."

He put his hand on my shoulder. "The soft drifts only want a sense of the thing. They think an eighteen-incher's a whale. The hard drifts have big bankrolls, spend to get what they want, and most of them know what they're doing. Not at our level, but close enough." He paused and sighed. "The problem with hard drifts is that they think they know it all. Still, they're not stupid and you have to be careful. Sturdivant treats the hard drifts like close family."

"At the same time we're to deny them what they pay for?"

"Capitalism," he said. "Profit requires a gap between what the seller sells and the buyer buys. No gap, no profit, and the buyer's out in the cold because there's nothing worth selling. The truth is, these people need us only because they think they need us. It's all an illusion. Pure service, which makes it tenuous. There's no product in this. Nature owns the fish. We simply provide the service. The fish are there for anyone who cares enough to figure them out. Life as a series of transactions. General Motors and Sturdivant's Guide Service, same-same."

"Some world," I said.

"I didn't make it," Collister said wistfully. "I just want to live in it the best I can."

My first hard drift's name was Samuel Creamer of Morristown, New Jersey; he owned textile factories in Calcutta, India, and created fabrics for designers in New York, Paris, and Milan. He was fortyish with white streaks in wavy black hair.

Per procedure, I met Creamer for breakfast, which consisted of a buffet with several kinds of meats and potatoes, smoked fish, plain yogurt, fresh fruits, omelettes made to order, blueberry pancakes, fresh muffins, and sweet rolls. Creamer took some fruit slices and black coffee and ordered a four-minute soft-boiled brown egg, which he cracked open on an unbuttered whole-wheat English muffin. "Fishing been good?"

"Not really. It was cold and rained all summer, then it turned hot and dry and that slowed it down even more." I observed a certain precision in his hand movements.

"Hatches?"

"Nothing we can count on. Some tricos in the morning, caddis in the evenings, some small BWOs if the clouds sock in. We'll have to search with nymphs and attractors. We'll need to fish deep."

"Sounds good to me. Sturdivant says there are twenty-pounders in the Dog. I told him I'd be happy with a ten. I saw that fifty-pound thing in the main lodge. Is that the old man's idea of promotion? The Dog doesn't seem like it holds enough water for that size of fish. Growth slows in winter. Hell, I'll be happy with a ten-pounder," he repeated. Creamer delicately dabbed the corners of his mouth with a linen napkin. "I prefer realism to fantasy. It flattens the lows and makes the highs better."

I gave him the drift menu, which allowed him to pick the foods he wanted served on the river. Hard drifts chose their own meals, which Sturdivant's Hungarian chef prepared in the dining hall for the girls to deliver to the river. Lunch would be ready and waiting when we arrived, and the girls would stay to act as servers. Soft drifts could choose from a menu of gourmet box lunches, which the girls delivered but didn't stay to serve. Sturdivant's concept was upscale before the concept found currency across the land.

Creamer made his choices quickly, circling what he wanted, and pushed the paper back to me.

I checked my watch. "I'll grab our gear." If we weren't supposed to put drifts on big fish, why was Sturdivant whetting their appetites with that damn mount?

"How far's the get-in?" Creamer asked.

"We're putting in here, right at the lodge."

"Last night everybody was talking about Thunderwood Bridge," Creamer said. It was not designed as a direct challenge, but he clearly wanted a rationale. I guessed that Creamer was a consensus manager.

"Too many small fish."

"You really think we can get into a ten-pounder?"

I tried a smile. "I can't say we won't."

"Be great if we got a big one and the others were skunked."

Competitive fires burned quietly in Mr. Creamer. I tried to imagine him seeing the sights of Calcutta for the first time, starving people, corpses, sacred cows wandering loose, the sick-sweet scent of funeral pyres blending with the acrid smoke of cook fires and noxious fumes of open sewers. And, having experienced all this, going back. Creamer looked soft, but there had to be strength there and the sort of courage required to go your own way.

In the kitchen, which was the largest and best equipped I had ever seen, a girl with light brown hair was arranging luncheon settings in picnic baskets. Her name was Kelli; she wore dangling earrings, upside-down cats. "Where's your stop?"

There was an annotated river map stretched across an entire wall. I thought about the float and tried to assess Creamer. I had told him we would take it slow and he hadn't objected. I tapped the map. "Holy Island."

"That's not very far down the river," she said, arching an eyebrow. "Most guides go farther down."

"We're gonna take it slow."

She shrugged. "Noon okay?"

"We'll be there. There's a place on the west end, in the pines above the sandstone."

"Very cool spot," she said. "I'll be ready for you guys by noon. Good luck."

"Thanks," I said, stopping at the door.

"Sure," Kelli said. She was young, easy on the eyes, midtwenties tops. In fact, all the girls who worked as servers were attractive and young, all similar in appearance, and all outgoing and at ease with people.

Sturdivant was at his usual station inside the walls of display cases. "Have you met your drift, Mister Rhodes?"

"Breakfast by the book."

"Creamer's a generous man when he's pleased," Sturdivant said.

From which I inferred the reverse. "I'll keep that in mind. Any other words of advice?"

"Dark day, dark, sunny day, bright," Sturdivant said.

This was the sort of simplistic advice that was regularly printed in fishing magazines. Most of the contributors to such journals were better at writing than fishing, but nobody seemed to understand this or, if they did, to care. "Thanks. I'll guard the secret with my life," I said.

Creamer handled his nine-foot rod pretty well, waded quietly and carefully, rarely disturbing the water, and worked his flies with impressive accuracy. Seeing that he was self-sufficient, I concentrated my energy on locating fish. It had been my experience that fluctuations in water temperature produced increased feeding activity; the sharper the changes, the more active the fish would be. Flat temperatures, even those considered ideal by fish biologists, just didn't excite the trout. Given the month's rain and the high water level, I guessed that the steepest part of the warming curve would occur between ten A.M. and noon. We had had hot weather for a short time now and the water levels were dropping, but the river remained high.

There was still an hour before lunch and we were less than ten minutes from the island. Creamer had brought three small fish to the net but spent too much time trying to make sure I approved of what he was doing. The overcast had blown off suddenly, leaving a brilliant blue sky. We were beached on a gravel bar across from a steep wall of staggered slate. I had never taken a fish in either the head or tail of the long pool, but I'd picked up some fish in the middle, below a cluster of sumac.

"This could be the spot," I told Creamer. I gave him a small orange Muddler. When Creamer got the fly connected to the tippet, I squeezed a bead of lead onto his tippet above the fly. "Make short casts," I explained. "Bounce it off the rocks if you can, let it sink, pulse your rod hard, then strip the line. Let the rod tip move the fly; strip to recover line, not to move the fly, and keep the loose line in front of you so it doesn't tangle. The weight creates an erratic, sharp movement if you let it work. Go fast. If you see a follow, pulse the rod faster. Make the fish make a decision. They'll be deep in crevices at the base of the rocks and they won't come out unless they see an easy meal. Don't be in a hurry. You may make a hundred casts along here, maybe more. Get your mind set on a six- to eight-foot section of the wall, work it with a few casts, and move to the next section. Be methodical and thorough. Cover all the water. If you hit a good fish, don't horse it and don't let it get back to the rocks, because it'll try to rub you off. The center of the pool is fairly clean; just keep the fish off the wall. That's home and that's where it'll want to be. When it's played out, work your way onto shore and swim it in. Don't screw around with the net."

"It's not very elegant," Creamer said.

"You can have big fish or you can have elegance," I told him. "You seldom get both. Little fish are predictable. Big fish aren't and no two of them fight alike. You need to reduce the elements that can go wrong. Nets are usually trouble. With big fish you have to do whatever is required. Trust your instincts."

Creamer attracted a twenty-inch, three-plus-pound fish after only a few casts and obediently drew it into shallow water before releasing it with a shaking hand. "You're going to hit a big one," I told him. "I'll walk overland to make sure our lunch is set."

"What if I hook a big one?" Creamer asked, obviously edgy about being left alone.

"Do what you just did. You don't need me," I added.

"What about the pictures?"

Nearly all drifts come for trophies, but you couldn't take fish from a no-kill stretch. Instead photographs and measurements were taken and sent off to a taxidermist in Pennsylvania, who used fiberglass to create a lifelike replica of the take. The taxidermist could estimate weights accurately with photos and good dimensions. The idea was to get a trophy without killing a fish. Sturdivant paid for hard drifts' trophy mounts and often had duplicates made for the lodge. It was all part of the service and the hustle, and I wondered what Sturdivant would do if we pulled in a monster bigger than the mount in the lodge. I pointed to the shore rocks where I had placed two cameras, a Polaroid and a German-made thirty-five millimeter. "Loaded, on, and totally automatic."

"It'll stress the fish to take it out of the water."

"Big ones don't stress like smaller ones. Don't worry about it. Catch one first and you can worry about the details afterward."

Creamer hesitated. "I'm not sure about this. I paid for a guide for a full day."

"Can I be straight?"

"Of course."

"The first time you went to India. Did you have a guide?"

"Of course. It's not possible alone, not the first time."

"But you kept going back and eventually you didn't need help, am I correct?"

"Yes."

"This is the same thing. You don't need me around. I've watched. You know what you're doing; now just do it. You trust yourself with fabrics, why not out here?"

"Aren't you afraid you'll lose a customer?"

"If you land a big one, you'll come back, but I won't be your teacher. I'll be more in the role of caddy."

Creamer chuckled and shook his head. "You're one of a kind, Rhodes."

"We all are," I said, checking my watch. More time had slipped by. "I'll push lunch back to one. I'll be back later." I flipped a small plastic container of streamers to him. "Switch to gold or chartreuse if you don't get hits or you don't catch a larger fish. Give the orange another half hour."

Creamer stuffed the box into a vest pocket and gave me a crisp salute.

Kelli was where she said she would be. A table and folding chairs had been set up. There was a linen tablecloth with silver threads, bone china, and place settings for five courses. A deck umbrella lay furled on the ground. The girl was dressed in a white peasant's dress with a pale yellow smock. White flats lay in the grass beside a log where she had stretched out. The dress had been pulled down her shoulders and tucked into her crotch to allow her legs to catch the sun. She sat facing the river, her back against a log, taking long pulls on a cigarette.

"Kelli?"

She immediately lowered the cigarette and raised her other hand to her chest, which sent her tumbling sideways.

I ran to her, but when I looked over I found her laughing silently. "You scared the *shit* out of me!" she said.

I held out a hand and pulled her up, but when she landed on her feet I jerked her off balance and grabbed the hand with the cigarette, which was hand-rolled, small, with an unmistakable odor.

"Wacky weed."

"You got me," she said. "I'm not hurting anyone, but Sturdivant's death on anybody who doesn't follow his rules. He's like, old fashioned? You gonna narc on me?"

"Your secret's safe," I said, releasing her wrist.

She held the joint out to me. "Want a hit?"

"I'm high on life," I said, "and equally old fashioned."

"Me too," she said with a happy squeal. Then, turning serious, "Where's your drift?" She looked past me toward the river.

"We're going to push lunch back. Will that mess up your schedule?"

"No prob," she said, taking a deep hit. "*My* schedule? All that counts are guides and drifts."

"I want the drift kept happy. He's about to catch a big fish and he's going to arrive thinking this has been perfect and I don't want to ruin his moment."

"How do you know he's going to catch a big fish?"

"I just do." Which was true. I couldn't explain it, but minute by minute I felt the certainty growing.

"Are you psychic or something?"

"I seriously doubt it." If I was, I would have solved M. J. Key a long time ago.

"You could be," she said. "It's weird knowing stuff before it happens. That happens to me sometimes."

She was pleasant and attractive in a wholesome, home-town-girl way, but she had hard brown eyes that tracked my every move. "Where are you from?" I asked her.

"Bloomington, Indiana. IU?" she said. "Basketball, Go Hoosiers?" She raised two arms like a halfhearted cheerleader. "This job is a stepping stone," she said. "Someday I'm going to open a gourmet catering service in Oregon. I've researched it. There's scads of sportsmen out west with money to burn. It'll be like Sturdivant's, only classier." Her face suddenly lit up. "I'll call it the Classy Lady. Do you like that?"

"Not bad."

"Everybody wonders about you," she said. "You know, like all the girls in the kitchen? Like all the other guides. *Everybody*. Nobody can figure you out. The guides, they all know each other and they say none of them know you. 'Course, they're real jerks. It's like sick how they act, you know, their shit doesn't stink?"

I didn't say anything.

"The girls think you're sort of delicious looking," she said. "When you came in this morning I thought you were nice. Not bossy or anything. I like that."

I checked my watch. My drift would be wondering where I was.

"Well?" she said.

"Well what?"

"If you're like psychic, you'd know."

"I'm not."

She looked irritated.

"I'd better check on my drift," I said.

Creamer's smile told the tale. He waved and enthusiastically pumped the air. When I got to the boat Creamer grabbed my hand and began pumping. "Two whoppers!" he yelled gleefully. "Can you believe it?" He took Polaroids from his pocket, shoved them at me and went splashing into the water. "Here," he shouted, "up here."

I looked at the pictures. I was pretty good at guessing length, even when fish were finning under water, and could estimate weights based on length and girth. A scale would have been accurate, but we wanted to handle the fish as little as possible, so we estimated as best we could. The first fish was twenty-six inches and around nine pounds. The second was much longer. Thirty inches, but maybe only eleven or twelve pounds because it was lean. "Eleven pounds and change," I said, tapping the photograph.

"I shot the whole roll of film," Creamer said. "I owe you."

"It's included in the fee."

Creamer splashed back toward me. "Screw the film. I mean *you*. That chartreuse, Jesus! First cast, the fish rolled behind the streamer. I threw again, another flash. He was definitely interested. Third time, I sped up the retrieve and bam! I'm afraid I got excited and horsed him onto the beach too soon. He broke the tippet on the gravel, but I kicked him out of the water. It was strictly amateur hour. I hope he isn't hurt."

Creamer suddenly sat down in the water. "I was ready to quit, but I thought, what the hell." He pointed across the river. "I saw a fissure down there. See the rounded area?"

I had seen it and knew he would too.

"I thought, that's a virtual cave. I've seen similar formations in southwest France. First cast, this thing hits so hard it nearly rips the rod out of my hand and I'm thinking, how much backing do I have, one-fifty, two, two-fifty? I don't have a clue, but I remember what you said, keep him in the open, let the drag do its job. I got calm, my head cleared, I did it by the book, played him out, turned him in, eased him up, took him out. I've never seen anything so beautiful. I'm starved," he added, staring downriver.

He was smiling and content when we got into the boat and drifted down to lunch.

Kelli was standing on shore at the downriver side of the island, which was actually a peninsula shaped like a hammerhead, holding a tray with two fluted glasses filled with champagne. I thought of James Bond movies and started to laugh. I beached the boat and stowed the oars. Creamer vaulted out and took a glass. I had to hand it to Sturdivant. He knew how to create an aura. Kelli looked like a very sexy saint.

"Luck, gentlemen?" Kelli asked.

"He's the best," Creamer said enthusiastically.

Kelli's eyes flashed briefly when I looked at her, but the pleasant, relaxed smile stayed perfectly in place. I took the other champagne glass and executed a small bow. "Mademoiselle."

"Merci," she said. "Shall I serve, gentlemen?"

"Mister Creamer?"

"Call me Sam," Creamer said. "I'm famished. What a *fantastic* day!"

This was how hard drifts and their guides dined at the riverside: Cuvée Louis Pommerol 1965 to freshen the palate; Wisconsin whitefish roe on rye bread squares, with lemon, Belgian endive, grated Spanish onion, and chopped hard-boiled egg yolks, all of this served with ice-cold Finnish vodka; as a main course, chicken salad with red pepper vinaigrette on a bed of Maine fiddleheads; a small pan of Virginia spoonbread made with white cornmeal, washed down with chilled Scottish Silver Birch; dessert of apricot lace cookies served in a gold-foil tube with SAMUEL CREAMER printed on the tube, left to right; and, to finish, a cup of strong, fresh coffee.

After lunch Creamer sat on a boulder and smoked a black cheroot. "How far back to camp?" he asked, watching an attempted smoke ring dissipate before it could take form.

Camp? The word struck me as ludicrous. Sturdivant's was anything but a camp. "Twenty minutes. Climb up the ridge and head east."

"I'm thinking I might walk downriver, Bowie, then work my way back upstream. I'll go to purple and black Muddlers as the shadows come in, work the holes slowly. That sound like a workable plan to you?"

"Should do," I said. "There are some interesting holes below here."

"I'd like to do it myself."

"You sure?"

Creamer sat up and extended his hand, "Positive, Coach."

I asked Kelli if I could help her carry her gear back.

"Sturdivant wouldn't go for that."

"I won't tell."

She had a pickup truck parked up the hill. Sturdivant's logo was painted tastefully on the doors. I helped her carry her things.

"Your drift seemed pretty happy," she said. "And nice. A lot of them aren't. They spend a lot of money and think they can have anything."

"Do they ever bother you?"

She shrugged. "I can take care of myself."

I wondered.

I went back down to the river, got into the boat, and headed for the pickup point. Creamer gave me a wave and a smile as the current took me past him. I couldn't believe that people would pay a thousand dollars a day for what was essentially free. Collister was right about that. It did not feel right, but I was determined to stick with it and find out what Sturdivant would reveal about the snowfly. I had hoped that Hannah and I had buried my obsession with her father's flies, and for a while I thought we had, but the big fish mounted in the lodge had rekindled the smoldering fire.

With soft drifts everything was relaxed and informal, but dinner with the hard drifts was formal and, as it turned out, tense. Guides and drifts were seated at a long, polished table, dining banquet style. I watched the serving girls bring in the food and spotted Kelli, who smiled away at the drifts at the other end of the table and did not look at me.

Sturdivant sat at the head of the table; he wore a black satin running suit with white trout embroidered on the shoulders, tasseled alligator slip-on shoes with black silk socks, and dark glasses. There was friendly banter around me, but I didn't join in. I preferred to observe. Creamer was beside me and also content to listen and eat. There was a lot about this whole operation I didn't yet understand and I felt keeping my mouth shut was the best way to learn.

A square-jawed woman with flaming red-orange hair sat between Collister and me. She had feline mannerisms, those not of a housecat but of a puma, bursting into ear-splitting squeals at any hint of a joke. Her hair was short and heavily moussed forward. Like Woody Woodpecker. She wore gold and jade rings on all of her fingers.

"Go all right?" Collister asked past the woodpecker.

I nodded. "You?"

"Carl helped me collect my twenty pretties," the woodpecker said, interrupting and grabbing his arm. "It was *great* fun," she added. "And I'm just learning," she said. "On dry flies," she went on. "Olives, I think? Just *fantastic*. Talk about a rush! It's nearly as good as sex," she said, shaking her head. Her rigid hair looked like a tomahawk being lined up to hack at something. Then she giggled. "Well, *almost . . .*"

Collister wore tan pants and a black shirt. "Congratulations," he said to the woodpecker. He lifted his glass and she hers. The touch released a single clean, pure note. I saw that he held the glass to his lips but did not drink.

The food was beautifully presented, served by the same girls who served lunches on the river. After the table was cleared, Kelli and the other girls brought trays of cognacs and boxes of cigars, and circulated among the guests distributing them.

Samuel Creamer had moved next to Sturdivant, keeping the old man nodding attentively to a steady stream of conversation. Eventually Sturdivant struggled to his feet and held out his hands, silencing the congregation.

"I trust our kitchen has proven satisfactory," the old man began. "To our old friends we say welcome back and to our first-time guests we say welcome. At Sturdivant's we have no other reason for existence than to satisfy our guests. There are grander and more elegant lodges and there are more beautiful settings, but nowhere in the world do trouters receive higher esteem, and nowhere in the world will you find finer fish than our beloved Dog trout. You pay dearly for this, but how dearly is largely up to you. Assembled at this table are the finest guides in the world, but that is only my view. I acknowledge my biases," he said, pausing for effect.

"When I created this establishment," he continued, "I realized that only the finest of everything could assure success. I pay my people well, but pay alone is not sufficient to maintain excellence. I said to myself, there must be incentives, but incentives from me could become entitlements. What we needed here would be pure competition, with the customer making the final judgment. My investment guarantees the best people; your rewards guarantee their undivided attention and effort. If they serve you well, you reward them accordingly. If you are unsatisfied, well, that's the way of the world. In order to maintain competition, I insist that rewards be distributed publicly. It is now time to see how clever Sturdivant has been, yes?"

This drew polite applause and smiles all around.

"Sturdivant is a gentleman," he said. "Sturdivant does not embarrass his guests. I would ask you to retire to the garden deck, where our young ladies will see to your needs. We would ask you to come in one at a time and to evaluate your day. You must be candid. We welcome your criticisms; only by acknowledging our shortcomings can we improve your experience. At the conclusion of your presentation, you will give me the envelope provided upon your arrival. When this transaction is complete I would ask you to retire. My house is your house," he added. "Checkout time is noon. When you are gone, I hope you will take fond memories and that you will come again next season."

He sipped his cognac before continuing. "I am frequently urged by many of you to allow guests more than one day a season, but I recognized long ago that a single day of the greatest value is superior to a longer visit. You, my friends, get one try at the river a year. My guides get one try at you. Such delicious tension affords a mutual effort toward excellence. It is the Sturdivant way, unique in the world. It is, my dear friends, the purest experience in the angling world, among we Brothers and Sisters of the Angle, as the eminent Mister Walton recorded it so long ago."

A hard drift, even a king, could come to Sturdivant's only one day a season. In this way Sturdivant created demand among people whose resources assured they would rarely face such limiting circumstances. I was surprised when he first laid this out to me. I decided then that my employer, however ipse-dixitistic, was a brilliant promoter. Nothing so far had happened to change my mind.

I wondered again why Sturdivant had chosen me, a drifter without credentials, to sit among this group.

The first hard drift to come was the woodpecker. "I'm new to all this," she told us. "I caught twenty gorgeous fish. They were small, I'm told, but size in many things is not the point." She emphasized this with a lascivious grin. "I'll be back," she said in Collister's direction. "Next season." Having passed her envelope to Sturdivant she raised her glass in salute and glided across the carpet and out the door.

This was how it went, one drift at a time, until Mr. Samuel Creamer stood before us, looked at me, shook his head several times, silently passed his envelope to Sturdivant, and departed without uttering a single word.

I felt all eyes on me. "What happened?" Collister asked.

I shrugged. The final two drifts talked eloquently of their experiences. Phaedra Allen had connected one of them to a seven-pounder; Edmann, the Montanan, had seen his client net a half-dozen fish in the five- to six-pound category and had hooked him to a larger fish, which had broken off.

"It is my most fervent hope," Sturdivant said after the last presentation, "that you will not let your rewards prevent you from being hospitable. We are professionals here. No need to say more. You may now open your envelopes, ladies and gentlemen. Let us see how you have done."

I checked the time. The long night had left me edgy. I watched the others open their envelopes and announce the amount of their tip. Collister's woodpecker had rewarded him with four hundred dollars, twenty a fish. "Not bad," he said. Bennett's drift, who had complained sharply about his guide's fly choices, had coughed up $650. Edmann got a thousand, as did Phaedra Allen. Dusty Whipkey got a mere hundred, but laughed it off. "It's a hundred more than I had in my pocket this morning," she said.

"Mister Rhodes," Sturdivant said. "Would you care to share your fortunes with your colleagues?"

"I haven't looked," I said.

"Please do so now." Sturdivant's voice had the raspy edge of sandpaper pushed across pumice. There were forced smiles all around. What had Kelli said? The other guides talked about me?

I tapped the envelope on the table, tore off the end, and blew into it. When I saw the number on the check I blinked.

"Well?" Sturdivant asked.

The note read, "Better than Beluga caviar and worth the price." "Twenty-three thousand," I announced, reading it again to be sure it was real.

Sturdivant slumped back into his chair, slapped the table, and bowed his head. "Excellence, Mister Rhodes. My God, *excellence!* We congratulate you." The guides lifted their glasses, but there was no pleasure in their eyes.

"This is fucking crazy," I told Creamer when we met on the deck.

"It's only money, Rhodes. It costs me that much to ski for a couple of weeks in France with my wife every year and she's a hell of a lot less fun. You get me a twenty-pounder next year and I'll buy you a damn palace in India. That's a promise."

Creamer had one drink. "Sorry to be a party-pooper, Coach, but I have to get out of here early in the morning. It was a hell of a day," he added as we shook hands. We had gone from Rhodes to Coach in one day, all because of fish. What a strange and inexplicable world.

The party was going strong when Kelli sidled up to me.

It was a cool night with a clear sky. I could see stars blinking through the trees.

"Is it true—how much you got?" she asked. "*Everybody is talking* about it."

"Yes."

"Damn. Is this a screwed-up world, or what?"

"It has some peculiar wrinkles."

"You want something to drink?" She held up a small tray with snifters of cognac.

"No thanks."

"Are you married?"

"No."

"Ever been?"

"No."

"I'm engaged," she said. "His name's Rick."

"Congratulations."

"It's probably a mistake," she said. "I've been here all summer and the only time we talk is when I call him. I'm thinking this is not a good thing. Have you got anything against marriage?"

"No?"

"I've got doubts. You know, like being with one person for the rest of your life? Can people really do that?"

"Some do." I thought of my father and Queen Anna, the Chickermans.

"Do you like what you're doing?"

"It's pretty good so far."

"Are you going to stick with it, you know, come back next season?"

"I don't know yet. It's getting late. Maybe I'll wake up one morning soon and think it's time to go."

Kelli frowned. "You mean after the season's over."

"Whenever it's time. Tomorrow, in a week, who knows?"

"And leave your money behind?"

I tried to see her face in the dark. "How's that?"

"You don't know?"

"I must not."

"If you leave before the season ends, Sturdivant keeps your tips."

"He can't."

"Did you sign a contract?"

"Some papers."

"Then it's legal. It's the same for all of us."

"Why?"

"To keep us here. He makes a fortune because of us. No us, no fortune. Actually," she said, correcting herself, "no guides, no fortunes. We girls are just accessories. He's real picky about his help."

"I have the check."

"Look at it. It's not signed. Sturdivant gets the signed checks. You think it's possible to make a lot of money without being ruthless?" she asked.

"I've never made a lot of money."

"You did today."

"But it's not mine yet."

She laughed. "Sturdivant gives me the heebie-jeebies," she said. "Do you know that he takes boats down the river alone at night? I've seen him."

"How does he do it?"

"I don't know and I don't think I want to know," she said.

We stood in silence and I could feel her staring at me. "Got a drift tomorrow?" she asked.

"A New Yawkah," I said, mimicking the city accent.

"They're the worst," she said, squeezing my arm.

When Kelli left to help with cleanup I walked over to the guide house, where there was a room for the guides in the basement. There we had reports of insect hatches and every fish caught during the season. Guides with the most seniority got first pick of the runs. I looked over the reports, saw where the others were headed, and decided to take my New Yorker to the same section of river as Collister, following him down by two hours to give the fish a chance to settle.

I had worked every day. I found the work easy enough; I was tanned and fit, eating haute cuisine and banking salary and accumlating tips, running fourteen hundred to three thousand dollars a week, not counting the small fortune from Creamer.

All of the guides went to the river on their off days, but when they were off and I had a drift, I never saw them and wondered where they went.

A heat wave arrived in late September, and with it came Indian summer. The river was low, evaporated by ninety-plus-degree days, and fish of any size were hard to come by. Some of the drifts wanted night trips, but Sturdivant's rules forbade them; he said insurance was high enough as it was. Night drifts with amateurs could be dangerous, he said. Some of my drifts had tried to cut private deals with me, but I adhered to Sturdivant's policy. More often than not, those who wanted to run by night were the most incompetent by day. The risk wasn't worth a few dollars. Still, brown trout fishing was better after sundown because the big fish tended to be nocturnal, and I remembered Kelli telling me that Sturdivant himself was slipping onto the river at night. It was his right, of course, but how did a blind man negotiate a fast, winding river alone? Maybe Kelli had seen something and jumped to the wrong conclusion.

Finally I had a two-day hiatus and no clients. By my calculation it had been nearly ten weeks since my arrival. It had been months since I had been intimate with a woman and although Kelli was becoming more and more overt in her flirtations, making her availability and interest about as clear as they could be made, I had ignored the openings she created, which was not easy to do. The truth was, I was horny and lonely.

My first night off I stayed at the lodge, ate with those who didn't have clients, had a couple of beers, and retired to my cabin to read. I went to sleep early and woke up the next morning knowing that I had to get out and do something.

I borrowed one of the lodge's pickups and spent the evening of my second day off drinking slammers in a tavern north of town. There was plinkety-plunkety-twangalang music, the patrons waddling the two-step, all pairs, near as I could tell, and mostly older folks. There was something obscene about septuagenarians in fringed mini skirts and white slouch boots. The bartender was a red-headed woman of fifty, lean and rawboned. She wore a plastic name tag. It said EARLEENE.

"Earle the Girl," I said. "What time do you get off work?"

"Way too late for you," she said with a practiced smile and the warmth of an Arctic winter. "Bub."

"You don't find me charming?"

"I find you extremely shit-faced. You might try sometime when you're sober, though I doubt the result will change. A drunk jerk is still a jerk when the booze wears off."

"But you don't know what you're missing."

"I'll try to live with my loss," Earle the Girl said.

"I wan' 'nother drink."

"You're cut off, Bub."

I became semiconscious in a chicken coop of iron mesh as thick as my thumb with a clean, pale blue cement floor and a sparkling white urinal in the corner. My first thought: The chickens here must be housebroken. Disinfectant hung in the air like gas. I was no stranger to hangovers, though it was not at all clear that I had yet passed to the pure hangover stage. Insanity was a possible explanation. Or abduction. I rubbed my eyes and rolled to the floor on all fours. Not a chicken coop; the belly of a destroyer. Family lore: Uncle Jess had gone to sea in a tin can and come home with lungs filled with asbestos and a blind hate for closed spaces, no explanations given. How had Jess fit in a tin can? I had been six then and my question ignored. At his daughter's wedding reception Jess had risen to offer a toast and, instead, informed the celebrants that when the ship crossed the equator, the crew had shed their clothes and "rubbed their peckers" on a cook named Rafael. Jess spent a lot of time visiting the VA hospital in Battle Creek. I hoped my ship was not nearing the equator.

"Praying?" It was Cashdollar.

I tried to look up, but someone had pounded a nail into my medulla. "Are we nearing port?"

"It seems that you have a real talent for extremes."

"Where am I?"

"County jail."

With effort I managed to look up at her. "Why?"

"Driving while intoxicated, although technically I would call it crashing while intoxicated. You wrecked your vehicle, which should've killed you, but God seems to favor fools and blind drunks."

"Not mine. Borrowed from the lodge." I remembered needing to piss. "I don't remember much," I said.

"You hit your head, which seems to have the resilience of a stainless-steel bowling ball."

"Obliged," I said, sinking back to the floor.

"Still drunk?" she said.

"I'll take the fifth."

"I think that's what got you here." She was grinning.

The judge sat behind a card table. He had the face of a frog and no neck. "No priors," he said. "No infractions. What's a man of your stature doing stone-cold drunk behind the wheel of a motor vehicle?"

I had no idea. "No excuse, Your Honor."

"Good attitude," he said with an emphatic nod. "I'd suggest you take this as a message from God. People are frail. Sometimes the train that is their life jumps the tracks. Put yours back on the tracks, Mister Rhodes. A man who saves lives of strangers ought not to be standing in front of me like a common sot. People like you and me, we're role models. I'm gonna fine you two hundred dollars and costs. Driving privileges suspended for fourteen days. Shoe leather will help you get your feet back on the ground. You stay clean for six months and your record will be expunged. Do you understand that word and does that sound fair?"

"Yes, sir, and yes."

"Then get the heck out of here, son. I'm going bow hunting and you need to see the cashier."

My head ached. The cashier volunteered four aspirin tablets and a paper cup with water.

Deputy Cashdollar was waiting outside, standing beside a dented and faded green jeep. She opened the passenger door as I approached.

"Did they tell you there's a slight concussion?"

"They could have," I said. "There was a lot of information flying around and not much landing. Sort of like caddisflies."

She burst into a laugh and said, "Get in."

"This isn't necessary."

"It's better than walking thirty miles, which is moot because you're grounded for two weeks and your pickup has gone to parts hell."

I was incapable of arguing. It made me dizzy to close my eyes.

She drove a few miles and pulled over, making me get out and look into a ravine. There were tire marks on the lip and not again until a considerable piece downhill. Two poplars at the bottom were shattered and propped up by the branches of surrounding trees, a lesson in the value of extended family.

"You must've fallen asleep, slowed, and drifted over the edge. Even at the speed limit, you'd have gone airborne."

"Lucky me," I said.

Five miles down the road she showed me the remains of the pickup I had borrowed from the lodge. It had become a flatbed. "I lived through *that?*"

"You were on the floor. We had to cut you out."

"We?"

"The romance of the road patrol. Dead bodies and broken cars. It's nice to have the order reversed for once."

"You sound almost happy to see me," I said.

"I have a well-established record of questionable judgment," she said with a chuckle.

She asked if I minded a stop at her house. I didn't. Her house sat on a bluff overlooking the river. It was a huge place, sort of what I thought of as Queen Anne–ish, with at least a dozen rooms and a spacious widow's walk on top. Only two or three rooms had furniture; most were in varying stages of reconstruction.

"It belonged to a heart surgeon from Ann Arbor. His wife used to spend summers up here and he'd come up to join her now and then. One time he walked in and found her doing squats on a naked carpenter's vertical joist. Threw him out, beat her to death with a crescent wrench. Second-degree murder. He did his time and moved to Colorado where he bankrolled a clinic that fixes rich women's noses. He can't practice medicine, of course, but he can still make money. That's America. He had two miles of frontage, which he deeded to the state in exchange for back taxes. The state was going to tear the house down, but I bought it cheap and had it moved here. It cost me so much to move it, there wasn't much left to recondition it. It was empty for ten years and it wasn't a pretty sight. I've put everything I have into it, but it's a slow go when you do your own work and you're infected by perfectionism."

"I like it," I said, which was true. I had always preferred old houses with character to modern slapdash throw-'em-up-and-sell-'em-quick construction. "I don't recognize this part of the river."

"We're nine miles west of Sturdivant's. He owns five miles of frontage over here, on both sides of the river. It's worth a fortune."

"Do you have river frontage?"

Her face turned sour. "My dad sold the river property to Sturdivant a long time ago."

Whenever I turned, I confronted Sturdivant's uncanny knack for acquiring wealth. "The old man seems to have a lot of irons in the fire."

She nodded solemnly. "He considers the river to be his and a lot of it is."

"You don't sound happy about that."

"It's none of my business." She opened a steamer trunk and groped in it. "Lose those clothes," she said over her shoulder.

"I'm okay."

"I'm not. You peed your pants when you ran off the road. You stink, Rhodes."

The loaner shorts were a size too large, and I wondered who they belonged to. Cashdollar led me up to the widow's walk and hand-cranked the windows open. There was a daybed along one side and a fly-tying work-bench along the other.

"Yours?" I asked.

"My dad's," she said.

She seemed ready to say something, but turned away. "I had a long night," she said from the stairs. "A nap will do us both good."

As her head disappeared, I walked to the stairs. "What's your first name?"

She looked back at me. "Ingrid."

"I sort of remember getting into the truck to drive back to the lodge last night, and that's about it."

"That's what a whack on the head will do for you." She gave me a sym-pathetic look. "Take a nap."

"I will. Ingrid?"

"Yes?"

"Thanks."

She smiled. "Think of it as your tax dollars at work."

Before I could sleep, I needed to talk to Sturdivant. There was a phone in the widow's-walk room. It had been stupid to get drunk the night before a client, but I had the desperate wants, couldn't bring myself to give Kelli a tumble, and ended up in the bar. Not smart at all, and now I knew I had to face the music.

"Where the hell you at?" Sturdivant wanted to know. It was odd how his vocabulary seemed to shift with his mood. "Whipkey had to take your drift. Lucky for us, she had a no-show. You know my rules. Miss a drift and you're history." He was on his high horse, boss-on-a-box, and I had no defense.

"I was in jail."

Silence. "Explain."

"I wrecked the pickup. I had a few too many drinks last night, fell asleep at the wheel, ran off the road."

"Are you injured?"

"Bumps and bruises. They jerked my driver's license for two weeks, but it could've been worse. I'll be back tonight."

"Do you require a rescuer?"

"Thanks, but I've got a ride. If it doesn't work out, I'll call."

"Check with Mister Medawar when you return," Sturdivant said. "You've got a demanding drift tomorrow. You will, of course, meet your drift for breakfast and you will be charming, am I understood?"

"You are."

"I'm a forgiving man, Mister Rhodes, but I assure you that a repeat of this episode will leave you on the outside looking in."

"I appreciate your understanding."

Sturdivant grunted gutterally. "You make money for me. That's what I understand. Sorry you had trouble, but the river doesn't like fickle lovers. Stay on the river and you'll have no problem. Get away from the river . . ." He didn't finish. "I'm relieved that you're okay, Rhodes. It would be a distinct inconvenience to replace you now, but I will if that's what it comes down to. You'll do well to remember that."

Could it all boil down to money for him? I still did not understand why Sturdivant had hired me; now I had broken a major lodge rule and he was giving me another chance. I stared at the telephone.

I awoke in the sun, sweating. Cashdollar was at the fly bench, her back to me. She wore a halter top and jean shorts, which revealed a figure heretofore entirely hidden by her uniform.

"I thought the bench was your dad's."

She looked over at me. "It's mine now. He passed away two years ago."

"I'm sorry."

"Feeling better?"

"I think I'm on the mend."

"You can't rush body chemistry. There's nothing like time and sleep for a hangover."

I got up and looked over her shoulder. She was tying a caddis emerger. "Do you tie the snowfly?"

She laughed out loud. "Yeah, and snipes too!"

I let the subject rest. She obviously didn't believe.

Ingrid made BLTs on toasted white bread for us. Afterward we walked down the back of her property, along the Dog River. The trail curved along a towering bluff covered with jack pine and scrub oak. Several whitetails kicked up ahead of us, showing their flags as they fled. The woods were covered with brown ferns. Eventually we hit a fence.

"It's Sturdivant's from here on. Downriver, too."

The river was narrower here than below the lodge.

"Interesting water."

"Miles and miles of private," she said. "No access for the unwashed public."

She drove me back to Sturdivant's late in the day. "I'd like to pay you back," I said. "Dinner?"

She seemed to think about it. "I think I'd like that. When? I don't like things open ended."

"Not sure. I work every day there's a customer. It might not be until the rush is over."

She said, "That would make it mid-November. It's a date. If something comes open before then, give me a call."

"I'll do that."

On October 13 I had a drift from Detroit, an elderly man nearly incapacitated by arthritis.

"I don't know how much fishing I can do," he announced, "but it's a nice day to float down a beautiful river. I used to fish the Dog in the nineteen-thirties and I had it pretty much to myself in those days."

"You're paying a lot of money for a ride down the river."

"You get to a point in life where money loses meaning. I've had a lot of luck in real estate. At my age, trading money for any good experience is a fair deal."

The drift's name was Merchant, a name that seemed vaguely familiar, but I couldn't place it.

We had a pleasant day. I moved us from hole to hole and held the boat out in the current so he could fish weighted flies deep. We had some luck, twenty fish, some of them reaching fourteen inches. He was a happy man.

Kelli, who more and more managed to be the one to cover my clients and me, brought us lunch, setting up on a grass-covered flat island in a huge bend. Merchant took a nap after lunch. Kelli hauled a load up the hill to her vehicle and I followed with the folding table. I was tired when I got to her.

"There's not much season left," she said. "Did I tell you me and Rick called it off?"

"No. Was it a joint decision?"

"Nope, it was my decision and Rick, he didn't argue," she said. "I didn't feel sad afterward, which I guess is a pretty good sign that it was over."

"You'll go back to school when the season's over?"

"No, I'm heading out to Colorado," she said. "Ski resort in Steamboat Springs. Assistant manager for catering. The pay's not all that good, but it's a great place."

"Gathering more ideas for the Classy Lady?"

She smiled at me. "I guess you've got to circle some dreams for a while. I thought you'd want to know something else," she added in a conspiratorial voice. "Sturdivant's going out at night."

"On the river?"

She nodded emphatically. "I followed him. He goes in upstream way west of the lodge and gets out about a half mile above. Medawar meets him."

"Maybe he's not blind."

"More likely he's not *human*," she said in a whisper.

I put the table in back of the truck and helped her load and pack the gear. Afterward we sat on the edge of the downhill trail. My drift was curled up on a blanket by the boat.

"You always make your drifts happy," she said. "That's a real gift."

"It's not that tough. If they catch fish, they're happy."

"I don't think it's that simple. There's something about you that makes people feel relaxed and comfortable. You're not like the other guides."

"I just give them what they want."

She went silent. After a long time she said, "What do you want?"

It wasn't a rhetorical question.

"I'm not one to look into the future."

"I mean right now."

I stared at the river.

"How come you haven't hit on me?" she said.

"You're engaged."

"Not anymore."

I didn't want complications, but I was weakening.

"I'm not pretty enough for you?"

"That's not it."

"What, then?"

She wanted more of an explanation, but there was nothing I could say that would make sense.

"Well," she said. "I've done all I can except rip off my clothes and jump your bones. You'd best stay alert for an ambush," she said with a laugh.

She got up and went to the vehicle. I heard the door open. I also saw that my drift was sitting up and looking around and that it was time to get back to work.

"Good nap?"

Merchant smiled. "Comes a time in life when a good sleep beats just about everything."

At three P.M. Merchant got a very large fish that threatened to run the backing off his reel, but luck and shallow water intervened and the trout, seeing the bottom slanting upward, turned and came back to deeper water. I breathed easier.

It was a substantial hen with a huge girth, a ten-pound fish. Merchant stared at the trout.

"Photo?" I asked.

"The memory's plenty for me," he replied. "Do you see many fish of this size?"

"Rarely, but they're in here and some are larger."

"Larger?" He seemed exhausted. "I'd like a little rest."

"Coffee?"

"Yes, please."

I had three thermoses on every float trip and some days they were not enough. The thermoses were made by a company in Pittsburgh and could hold heat for twenty-four hours. Determined that equipment failure would never stand in the way of customer satisfaction, Sturdivant equipped us with the best. Even the boats were custom-made, lighter, higher riding, and more maneuverable than most driftboats on this river or any other.

Merchant held the thermos cup in both hands. "Do you take pleasure in your work? I think you must. You're very good at it."

It was a job, but was this work? I had never really thought about it. "It's got its points."

"It's your passion, I suppose. Mine is land and real estate."

"You're a developer?"

Merchant smiled. "Goodness, no. There's far too much risk in that, and even if you turn a profit it can take a long time to see it. I buy what's already there. It's not very exciting, but there's an element of art in knowing a fine property. I used to look at every one myself, but now I have people to do that for me. Still, I insist on photographs and reserve the veto on all property acquisitions. I'd like to say I had a vision, but this all just sort of happened. I loved to hunt and fish when I was young. I had no money then, so it was tents or sleeping bags under the stars. But it seemed to me that if there were more and more people and the same amount of land, there would be increasing demand. We have a beautiful state and it always impressed me how people stay in state for vacations. I also knew a lot of people who owned cottages and passed them on, generation to generation. Most people don't want the cost or trouble of maintaining a place year-round. And if they head north, they don't want to be packed into fleabag motels or cabins two feet apart. So I started buying. I make good money now, but I think I also provide something of value. Like you."

Vacation places! *Ovid Merchant*. Now I remembered. "You're from Southfield?"

"Yes," he said, looking slightly surprised.

"You have places near Grand Marais?"

"You've stayed in one? I prefer Lake Superior to Lake Michigan. It's the purer experience."

"Some time back there was a woman who stayed in one of your properties near Grand Marais. Her name is Key. I mean, that's the name she used."

"I don't know the people who rent. I used to, but now there're too many for that."

"She and I grew up together and sort of lost contact. I had someone check with your management company in Marquette, but they said she paid cash in advance. There was no address for her, no way to contact her."

"That's unusual," he said, looking slightly perplexed. "That's not my policy. I believe in direct-mail follow-up. If we don't have the address, how can we market and get return business?"

I wasn't interested in his technical problem. "I would really like to locate her."

He poured out his coffee. "Well, I can't promise anything, but it would be a pleasure to look into it for you." He looked around.

We did not fish the rest of our float to the get-out point. At dinner that night the ten-pound fish raised eyebrows. So did our total catch, which was triple that of any of the others.

Merchant tipped me five thousand dollars and left the group shaking their heads again.

After dinner, Sturdivant pulled me aside. "You have had a remarkable season. Ordinarily I do not extend reemployment offers until the season is over and official evaluations completed, but tonight I am making an exception. I want you back, Mister Rhodes, and because you're first to be asked, that will make you my senior guide, affording you first choice of everything. Every one of your drifts has rebooked for next season. This is unprecedented. What say you?"

Next season? "I think we should keep tradition and talk again after the season is finished."

He was not happy with my answer. "As you wish," he said.

I had a drink with Ovid Merchant and thanked him for his generosity. "I've signed up for next year," he said, "but at my age, who knows what a year will bring? All I can promise is that I will look into the matter we discussed earlier. Where will you go when you're finished here?"

I told him how to contact me in Grand Marais.

At midnight Kelli knocked lightly on my screen door. "Bowie, are you awake?"

"I was just finishing my drift plan for tomorrow."

"Sturdivant's gone out again. You want to see?"

"You bet." The unexpected job offer for next season had me puzzled and intrigued. It seemed to me that he wanted something from me, but I could not figure out what. I grabbed my windbreaker.

"I'll meet you up at the highway," Kelli said. "By the bridge. Ten minutes?"

"See you there."

She drove me to where Sturdivant had put his boat in. His truck and trailer were still there. "Somebody will bring Medawar to the rig in the morning and then he'll drive the rig downriver to meet him."

"You've followed him before?"

"The Bible says, 'Be not curious in unecessary matters: for more things are shewed unto thee than men understand,' but I guess I can't help myself. You wanna know who's sleeping with whom?"

"No thanks."

"Well, you're not sleeping with anybody."

I laughed quietly. "Maybe you should join the CIA."

I wanted to see what Sturdivant was up to. I wanted to know how a blind man negotiated a river in a boat, but there was no way to know where he was. The best I could do was to go into the river above his get-out and hope for an intercept, preferably at sunrise when we could actually see.

"Shall we try to see what he's doing?"

"I'm game," Kelli said. "For *everything*," she added in a whisper close to my ear.

We parked her car on a two-track several hundred yards above Sturdivant's pickup point and walked cross-country over private land heavily posted with NO TRESPASSING signs.

"This is neat," Kelli said as we walked through the dark.

"If we run into trouble, split up and meet at the car."

In the darkness her eyes were better than mine. I let her lead.

We heard the river before we saw it. There was a sliver of moon low in the clear sky. We climbed down to the river and went upstream and down, looking for places to beach a boat. There were only two spots and one of these was just above a wide bend in the river.

"Let's park it here."

We found a spot behind a tangle of driftwood and settled in.

The nights were cooling. We sat close to each other. There was dew forming. "A fire would be nice," Kelli said.

"It's private land."

"We could make another kind of fire."

"We might miss Sturdivant."

"That would be okay by me."

We both laughed.

Insects buzzed all around us. I had no worries about oversleeping; the ground was hard and cold.

As the sun came up, Kelli snuggled under my arm and we watched the river.

We heard a whistle before Sturdivant came around the bend. He blew the whistle every few seconds and looked straight up into the morning sky, which fanned pink and gray in the east. The boat slid onto the gravel beach and the huge man stepped out and made sure his chains were set.

Sturdivant retrieved his rod and waded into the river. The fly was large and white, like a wad of fresh-picked cotton. He made short casts into a run, but there were no takes and after a while he clambered back into the boat, started tooting his whistle, and disappeared downstream.

"That was like, totally weird," Kelli said.

I thought: Why the white fly? Why here and why now?

We took another route back to the lodge so as not to encounter Medawar. Kelli dropped me at the bridge and I cut through the woods to my cabin. I knew I had to get Sturdivant aside, but I needed to pick the right time.

When I went to meet my drift I was tired. He was a young guy from Fort Wayne with a Canadian accent.

"You look happy," he said. "Does that mean a great night behind or a great day ahead?"

"A little of both," I lied. I knew the day would be a struggle and I would be fighting sleep. When I saw the transplanted Canadian cast, I knew it would be even worse. He bent his wrist, went too far back with his backcast, and slapped the water like Lash LaRue with a whip. It was an awful day. But we caught a few fish and the drift was happy.

I had dinner with Ingrid Cashdollar on Halloween. I was supposed to have a drift, but my client suffered a heart attack on the flight from Oklahoma City to Detroit. Sturdivant tried to get a replacement but without success, and I was glad because it would give me a couple of unexpected free days.

My driving suspension was long past, but I still had no car of my own. Collister, who had taken to calling me Crash, reluctantly loaned me his Oldsmobile. "Hope the bastard starts," he said. Of all the guides, he was the only one I could relate to.

The restaurant was at the end of a gravel road twenty miles from Dog River and the lot was packed. I arrived early to get our table, but Cashdollar was already there. She wore a tight angora sweater and a short skirt. She was a muscular, compact woman with wide shoulders and an inordinately small waist; she knew how to dress to favor her figure. She greeted me with a friendly smile.

She ate sparingly and apologized. "I've got the sort of body that could go square in a New York minute."

I laughed. "I doubt that."

"How's the fish business?"

"Busy. Can you tell me more about Sturdivant?"

She played with the swizzle in her drink, a plastic wand with a pineapple on top. "Not much. He's been here forever. He arrived after the war and built the lodge from scratch."

"Was he blind then?"

She nodded. "From the war, people say."

"What does Sturdivant say?"

"Nothing. People thought he was crazy when he first came, but every year he seemed to have more and more business. In the nineteen-fifties a few people started recognizing that there was money in fish. Over the years businesses came and went. Only Sturdivant has lasted." She looked across at me. "Why the interest?"

"Do you have any idea how it all works?"

She shook her head. "His people don't much mix with townies, present company excepted."

"We're supposed to make sure our clients catch fish, but not big ones."

"You're kidding?"

"Nope, that's the rule."

"Do you follow the rule?"

"Not at all, but he's asked me back for next season. As his lead guide, no less."

She whistled softly. "After just one season? You must be good."

"I don't think that's the reason."

"Then what?"

"That's what I'm trying to figure out."

After dinner we went into the bar. The band was all female, the Fishnets, costumes to match. We danced and nursed drinks. I told Ingrid about Sturdivant's night forays.

She had never seen Sturdivant at night, but she had heard the whistle below her house.

"Must've been him," I said.

"Sort of like a bat," she said. "He's really strange."

"We can't take clients at night, but he goes out alone after dark. Blind."

"Maybe he just wants it all to himself."

"He fishes at night with huge white flies."

"How do you know?"

"I've seen him."

"Ah, spying on the boss?"

"I was curious."

"You know where that can lead."

"It seems like a cop would be at more risk of that than me."

She nodded. "Don't think cops don't worry. Every time I pull somebody over or go up to a house, I think this could be it. Really bugged me when I first started. The trooper job was the worst. Too many locos out on the interstates. This is better, a lot more predictable."

"But not entirely safe."

"What is?" she asked. "I've learned how to be careful," she added.

"I've never met a woman cop before," I said.

She gave me a pained but playful grimace and fluttered her eyelids to mock me. "What's a nice girl like me doing with a big old gun, right?"

I laughed. "Something like that."

"Dad was a cop. I guess I just followed him. You watch, down the road there will be more female cops. Being a good cop isn't about being tough and kicking ass. It's about listening and talking and calming people down and solving problems. A lot of women are better at that part than men. I like working as a deputy in the country. In this job a cop is a friend, not an enemy to people."

I had never heard a better description of police work.

We danced close on the slow dances, pressed to each other, her head lightly on my chest.

"Sturdivant was sick a couple of times," she told me when we were off the dance floor, between numbers. "Each time he closed up for the whole season."

"Must've been serious."

"No, it was more like bullshit. He was there the whole time. People saw him fishing from time to time."

"When was this?"

"Once sometime in the late nineteen-fifties and again in the sixties. I don't know the exact years."

We danced through the final set, not talking, enjoying the rhythms and closeness. It was one A.M. She looked at her watch first.

"Gotta go?" I asked.

She said, "Last call, so to speak."

"It's been a great time," I said. I felt nervous and had a reasonable idea why.

She turned around. "I know somebody who could tell you more about Sturdivant."

"Who?"

"She lives in Manistee. She worked for him a long time."

"How do I get in touch?"

"I'd have to take you," she said. "I don't think she'll talk to a stranger cold."

"When can we see her?"

"We could go tonight," she said, with a smile.

"It's pretty late."

"She won't mind and you'll be safe with a cop."

I laughed and said, "Okay."

We went in her jeep and didn't talk much. It took us nearly ninety minutes to get to Manistee. The house was on a tree-lined street, east of the center of town. There were lights on in the house.

"She's a confirmed insomniac," Cashdollar said.

The woman's name was Gally and she looked to be in her seventies. "Damn, is that you, Ingrid?" she said when she opened the door. "Don't you look the pretty picture," she said, looking Ingrid over.

I was introduced. "This is Bowie. He's my friend. He wants to know about Sturdivant."

The woman made a face. "Come on in here. I'm freezing with the door open."

It was an old house with a musty smell. We sat in the parlor. "Sturdivant's mean," she said.

"Is he blind?" I asked.

The woman grinned crookedly. "Legally blind, but he can see some and if you ask me, maybe he can see a whole lot. It sure seems he can always see what he wants to see. You seen him at night on the river, have you?"

"With his whistle. How did you know?"

"I remember when he started that."

"It's a put-on?"

"With Sturdivant anything is possible."

"Ingrid says he closed the place for a couple of seasons."

The woman nodded. "I was there the first time."

"Was he sick?"

"Not that I ever seen. He just didn't want people around his place. He fished every night and I cooked for him and he was in a foul temper the whole time. He said, 'You want to keep getting paid, you just keep telling people I'm sick.' So I kept my mouth shut."

"He fished alone?"

"Yep, usually he did, but there was a fella used to drop by sometimes and the two of them would go out. Had an accent. Little fella, heavyset."

"You met him?"

"Just seen him. Sturdivant got real edgy whenever he was coming. Nervous. I could always tell."

"Did he come to fish at other times?"

"Just that year Sturdivant closed up."

"Do you remember the man's name?"

"Never heard one. I asked Sturdivant who he was and he told me to mind my own business."

"The big fish hanging in the lodge. The one by the fireplace."

Another nod. "That came after that season closed."

"Was it really caught in the Dog?"

"He never said and I never asked."

The conversation petered out after that. She and Ingrid swapped a few memories and the old woman said she was tired. She went with us to the door.

"If you think of anything else about the man who fished with Sturdivant, I'd like to know."

"You can call me," Ingrid told her.

"There's nothing else to remember," the woman said. She tugged on Ingrid's sleeve and whispered something I couldn't hear.

In the jeep Ingrid said, "Gertie said the man who fished with Sturdivant? He carried a cane. It was black, she said. And crooked, whatever that means. It had an ivory handle with a design."

I had a hunch. "Gold inlays, in the shape of three diamonds?"

She stared at me. "You know him?"

"Less and less," I said.

It had to be Gus Chickerman.

There was only one day left in the lodge's season. The state trout season had closed six weeks before, but our water was catch-and-release and would stay open all winter. Years before, Sturdivant had convinced the DNR to leave the river open and they had agreed. This classification on the Dog was an experiment, but years later rivers all over the state would follow suit and operate year-round under special regulations. Even with the water legally open to fishing, Sturdivant closed the lodge just before deer season in mid-November and did not reopen until spring. I assumed part of the strategy was to limit supply in order to increase demand. But there could be other reasons as well.

My last drift was a surprise: Sturdivant himself. I had thought it was to be the president of the University of Virginia. "What's this all about?"

"I thought it was time we talked man to man."

Medawar drove us west to the get-in Kelli and I had seen. "I haven't fished this stretch before."

"Private property," he said. "Mostly mine."

We put the boat in and started downstream.

"Anchor her," Sturdivant said. I did as I was told. "You went to see Gertie Gally," he said. "She called me. I don't like snoopers, Rhodes. I know who the hell you are. You worked with Angus Wren."

"I never hid who I was."

"You damn well didn't declare it either," Sturdivant said with an accusatory grunt. "Why the hell are you digging around?"

"You asked me to stay, remember?"

He heaved a deep sigh. "You're just like the rest of them."

"Who?"

"Your erstwhile colleagues," he said. "Did they tell you it was my rule that you don't put drifts on big fish?"

"I heard that."

"But you didn't ask me for verification."

"I didn't need to. I put my drifts on big fish."

Sturdivant laughed. "*Twenty*-pounders? You think *those* are big?" The boat rocked in the current. "Twenty is a pipsqueak." Sturdivant was immense, three hundred pounds, at least.

"Big fish," I said. "Like the one over your fireplace."

"Yes, big fish. *Real* fish. Like that."

"Which you didn't catch."

He squinted at me and looked disgusted. "What does it matter who caught it? It *was* caught and that's the only fact that counts."

"But not by you and that sticks in your craw."

Sturdivant glowered at me. "M. J. Key caught it," he said. "On a snowfly."

"M. J. Key who used a black cane with an ivory handle?"

Sturdivant nodded and I thought, I'll be damned. Gus Chickerman was M. J. Key. At least one of them.

"But he didn't catch it here," Sturdivant added. "He's a devious bastard, that one. It's true, he came and fished here. I first met him in Canada, way up in Northern Québec. I flew in to a river with a bush pilot and he was already there, and on his own. He told my guide and me about the snowfly. Hatches every ten years or so. At night and for only a couple of hours. Never before fall and never after spring. Key said he knew all about the snowfly hatch, even the schedule. He knew places where the hatch had happened. I thought he was full of shit, but after fishing in that river with him I decided maybe he knew something after all. He called me one year, said the next year would be the one."

"So you shut down for the season."

"I had no time for business. I wanted the summer to prepare myself. I had to be on the water and I didn't want to be distracted."

"That's the year he came."

"We caught fish, but we didn't catch *the* fish. There was no hatch."

"But you learned something about white flies."

"They work at night, dusk, dawn. It's sporadic. I have no idea why. Could be a hatch now and then, the way you'll see olives a month before their regular hatch. Or hex flies here and there, even in September, months after the main hatch is done. You don't see white flies on every river. Key traveled around. Kept a book. He was methodical, I'll give him that."

"Your data board in the guide house. You got the idea from Key?"

"I learned a lot from him. Why not?"

"He made you think the hatch would be here, but he came only a few times."

"One morning I got up and found the big fish on dry ice in a wooden box outside the lodge."

"Red herring. He wanted you to think the hatch was here so he could have the real hatch site to himself."

Sturdivant chewed his bottom lip and nodded. "And I fell for it."

"But the flies did hatch."

"Somewhere, and not far away, I'd guess. The fish he left was fresh."

"But such hatches come only once to a river."

"Who the hell knows the truth? He could've lied about everything."

"Ten years later you closed again."

"I couldn't take the chance that there wasn't a real ten-year cycle. That's how disinformation works. He had hooked me."

"When is the next cycle?"

"Season after next, if you're a believer."

"Why'd you hire me?"

"I recognized your name from the column. I knew Angus Wren. I was at his funeral, I saw you there. Wren and I had some differences of opinion and we stopped talking."

"He didn't like headhunters."

Sturdivant grunted. "Purity is a much-overrated commodity."

"Okay, Angus and I worked together So what?"

"I had a hunch. This season I wanted to check you out. If Angus hired you, you had to be good. If you were, next year I'd get you back and we'd get into the night routine."

"To get ready for the hatch."

"I confess that I did have that in mind."

"But you want the fish yourself."

Sturdivant's voice iced over. "I don't give a shit about who catches the damn thing just as long as we get the big one from the Dog. The fish will bring the business, not who caught it."

"Promotional leverage."

"There it is."

"It's all money to you."

Sturdivant laughed. "What else is there?"

"But the chances of the hatch happening here are slim."

"I talked to all the old-timers. Know them all. Plenty have seen some snowflies, but never a full hatch. The flies are here, down in the mud, sleeping, waiting. It's just a matter of time until the hatch happens."

"It may never happen in your lifetime. It may never happen at all."

"It will happen and you'll want to be here. You could make a fortune. You think you made a bundle this year? Peanuts, a drop in the bucket."

"I won't be back next season." The decision was made on the spot and I knew it was the right one. The snowfly had been pushing me around most of my life and now I saw how it drove Sturdivant's life. I wanted no part of it.

"That's it then," he with a grunt. "Let's go."

We drifted all the way back down to the lodge in silence. Sturdivant seemed morose. There was a final dinner that night, but I stayed away. In the morning there was a check waiting for me in the office. All of the tips there, including interest.

I considered calling Ingrid to ask her for a ride to the bus stop, but I decided at the last moment not to bother her. I didn't call her to say good-bye either. What would I say? It felt too awkward and given that, I did what I often did, I fled.

Kelli drove me to a crossroads called Vermilion to await a Trailways bus going north. It was snowing hard. There were red-clad deer hunters all over the place, giddy over the snow, which would make it easy to follow blood trails.

Kelli and I kissed good-bye and she said, "Last chance. My backseat's *huge.*"

But we left it at that one kiss and I got my gear out and watched her drive away.

The snowfly thing had been in and out of my life for as long as I could remember. Like malaria, flaring up when I least expected it. In two years there would be a hatch. I told myself I didn't care.

19

I got off the bus in Mackinaw City and went into a restaurant called the New Bridge. It was snowing and across the street, the community buck pole was accumulating grisly trophies, shadows dripping blood that coagulated and cooled black on the snow. The restaurant walls were decorated with saltwater seashells, the closest salt sea a thousand miles north or east, seashells displayed alongside shellacked deer antlers on plaques.

Two booths down a man in a red plaid hunting coat was telling several companions how his wife "came up on" a twelve-point buck mounting a doe on the edge of a pond and she couldn't bring herself to shoot until they had finished.

Said the man, "I told her the doe don't get no pleasure from it. And his wife said, 'Don't I know it.' " Hearty laughs all around. I laughed with them.

Fort Machilimackinac was in view across the street, below the approach to the bridge. Queen Anna had given me Kenneth Roberts's novels to read when I was in high school and one of these, *Northwest Passage,* had been made into a movie with Spencer Tracy as Major Robert Rogers, who led his rangers against the Abenaki Indians. I was in college before I learned that Rogers had not only been real but also had commanded the fort I was looking at. I never stopped at the straits without thinking about Rogers, who lived adventure after adventure but never seemed to fit in anywhere.

Decor and conversation as non sequiturs, seashells, buckhorns, and the battle of the sexes. The nonfits shoehorned into my mood. I had a room in the motel next door courtesy of a hunter's no-show. I was determined to make a plan.

Coffee was served by a six-foot amazon with close-cropped white hair. She had saucer-sized hands with giant red knuckles and refilled my cup only if I held it above the table and said, "Please," a reminder that the battle for control raged everywhere.

I used a paper placemat and ballpoint pen to jot notes.

"Are you a nimrod?" my amazon asked.

Nimrod of Genesis, hunter and king: I was neither. "Not really."

"Each to his own, I always say. I don't eat what I don't kill and I won't kill what I won't eat," she declared, a philosophy packed with ambiguity. A life based on presumed balance. I envied her.

I had kissed Kelli and the guiding life good-bye. Several stops and five hours later I was sitting among Coxey's Army trying to write down what I knew about the snowfly mystery. I saw it as a way of ridding my system of the Key virus.

The notes did not come easily because the thinking didn't come easily. It had been a long road, complicated by many sudden switchbacks and no satisfactory answers along the way.

I remembered the floater's widow in her red Caddie ragtop. She had started it all, snowflies and flashing beaver, in her mind an either-or proposition. I had passed on Kelli and not hit on Ingrid. Was I growing up? Queen Anna would be proud, and this thought somehow depressed me.

Red Ennis, thousands of miles west in a state of emeritus, held the opinion that those myths that persisted were usually based on something real. The question was what that something was, the qualifier buried deep in the pronoun.

Rose Yelton, bless her, had gone back to Red Ennis, written down the legend, and sent it to me, a parting gift. Or curse. It took time to get perspective on which was which and the jury on this was still out. My snowfly trail had nothing but question marks and dead ends for road signs.

The legend as I knew it:

Certain insects hatch on a ten-year cycle (or fifteen?), never rising twice on the same river (allegedly), between fall and spring (maybe), which took in a whole lot of months at northern latitudes. Meaning *only* on rivers? *Some* rivers. Some trout lived forty, fifty years? Not likely. Yet Angus and I *had* seen a hint of long-lived trout in Parley Finger's spitwad pond in southern Ohio. Trout rising only to a fly few people knew about? It was nonsense on the surface, but my interest had always been real, if not rock steady. I would tell Red Ennis that the some myths rested mostly on some people *wanting* to believe.

Lloyd Nash had shown me M. J. Key's 1892 and 1943 books. Lloyd knew of Key, a reclusive professor in the college's distant past. And there had been the Collection Room: White flies found, white flies lost. Probably snowflies, and probably they had once been Key's.

Danny, my Good Samaritan at the New York Public Library, had given assistance, then been chased off the hunt by the government. Why? Before she abandoned the search she had been really helpful, veri-

fying Key, his mysterious departure from MSU (then MAC) and his interest in codes. A spy perhaps? Nash had suggested this. Why else this government pressure decades later? Or General Centre warning me off the
search when I probed Key's relationship to wartime codebreakers in England. Or Charlie Jowett's late aunt, wartime denizen of Bletchley Park,
who was cagey in answering my questions. Key had been driven out of
the university because he was a Nazi sympathizer. Maybe. This could
just as easily have been government disinformation. Maybe they wanted
him for their own uses. I had seen the government's little games after my
departure from the Soviet Union. The government was like a river,
always making ripples disappear.

The Goodwins, Dickie and Gillian, owners of the Trout House on
the River of Trout, South Vietnam, Republic of. Planted by the eccentric
Englishman Sir Thomas Oxley. Talk about non sequiturs and coinci-
dences. There I had seen Key's unpublished manuscript, *Legend of the
Snowfly*. It had been in my hands, then it was gone. Misfortunes of war. It
had been real, but I would never know its value, if any, to my search. You
couldn't follow a map you didn't possess.

Raina Chickerman had appeared after my father's death. Why?
More puzzling: Raina as Miss Smith in Grand Marais in winter. Father
Buzz. Raina Chickerman. Second coming. Why had she been there? I
seesawed between certainty and uncertainty. Ovid Merchant could assist
on this. He had promised to try, and his appearance on the Dog River as
my drift was as strange as all the rest of the threads in this damn thing. I
needed Merchant's help. No way around that.

I had tracked the remainder of Oxley's collection to London, but it
had been sold to the Russians. I stubbornly pursued, and look where
that had led: My search had cost a man his life and nobody seemed concerned about that but me. The Soviets had panicked and dumped everything. I was lucky to get out. Thank Valoretev for that. I wondered where
he was. He and I might have become close friends. Queen Anna had
said, "When elephants dance, it's the grass that suffers." I had wandered
into the periphery of an ideological clash. Perhaps even prompted it,
though this seemed unlikely.

Oxley had been brokered to Lockwood Bolt, Elliot Lake, the outer
reaches by any definition, ultima Thule. Cold trail, hot tailings, Cold
War. Extremes and diametrics when you cared to look. For Bolt, purely
an investment, like soybeans or hog futures. Oxley moved again, from
Bolt to M. J. Key! Ghost as investor or meddler? Who *was* Key? And *what*?
Gus? Raina? All of the above?

Izaak Walton had written, "That which is everybody's business is
nobody's business." I wondered if the converse applied.

Angus Wren bought snowflies so people would not be tempted, one man's futile effort to halt a viral obsession. I had never seen any for sale, but Angus had been eighty-eight when he died and had been traveling for decades. Fact: Some people tied the flies. And had for a long time. Why? Because they believed in the hatch. No other explanation possible, unless the flies were tourist jokes, like jackelopes you could find in Texas.

The Chickermans died, consumed by fire. And their only child never bothered to show up. Again, *why?* Lawyer Eubanks stonewalled me on her whereabouts *and* on white flies. From Maria Idly's contacts I had learned that some sort of federal protection program was linked to the Chickermans, but no rationale or details. Much less context. But Eubanks had his own flies on display in his office, which was more like a museum. Smoke after the real fire. A literal fact sequence here. I was reminded of Red Ennis. Myths that persist were likely to have substance.

My sister, Lilly, confirmed that the late Roger Ranger used to see Gus Chickerman crawling out of local streams. And that Gus used to travel a lot, both of these facts previously unknown, and both wholly unexpected. Gus gone, long trips, where a mystery. He fished? Why did he keep this a secret? And *way* up Whirling Creek, a documented killer. Who *was* Gus Chickerman? And *what?*

Buzz had helped me get the link of Miss Smith = M. J. Key = Raina Chickerman? A suggested loop, a would-be circle lacking evidence for closure.

According to Hannah, Angus Wren probably never knew Key and surely loathed his values. Headhunter, seeker of trophies. Angus = pure. Key = not pure? Whose definition? Angus knew Sturdivant too, but this wasn't a surprise. Angus knew a lot of people, big and small, presidents and peasants.

Sturdivant knew someone named Key, carrying the same cane as Gus. The Key whom Sturdivant knew was definitely a headhunter; the gigantic stuffed trout in the lodge attested to this. Not caught in the Dog. Then where? Sturdivant, the blind man in a boat, whistling in the darkness in pursuit of profit. Used his whistle and sound to navigate the river at night, walk in the woods. I had figured this out all on my own. Chickerman as Key had *misled* Sturdivant. Sleight of hand, applied to greed. Supports contention of Angus Wren. Key = not pure. Nor Sturdivant. Any of us? I couldn't say.

"You're wasting paper," my amazon said, interrupting me.
I presented my cup for the fourth time. "Please."
"Men's is down the hall, left," she said.

Key: published 1892 and 1943. A Key (probably Chickerman) fished the Dog in the late 1950s, said Sturdivant, confirmed more or less by the woman named Gally, Ingrid's friend, who'd promptly informed Sturdivant. I had no idea why other than that he was "the" man in the area and people tended to want to stay on the good side of people with power.

Don't dare think about Ingrid now, I told myself. I should have called her. Keep plowing along.

Key as multiple personality? Was there such a thing? A cat, maybe. How many lives were left?

The unpublished manuscript. This existed. A second copy, last acquired by M. J. Key (*damn* loops), gender unknown. Burying evidence of herself, himself, themselves? Raina? Smith = Key = Raina = Smith. My eyes had seen Raina as Smith. Cops always said eyewitnesses were notoriously unreliable. Reporters included? Yes. Gus as fisherman. The things you never know soon enough.

Two avenues remained: Raina Chickerman and the unpublished manuscript. Correction: Make that one avenue, obscured, grown over, covered. But *real*. Had to be. Find one, find the other? Ovid Merchant as loose end to be spliced in? He was a strand of hope, maybe my last one. What were the odds of him remembering his promise?

The draw of a liberal arts education: Get a little of a lot, B.D., Bachelor of Dabbling. The downside: Facts whip through the mind like jellyfish in a riptide. Occam's razor: If you get two satisfactory solutions to a problem, take the shorter, simpler one. But this wasn't math and there were no obvious answers, long or short. Life refuses to adhere to formulae.

Resolve, absent direction, equaled chaos. This was reality, not theory. For now, the only answer seemed to reside with Ovid Merchant. He was not my best bet; he was my *only* one.

My brain was beginning to skip and dart. Time to quit. I folded my notes, paid my bill, and went outside where a crowd had gathered at the buck pole, snow gathering equally on hats and corpses. A flatbed truck was parked nearby. Curious onlookers were staring at an immense carcass with snow piling up on it. A conservation officer in a shapeless green horse blanket addressed a small man in a flaming red snowmobile suit. They stood by the flatbed.

"It's an elk, you fucking mutant!" the angry CO said.

Replied the hunter, "Can you eat it?"

"Not from jail," the CO said.

Some mysteries are more easily solved than others.

I called Fred Ciz from Mackinaw City and caught a Trailways bus to Newberry. Fred met me in front of the Lumberman's Hotel. He looked thinner, older.

"You look like a right-hand foot in a left-hand shoe," I told him.

"You don't look so peachy keen yourself," he said.

We embraced like brothers.

The first order of business when coming home is the ritual catch-up.

Fred began immediately. "Subscriptions are up eight hundred from all over the state. Thanks to Karla. That gal's a born promoter. And forty-two new building permits last summer. Selling *and* building now, since she hooked up with a fella named Van from the Soo. He builds, she sells." Fred glanced at me in the passenger seat. "They're an item," he added. "Is that the right lingo nowadays?"

"Close enough."

"That too," Fred Ciz said. "Buzz is Buzz, as busy as ever."

"Janey?"

"Some answers you've got to get on your own." He looked straight ahead and changed subjects. "I read about Angus Wren. I'm sorry. The column not work out after that?"

"Family disease. Greed."

Fred cracked a smile. "Looking for work?"

"I wouldn't mind helping. No pay."

"Grab the brass ring, did you?"

"In a manner of speaking."

We had dinner at Staley's. Fred, Buzz, Karla, and her boyfriend, Van, Janey, and me. Van wore an ill-fitting blue corduroy suit and white socks that looked like they were purchased a dozen pairs at a time from the Monkey Ward catalog. He was tall and heavy, older, and he doted on Karla. Janey wore a dress that hung nearly to the floor and was terminally wrinkled. Her hair was long and straight. No makeup. Her clunky sandals over wool socks seemed to make her tilt backward like she was walking into an eternal wind, which for her life was an apt metaphor. She did not look at me. I answered some questions and asked others and we all got caught up. It was a true Staley's dinner, steaks rare, scallions and 'shrooms, baked potatoes, thick sour cream with chives, a metal-capped bottle of red wine.

Buzz had been offered a diocesan job in Marquette and turned it down. "Little enough time for trout as it is," he explained.

Karla's kids had settled in and Van had two of his own, girls in their late teens. I gathered they were cohabitating, blending offspring, seeking cohesiveness. I was happy for them. And only a bit envious.

A young, wealthy entrepreneur from Cleveland had bought four thousand acres in the county and was fencing it in. The townies yanked down the fence sections as fast as they could be put up. Fences in the U.P. were taken as an act of war: The interloper's money would not guarantee success. The same as in Vietnam.

Newberry High had a halfback recruited by Wisconsin. Michigan and Michigan State had ignored him. Never mind that the Yoopers had more of an affinity for dairy herds to the west than car makers to the south. The kid's snubbing was a point of honor.

Last winter a woman named Delilah had shot a 650-pound black bear that had been raiding her garbage. One shot, in the left eye, with a .222 Hornet, the small caliber and accuracy a source of immense local pride.

Steelhead and salmon were running up the Little Two Hearted, attracting snaggers by the hundreds.

The rivers had been high all summer and Buzz bemoaned the smallness of the trout. "Petty 'bows," he said. "God's dinks."

An albino buck had been seen several times near Lake Mitawichen. Popular opinion held that scavenging Indians would kill it and eat it. There was no romance about Indians up here, and even less sympathy. They'd barbecue a white buffalo just as fast. Food first, gods later, as anticipated by Maslow. I understood both views, but most admired practicality.

All the trivia of home, half facts pulled through the screen of collective identity. I loved it all, took comfort in the pointless detail.

After dinner Buzz headed for church and Fred for the office. Karla and Van didn't announce their destination but their eyes told the tale. I faced Janey alone.

"How're your kids?"

"Older," she said. "Doing fine. You've been gone a while."

"It didn't work out the way I planned."

"What does?" she said. "Fred showed me some of the columns you wrote. They were good. I like what you do with words."

"And you, how are you doing?" I asked.

"I like the job. For a long time I felt like I was stumbling along."

"And now your feet are solidly under you?"

"Getting that way," she said. "Thanks to you."

"All I did was nudge an idea."

"Don't interrupt me," she said with surprising force. "If Staley's hadn't been continued, I don't know what might have happened to the town. You and Karla came in and made some things happen. I see pride again and I like it. This is no small thing. For the town—or for me." She reached for my hands. "Thank you, Bowie."

It was the first time she had ever used my given name. I quickly changed the subject and got up and fetched fresh coffee for us. We made more small talk, catching up on her kids and the problems and challenges of running the Light and when I departed she gave me a chaste hug.

I was living at Fred's place again and helping him with the paper. It was February and we had an immense pack of snow, close to two hundred inches, mounting and counting. The snowbanks had risen to ten feet and the county sprayed them with purple dye to help drivers see them. We hung purple ribbons on vehicle antennas to keep the county snowblowers from eating them. In mid-January there had been a three-day whiteout, all of us buried and marooned in place. It made me think of Pompeii, only at the other end of the temperature spectrum.

All the while I worked hard and time passed and I brooded about the snowfly and Raina Chickerman. The two subjects did not dominate my every thought, but neither were they far away.

On February 1 I called Southfield and learned that Ovid Merchant and his spouse had gone to Florida until the northern ice broke up, which could be months ahead. I talked to one of Merchant's employees, a man named Allen, an accomplished prick.

"Mister Merchant promised he'd call," I explained. "He was going to get some information for me."

"Then I'm sure he will."

"But I need to talk to him *now.*"

"Do you take business calls on *your* vacation?"

I told him I did.

"Pity," Allen said. He was an effective gate guard. I had no choice but wait for Merchant to call me.

True winter, no hope from any direction. I was hunkered down until spring could force its way in. I saw Janey almost every day and learned she had a great sense of humor to go with her smarts. We became friends and a couple of times when the weather allowed we drove into Newberry to take in a movie. It was strictly platonic.

I drove west to Houghton on February 14. The old mining town was snowed in, like the rest of the north. And hilly, which made it worse. I visited the library at Michigan Tech and talked to an old fellow named Pelkie. He was an acquaintance of Buzz, a retired railroad engineer who worked as a volunteer at the library. I looked in the card catalog for Key's books, but there were no listings. I asked Buzz's pal to check his other sources and he came back shaking his head, saying there were no listings anywhere, which struck me as odd, and I ascribed this to Pelkie's being old and a little addled. Besides, I knew that libraries discarded old books from time to time. I asked him where I could find the best library on fly fishing. He'd have to noodle it, he said, get back to me. This was becoming a familiar refrain. He never did.

On the way back to Grand Marais I began to think about Ingrid. I had no intention of calling her, but as I drove through the snow and darkness the idea got rooted in my mind and by the time I got to Marquette whim had transformed to overwhelming need. It was midnight and she was home, asleep.

"If this turns out to be a dream, I will be seriously ticked," she said.

"Meet me in St. Ignace," I said. The invitation was out before I could debate it, an example of the subconscious asserting its needs. "I'd like to see you."

"*Jesus*, Bowie Rhodes. *You* want! You *want?* Just like that? You bug out and don't say good-bye or kiss my ass, and not a word since, not even a card on Valentine's Day, which was yesterday, and Christmas, which was months ago, and now it's *meet me?* What is it with you men?"

"What do you say?" I was in no position to argue for the honor of the entire gender. Besides, I was guilty as charged. Her voice sounded wonderful.

"When?"

"Tomorrow in St. Ignace at the Wanderer Motel."

A long pause. "I've got a lot of sick days in the bank, which is apropos, because I must be sick to agree to this."

"Is that a yes?"

"Don't give me reason to rethink it."

I sat in the café of a truck stop, north of the off ramp of the Mackinac Bridge across U.S. 2 from the motel. The Wanderer had several units built in the approximate likeness of tepees. I was waiting for housekeeping to finish cleaning two of the units.

There was not much traffic coming north across the bridge that joined the state's two peninsulas. The Ojibwa, who had lived here when the French arrived in the seventeenth century, had not lived in tepees, but Ojibwa and Mohawk had died building the bridge centuries later.

Ingrid arrived at noon and joined me in the café. She seemed smaller than I remembered, her neck long and firm, her hair short and swept back to give the impression of constant motion. She gave me a half smile when she saw me and slid into the booth across from me.

"Are you hungry?" I asked.

She shook her head. "Butterflies. That's supposed to be a sign."

"Of what?"

"I haven't got a clue," she said nervously.

"I'm sorry," I said. "About the sudden call."

"I'm here," she said, "and I have to say this to you: I rarely let my impulses have their way."

"But this time you're making an exception and I'm glad."

"I didn't think it through and now I don't want to. What's your agenda, Rhodes? Be direct."

I pointed. "I have rooms across the street."

"That's damn direct," she said quickly.

"I didn't mean—."

She was blushing. "That's not what I meant either," she said.

"We can sit here and talk."

"The room's good. I want to get these boots off. I hate cold weather. I go barefoot at home most of the summer."

"There are two rooms," I said.

"You're a gentleman. Let's take a look at those rooms."

The rooms adjoined in Tepee Number Fourteen; the rooms were numbered ninety-one and twenty-two, the logic of this escaping me. They were minuscule, each with twin beds, a small table, two chairs, and a three-year-old calendar with photographs of clumps of forget-me-nots.

"Opulent," she said, setting her small bag on the floor. She went to the window, stared out, then drew the curtains closed. "Why *did* you call after all this time?" I saw her eyes examine the small beds. She said, "I didn't hear anything from you for . . . how long? Six *months*. And here we are. This isn't me. It can't be."

"I was thinking about you. And then I was calling."

She carefully took off her jacket, sat on the edge of the bed, kicked off her boots, and rubbed her feet. "Okay, both of us can be impetuous, but what's your motive, Rhodes?"

"I'm sorry," I began to say.

"I'm not and, besides, cops hate apologies and denials. Everybody's always sorry for what they didn't do. It's a miracle human beings ever take responsibility for anything. 'I'm sorry, officer, I didn't do it.' What the heck does *that* mean?" She jerked her shirttails out of her jeans. "You left Sturdivant's without a word. *Then* what?"

I sat down on the bed facing her and began. I told her I had been a columnist before I came to Dog River. UPI had been cutting people and I had been lucky to get the job and had loved it. Then Angus died and the legal war began and I was out and I ended up in Dog River purely by accident.

"Those men I saved? I don't remember a thing about it."

"You saved them," she said. "And nearly drowned."

What to say next? "All my life," I began, "I've been chasing something."

She rolled her eyes. "The snowfly. You think you're the only one?"

There were others? I had never considered this before. "What do you mean?"

"You asked me that day at my house if I tied snowflies. Only believers ask this. Over on the Au Sable a few years back there were a bunch of bums living along the river and the USFS kept chasing them off and they kept coming back. They were waiting for the snowfly hatch. A couple of the bums froze to death that winter. When spring came, they were gone."

Others chasing the snowfly. And they were there during winter. Evidence or wishful thinking on my part? I felt a charge of anxiety. "You don't believe the legend?"

She listened attentively. "No, but there are worse things to believe," she said. "All people need dreams."

"What if the dream's a nightmare?"

"You don't look any worse for the wear," she said. She ran a hand through her hair. "People say God doesn't make junk, but he sure does seem to pitch a lot of it. Curveballs, screwballs, dropballs, sinkers, sliders, even spitters, the whole divine mess. God, fate, call it what you want, doesn't make life easy, but I think people ought to finish what they start."

"Philosopher cop."

"Who better to philosophize than somebody who gets a daily look at the real price of life?"

"It must be nice to know who you are and what you want."

A wry smile formed. "Right, and then one night you get a phone call and you're up early the next morning splashing Shalimar between your boobs and driving north fifteen miles an hour over the speed limit. Explain *that*."

"I can't."

"And neither can I and sometimes you just *know* something and there's no logic and you either trust your instincts or you don't. *You* called me. And now that I'm here, maybe we should just go ahead and finish whatever it is we've started."

I was shaking when I sat down beside her and took her hands in mine. "I meant to call you before this."

"A big-shot columnist should have a better line than that."

"I mean it. We had a nice time and I moved on. But I kept thinking about you."

She laughed and looked into my eyes. "I think Nanook needs some Nanooky."

Our laughs turned into a kiss that melted my brain.

"Bingo," I mumbled.

Ingrid pushed me back. "Does that make me the cheap prize?"

"Bingo fuel. It's pilot talk for having enough gas to get where you're going, but not back to where you started."

She touched her hand to my cheek and whispered, "Bingo."

Afterward, we lay intertwined in the too-small bed. "Well," she whispered, "what comes after bingo?"

"Touchdown at destination."

She nibbled my ear and cooed, "I like making touchdowns."

The next morning over breakfast I told her the whole story of my chase after the snowfly, Raina, the floater, M. J. Key, Eubanks, Ovid Merchant, all of it.

She dug into her purse, extracting a pencil and notepad. "Let's have the particulars on Merchant." When she had them, she went to a pay phone and dialed. I stood next to her, rubbing her lower back. "Is Sergeant Briggs in? Oh, Doug. This is Ingrid Cashdollar. Great. I need some assistance locating a man. Ovid Merchant of Southfield. He's in Florida for the winter and I need his address down there. Okay, I'll wait." She smiled at me while we waited and when the voice came back on the other end, she put her pad on a shelf under the phone and got her pencil ready. "Shoot." She wrote quickly and said, "Thanks, Doug.

"Troopers in Royal Oak," she told me. "They called the post office in Southfield." She handed me her pad. "Elementary, my dear Watson."

Her note said, Ovid Merchant, Sandflea Island, Florida.

"How would you like to go to Florida?" I asked.

She rolled away. "First St. Ignace. Now Florida. This is going a little too fast."

"Can you get off?"

She studied my face for a long time. "Not a problem so far," she said, chucking my arm and pulling me out the door toward the motel. "I feel a touchdown approaching."

Ingrid arranged for time off and we stopped at her place for clothes then drove to Detroit, where we left her car. We flew from Detroit to Atlanta then on to Mobile, where we rented a car, bought maps, and drove east. Sandflea Island was aptly named. It was just off Florida's panhandle, a small spit of white sand, scrub brush, and mangroves on the landward side. The only way out to it was by boat. I rented one with a small outboard from a marina called Wilbur's. The engine putt-putted confidently, swirling tendrils of stinking blue exhaust. Terns followed our tiny wake, skimming the water.

There was only one house on the island, and no security apparent, in stark contrast to how difficult it was to get a message to Merchant by telephone. We trudged across the scrub flats and saw blue roof tiles flashing through the brush and trees.

It was a sunny day with a timid Gulf breeze. I spied my drift in a faded beach chair on a lawn that was more sand than grass.

"Mister Merchant?"

He stared out into the Gulf, which was coated with a Technicolor slick.

"You people!" a female voice shouted from the house. "You people get away from there!"

An elderly woman with frightened eyes appeared, brandishing a dust mop.

"I'm Bowie Rhodes," I said. "This is Ingrid Cashdollar. I fished with Mister Merchant at Sturdivant's last fall."

The woman lowered her weapon. "Oh my! I apologize. We weren't expecting anyone. He talked about you," she said. "You're much younger than I expected."

"We were in the area and thought we'd stop for a visit. I'm sorry we didn't call ahead."

She looked sad and perplexed. "A call wouldn't have made a difference," she said.

I looked at Ovid Merchant for the first time. Spittle covered his chin. His mouth hung open.

"He had a stroke," the woman said. "He's here, but not here. I asked the doctor where a mind goes when this happens. He said, 'Looking for Jesus.' I said, 'We're Jews.' The South," she added disgustedly. "Ovid and I fought over this place. I said, 'Jews belong in Palm Beach.' He said, 'This is the Redneck Riviera and we're redneck Jews.' Ovid had a unique view of the world that helped make him a success, I suppose, but I never understood him."

"He was supposed to get some information for me," I said.

"He was quite a trader," she said, nodding in his direction. "I give you this, you give me that. He should've traded horses. I used to tell him that. He said, 'Horses eat.' See what I mean about his mind, how it was?"

Ingrid and I exchanged glances. "He had girlfriends," the woman said. "Oh yes, a real schtupper, he was, collecting his cutie pies. I always meant to tell him what I thought of that," she said. "Now this. Damn him."

She aimlessly dabbed at the sand with the mop, then looked up. "Wait here!"

"Yes, ma'am."

She came back with a tray and two tall glasses. "His favorite." She held them out to us. Unsweetened grapefruit juice. Ingrid sipped politely and put the glass back, hardly touched.

"Thanks for the drinks. We're sorry we barged in."

"He wouldn't know," she said.

Ingrid looked at me and rolled her eyes. We started to walk away.

"You're Rhodes," the woman said. "Right?"

I turned. She was holding an envelope, which she held out to me.

"I can't believe I forgot to mail this." She sat down beside her husband and spoke slowly and loudly as if volume could drive her words into his injured brain. "There," she said. "I did it. Now don't kvetch." She patted the back of his hand tenderly.

Ingrid and I were back on the mainland before we spoke again.

"She shouldn't be out there alone like that," Ingrid said.

I thought: In one way or another we're all out there alone like that.

I didn't open the envelope for a long time and Ingrid didn't ask. Our ease with each other brought me unexpected and sublime comfort. We fit each other.

Eventually I could no longer ignore the obvious and pulled the car over to the shoulder of the road. There were white birds with long necks in the low branches of dead trees at the edge of leafy swamp water.

I pointed to the birds. "Witnesses."

Ingrid smiled.

There was a note inside, folded once. My name was on the outer fold. Inside it said, "Chickerman. Box 45. Rhinecliff, New York." Not a city girl after all.

Back at the Mobile airport, Ingrid seemed antsy. "This was it, Florida, one day, scoop and run?"

"This is Alabama. The real Florida is next," I said.

"You who've never been there before."

Ingrid made me smile. Her jabs were playful. There was a delicious tension between us. "In my mind I've been a lifelong resident."

She squeezed my arm and shook her head. "You're batty, Rhodes."

We flew from Mobile to Miami and on to Key West; all seats sold out on all flights. We were pasty white, snow geese migrating single-mindedly toward the caresses of the winter sun, which camped resolutely over the equator.

It was late and dark when we thumped down on the runway in Key West, Ingrid asleep against my left arm, which, in turn, had gone to sleep and tingled. We walked slowly across the ramp. The air was thick with the ocean, a mixture of life and death in varying ratios.

"*Real* Florida?" she asked sleepily.

"Smell it," I said, inhaling.

"Do they have beds?" she mumbled.

We rented a small Ford, drove up the archipelago, found a vacancy at the fourth or fifth motel we came to, and checked in.

Passion has its own moods and timing, spooned together, our breathing in sync. By morning we were standing together at the sliding glass doors, sun streaming in. "The real Florida," she said. "I hear the sun calling my name. I always wanted pink boobs in March."

"Work first," I said.

"Spoilsport," Ingrid said.

We drove to a hamlet above Marathon. I knew Carl Collister lived nearby at Jeannie-Gone Key, but the maps showed no such place. The village where we stopped was called Drift Bay, but there was no bay in sight. I went into a place called BAIT-N-BEER-N-BOATS. The fishy odor inside confirmed that the establishment was what it purported to be. There was a nicked Formica counter with a woman behind it. She had a plate of fish sticks in front of her and was dipping them into a jar of tartar sauce. She looked at me, kept chewing, her jaw working sideways, defying its hinges.

"I'm looking for Carl Collister."

She blinked several times. "You'd be wantin' Jeannie-Gone Key," she said.

"Where's that?"

She lifted a foot, took off a faded pink flip-flop, rubbed between her big and second toes, dropped the flip-flop, speared it with her foot, picked up a fish stick, and used it as a pointer. "Half mile south, dusty road right, all the way to the end." She bit off the end of the fish stick.

When we turned onto the road Ingrid took off her clothes and wriggled into her bathing suit. Jeannie-Gone Key consisted of a trailer on a low bar of crushed coral and sand. The trailer was in bad shape and looked like a discard from a hurricane. An unpainted wooden footbridge led out to the trailer. Collister's Olds was parked by the bridge.

We crossed over and Ingrid whispered, "I need sun," and left me.

I knocked on the door. Collister appeared. "I'll be damned," he said when he saw me. "It's Crash himself." He didn't look happy to see me. He hadn't shaved in a while and was carrying a can of beer.

"I need to talk to you."

"So talk," he said.

There was a screen door between us.

"I quit Sturdivant," I said.

"He fired my ass," Collister said.

"I didn't know."

"Fucking Sturdivant. The lowest-rated guides get the gate. Another example of pure Sturdivant bullshit capitalism. I never should have gone up there. We do dumb things in the hunt for moola."

I didn't know what had happened to any of the guides. "He offered me the head guide job," I told him. Not only had he tried to recruit me into his personal snowfly hunt, he had paid me outside the rules. We were supposed to remain until the end and I had departed one day early. Meaning the pay was a soft bribe to encourage me to someday write favorably about the place. Sturdivant rarely missed an angle. He would probably be a killer chess player.

"We heard. That had all of us puzzled. Some of them were mighty pissed."

"Snowfly," I said.

Collister rolled his eyes. "*That* shit again. What the fuck is it with you Yankees? You want big fish? Try the damn ocean. It's full of them."

"Sturdivant thinks there'll be a snowfly hatch in two years."

"Like I could care," Collister said. "All you assholes sneaking off at night. I just didn't get it. Still don't."

"All who, sneaking off?"

Collister's brows furrowed. "You. Them. All of you."

"Not me."

"Your cabin was always dark, just like the rest."

"Not because I wasn't there." I looked over at Ingrid who was sliding down her suit top. She was sitting on the sand, looking out at some scruffy mangroves, facing the sun.

My former colleague studied me for several seconds. Half grin, nod of the head. "Ginch? Who was it?"

"No, it's called sleep."

"With one of the guides?" he asked. "Or one of the flunkies. They were fine."

I said, "Alone."

Collister studied me. "Maybe I was wrong about some things. You never did fit in, catching those big fish, with the rule and all."

"There was no such rule," I told him.

He sucked in his breath and frowned. "Fuckers told me there was."

"It was the guides' rule, not Sturdivant's."

"Bastards," he said. "Why?"

I shrugged.

"Bastards," he said again. "Bastards."

"I need help," I told him.

"You should've told me about the rule."

"I didn't know about it until I was done."

"Bastards," he repeated. "What help?"

"The snowfly."

Collister closed his eyes and snorted. "It's so much *bullshit!* You fish for specialties, you always get nut cases. There's always some half-assed legend. With bonefish, it's the silver squid. Supposedly come up on the flats every five years, but there's no such thing. You hear this kind of baloney everywhere in this business. Reality isn't enough for some people. The best education and brains in the world don't make some people immune from idiocy."

"All I said was 'snowfly.' I didn't say I believed it. I just want to pin it down."

Collister shook his head. "Big fish are an addiction. People lose touch with reality, people who're otherwise perfectly reasonable."

"I'm telling the truth, Carl."

"I was a cop before I went professional," he said. "Junkies and perps all swear they're telling the truth." He sounded like Ingrid.

I decided to change tactics. "Don't you ever want to take one of those jerks aside, tell them, here it is . . . in black and white . . . no silver squid."

"Rules of logic," Collister said. "You can't prove a negative."

"It's not a negative if the legend started somewhere, if you can nail down where it started, who started it, and maybe why."

"The squid's not like that."

"I think the snowfly is."

"If you know it, why come all the way down here to bug me?"

"I think maybe you could know somebody who knows somebody, drifts, other guides, outfitters, whatever."

"Yeah, what's in it for me?"

"Not a damn thing."

"Hmm," Collister said. "What is it you want to know?"

"I'm looking for a comprehensive trout-fishing library."

"Yale," he said. "That's the biggest and the best."

Ingrid would not be happy about going back north. "What's down this way?"

"York," he said, not missing a beat. "York Gentry guided everybody who was anybody and everybody who thought they were somebody. He had a nose like an anteater, an ungodly big nose and as ugly a sumbitch as ever was born. He was Hemingway's favorite. They were real pals. They used to go out on the *Pilar.* Once Hemingway brought a Cuban floozy with him and introduced her as his fiancée. He was between wives at the time. Only this wasn't his fiancée, she was a hooker from Havana. The whole time she's on the boat she's pawing Yorkie's Tootsie Roll and Hemingway's growling about some Spanish dude who diddled one of his girlfriends when he lived in Spain and how he shot off the Spaniard's dick! He didn't tell Yorkie the truth for two years." Collister laughed heartily. "Yorkie had a shitpot full of books on trout fishing."

"Where does he live? Gentry, right?"

"Another time Yorkie was in Iceland with this Saudi prince? The guy was a big-time asshole and he was missing Atlantics left and right. Hopeless case. Yorkie takes the guy's rod, makes one cast, a fish hits, he sets the hook, hands the rod to the guy, and says, 'He's all yours, Sinbad. Don't bother to rebook next year.' Old Yorkie stomped off and left the guy there and when a check came in the mail, he sent it back. He and Papa were like that, men of principle, and hardheaded to boot."

I could sense that Collister's stories could ramble on for hours.

"You said there was a book collection. Where's Gentry live?"

Collister stopped. "Hard to say. Heaven maybe. Or Hell. I don't have an opinion one way or the other. He's gone."

"Fishing?"

"Yorkie croaked, but that's not all."

At Sturdivant's Collister had seemed more solid and reliable than the others. Now I was beginning to question my judgment. "Dead is dead. What else can there be?"

He said with a conspiratorial laugh, "Hemingway, he's not dead! At least not the last time I heard. That deal out there in Idaho? Not him. He staged the whole damn deal. It was just so much bullshit. I guess he got sick of being the big-shot writer, sick, doctors pawing, critics kicking his ass, his editor wanting more, ex-wives taking what he had. You know they were giving him shots at Mayo? All he wanted was for people to leave him alone so he could chase trout. So he made it look like he'd killed himself and now he's a free man."

Collister's grip on reality was evaporating in front of me. He didn't believe in the snowfly, but he was sure Hemingway had faked his death. "Ernest Hemingway is alive? Says who?"

"Yorkie. He used to go meet him here and there. They chased fish together and let me tell you, that was a pair to draw to. Yorkie looked upon himself as the author's protector, not that he needed protecting, except from himself."

"York Gentry and Ernest Hemingway."

"Jesus, listen up. Hemingway just pretended he was dead. Yorkie was alive then. They used to meet at different places. Now Yorkie's gone."

"And nobody ever figured out any of this?"

"Some people know, but Hemingway used to be a reporter. Maybe some of the brotherhood wanted to give him a break and let the dog sleep."

I couldn't believe what I was hearing. "Maybe Yorkie faked *his* death."

Collister gave me a blank look. "Why the hell would he do that?"

"He was famous, like Hemingway."

Collister laughed. "Yorkie would've loved being famous, but he never was. Hemingway hated the spotlight most of the time. Yorkie got drunk and fell off his boat two years ago. He was never found, but bodies in shark waters seldom are. Do you want help or not?"

"Sorry. The Hemingway thing threw me."

"That doesn't mean it's not true."

Which was exactly my point about the snowfly. "I just want to know where Gentry's books are." I also had an urge rising to put my fist through the door screen and Collister must've sensed it because he held up his hands and smiled.

"Easy there, Crash. Yorkie loved fishing. Truth is, I don't know that the little peckerwood could read a word, but he had this big-ass library in a building next to his house. Now it's a half-ass museum. What books he didn't have, he compiled in a list. You know, everything ever written about fishing. Thing is, it's private. You gotta have a connection to get in."

"Where is it?"

"Key West," Collister said.

"Can you get us in?"

"Why the hell would I want to look at a bunch of old books?"

"Not you and me," I said. I invited him outside and pointed to Ingrid. "Her and me."

"I'll call ahead for you," he said, riveting his eyes on Ingrid. I couldn't blame him for staring.

"How about calling now?"

"Maybe we should take her a glass of juice or something," Collister said.

"Please, Carl. Make the call." Hemingway, for Chrissakes. I decided not to tell Ingrid about that part. She'd think I needed a shrink. And maybe she would be right. This snowfly thing had moved my bubble way off center.

"No problem, Crash," Collister said.

York Gentry's place was close to water, not far from Harry Truman's vacation White House in Key West. There was a large, plain metal building behind the small pink cottage that had been his house.

"There sure is a lot of running around on this vacation," Ingrid said as we parked.

"This is the last stop," I said, hoping I was right. There was a blue 1956 DeSoto parked in the small gravel lot beside the building. Ingrid made a pass by it and peeked in as we headed up to the larger building.

We were greeted by a youngish man wearing a faded Green Bay Packers hat. He seemed nervous, his arms darting here and there.

"I'm Rhodes," I said. "This is Ingrid Cashdollar. Carl Collister called about our visit."

"I'm Adams."

"Nick?" I said, intending a joke.

He gave us a stupefied grin. "How'd you know?"

This was getting weirder by the minute. "I'm trying to trace an unpublished manuscript, *The Legend of the Snowfly,* by M. J. Key."

Adams said stiffly, "We'll have to go to our whatchmacallit—card catalog. Mister Gentry's collection is big, but he didn't own everything."

"Did you know him?" Ingrid asked.

"No, ma'am. I'm just doing a favor for somebody."

There were books everywhere in the building, more on floors than on shelves. The place looked in disarray.

Ingrid whispered, "Some museum. I've seen dumps organized better than this."

Adams went to a wall of metal cabinets and pointed. "File cards. If a book isn't listed in there, it doesn't exist." He stepped aside, making it clear whom he expected to do the work.

"What do you mean, if it's not here it doesn't exist?"

"Mister Gentry didn't want to own everything as much as he wanted to know where everything was. Most of the cards refer to books that aren't here."

I started thumbing through cards. Whoever filed them had not done a very good job. They were not quite in alphabetical order.

Ingrid wandered around while I searched and I heard her ask Nick Adams, "Are you a fisherman?"

"No, ma'am," he answered.

I found no entries for Key's published books or for the manuscript. Strange. The same thing had happened at Michigan Tech.

Ingrid was suddenly beside me, her hand on the small of my back. "Do any good?"

"Nope."

She whispered, "I doubt our genial host will be much help."

"What?" I looked over at her.

"He just split," she said with a nod toward the front door.

"Maybe it's lunchtime."

"It's four o'clock, Bowie."

"This *is* Florida."

She rolled her eyes and clutched my arm. "There's a sign on the door we came in that says they close at five. So why is he leaving at four?"

I was trying to think about Key. "You're the cop. You tell me."

She smiled, but there was no mirth in it. "He said he's not a fisherman."

"Lots of people aren't."

"Then how come the backseat of the DeSoto is loaded with fishing tackle?"

"Maybe he borrowed it from somebody."

"If it quacks like a duck," she said, her smile gone. "I'm going to look around. I've got a feeling."

Not a good one, I surmised. The answer was in a room upstairs. An old man was curled up on a ratty couch. Ingrid poked him and got no response.

"Deep sleeper?" I asked.

"Call for an ambulance," she said, kneeling beside the man.

I thought she was kidding.

"*Now!*" she barked in her cop voice.

A local cop named Fowler came. He was humongous with long greasy blond hair, a rumpled uniform, and SEMPER FI tattooed on his left forearm. He wore shorts and sweated like he had just run ten miles.

The old man on the couch was the real curator and his name was Adams, Harold, not Nick. The identity of the young man with the DeSoto was anybody's guess. Harold Adams had been drugged, which left his memory patchy as he was driven off to the hospital in an ambulance. Ingrid and I recounted our story several times for Officer Fowler, who had a tendency to address Ingrid's breasts when he was talking to either of us. Curator Adams was not going to be much help until morning and we were politely instructed to remain in town. Fowler thoughtfully arranged a room for us at the Flamingo View Court, which was pale blue in color, had no view, no flamingos, and no court.

We ate spicy conch fritters and shrimp salads for dinner and went to bed early.

I awoke with Ingrid in the crook of my arm, her mouth open, her breathing deep and even. I was getting accustomed to having her close and I loved the natural perfume of her skin.

She awoke later with fluttering eyes and stared upward and said, "Great. Giant cockroaches on the ceiling."

"Palmetto bugs," I said. They were everywhere.

"What's the difference?"

"A rose by any other name. That cop really looked you over yesterday."

"I'm a one-man woman," she said, nibbling my ear. "Serially speaking."

"I'm moved," I said.

"You will be soon," she said, sliding her hand down my belly.

Later that morning we met with a detective with a Van Gogh beard at the library. Harold Adams was there too. He still looked shaky.

"What a mess," Adams declared, looking around.

"Sleeping pills," the detective said.

Harold Adams added, "The jerkwad was here when your friend Collister called. He said the heat had gotten to him and he just wanted air conditioning. I could appreciate that."

Ingrid looked at the detective. "What about the DeSoto? There can't be two bright blue ones like that in the world, much less in the Keys."

"We've got a BOL on it," the detective said. "We'll find it. Eventually."

His response reminded me of Ingrid's when my car was stolen in Dog River.

We told our story again and the detective left.

"He was after something," Ingrid announced.

Adams looked at her. "The detective?"

"No, the other Adams."

"Could take me a while to figure out if anything's gone," the older Adams said.

"Couple of days?"

"More like three," Adams said.

"Good," she said, looping her hands through my arm and looking up at me. "That means we are on vacation for the next three days, right?"

"Right," I said.

We found another motel with a semiprivate beach and Ingrid was out on the sand and crushed shell dust almost before we were checked in.

"You'll burn."

She glanced up at me. "What's a vacation without some self-inflicted pain?"

"You'll be sorry."

"Vinegar salves all," she said with her usual style.

I couldn't sit in the sun the way she could so it was my job to shuttle back and forth from the beach to Sunny's Clam Bar, fetching drinks. We drank Ron Rico dark mixed with orange juice, Ingrid's idea: We called them Ingrid Libres. Each glass came with a tiny turquoise-and-coral paper parasol. Ingrid planted them in rows in the sand, a graveyard for "small dead soldiers." After our fourth drink, she shucked her top.

Curator Harold Adams eventually came to see us. Mostly he stared at Ingrid. I had been over to the library several times over the three days, but he had shooed me away.

"There's no card for the manuscript in the index, and none of Key's published books on the shelves. Was, but not now."

"Meaning?" I asked.

I noticed his eyes move in sync to a rivulet of perspiration running off the slope of Ingrid's left breast.

"Uh, well," he said. "I know we had Key at one time."

" 'Had'?"

"Not now. The index card for his manuscript is gone. I know, because I remember that snowfly silliness. Only one manuscript is known to exist, but its whereabouts has never been verified and even if Yorkie had known where it was, he didn't have the kind of money you need to buy really rare stuff."

He was wrong about the number of manuscripts and I knew where both were or had been, sort of. "The cards and books have been misplaced?"

"Gone," he said. "As in purloined."

"But you remember a card for Key's manuscript."

"Sure do. Yorkie used to talk about the snowfly all the time."

I stared at Ingrid, who gave me an overly sweet smile. "You knew Gentry?"

Adams nodded. "Sure did, and he was fixated on that bug. Papa too."

"Papa, as in Hemingway?"

"Yep, the two of 'em, but they both died before they could chase after the god-blamed thing, which is just as well."

I suddenly felt weary and sank to the sand beside Ingrid. Collister had told me Gentry and Hemingway were close and I had doubted him. Now I was hearing they were both interested in the snowfly. Collister swore the snowfly was bullshit, but insisted Hemingway had faked his suicide. Would I ever untwist all of this?

"Do you think the 'other' Adams took the card?" I asked the curator.

"If I was a betting man, which I ain't."

When he walked away, Ingrid lifted her sunglasses. "Does this mean our vacation's over?"

I had a powerful urge to move on, to hunt and chase. But what and where? Velocity without direction was not progress. "How do you feel about staying through the weekend?"

She said, "Why don't we discuss this in our room?"

It was a long, leisurely discussion with few words and a great deal of laughter.

The following Tuesday morning we were at Ingrid's house west of Dog River. She was putting on her uniform. She carried a Colt .357 magnum in a black holster and I couldn't stop staring at it. It was so huge and she was so small. Guns had always unnerved me, especially in Vietnam, where they had been ubiquitous. My father had been a hunter and I had grown up in a community of hunters, but I had never been comfortable around firearms. The old man and Queen Anna both insisted I learn to shoot, and I had. The old man said I was a natural, but each can and bottle I shattered turned into a living creature in my mind. For me, the psychic weight of bullets in a gun quadrupled its weight. I had no ethical hangups over hunting and hunters. It just wasn't for me. You couldn't release the dead.

"You ever have to use that thing?" I asked her.

She looked at me quizzically. "Never even unholstered it. Why?"

"Just wondering."

"Girlfriend cop as personal problem?"

"No, nothing like that." I told her about my folks, my learning to shoot, Vietnam.

"A gun is just a tool, Bowie," she said, sitting down beside me. "No more, no less. A cop's real weapon is talk, not lead."

I wasn't reassured. "Would you use it?"

"You mean, *could* I use it. I don't honestly know, but I have to think I could, if it came down to that. If I couldn't, I should find another line of work. You can write about bad guys from a distance. I have to smell their sweat. Why are we talking about this?"

"Are you a good shot?"

"I'm not Annie Oakley," she said with a forced smile. "Is there something you want to tell me?"

I wanted to tell her to take off her uniform and gun and get back into bed. I wanted to fold my arms around her and keep the world away from her. But I couldn't say what I felt.

"It was a great vacation," I said.

She kissed me tenderly and whispered, "Worrywart." Then she was up and all business. "See you tonight."

"I have to go to New York," I said. This was the first time I'd mentioned it.

She took it in stride. "When will you be back?"

"You mean, *will* I?"

She smiled. "You'll be back, big boy."

"I don't quite know when. I'll call you."

"This time I know you will," she said.

I walked her out to her cop car and we kissed good-bye. I had never told a woman I loved her, but I was about to. Ingrid put her hand over my mouth and smiled. "Not now, not yet, not like this." My mind reader.

20

GRADY Yetter had once told me you could tell the world's current geopolitical losers by the language predominating in New York cabs. On my hop from La Guardia into Manhattan, my driver was South Vietnamese.

I had a reservation at the Visigoth, a small residential hotel on Bleecker Street in Greenwich Village. I called Yetter from a pay phone.

"Jesus," he said when he heard my voice. "You're alive?"

Did I detect less humor in his voice than usual? "No thanks to you."

"Always the carping. It looked like a good setup." He added, "If you're looking for work, it's still bleak here."

Such directness was not like him. "Just dinner," I said.

There was a pregnant hesitation in his voice. "You're here?"

"Hey, I'm your find, remember?"

He reluctantly agreed to meet me and I smelled trouble.

We met at one of his Irish watering holes on Second Avenue. We shook hands. He piled his overcoat in the corner of the booth. I already had a glass of Guinness on the table for him. He took a long pull that left froth on his upper lip.

"So," I said. "You look good."

Yetter stared at his beer. "What do you want, kid?" His eyes stayed down.

"I have to want something? Old pals can't have dinner, swap war stories?"

"I couldn't hire you back if I wanted to. I don't know what you did over there, kid, but you obviously broke some big ballskis."

"You want the story?"

Finally, he looked up. "No, kid. I don't *ever* want to know. Our suits and lawyers have been visited by spooks. They didn't specifically order you kept off the payroll, but they said you should never leave the country again for UPI if we don't want the FCC and IRS and who the hell knows who else shoving their microscopes up our keisters. You pissed off the Russians *and* Washington, kid. That's quite an accomplishment. I've been in this business forty years. I think my reporters should make snakes rattle, but this . . . *this* went way beyond that. I don't know what you did, but son, you've sure got the federal snakes buzzing. Take my advice, get your ass back to middle America and stay put."

"Or?"

"Just do it, Bowie."

I didn't follow Yetter's advice. Instead, I went to the New York City Public Library when it opened the next morning and asked to see the head research librarian.

His name was Robert Peterson and he wore a gold loop earring in his right ear. It caught the light when he moved his head. I told him I was a journalist looking for information on M. J. Key, published works and unpublished works, and that I had been led to believe the library could help.

He was gone for about an hour and sent a woman to tell me to come back later that afternoon.

"Nothing," he said, when we met again.

"What about other institutions? You're connected to other places, right?"

"I've checked. There's nothing. There's no M. J. Key on our shelves. No M. J. Key in our catalogs. No record of any M. J. Key publications, published or not, in the index of the Library of Congress. Nothing in our sources on out-of-print works. You must have the name wrong. Or something."

Or something, was right. Key was disappearing from library references and I had a hunch the government was behind it. Danny had found Key's works here before, and now references to them were gone. Was this widespread, and if so, why? I didn't know how many of Key's books had been in print, but there was no way they could all be collected physically. Not even Uncle Sam could do that. Not that they had to physically remove the books. All they had to do was remove card-catalog entries and cross-references. Not a small job, but doable if this was what they were up to. The old fellow at Michigan Tech had similarly come up empty. At the time I thought it was his incompetence; now I had to wonder. And somebody had removed Key's books' index cards from York Gentry's collection. Was all of this connected? I had no way of knowing unless I kept pushing ahead. The more barriers that got thrown in my way, the more determined I was to break them down or find a way around them.

The CIA had debriefed Valoretev and me in Sweden. And the government was threatening UPI if they employed me again. I thought about this and all I could come up with was M. J. Key. I had wanted to interview Brezhnev and this had cost a man his life. My dogged pursuit of the rubber-bullet story in England had cost Jen Chia Yi Yi her life as well. My refusal to back off had left blood on my hands, and it was clear now that the Key manuscript was anything but a simple fishing book. On the other hand, the Russians had let it go back to the West. Did they know what they had, or had it been bought for the Kremlin strictly as a collector's item, as Valoretev had said? What the hell was in the manuscript that was making my own government so determined to make all mention of it disappear?

I called Ingrid but got no answer. She was probably still on patrol. You could never find a cop when you needed one. And she was conscientious. She would never quit early.

Neither would I.

I went over to Grand Central Station that evening, stopped at a newsstand, and looked at a New York State atlas. The next morning I took the New York Central an hour and a half north.

The village of Rhinecliff was built on a bluff overlooking the Hudson River; it was spring, newly bloomed forsythia blazed yellow, and there were buds on the trees. The station was several hundred yards north of the village square and I enjoyed the walk in soft air. I noticed that all the houses had mailboxes. Not a good sign for what I sought.

The village square was triangular. There was a stone monument to the war dead in the center of a patch of old grass. The post office was between a hotel and a bar.

There weren't all that many brass boxes in the post office. Each had four knobs to rotate to a combination number. I found Box Forty-Five and peeked in. It was empty.

I went to the service counter and tapped the hand bell on the counter. A man in a green eyeshade appeared. I told him I was thinking about moving to the area. Did residents have a choice of boxes or delivery?

"Everything's delivered," he said.

"Then why the boxes?"

"Seasonal people," he said with disdain.

"Do you know Raina Chickerman or M. J. Key?"

"Sorry," he said. "I'm not the answer man."

"Is there a newspaper in town?"

"There's the weekly *Gazette* up in Rhinebeck."

"How far is that?"

"Four, five miles."

"Is there cab service?"

"From the train station," he said.

"I was there and didn't see any."

The man shrugged.

"How about a pay phone?"

"Outside the Sugar Cone." Before I could ask what this was and where, he pointed. "The ice cream shop is back up the hill and to the right. You can't miss it."

The telephone was inside. I got a directory from the girl working the ice cream counter and called the *Gazette*.

The editor's name was VanDenBerg. I told him I was a reporter from Michigan and asked to use his morgue. When I got back to the train station there was a cab. The driver wore a baby blue porkpie hat.

"You from L.A.?" the cabbie asked.

"Michigan," I told him.

"Tigers," he said. "They're okay. I guess I can take ya. Friggin' creeps from L.A. can walk." Another clan encountered.

Milt VanDenBerg (he told me he was named for Milton Eisenhower, not Milton Berle) gave me a cup of coffee and took me to his microfilm file.

"Looking for something in particular?" he asked.

"Two people. M. J. Key and Raina Chickerman."

"Never heard of 'em. You try the City Directory?"

I drew a blank. "What's that?"

"Lists everybody. Got one in every town in America."

"You've got one?"

"Yes, sir."

I looked, but there was neither Chickerman nor Key. I did, however, find an R. Smith, which was the name Raina had used in Grand Marais. The address was Box 45, Rhinecliff. My heart raced.

I told VanDenBerg I had found a name, but only a box number.

"That would be a city person," he said. "We get a lot of 'em. Probably comes up weekends and summers. City people got their own ways." The values were obviously not shared.

"Do they use a box if they don't want their mail delivered?"

"Wouldn't surprise me any," the editor said. "Could be they sublet a different place every summer. City people like to jump around. Real grasshoppers."

"Is there a listing of sublets?"

"Only if a Realtor handled them, but we've got so much demand up here that people don't need to throw money away. It's cheaper to run an ad with me. I've got subscribers all over the place."

"Are your subscriber lists public?"

"Nope, that is a matter of privacy. And you could be the agent of a competitor."

"I'm not. Could you take a look for me?"

"Not sure I could do that."

"I can pay."

"That would be unethical."

"For your time and effort, not the names. Call it professional courtesy."

"I can do *that*." He waited until I gave him a twenty and wrote the names for him.

When he came back, he was smiling. "No Raina Chickerman, no M. J. Key, no R. Smith."

Which amounted to another wall, hit nose-first.

"Sold an ad to another Chickerman, though," he added after a long pause.

"Who?"

"Time's money."

"Gus Chickerman," I said and I saw by Milt VanDenBerg's face that I had guessed it.

The editor gave me an address and I knew Raina wouldn't be there but I had to look. I took a cab to the house, had the driver wait, and walked the grounds. The place was small, more cottage than house, and it was empty. All the shades were up. A mildewed FOR SALE sign was stuck in the front yard beside a hedge gone wild.

I wrote down the name of the realty company and paid a visit. Another twenty bucks got me the name of the person who wanted the house sold: Eubanks!

It remained a wall, but now I knew she had been here and that Raina's movements had not been the mystery her late parents had led me to believe. And Eubanks was involved.

I caught a cab back to Rhinecliff and took the train north to Albany. It was easier to get a flight from there than to go back into New York City.

On the flight from Albany to Detroit I sat beside a woman with pale blue hair who silently read a Bible, moving her lips and tracing each word with her forefinger. She stopped reading when we hit some air pockets. She closed her eyes tight and began to lose her color.

"It'll settle down," I told her.

She did not look at me.

When the air grew smoother, she immediately went back to reading.

After a moment, she snapped the book shut with a pop and looked at me. "Are you a Believer, sir?"

When I didn't answer, she said, "Do you put your life in the hands of the Big Fisherman?"

"M. J. Key?"

She said, "Blasphemer."

I had always loved reading detective stories and I had known my share of cops and security types; stories found neat resolution, tightly engineered by their authors, but real investigators, cops or reporters, rarely found easy or quick answers. Less than two-thirds of murders in cities were ever solved. Reality was eternally messy.

I claimed my car in Detroit and pointed myself north. I could not wait to see Ingrid. By Alma it was snowing. By Mount Pleasant the snowstorm had intensified, making it impossible to see, but blind as I was to the outer world, I had a crystal-clear view of my inner world and it was a startling sight. I had missed Ingrid as I had never missed anyone in my life.

I also thought about something else. My old man had always said, "What goes around, comes around." I had been butting up against M. J. Key since college and I had no doubt that this wouldn't be the last time. Raina Chickerman was the key to Key. I didn't know how or why, but I knew it was true.

It was nearly sunrise when I got to Dog River and headed west. I drove toward Ingrid's, but the snow had drifted high and a half mile away was as close as I could get. I walked the rest of the way leaning into a howling wind and when I climbed onto the drifted-over porch I pounded on the door.

"You're freeezing," she said when she opened the door.

Snow was melting on my face. "I love you," I said.

She looked at me for a long time.

I asked, "Now, like this?"

Ingrid held out her arms and smiled. "Exactly the way I imagined it."

21

S PRING in northern Michigan comes only after a long, painful labor, and
like any difficult delivery its arrival is greeted with a combination of
joy and exhaustion, followed by postpartum blues. Ingrid and I had
settled in and, by the time the first robins showed, we were both ready to
fish. The day after I first told Ingrid I loved her, I called Fred Ciz, gave him
my new address, and told him I'd be up to visit sometime that summer.

I took Ingrid to meet my sister, Lilly, and after that they were on the
phone at least once a week. Lilly and her children came down to visit at
Easter. Ingrid's big house on the upper Dog River was overrun with little
bodies in sleeping bags. We cooked hamburgers over charcoal and I was at
peace.

"There's more to a relationship than this," Lilly said, softly scolding.

"I'm discovering life."

Lilly said, "You look happy." I could tell she meant it.

A week after Easter Fred called.

"Amp's dead," he said. The deputy, who had been in Vietnam, had gone
down with a heart attack trying to referee a domestic dispute and died on
the spot. I hadn't known Amp that well, but he had always seemed competent, an integral part of the fabric of Grand Marais. Amp enforced the law
with common sense and care and I admired him.

"When's the funeral?"

"Next Tuesday."

"We'll be there."

"We?" he asked.

"You'll see."

Ingrid went with me. We had the wake at Staley's, which was packed
with cops and DNR people in uniform and Amp's friends and relatives from
fifty miles around. CO Service was there and we talked and decided that we
would try to get together sometime other than at funerals. As it happened, I
would know Grady Service for a long time.

It became clear at the funeral that Amp had been a hero. He had won
the Distinguished Service Medal, two Silver Stars, a Bronze Star with a *V* for
valor, three Purple Hearts, and never said a word about his military service.

The Army had wanted to send a ceremonial burial detail up from Detroit, but Buzz and Fred refused and said they would take care of it, which they did. Some vets from the Newberry VFW post handled the detail. "Taps" was played, rifles fired, the flag folded into a smooth triangle and presented to Amp's mother. Wet eyes everywhere.

The wake was rowdy. Karla, Buzz, and Fred were all over Ingrid. Janey circled cautiously around her but seemed to warm to her by the end of the evening. At one point I saw Karla pigeonhole Ingrid. There was an animated discussion punctuated by bursts of laughter and it unnerved me.

In the bedroom at Fred's that night, I wanted to know what Karla had told her, but couldn't bring myself to ask. Ingrid had been able to read me from the first moment.

"It's none of your business. Woman talk."

In the morning we had slight hangovers and a visitor. Luce County sheriff Donal Hammill had a red face, a mashed-in nose, and small ears that stuck out like buds. Fred served up breakfast and Hammill drank six cups of coffee and ate six fried eggs and six pieces of buttered white bread, toasted dark. He must have had the metabolism of a shark because he couldn't have weighed more than 160, firearm included.

"Most important meal of the day," he said when he was done.

"Breakfast?" I asked.

"Nope," he said with an impish grin. "The one you're eating at the moment."

It was easy to see why Amp had been hired. His boss had the same direct and easy manner. Eating done, he turned his attention to Ingrid.

"Rumor has it you pack a badge."

"Rumor is fact," she said. "Which is rare."

"I might as well get to the point," Sheriff Hammill said. "I've got an opening. Pay's crap, and so's the work. You interested?"

"Maybe I'm not qualified."

Hammill grinned. "I talked to your chief last night. I talked to people in Detroit too."

"You've been busy," Ingrid said.

"Are you interested or not?" Hammill asked.

Ingrid looked at me. "It's your decision," I said.

"I'm interested," she told the sheriff.

"Good. Come see me tomorrow afternoon and we'll talk."

"What about your house?" I asked her when we were alone.

"I don't let things define me, Bowie. The house will keep. You love it up here and I've got a feeling I will, too. What's to think about? You think your friend Karla can find us a place to live?"

Which is how we came home to Grand Marais and thoughts of Raina Chickerman and the snowfly slowly faded. I had love, friends, and money in the bank. In time, I knew the snowfly would be behind me.

By the middle of July the blackfly infestation had subsided. Ingrid worked a regular day patrol in the northern county, but anytime anything happened up our way, she got the call. It was High-T season, meaning a long ton of tourists in camper trucks doing stupid things.

We rented a small log cabin a block from Staley's and though we were happy, we never talked about marriage.

The phone rang on a Wednesday night as we were making love in the kitchen. This wasn't unusual. Ingrid was spontaneous and passionate. Her work often butted in.

"Damn," she said when she hung up the phone.

"Gotta go?"

She nodded. "I hate those words."

Ingrid did not talk a lot about her work and only occasionally felt the need to vent.

"Got a body," she said. "More like a skeleton, I imagine. Been there a while, they say. Could be a hunter from last fall."

"Somebody known to be missing?"

"That would be too easy," she said.

She returned about four A.M., woke me, took my hand, led me into the kitchen, and started undressing. "Now," she said, "where were we?"

A week later I was using a dry Royal Coachman on the West Branch of the Fox River. Ingrid, Buzz, and I were only five or so miles north of Seney, whose infamy had peaked before the turn of the century, when white pine was king, loggers terminally thirsty, and the town boasted fifty bars strung out along two miles of nasty dirt road. Now the road was paved, there were only three taverns, some Mennonites looking to homestead, and a few remaining loggers jobbing pulp for a couple of local mills. Pulping was beer money to add to the dole.

Ingrid had waded upstream ahead of me. She believed in covering as much water as she could, while I preferred to go slowly and study the river and let its secrets unfold at a more leisurely pace. There were plenty of brookies and a few browns in this part of the Fox, each with its own niche. Of course, it didn't escape me that Ernest Hemingway had been up here long ago, maybe stood at the same bend, freshly returned from his stint with the ambulance service in Italy, where he had been wounded, gotten hepatitis, and come back to the States to lick his wounds and bask in self-proclaimed glory. He came up to Seney by train and camped along the river with a couple of pals and caught fish and brooded and maybe dreamed of greatness or killing himself. Unless you believed Carl Collister, and I wasn't buying his fantasy one bit.

From what I had read about Hemingway, there were two things always on his mind, be great or die, or be great *and* die, the line of demarcation never too clear to me. I had seen soldiers with the same dementia in Vietnam. The only soldiers I knew who conjured greatness out loud usually ended up dead soon thereafter. But Hemingway wasn't a soldier, then or later. He was more like a USO doughnut dolly or a Red Cross hireling and later he was a war correspondent, the same as me, which was definitely not a soldier. Reporters watched and soldiers *did,* a much greater divide than mere words can convey.

Of course Hemingway had killed himself; suicide ran in his family the way six toes, tiny peckers shaped like plantains, or a propensity for contracting upper respiratory infections afflicted others.

"I thought we were fishing?"

Ingrid's voice snapped me back to reality. She had returned silently and eased down beside me on a sturdy cedar sweeper.

"I was daydreaming."

"About me?"

"Sure," I said.

"Right answer, honey."

Buzz eventually came back, surprising us by arriving overland, making a great deal of racket and tumbling the last six or eight feet down the steep sandy embankment.

"No hills in the river," I said when he had recovered. "It's easier walking down here in the water. You might want to try it."

He was in no mood for banter. In fact, he got up and trudged sullenly down the river ahead of us and did not speak. Maybe the fall had put him in a bad mood. Or he had not caught fish. He hated to get skunked. My musings certainly hadn't helped my mood. The Hemingway thing gave me the creeps. He faked his suicide to pursue the snowfly? I shook my head at my own gullibility.

It took quite a while to identify the body that had been found south of Grand Marais weeks before. The dead man was Mickey O'Brien, an elementary school principal from Red Hook, New York. His wife told Ingrid that her husband had gone on a fishing trip three years before and never returned. She had filed a missing persons report, but until the body was found there had been no trace of him. He was supposed to have been fishing on the Au Sable River in lower Michigan.

In the back of my mind though, I remembered Ingrid telling me that the mysterious trespassers had left the area. The body was identified through dental records, which was a good thing, because there wasn't much else to go by. The dead man's wife told Ingrid that he had become increasingly obsessed with "some stupid fishing thing." She also asked if the remains could be shipped to New York and Buzz stepped in to help her make the arrangements.

I reminded Ingrid of the story she had told me about a couple of snowfly chasers freezing to death near the Au Sable and asked her if she thought the events were connected. She said, "The Au Sable's hundreds of miles away. If he was fishing down there, what's his body doing up here?"

I was tempted to call the woman and talk to her about her husband, but I refrained. Was the snowfly involved? Maybe. Did I care? No, I told myself. Maybe he had been with Hemingway, I thought, making a joke of the whole thing.

Ingrid was called out early in the morning to a traffic accident. A flatbed truck had struck a Ford camper head-on, with predictable results.

Buzz came by at midmorning, looking washed out. He asked for a cup of tea and was uncharacteristically quiet.

"You look like they just made you bishop."

The priest managed a weak smile.

"Friends talk to each other," I told him.

"So now you're Mister Garrulous," he grumbled.

Whatever was on his mind wasn't going to be pried out. We sat in silence. Eventually he looked up at me. "That time on the Fox?"

"Which time?" Ingrid, Buzz, and I had been to the Fox River several times.

"The time I fell on my tookus."

"What about it?"

"I got lost."

"That happens to all of us."

"You're happy?" he asked.

I thought the subject was going to be his terrible sense of direction, which was legendary. "Don't I look it?"

"Ingrid's a fine woman."

"I know. What are you getting at?"

"You haven't married her."

"Is this going to be a morality lecture, Father?"

He stared at me. He wanted another response, but I didn't have one and I resented his butting in.

"What the hell do you want, Buzz?"

"To be sure," he said, "of you and Ingrid, that the bond is strong enough."

"Buzz, what are you saying?"

He looked at the ceiling as if he was trying to decide something. Had he looked for God's guidance? "That day on the Fox," he said, "I saw someone."

"What's that got to do with Ingrid and me?"

His eyes were piercing as they locked onto mine. "It was *that* woman."

"*What* woman?"

He paused before he spoke. "Smith. Key. Whatever her name is."

My stomach fluttered. "On the Fox?"

"I saw her get out of the river ahead of me. She had a fly rod. I tried to follow her."

I closed my eyes. Buzz had come down the east bank. "Where did she go?"

"Into the bush. I lost her. I thought maybe she was headed for a vehicle, but there are no roads back that way, not even a grown-over tote road."

Raina Chickerman. Again. I had tried to repress the whole thing. Would Raina never leave me alone? "Why didn't you tell me this before?"

"I wasn't sure it was her," the priest said.

"Why're you telling me now?"

"Because now I'm sure, is why," he snapped. "I saw her again."

"When?"

Buzz chewed his lower lip. "Yesterday. She was headed into the headwaters of your river."

"The No Trout?"

The priest nodded solemnly.

My mind was running in multiple directions. Snowflies? Not till next season, Sturdivant said. Of course, Gus Chickerman had toyed with his mind. This year, next year, ever: Who knew? Raina was headed for *my* river.

I couldn't afford to wait for Ingrid to come home. Buzz had seen Raina Chickerman from the road. She had been on a trail leading toward the river. She had a backpack and bedroll and a rod tube tied to her pack. The trail was way upriver, in an area I had never gotten to. Maybe it wasn't Raina. Buzz could've been wrong, and said so, but I had to know and I couldn't wait around to discuss it with Ingrid. Raina had a twenty-four-hour lead. I felt guilty about running out, but some things you just have to do. If Raina was here, I imagined I had a new window of opportunity and I had to hurry to get through it before it closed. Obsession at its worst.

22

I wanted to find Raina Chickerman and confront her once and for all. No, it was more than that. I *had* to find her and force an explanation. I told myself this was all I wanted, but it wasn't until I reached the river that I realized I had two rods in tubes, four reels, and a passel of flies and that maybe all this was about something else, moving shadows in deep water. I didn't consciously remember grabbing my gear, but I had. The old man had warned me that trout could turn perfectly sensible human beings into deeply troubled wanderers—his point, if not his precise words. There was more to this than Raina.

The snowfly had hooked me. The hooking was different than that which Sturdivant suffered, but it was just as real in its hold on me. I saw now that the snowfly got people in different ways. Angus Wren was as obsessed as Sturdivant, only from the other pole. The effects of the snowfly were insidious.

I chastised myself for not leaving a note for Ingrid, but knew if I had taken the time to write, or waited for her, I would never have gotten out of the house. The truth was, I didn't want to be talked out of it.

It was twilight when I neared the river. I had walked hard and taken no rests. It was possible to make good time because the DNR and USFS had roughed out a trail part of the way. Eventually hikers and campers would have neat little paths all over the backwoods. I hated the scheme because paths were sidewalks and people needed places to go where there were no sidewalks. At the moment, however, I was glad to have easy going. I had not forgotten the difficulties of my last expedition in the No Trout River. I knew that once I got to the river, I would need to be cautious. Now Raina Chickerman was ahead of me and all of this augured trouble.

I pulled up short and used the remaining daylight to set myself up. I was no soldier, but I had learned a few grunt tricks in Vietnam. Lurps sometimes spent a month in enemy territory gathering information. Their specialty was invisibility and I was determined to emulate them.

Wire could save your life or take another's. I kept two rolls in my pack, small gauge, high tensile strength, hard to detect. The approach was low tech and effective. I strung two circles of wire around my position, one perimeter twenty yards out and the second one at ten yards, then stretched the ends of the wires back to me. The loops were strung low, about six inches off the ground, terminating at forked sticks on either side of my pack. I tied each wire to one of the cups from my thermos and put several double-ought buckshot in each. If a wire was tripped, I would hear a rattle and it would alert me. I would sleep dressed and sitting up against my pack. Nobody would surprise me this time. I stuck several pine branches in the ground behind the pack to obliterate my silhouette and rubbed swamp muck onto exposed skin and into my hair to keep off mosquitoes and kill any sheen. Invisibility was about making the smallest imprint possible. This time I meant to have every edge possible and I was confident that I was secure when I settled in for the night.

I should have remembered an interview I'd once had with an Air Force pilot, a major who had flown combat in Korea and was doing it again in Vietnam. All pilots were taught a special form of hand-to-hand combat, a blend of judo and karate and street fighting, invented to keep them alive if they were forced down on enemy turf. I had asked how proficient he was.

"They teach you just enough to get you killed," he said.

At night in the forest, insects land on your face and you swat them away. It's reflex. The next morning you don't remember.

I was in deep sleep when I swatted and hit something both hard and coarse, hard and coarse and hot and wet, something that snarled and froze me in place.

My first thought: The fucking wires didn't work.

My second thought: Play dead.

My third thought: This could be an easy role. And a short one.

The snarls came and went like a distant freight. I thought of the Doppler effect. I looked into glistening red eyes under a white moon and felt undiluted terror. I tried not to breathe, struggling to will oxygen into my lungs through my skin, then I remembered I was caked with swamp muck. I could think, but I couldn't reason, my logic pancaked by pure adrenal flow, time suspended. I wanted the moon to dislodge, fall, kill us both. I did not want to die as a component in an anonymous food chain. After death it would be acceptable, pure microbiology. Before death, I wanted to scream.

Somewhere beyond the steamy snout and reeking breath, I heard a scratchy voice, whispering, a voice vaguely familiar, comforting because it was human, threatening because it was something else. I knew I had heard it before.

"Dammit, Betsy. How many times I gotta tell you? Don't play with your food."

These words I heard as a murmur, a breeze over dry leaves, but they were answered by a sharp tonal shift and a shower of gluey drool. The beast pulled back several inches, bared jagged fangs, the ivory glowing pale blue in the moonlight.

"Gonna eat, eat. We ain't got all night."

Carni, Latin for "meat," an amorphous and all-inclusive term.

The jaws closed sharply. Clack-clack.

I tried to say something, but gagged instead. Dry heaves. I fell forward, prostrate, prayerlike, a Muslim bowed toward Mecca, gasping for breath.

A hand clasped my throat, bony and callused, probing roughly.

"Don't feel wet. She rip your throat? She gets excited, see? Fancies herself a man-eater, but near as I can tell, it's mostly wishful thinking. Used to be a regular pain in the ass, but she's old now. Hell, we're all old. Got the lumbago in her hips. She can't chase things down the way God intended. But you were settin' smack in her favorite place so I speck I thought God Lupus left you as a gift." While the man cackled at this, I was recovering my wits. "Look at a wolf and what d'ya see?" he went on. "Dog, most would say, woof-woof. Nope. Four-legged man. Wolves think. Sometimes Betsy just sits and ponders, like there's a whole bunch she ain't quite worked out yet, though this is mostly spec-a-lation on my part."

Wolf. The dry heaves returned.

"You hurt?"

"Not so you can see," I said weakly.

The low moon was fading to pale blue. The eastern sky hinted color, but it was still mostly dark. The wolf sat nearby, watching me, panting silently, her tongue extended and bouncing.

"Didn't know they had wolves here," I said.

"*They* don't. Don't nobody *got* wolves. More like the cat thing, y'see? Not pets. Companions by *their* choice. She showed up one mornin' and stayed. I can't say why on either count. We get on each other's nerves at times and that's a fact. She can be worse than a wife."

The animal suddenly darted over to me and I stiffened. Her muzzle was down and she sniffed tentatively. I couldn't look into her eyes. She slurped my chin and sat down beside me.

"That's a wolf for ya," my savior said. "She's just tryin' to say howdy."

390 ❖ JOSEPH HEYWOOD

My benefactor said his name was Harkie. He had a huge, protruding nose, long and pointy to the extent that I couldn't help but stare. It took thirty minutes to walk uphill to a dwelling I would generously describe as a hut. It was more like a pile of limbs with a space inside, twenty feet by ten, with black tar paper draped over the place. It was full of holes and gaps and looked like it would collapse if a butterfly flew past.

"Just Harkie," he said. "One man, one name, all alone and liking it that way. Been here . . ." He closed his eyes. "Hell, time don't mean diddly to Harkie. Space counts, not time. Liked it here once, but Harkie's thinkin' it's time to move on. Too crowded."

"Crowded?" We were in the middle of nowhere.

"First some split-tail, now you. People runnin' all over the damn place." He was thoroughly disgusted.

"Did she have black hair?"

"Had a black heart is what! Drew down on me with a sawed-off scatter-gun, she did, and Harkie just trying to conversate," he added. "Gets rusty with only a wolf to practice on."

"She was armed?"

"Does that asshole Fee-dell like cigars?"

It had to be Raina Chickerman.

"Where'd she go?"

We were halfway up a tall ridge. The river below looked pale orange. Harkie jerked his head north toward Lake Superior. "That way, maybe. I didn't pay her much mind."

"You talked to her?" I asked.

"I already told you, that one didn't want no talk," Harkie answered. "Nor nothin' else, I speck. Glad she moved on. She crowded Harkie's space and got the wolf considerable twitterpated."

Harkie fed me overcooked, tight-grained slices of dark meat and small potatoes, everything fried together in lard in a huge black skillet. The smell of the cooking made my mouth water. The fire was inside the heap of branches that served as his hut. A metal pipe and scoop were propped over the fire to capture smoke. It was a hovel.

I took a good look at the man. He was scoliotic and weather-beaten, with deep creases in his skin, which had the texture of saddle leather. Cracked fingernails, caked with dirt, the antithesis of fastidious. He looked old and frail from a distance, but his arms were knots of hard muscle and I had no doubt that he could handle just about anything. Especially if he had a weapon to pound somebody with. Every time he spoke I was sure I knew his voice. I looked at my host, closed my eyes and listened, and wondered if he had been my assailant years before on the river. If so, why was he breaking bread with me now? I was reminded of Collister's description of York Gentry's "ungodly big nose"—like an anteater's, he had said.

"Two-name meat," he said when he gave me the food. "High-speed beef in here, venison out there." He waved his hand for effect.

The hut was bleak and cluttered with debris. The dirt floor was worn smooth. He'd been here a while. An old red door lay across two sawhorses to serve as a bed. He had some dented utensils, a few tools, two rifles and a shotgun, all in need of rebluing, several fishing rods, all with bait reels. Some candles. Harkie's teeth were jagged and yellow. He speared potato slices with a knife and nibbled inward from the edges.

"You trackin' the split-tail?" he asked.

The wolf came in and sat near him. She was an immense animal.

"I came to fish," I told him.

I noticed yellowing pike skulls hanging above us; they were eyeless, with sawtoothed jaws, freshwater barracudas. Curled, dried skin stuck to the bone.

"Not my nature to be advicin' strangers, but back in these parts, passin' through's a risky game. Dig in and make your claim or get out. Won't be long till the white buzz comes." Snow? I wondered. Or the snowfly?

The wolf yawned and pawed idly at him. He gave her some meat and she trotted outside.

"That animal makes me plumb dizzy," Harkie announced. "One winter she come in, lasted maybe an hour. I had us buttoned up and she like to have wrecked the place tryin' to get out. Wolves got their own ways. Got to remember that. People're different, always tryin' to figure out who they are. Not wolves. They just know and keep true to it. People think too much on things they ain't never gonna figger out."

It was impossible to guess the man's age, but he moved deliberately and worked the same way, as if he had calculated the precise amount of energy required for every task. And, I was sure, he always kept something in reserve.

"Can't stay and jaw," he announced. "Harkie's got things to do."

"Where's my pack?" I'd been too unnerved to notice exactly where we had come from. We had walked uphill and sort of west.

"Harkie's no thief," he said. "Your stuff would be right where you left it."

His claim seemed ridiculous, in the face of facts. My benefactor had sundry items he sure as hell hadn't found lying around in the woods. The meat could be explained but not the potatoes, lard, or sawhorses. He acquired these somewhere and I doubted money was involved.

He went outside and I followed him. He was headed toward what I thought would be downriver. I could faintly hear moving water now that I was outside. The wolf snarled and whined.

"You show him," Harkie said to the wolf. "I ain't your keeper."

"What's upriver?" I asked before I left.

He didn't look at me. "Beats me. I told you the woman went downstream." No, he had bunted at that earlier, pretending he had paid no attention. Besides, I hadn't said anything about Raina. He didn't want me headed upstream. Was he protecting her? Nothing would surprise me anymore. I also had a rising suspicion that Harkie was York Gentry, who was thought to be dead. "How's the fishing here?"

"Depends on who does the doin'." He looked back at me.

"Why didn't your wolf defend you when the woman pulled the gun?"

"Both of 'em's females."

"Thanks for the chow."

"Don't come back," he answered.

The wolf both led and followed me. My gear was where I had left it.

By day Betsy's eyes were the color of amber, her coat dark, nearly black. I tried to make eye contact, but she kept her distance and clacked her jaws from time to time, enjoying her dominance and my insecurity.

The river was too serpentine to walk with any speed. The banks were overgrown with vines, thistles, pricker-laden berry bushes, and tag alders. I stuck to high ground and walked a sort of S-pattern so that I was constantly weaving back and forth across my intended route. If Harkie was following, I'd have a better chance of spotting him this way. As long as I could see a glint of water in the distance to my left, I could follow the course of the river. Late in the day I moved down to the river, found a promontory, and made camp beneath it. I picked a place with open ground all around. Once again I strung my wire. The wolf came down to the river and watched me drift a fly along the seam of a dark glide. I caught several fish in no time at all. I scraped a hole between two fallen logs and kindled a small fire with minimal smoke. I had the trout gutted and cooking in no time. The wolf noisily sniffed the entrails, which I'd thrown aside, then inhaled them in two gulps and wagged her tail.

I slept against my pack and drifted in and out of an odd dream. Gillian and I were sharing a smoke on the roof of my place in Saigon.

"Truth is a much overrated commodity, darling. There's no way to know if you have your hands on truth or just what you want to be true."

"Facts are truth."

"Yes, but in what *order?*"

It was a bizarre dream, too vivid for comfort. She had said one other thing in the dream.

"If you find love, Bowie darling, don't leave her. Not ever."

I woke up regretting that I had not left Ingrid a note. I knew I should not be chasing Raina. What was Ingrid thinking now? What the hell was wrong with me?

The wolf came up from the tag alders at sunrise with water dripping from her snout.

"Anything you'd like to say on behalf of your gender?"

She tilted her head and snapped her jaws several times.

I went to retrieve my wire. Harkie had clumsily tried to convince me that Raina had gone downstream, but my gut said up. I was homing in on something. What that was remained an open question.

Betsy abandoned me during the next night. Another time, in another place, a soldier pointed to a distant copse. "Bad guys," he said. I did not know his politics, rendering the reference ambiguous. But boundaries we can't see can be as real as those that bend light.

My warning system worked. Toward morning I heard the cans jingle, immediately dumped the lead shot out, and got cautiously to my knees to see if I could spot what had tripped them. I heard steady footsteps, careful, furtive strides crunching twigs and dry duff. Cat and mouse, and this time I was the cat. There was a partial moon. I got to my feet and began stalking.

Fifty yards in from the river there was a clearing. I saw a silhouette move along the edge, switched on my flashlight and yelled, "Hey!"

At that moment I was hit hard in the right shoulder and knocked left. I stumbled under the force, frantically trying to recover my balance, but the ground gave way beneath me and I dropped.

The landing was hard and knocked the breath out of me. I heard a demonic laugh above me.

"Asshole!" I half grunted, half shouted.

The answer was a gunshot above the hole, the muzzle flash momentarily lighting the opening. Nearly simultaneously, something splatted on my head. I recoiled, trying to brush it away. My hands groped around for it.

Cloth. From a spirit hole to a trap, I thought, but this time I was not feeling contemplative.

"Best put that on your head," a voice cackled from above. "While you still got one." It was Harkie.

"Fuck you," I shouted angrily.

A second gunshot lit the hole again and I quickly pulled the cloth over my head. It was a bag. I was afraid but not paralyzed. If Harkie wanted me dead, the deed would already be done.

A rope slapped me on the shoulder. "It's looped. Put it around your waist and be quick. We ain't got all night."

I obeyed, felt the rope tighten and reached up with my hands to get a grip. He had said "we," not I. He had help.

As the rope helped me swim over the lip of the hole into a bed of damp ferns, a foot pressed on the back of my neck. My arms were roughly pulled forward, almost elbow to elbow, and my assailant began to wrap me in rough rope, working fast. My arms were lashed together then pushed against my chest. More lashings were wrapped all the way around my body. You don't know how much you use your arms for balance until you lose the use of them. I was a mummy in hemp.

My arms secured, another rope was looped around my neck and cinched tight.

"Told you to go downriver, didn't I?"

Trussed is a term of degree. Like tied up without wiggle room. Skewering is pinning a dead chicken's wings to its body. I was not technically skewered, but just as helpless.

I was jerked to my feet, then pulled, and away we went, with me stumbling continuously, knocking against things, barking my shins. We walked for what had to be hours. Several times I fell down, only to be hauled up. Eventually I began to smell smoke and later, when we finally halted, I felt heat from a fire. I was tired and sore and working too hard for air inside the bag.

A poke in my back sent me lurching forward; I tripped over something and fell face-first.

A voice said, "Every situation has inherent inelasticities. That which cannot be remedied must be endured. Believe it, dickhead." I heard whispering voices, which grew into angry shouts. A debate was in progress.

"Our rules are clear. No conscripts. A man walks in on his own, or he don't walk at all."

"This is my business," a woman answered. Raina Chickerman's voice!

A different voice intervened. "Give 'im the bag. That's how it's always been."

"Don't be ridiculous. He's mine," Raina's insisted. Where was Harkie?

The toe of a boot or shoe kicked me in the ribs. "On your feet, you sad sack-a-shit. Lettin' yourself be taken by a woman." The speaker made an exaggerated tsk-tsk sound. "You should be ashamed."

I heard sniggering around me, on the periphery.

"The fuck we want with a dude gets took by a woman?" someone asked.

"The fuck we 'spose to do with you, *man!*" the first male voice shouted into my ear.

Purely rhetorical, I judged, and elected to remain silent in an effort to collect brain cells and my wits. I was still breathing hard from the long hike, and sweating. I was not afraid as much as curious.

"Reasons aren't important," Raina said. "I brought him, which makes him mine. Nobody has a say in this but me."

A gestalt: My quarry had become my captor. She was working with Harkie. I had heard his voice.

"We have the rules," someone said.

"There it is," another voice said.

"*Your* rules, not mine." Raina had modulated her tone to near-sweetness, but I knew there was steel backing it up. Buzz had been right. But if he was so worried about Ingrid and me, why had he told me? He could have kept quiet and I would never have known. Another puzzle.

"Out there, you can do what you want. But you're here and it's our book. That's how it is."

I heard the slide of a firearm work. "I do what I want, wherever I am," she said. It was Raina, all right.

The main voice softened. "Maybe we'll have to take care of both of you."

"Then make it a threesome because you'll be going with us." No give, no fear. *Definitely* Raina Chickerman. I almost told the voice to believe her. I did.

"Let her keep him," a different voice said from the shadows. "Couple of days, she'll get tired of him."

"Rules are rules," the main voice said, insistent, but less stridently. "Walk in on your own. We all have to choose to be here."

"She'll whack your ass," another voice called out. "She'll do it, Red."

The main voice was in my ear again. "What's your name?"

"Key."

A hard blow knocked me backward. So much for testing them. "Gotcher wallet, shit-for-brains. Says Rhodes."

"It *is* Rhodes. I swear."

"Ain't polite to swear," somebody called out. I heard fragments of laughter.

"You the law, Rhodes? Fish cop? Forest service puke, maybe?"

"I'm nobody."

"That fits," somebody shouted.

"Let me through," a voice demanded. I heard scuffling.

"Bowie Rhodes!"

I blinked at the familiarity of the new voice. "Yes?" My mind was spinning. *Another* familiar voice?

"Have you fucked Chairman Brezhnev's wife lately?"

"Valoretev?"

He slapped my back. *"Da!"*

"Val?" Was this possible?

His hand was on my shoulder. "I know this man. He has courage and he is my friend."

The main voice barked, "Both of you can take responsibility, but he's not one of us. Teach him how we do things here." Both. Valoretev and Raina Chickerman. Had I slid into *The Twilight Zone?*

I was being led again, stumbling along. "Dammit, Punky, get this damn thing off my head."

"What is this Punky?" Valoretev asked.

"It's okay," Raina said.

The bag was whipped off and I gasped for fresh air. It was evening, still light, the sun almost below the ridgeline to the west. I wasn't uncovered more than a few seconds when I saw a face I recognized and felt a rage explode inside me. I didn't think: I lowered my head and bulled my way forward, smashing the top of my head into the man's face with a sickening crunch. We both went down. My sudden move had ripped my leash away from Valoretev. I struggled to my feet and knee-dropped the man on the ground, trying to drive my knees through his head, but a shoulder knocked me sideways.

"Hold him," Raina said calmly.

My adrenaline burst was not yet done. I looked over at the man, screamed, "Nick Adams!" and tried to crab-crawl on my side to scissor-kick him, but again I was restrained.

Valoretev sat on me, laughing raucously, then hoisted me up by the armpits and pushed me along. I tried to pull away several times to get at the man who had misled Ingrid and me in Key West. But Val was too strong and moved me steadily away. I had to take consolation in the blood cascading down the fingers of the man holding his face. It felt good to strike out.

I was certain that everything was about to fit together, but how?

It was a short walk to a small cabin built under huge, sagging white birches. There were no windows and the place was dark, with vertical logs, in the old French *coureurs de bois* manner, thick chinking aged dark by soot. Dark blue-green moss covered the roof and outside walls.

The floor was made of planks that sagged and squeaked under our weight. I felt the leash soften and watched Raina moving around me. Light flickered from a match and a lantern hissed to life. I looked around the room. Val was no longer with us. There was a table with two chairs, each painted a different color, small beds in two corners, a woodstove in the middle, clothing hung on wall pegs, animal skulls tacked to a beam overhead, a dented metal tub in the corner. There were several fly rods on pegs along another wall. Expensive stuff, split bamboo, shining pink in the shimmering light. One wall was stacked nearly to the ceiling with wood. The ceiling was open to the roof above rough-hewn square-planed beams. The scent of pine and cedar was heavy in the air.

"That was an exceptionally childish display," Raina Chickerman said, pushing a chair over to me and holding my shoulder to steady me as I sat.

My anger had not entirely abated. "That asshole drugged an old man in Key West."

Raina seemed to measure her words. "By that standard, every surgeon in the world should be popped in the nose. The old man wasn't hurt. He simply got a longer nap."

"You knew!"

Raina Chickerman was small, not up to my chest, with short black hair and dark skin. She wore camouflage fatigue pants and a black T-shirt.

"Does knowledge invariably imply culpability? I didn't have anything to do with it," she said, turning away to light a wood fire in the small stove.

"Bullshit!"

"You don't argue any more effectively now than when we were children. Volume still doesn't equate to logic."

"You've been dogging me for years."

"Coincidence is not a precursor of theorems," she said.

She boiled water, poured some into two mugs, and filled them with small, aromatic red-green twigs, which she swizzled around. I smelled sassafras.

"What the hell is going on?" I demanded. "Why are you doing this?"

"Drink," she said. "It's hot and maybe this will help disabuse you of your Ptolemaic perspective."

"I have a right to know."

She looked across the table at me. Her normally blue eyes were intense and seemed to change color from blue to green.

"Do you?"

"Why?" I repeated.

"Fate," she said. "Now drink."

I held up my wrists. My arms were no longer pinioned to my chest, but they remained bound to each other.

She sighed unsympathetically. "Make the best of it." She sipped from her cup and relaxed against the back of her chair, watching me. It was the same look she had fixed on me when we were children.

I tasted the bitter liquid. "This tastes like shit," I said.

"So much anger," she said.

When we had finished, she guided me to one of the beds. "Yours. It'll be warm in here tonight." She crossed to the other bed and lay down. "You were meant to be here," she said, her last words of the night.

I was tired and too sore to argue but had a difficult time sleeping. What the hell had I gotten myself into? What were these people doing out in the forest living like this? What was Raina's connection to them? What would Ingrid think if she saw me like this?

Valoretev came into the cabin at daybreak. I had hardly slept and ached from the previous day's exertions. There was no sign of Raina; I had no idea when she had left the cabin. It had been the same when we were children; she could come and go like a thought.

"You are a crazy bastard, my good friend Bowie Rhodes," Val said with his infectious grin. I took a good look at him in the morning light. His hair had grown long and his beard and mustache were starting to gray. His eyes were sunk deep and dirt was ground into his skin, which shone like grease. He carried a carbine, slung tightly across his chest; a huge knife was upside down in a scabbard on his left leg. We walked to the bank of the river. He took a pack of my own cigarettes from his pocket and lit one for himself. I hadn't thought about my gear since being knocked down two days before.

"Where's my pack?"

"Safe," he said. "I see you still carry your rod from Russia. It has been good to you?"

"Yes. How about a cigarette?" He opened the pack, tapped out a cigarette, and pushed the pack into my shirt pocket. He then lit the cigarette and put it in my lips. He kept my lighter.

"Cut my arms loose," I said.

Val smoothed his beard and looked at me warily. "You won't run, will you?"

"Not until I get an explanation."

It felt good to have the use of my hands again. My fingers tingled as unrestricted blood flow returned.

Val said, "You come for the beautiful fish, yes?"

"What beautiful fish?"

"We are friends," he said. "Don't play stupid."

"This is crazy."

Val pondered my words. "Traveling with Gentry's wolf is crazy. That animal is a killer."

"Gentry? You mean Harkie."

"Yorkie, Harkie, American nicknames very much confuse me. He is a crazy old man."

So the old man was York Gentry and if he was alive . . . "Fuck!" I said out loud. The implications were . . . unthinkable.

"Is Harkie part of *this?*" I couldn't think of a better word.

"He serves a purpose," Val said.

"He or one of the other cretins nearly killed me."

"If Harkie wanted you dead, you would be so. I think he only wanted to enlighten you."

"The way the KGB wanted to?"

Val grinned and winked. "The KGB never got the chance. Besides, that which does not kill us makes us stronger."

"How does Nick Adams fit?"

The Russian looked at me blankly, then snapped his head down in an understanding nod. "*Da,* the poor boy whose face you broke. He is Harkie's illegitimate grandson."

I had to ponder this concept. "Harkie and Raina work together?"

"No. Harkie is with us."

"But Nick Adams came to Key West to get in my way. Raina must've sent him."

"Raina? Why do you say this name?"

"Raina Chickerman."

"Her name is Key," Val said.

"Her name is *not* Key," I said emphatically. "I have known her since we were children."

Now Val looked confused, but he quickly shrugged. "It doesn't matter, her name. She has arrived only recently. She does not stay with us. She comes, she goes. I love the freedom in America. Why did you follow her?"

"That's between her and me."

"Why?" he repeated.

"Mind your own business," I said. *"Comrade."*

He patted my back affectionately. "It will be all right, my friend."

"What happened with you and the CIA?" I asked him.

Val laughed. "They are *babushkas*. They talk and talk and talk. So many debriefings, so much repetition. I grew weary of the games and said good-bye."

"They let you go?"

"It was not their place to decide," he said indignantly. "I was not a prisoner."

"They'll find you."

He grinned. "Let them look. Did I not get us out of the Soviet Union? It is easier to evade your CIA than to get your girlfriend alone when the KGB is interested. Your people are boy scouts."

"Why are you here, Val?"

"Catching trout," he said, with a huge grin. "Fine American fish in free and clean American water, just as my friend Bowie told me. I choose to ignore the German origins of these beautiful trout," he added. "This is why I left the Soviet Union. To catch trout and to live free and to tell the truth. This is truth. Men who live lies cannot recognize truth. This side, that side, all sides are same. I will never live a lie again."

"You used me to get to freedom," I said.

He flicked a huge hand in the air. "I did not need you to accomplish this. I chose to help you, my friend."

"Your people killed a man."

"Both sides kill."

"The man died because of me."

Valoretev looked hard at me and grasped my shoulders. "He died because of the system, not because of you."

His words did not salve my conscience. "Both sides will hunt you down," I said.

Val grinned and whispered, "Who dares hunt the hunter?"

A small breeze skittered up from the south, tantalizing us, then lay down. The air was viscous, the weight of atmosphere on Mercury. Life as nightmare. I had come a long way and a lot of years in my on-again, off-again quest for Raina and the snowfly, and I felt I had somehow gotten exactly where I deserved to be: nowhere. Val and I returned to the cabin where he retied me with deep apologies. "When Key returns, she will release you."

"Where is she?" I asked.

"Fishing, of course. She is always fishing. Alone," he added.

Mosquitoes drained my blood and I worried about Ingrid. At first I was certain that a search for me would be mounted immediately. Then I remembered my gear. When Ingrid saw that my rods were gone, she would assume I had gone off to fish. She would not like being left behind—in fact, she would be pissed off—but I also knew that she would not assume the worst, at least not right away. Would Buzz tell her about Raina? Why had he told me?

I did not see Raina again until that evening. The sun was low and brilliant, backlighting the trees.

I wanted her to talk to me, to answer my questions. "This is the same group that was down on the Au Sable and had the authorities up in arms."

She looked at me disinterestedly.

"A couple of them froze to death. The body of a man named O'Brien was found up here this summer, south of Grand Marais, a man from New York missing from his home for three years."

"You think you've fallen in with kidnappers?" She didn't try to hide her amusement.

"Raina, what are you doing here?"

"Hunting," she said with a tone I had once known well. She would talk when she was ready to, and not before.

Later that night Val awakened me. Raina wasn't in her bed. He took me through the forest to a building that was no more than a roof under the trees. It was lit by lanterns and tallow candles.

"Please show respect," Valoretev whispered in my ear as we entered.

There were more people than I anticipated, but no Raina. I saw a man sitting on a rusty lawn chair. I couldn't make out his face.

"You'd be Rhodes," he said.

I nodded. When I got into better light, I saw his face and gaped openmouthed. The sparse hair on the head was snow white, his beard thick and white and yellowing, his eyes pale brown, like beer diluted by water.

Ernest Hemingway stared at me through sunken, hollow eyes. He was older, his face puffy and red. Veins showed in his nose and cheeks. Liver spots dotted the backs of hands. He wore faded, baggy canvas shorts. His bird legs showed webs of varicose veins. His huge feet were stuck in torn moccasins and a threadbare blanket was wrapped around his shoulders like a shawl.

"People know you're alive," I said.

"Loose lips," he said. I was shocked at the high, almost adolescent voice. I had somehow always imagined a deep bass. "Certain people could never keep secrets, but so many lies have been told about me, who the hell would believe another improbable tale?" The famous author still had a substantial frame, but no shape. All his bulk had collected in the middle of his torso. There was a nasty scar on his forehead and his nose was bent, like someone had twisted it and it hadn't come undone.

"Harkie says you were after the woman."

"Not Harkie," I said, "York Gentry."

Hemingway nodded. "Bad business, dames. They get your blood up or turn you snow-cold. I took shrapnel in the groin once. Jesus, my testicles swoll the size of grapefruits and I kept the inventory, but there were sure times I wished I hadn't. This woman is not my type. Maybe she's nobody's type. What do you want with her?"

"That's my business."

He was a slow, deliberate talker, his tone relaxed and conversational. "Here, *your* business is *our* business. I never had much use for commies, but the Red bastards were right about the strength of community, sport. Go to Africa and you'll see it in the animals. Interconnectedness. One for all, all for one."

"What happened to rugged individualism?"

I thought I detected the beginnings of a sneer. "I was what I was and now I am what I am. Which is to say, I'm none-a your business either, kid."

"Quite the friendly crew you've got here."

He said, "You're just sore because you got yourself snatched by a dame. I would be too, and believe me, I got taken by lots of them!" A smile formed and his eyes suddenly twinkled before darkening again. "The men here are committed, Rhodes. They're the real thing, the purest concentrate of American stew, cooked slow and long in the melting pot, reared on self-reliance."

I said, "They look to me like they should *be* committed."

Hemingway laughed so hard that he began to cough; several people rushed to him to slap his back and give him water.

When he recovered, he asked, "What the hell are you doing here, Rhodes? You think I went to all this trouble just to be tracked down by some bumbling amateur?"

"This isn't about you," I said. I doubt he believed me.

He sipped his water. "There something *between* you and the dame?"

"Not in the way you think."

"There's always something between a man and a woman," he said. The old man closed his eyes and put his head back. "You're in a pickle, kid. We're a private concern here. If you're here for the dame, that's peaches with me, but I don't make the decisions. Were it up to me, I'd say fine, but it's not up to me. The men here don't want to be found. We have a mission and nothing is gonna get in our way. That's the whole point, see?"

I didn't see at all.

Two men helped Hemingway to his feet and tried to hold his elbows to provide support. He pushed them away and growled.

"Why did *you* come here?" I asked.

He cinched the blanket around his shoulders. "Lost my juice," he said. "Nobody's one person. The one that used up pencils went away. The one that remained needed something else."

"Bullshit," I said. "You're here for the snowfly."

He grinned crookedly. "We all have a word for what it is that we're after. Suit yourself, feel free to pick the one that pleases you."

He started to shuffle away, but lifted his elbows to halt his escorts and looked back at me. "A woman's a good thing or a bad thing. She can lead you places and you won't even know you're being led. That's the hell of it. I wrote every one of my books for my women, now look at what they say about me. This dame we got here, handsome as she is, she might take you places you're not ready to go. All good-lookin' dames eventually get old," he added wistfully.

I saw Val exchange whispers with Hemingway at the edge of the shelter and then he was gone.

Valoretev narrowed his eyes when he came back to me. "Papa is a great man. In Russia great men do things common men cannot understand. Mathematicians, theoretical physicists." He tapped his left temple. "Great men live up here, unencumbered. For Papa, it is trout. This is noble, yes?"

I had heard enough of Hemingway.

Val returned me to the cabin at daybreak. "Morning," Raina Chickerman said as we walked in. She was waiting there, just out of reach, and she looked tired.

"Why am I here?" I asked.

She said. "You wanted this. I heard your voice, saw your face, kept seeing you. There were too many intersections. Then you followed me and I knew. Actions outspeak words."

"Excuse me," I said, "but have you had your thorazine today?"

She smiled. "Got you here, but I don't have you, not yet."

"What's that supposed to mean? 'Have me'?"

"I think you know," she said. "Inside." She tapped her chest lightly. "If you have the courage to look in there."

"I don't know anything anymore," I said. Perhaps I never had.

She smiled. "That's as good a starting place as any. Get dressed."

"I'm not undressed."

She paid no attention and vaulted gingerly to her feet. "Here we work before we eat."

I followed her to the river. The water was the color of beef stock, the current sluggish. If the river had been wider I would have guessed I was downstream of where I had been previously, but it wasn't wider. There was a path worn along the river. Raina crawled down from the embankment to a pile of rocks and felt around with her hand, then caught a line and tugged until a pike splashed to the surface. She took the fish by the tail, swung it up past me, reached into her pocket, rebaited the hook, and let the weight carry it back down into the water.

The fish continued to flop.

She climbed up and tossed me a cord. "Pick it up."

"Yes, Mistress." I strung the cord through the fish's gills and mouth and looped the cord around my hand. She looked at me and shook her head.

We walked for nearly an hour, collecting seven fish, the largest in the range of a few pounds. I dragged them behind me and they gathered leaves as they fought for life.

"Now what?"

"We trade."

"For what?"

"All you need to know is inside you," she said. "It's always been in there."

There was no sun, the sky blocked by the gauze of high cirrus clouds drifting south.

After the river walk, we went back to the open building, where Hemingway had sat, the aging king on his makeshift throne. There were a dozen men already there. Raina took the fish, removed one, and put the rest on the ground. There were other piles of dead animals. Hares, a fawn with spots, several small coons, a large possum, more fish (some trout, but mostly white horse suckers), some piles of small red twigs, a gunnysack filled with the stringy roots of wild carrot, other things I didn't recognize. Flies everywhere, on everything.

Raina moved through the piles, picking a few things, then motioned for me to follow her.

We went back to her cabin.

"You must have a lot on your mind," she said when we got inside.

"Situational paranoia."

She looked at me and smiled. "They're not what you think."

"Vets?" I asked, this a desperate guess. I had heard rumors of communities of Vietnam vets, so-called bush vets. Feeling betrayed by society and their country, they supposedly fled into the country's forests and wildernesses to live as they wanted to, making their own laws. The rumors struck me as myth, but now I was not so sure.

"Some undoubtedly are vets, but as usual you're groping," she said. "You're not even close. They just want to live their way. There have never been that many of them and there aren't that many of them left. They live in the bush and rarely go out into the world. There used to be more of them and new ones came along every so often, but this is a hard life and it takes its toll. They live free and die the same way."

"The authorities allow it?"

"There have been confrontations. You were right about the Au Sable, but the government always gives up. America is no good at trapping shadows and it isn't worth the effort or expense to drive them off. They just move to another place and settle in."

"This is no way to live," I said.

"As bad as yours?"

The question took me by surprise. "You don't know anything about me."

"Don't I?"

"You're psychic?"

"Something like that," she said softly.

We had filleted northern pike fried in a pan, flatbread, and thin slices of potato cooked with the fish. She poured tea.

"It's made from bark," she said. "It tastes putrid, but there's vitamin C in it. Out here you sacrifice taste for efficiency."

"It would take a while to develop vitamin deficiency."

"You'd be surprised how quickly a body falls apart if you don't take care of it."

"You make it sound like I'm going to be here a while."

She looked across the table and fixed her eyes on me. "Are you?"

"I didn't choose to remain here. Remember?"

"If you say so." Obstinate as a child, obstinate as an adult. And still beautiful. Having thought this, I immediately thought of Ingrid and was ashamed.

"That's the reality," I told her.

"Reality is much overrated," she said. "You were tracking me. Not just here. For years. Why?"

"You cut me off from Key at every opportunity." I pushed my plate away, but she pushed it back. "When there's food, eat. There'll be times when there's nothing."

"I'm not going to be here that long."

"You say," she said.

That next afternoon I split wood with a sledge and steel wedge and lugged it back to the cabin. I was sore, achy, and hungry beyond description.

Raina Chickerman watched me work, making no effort to help.

"Tell me about M. J. Key," I told her. "You owe me that."

"Do I?" she asked.

I had nothing to lose. To encourage her, I told her how I had learned of the snowfly and followed it over the years. She listened raptly and when I had finished, she craned her neck and stretched.

"Have you ever gone all the way in anything, Bowie? Just once? When we were kids, you always held back. You had so much fire inside you, but you never gave it air. You were good at everything, but did you ever want to be the best? Did you ever feel the fire get so hot that you thought you'd die if it went away? I think you've always been afraid of falling short."

I said, "M. J. Key." I wasn't in the mood for one of her lectures.

Raina gave me a cold stare. "You think life's hard? It can be a lot harder."

"You didn't answer my question."

"You haven't earned the answer."

The rest of the day I worked in silence, driving the wedge with all the muscle I could summon, and by the time I was done my only thought was for food.

When we got back to the cabin, Raina said, "You cook."

A small hunk of red meat and several carrots and onions were by the woodstove. "Venison?" I asked.

She nodded.

"They don't grow the carrots and onions out here."

She looked amused. "They have outside help."

Meaning they either went out from time to time, or someone came to them. Buzz, for example.

"There are no answers in mere logistics," Raina said. "You want to be here." Stated with the certainty that had always been in her voice when we were children.

My cooking skills were marginal, but so were the circumstances and the food. I worked slowly. This was the first time Raina had seemed willing to talk and I wanted to make it last.

"How do you fit in here?" The men seemed to accept her, albeit grudgingly, but she didn't seem to be a full member of the peculiar community.

Raina grinned. "I expect opinions of how I fit would differ."

"Answered like a politician."

"We're all politicians," she said. "Let's leave it at I choose to be here, same as the others. Why did you follow me?"

"I've already told you. To find out why you keep dogging me. And to find out about Key. Val says you call yourself Key here."

"Are you sure that's all?"

"I've looked for you for a long time. A post office box in Rhinecliff, New York. You were on the Fox River a few weeks ago. You've been using the name M. J. Key."

"A few facts strung together don't amount to much, do they? Perhaps Key isn't your only reason for being here."

"What other reason could there be?"

"You brought your rods," she said. "Maybe you want to know something you think Key knew. Perhaps he wrote something about it."

The manuscript. "I won't deny that," I said cautiously. "I've been interested for a long time." Raina had always operated on a different plane than the rest of us. I needed to go lightly. "Remember when you told me that white flies were *Ephorons*? You lied to me back then."

"It wasn't a lie," she said indignantly. "*Ephorons are* white flies."

"But not snowflies."

She shrugged. "Semantics."

"I had the manuscript in my hands," I told her.

Her smile disappeared and her skin seemed to turn pale. "What manuscript?"

"*The Legend of the Snowfly*. I found it in Vietnam. It had once been in Oxley's collection. Apparently he had two copies."

Her eyes turned hard. "Then you already know what's in it."

I knew then that she had the surviving copy of the manuscript, but I realized that, until this moment, she had thought hers was the only one. I didn't have the acuity to use my new edge. "I was talking literally. It was in my hands, but I never got a chance to read it. It got blown up."

She exhaled with relief.

"Of course, you could always loan yours to me," I said.

She leaned back. "You want the secret of the snowfly?"

"Is there a secret?"

"The secret is that you have to do it on your own. You've gone to a lot of trouble to find out what you should've known all along."

"How can I know what I don't know?"

Raina said, "Perhaps we'll have the chance one day to discuss theories of ignorance as forms of knowledge."

This was vintage Raina Chickerman and I started to laugh but saw she was dead serious. "You're expecting a snowfly hatch here."

"There was always a pathetic side to you," she said, getting up and commencing to ignore me.

After we had eaten, she fetched a jar with clear liquid inside and filled two chipped teacups.

The liquid seared my throat and ignited a burgeoning fire in my belly.

"Shine," she said.

"They've been here long enough to set up a still?"

"Does it matter?" she answered. "Why are you obsessed with facts? Is this a result of your career choice?"

"What I see is a bunch of people who look like they're on their last legs and they screw around making hooch? It looks to me like a doctor could help these people."

"It's not their way."

"They just live like this until they drop?"

"Exactly."

"That's nutty."

She said solemnly, "If evolution is the law that governs all life, then doctors and medicine are unwittingly destroying the human species by allowing people to live who genetically should not. I mean, the whole point of natural selection is to select for strength. Medical intervention dilutes this. These men live naturally to the full extent of their natural allowance."

I shook my head. "The power of evolution requires reproduction. There are no women here. They can't pass their genes along, so what's the point?"

She looked over at me again. "You might look more at effort than outcome."

I rubbed my eyes and finished the drink. "You're the wizard behind the curtain in Oz," I said.

"You're making progress," Raina said with a sly smile. "But you still don't get it."

It was the horse latitudes at sidereal passage, long past last light and a long way until the new one. We had separate beds, Raina and I. A statistician once told me that two data points would guarantee a straight-line plot; more, and there was a serious risk of disorder. Well, we were here, just the two of us, and I was enmeshed in more disorder than I could tolerate.

"Why couldn't you leave me alone?" Raina said, turning to face me. "Or act like a man and decide earlier?"

Decide what? Her voice was distant, contemplative. "You were butting into my life."

"Don't play stupid," she said.

In this instance I was not playing. I tried to check my frustration. "You sent Nick Adams."

She rolled her eyes. "You are an idiot. I didn't send anyone anywhere. Hemingway sent him."

"Huh?"

"Hemingway knows about Key. He doesn't want others to follow him. And Gentry wanted his books back. Actually, Hemingway was pissed at the grandson for drugging the old man in Key West."

"What about what Gentry did to me?"

She said, "What are you talking about?"

"Gentry attacked me. I nearly ended up in the hospital."

"I was with him. He only bumped you a little bit."

"Not then. Before that. I was fishing on this river and he came into my camp at night and beat the hell out of me."

"An old geezer like that against a big virile man like you?" She smiled, disbelieving.

The old man had struck me hard enough with his shoulder to feel like an all-world linebacker. And he had hoisted me out of the hole like I weighed nothing. "Gentry's crazy," I said. "And dangerous."

"He's only protecting Hemingway. They both believe in loyalty and they've seen little enough of it in their lives. I can understand them."

I must've blinked. "I still don't understand the Key West thing. The kid took all references to the manuscript and to Key's books."

She moaned. "God, you are thick. He wants to spare others what he has gone through. He knows what it is to go all the way for something and he knows that it crushes most people."

"If he knows this, why does he stay?"

"Because he's committed. I swear, Bowie."

"All right, let's assume you're telling me the truth about Hemingway and what happened in Key West. Explain to me why the U.S. government is methodically removing all references to Key's works."

She leaned forward. "What are you talking about?"

I told her about my experience at Michigan Tech and the New York City Public Library.

"The materials are not listed in the Library of Congress?"

I knew I had her interest. "It looks that way."

She said, "Give me a smoke."

I tossed her the pack. She struck a wooden match on the table, lit the cigarette, and stared at the flame until it was nearly burned down to her fingertip.

Raina was quiet for a long time. "Eubanks said you were trouble," she finally said.

I elected to remain silent.

"There's nothing in the manuscript," she said. "Don Quixote. If the government is doing what you say, it's misguided and acting foolishly."

"You should know," I said.

She smiled. "You haven't figured it out yet."

Why did she keep saying this? "I know that Gus was Key."

"Gus wrote the manuscript," she said. "The government has never been able to break his ciphers. They're afraid that the manuscript contains some sort of key and they want it."

"They haven't approached you?" If I knew she had the manuscript, the government would surely know.

"Oh, they've tried," she said. "Through Eubanks, but the manuscript is mine, not theirs, and Gus swore to me there's no key to any code in it."

"But they think there is."

"And you think it contains the secret to the snowfly. People believe what they want to believe."

Or they're led to believe in a certain way, I thought. Before I could say anything, she began to talk. "My father was a scientist, a biologist and a physicist. He and my mother were Russian Jews who fled the Reds in the early nineteen-twenties. The Russians hated the Germans and my father figured Germany would be a safe place. But he had not counted on a Hitler. Who had?" she asked. "When it began to look like National Socialism would grab the reins of power, he took my mother and left Germany." She paused and inhaled, her cigarette glowing. "They were Jews by birth, but their records were buried somewhere in the chaos of Russia and they were not practicing Jews. Gus doubted the Nazis would ever find out, but he couldn't take the chance. My father was a prominent scientist for the Germans and might have stuck it out safely, but he had my mother to think about. They came to the U.S. and my father got a job teaching in East Lansing."

"As M. J. Key."

Raina smiled. "Do you know who Donovan was?"

"Wild Bill, leader of the OSS, father of the CIA."

"Gus loved puzzles and codes and he had some revolutionary ideas."

"He and Vijver."

She whistled in mock appreciation. "You've done some homework."

"I read their article."

"And what did you think?"

"It suggested there was a code buried in it and dared anyone to break it."

"There was," she said. "Gus knew about some of the German cryptography and he and Vijver wrote the article to spike Washington's interest. Nobody there could break it."

"And Donovan got the message."

"Somebody he knew recognized that Gus was on to something."

It was strange how she called her father by his given name. She flicked the cigarette butt aside and lit another. "It was 1938. Donovan had already decided in his gut that there was going to be a war and he recognized that Gus could be a tremendous help to the country. He arranged for my father and mother to leave East Lansing in such a way that people would not much want to follow them."

"As publicly accused Nazi sympathizers."

"Gus spoke English with a German accent, so it was easy enough to believe. At that point Donovan was without portfolio, but he was gathering assets for the country. You won't remember this, but when Roosevelt got elected to his third term, he promised that Americans were not going to fight other peoples' wars."

"Which didn't rule out *our* wars, if we got pulled in."

"You've got it. Donovan was convinced that the U.S. needed a new, centralized intelligence agency run by civilians, not soldier boys. Roosevelt picked him to run the show. My mother and father were then living under assumed names in New York."

"Rhinecliff," I said, guessing.

"Close enough. Remember, Roosevelt was from Hyde Park, which is just down the Hudson. My father was one of Donovan's first recruits. Gus wanted to play the cryptoanalysis game, but Donovan had other plans for him and when Donovan wanted something, he usually got it. He asked Gus to return to Germany."

I had lived beside these people and never known anything about them.

"My mother remained in New York and also worked for Donovan. Gus went back to Germany and took a position at a technical institute in Berlin. By then he and Vijver had refined their plain language codes. Gus wrote letters to people all over the world, all of them Donovan's agents."

"About trout," I said. "And all of it was code."

I could see Raina's teeth flash. "You were always smart, Bowie. Smarter than you knew or gave yourself credit for. The Nazis never broke the codes and Gus was never suspected. With his academic contacts he kept the Allies tuned in to a lot of things the Nazis were up to. Donovan said that my father was the most important spy in the war. Gus came home in 1945 and they gave him medals and he said he had had enough. He felt he had earned his place in America and we went to Detroit to live."

Now I had something to ask. Raina was born the same year I was. "If your father was in Germany, where did you come from?"

"Dirty mind, Rhodes. My father was a scientist. Scientists traveled, even during the war, mostly to neutral countries. Donovan arranged for my father and mother to meet. He was sensitive to such things. I'm the result of a reunion."

"M. J. Key," I said.

"Hold your horses, I'll get to that. In 1947 the government came calling again. This time the war was against the Russians. It was cold, but just as serious. They sent my father to Leningrad. His job was to gather information, but more important to stop certain things from happening."

"Such as?"

"I don't know. Spies don't talk in details."

"How did they get him into Russia?"

"Easy. He went in as the Nazi scientist he was. Remember, at the end of the war the Russians, Americans, French, and Brits were all grabbing Nazi scientists. Many of them went to ground. It was arranged in 1947 for my father to be found and sent over to the Russians."

Part of me wanted to believe her and part did not.

"My father got out in 1951 and told the feds he was finished. His nerves were shot and he wanted his own life."

"From Russia to Pinkville."

She laughed the old Punky laugh. "I never caught the irony before."

"Your name isn't Chickerman," I said.

"Well deduced, Einstein. That was Gus's invention."

"There were other transplants in upper Michigan and Eubanks was their guardian."

She nodded. "My mother and father were the last."

"Which is why Eubanks pulled up stakes."

"He what?" I detected a stitch in her voice.

"He left Traverse City."

"Yes," she said. "Of course, that's logical."

Didn't she know? This upset her. I decided she didn't and I sensed it hit her hard. Now she was alone, without her protector. "You went to a lot of trouble to get the Key manuscript and make sure I didn't."

"Don't be an imbecile. I had no idea you were after it."

"But you wanted it bad," I said.

"Not for the reason you did."

"Not for the snowfly?"

"God," she said.

"But Key was real, a Brit," I said.

"No, some people think that, but he was American born, with an English mother, and he was raised over there. Gus took his name to write the 1943 work. It was published as part of the British scheme to make the Axis think he was alive."

"But it was Gus who wrote the snowfly manuscript," I interrupted.

"Yes, Key no longer needed his identity. He was in the ground. And had been since before the war."

Which confirmed what Lady Hoe had told me. "Your father was using his name before that."

"Yes, Gus admired him. They were very close friends for a long time."

"So he took his identity."

"At times," she said defiantly. "Key traveled throughout Europe for con-ferences all through the nineteen-twenties and into the early thirties. Gus was in Germany then and he and Key became close friends, took vacations, fished together, England, Wales, Scotland, Ireland, Iceland, France, Bel-gium, Germany, Italy, everywhere. When Dad settled in East Lansing, he used Key's name to conceal his identity and to honor a great man."

"Key was at Bletchley Park."

Raina laughed heartily. "You get an A for effort." I didn't let on that I was guessing. "Key was in England in name only. Alan Turing was the driving force at Bletchley and Key had been his mentor. Key's death before the war was kept secret so that he could be kept alive. The Germans knew Key and feared his ruthless intellect. Bletchley sent out communications for the Germans to intercept so that they would think Key was alive and playing a crucial role in Allied intelligence. Nazi agents chased his name all over England and the Brits used this to trap them. Key was just bait," she said. "Gus said that Key would have appreciated this. When Gus wrote his code article he used Key's name as a way to assure government atten-tion."

Most of it fit together, even the government's paranoia. There had been two Keys and Gus was one of them. "I never knew your father fished."

She chuckled quietly. "Gus was pathologically private. The Germans used him, the Russians used him, and the Brits and the Americans used him. When he had enough, we disappeared. He wanted to dedicate his life to something that could never be corrupted. Even though he worked against the Nazis and Soviets, he also had to work *for* them in order to preserve his cover, and this always weighed on him. He could never forgive himself, but he tried all his life to make amends."

"With *fish?*"

"Why *not* fish? Gus and Key loved fish and it was a symbol powerful enough for Christ. Fish are about hope."

"If you say so."

"You, of all people, should understand."

I wasn't sure what I knew anymore. "What about the snowfly?"

"Good night," she said wearily.

The next day I watched Ernest Hemingway make clumsy roll casts into a slow pool in an oxbow of the river near camp. Two men were with him. Most of his casts fell short and others got hung in the tag alders, low brush, and dead timber along the bank and had to be freed. He stood silently and motionless while others came to his assistance. When the line was free, he began casting again, deliberately, mechanically.

During one of his frequent hangs, I approached him and waved.

"Hiya, kid."

"Doing any good?"

"I never philosophize when I fish," he said. "Doing is enough."

"Might do better here with worms," I said.

He laughed silently. "Using worms isn't trout fishing, but I'm no snob about it. Nah, that's not it at all. I had plenty of catching in my day. We all did back then, I guess. Now we're paying for it. You can't keep taking just because it's easy. I used to count every word I wrote. Precisely. Last thing I did every day. Wrong headed, I think. Too much emphasis on progress, too much on the future. Life is about now. We forget that sometimes. No fish today, but I still have good days. You count your fish?"

I shook my head.

"Good for you, pal. Anything you've got to count usually isn't worth it."

The fly was freed and when he resumed casting, I left him alone. But before I had taken too many steps I heard him shout, "Get away from me!"

He had a fish on.

One of his helpers had a long-handled net and was down on one knee on the embankment, but Papa kicked awkwardly at the man as he scuttled back. Still the rugged individualist after all. He was old and not well, but he wanted to do it on his own. I felt growing affection for the man.

I couldn't believe the transformation. The old man with the barrel body and stick limbs, the old man who, minutes before, had stood like a statue, was now rippling with life. Maybe Raina was right, that fish were about hope. The fly rod was bowed. The line ripped nervously across the surface of the river. Hemingway's arms held strong, his elbows in, braced against his ribs. He glanced over his shoulder at me, squinting and grinning, and returned his attention to the fish.

It was an extended struggle. I squatted to watch. Hemingway said nothing, but grunted steadily under the strain, keeping the line taut. Others drifted down to the river and stood quietly.

His arms were flabby and jiggling like Jell-O, his spindly legs bent for balance and set wide.

The fish vigorously surged upstream, then reversed course.

I looked around. The whole company seemed to have assembled. The sun was large and hot. Some of the men stripped off their shirts. Their ribs showed like winter-starved deer. The only sounds were Hemingway's labored breathing and the line cutting the water.

At some point Raina and Val joined me.

The old man stood his ground grunting, awkwardly shuffling his feet, raising dust. His arms were wet, angled, silhouetted. I could see that his elbows were beginning to fan out. The fish was sapping him, getting the upper hand.

"Hold him, Papa!" a man shouted. "You can do it!"

A towering man with a red beard went to the man and hushed him.

Hemingway fell, landing on his behind, but kept the rod high and tried to get up.

A high-pitched crack told us it was over. The line had broken.

He held the rod overhead, stared at the reel and threw the rig away in disgust.

Nobody moved.

He lay back, spread out his arms, and said with a pained smile, "That should do it."

Then his chest was still.

We gathered in the communal building. One of the men bathed the body. Hemingway looked asleep.

Valoretev stood stiffly near the body as it was wrapped in cloth. He was weeping. I smelled kerosene. Harkie-who-was-Yorkie was there, filthy and giving off a loathsome stench, his back bent and tears running freely down his cheeks.

There was no sign of the wolf.

Raina was beside me.

We took the body into the forest and put it on a platform of sticks. Wood was piled neatly under the platform. A pyre.

Valoretev said, "A great man rarely owns his own life. To die doing what you love most is to have a glorious death."

Then the fire was lit.

I watched Raina Chickerman stare rapturously at the dancing flames.

We were back in her shack. There was no light inside, no moon outside. We could hear the wind chattering in the trees as a storm built. Raina had a cigarette. The ember glowed brighter when she drew on it, a tiny beacon of life on the other side of the room.

"It was a good death," she said, her voice barely a whisper. "You were there when my parents died."

"Afterward."

"They were together," she said. "I was glad for that. They both had cancers, terminal."

This was news. "I expected to see you. I tried to get in touch with you, but Eubanks blocked my way."

"It couldn't be helped," she said.

What couldn't be helped—her absence, their deaths, both? I asked her, "Do you know how the fire started?"

"It was what they wanted. It was time for them to go," was all she said, and the words gave me a chill.

Was she suggesting they set the fire themselves? Or worse? I couldn't get the possibilities out of my mind. I fell asleep listening to a battering wind and awoke with a start at morning twilight to hear the steady gush of rain on the roof. It was leaking through in many places. My first thoughts upon waking were of Hemingway's pyre and of Raina's face illuminated by the flame. Had Raina set the fire that took her parents? It was too horrible to contemplate.

"It won't be here," Raina said from the doorway. "Not this year."

She was dressed, her pack high on her back, and she wore a black rain slicker and boonie hat. She also had her shotgun in hand.

"What won't be here?"

"Did we ever make love?" she asked.

"No."

"I thought we must have."

"No."

"I guess it wasn't meant to be," she said. "Are you certain?"

"Yes." I would have remembered this. I had fantasized enough about it during our high school days.

She smiled. "Some things aren't meant to be," she said again. She looked back at me and adjusted her pack frame.

"You're leaving?"

"I always know when it's time."

"Because Hemingway's dead?"

She smiled darkly at me. "Some things and some people never die. Ideas count, my dear Bowie, not names and personalities."

"Will I see you again?"

"Perhaps," she said. "Though there is no longer any need. You know about Key and the snowfly. You should be satisfied now."

I was suspicious as I watched her walk briskly through the rain, which was letting up. She did not look back and I had a strange feeling that she had deflected me again. From what, I was not at all certain.

My gear was piled neatly on her bed. I grabbed everything and went out into the camp. The crude huts and dwellings were empty, abandoned. Only Valoretev remained and looked ready to go.

"They're gone?" I said.

"Exile is change," he said. "The woman says this isn't the place and not the time."

"For what?"

"Snowfly," the Russian said. "The search continues."

"You're all here after the snowfly?"

He smiled. "It is our life," he said. "It is heroic, *da?*"

"You do what Key tells you to do?"

"Of course," Val said. "She is the one who knows."

It was crazy. "Where will you go?"

He held up his hands. "Ah," he said. "Names are unimportant. We're all searching for the same thing, each in our own way. All that matters is to know when you've found it."

The Russian held out his massive hand. We shook and then we embraced.

He started to walk away, but stopped. "We took Brezhnev's trout," he said.

"Brezhnev's trout?"

"*Da,* we poached his private preserve! No matter what else, we have that. God go with you, my friend."

Valoretev jogged into the thick haze clinging to the forest and disappeared.

I was almost to the river when Raina appeared briefly on the far bank. She did not wave and it seemed to me that she was looking at me for the last time. My instinct was to follow, and I took a step toward her but heard a sound behind me and, when I turned around, Ingrid was sprinting toward me and there were men trailing behind her. She leaped the final distance and wrapped herself around me, smothering me with kisses and just as quickly backed away and began pounding my chest with her fists.

We were in the graveyard in the forest.

Sheriff Donal Hammill stared at the blackened, exhumed remains of Ernest Hemingway.

"What the hell do we have here?" he asked me.

"Nothing to worry about now."

"I'll decide that," he said.

The body was never identified and is buried near Grand Marais.

Ingrid and I were in our house in Grand Marais. I stood in the shower until my skin wrinkled.

"How did you know where to look for me?" I asked her.

"Buzz," she said. "He thought you might have hiked toward the head-waters of the No Trout."

He hadn't told her about Raina.

I would deal with him later. But first I had to make amends to her and I began by apologizing.

"What happened out there, Bowie? Why were you there?"

Our reunion had been hot, then cold. She was angry, hurt, and confused, and I couldn't blame her. I had not only been stupid; I had been a selfish asshole.

"I'm not really sure," I told her. And then I told her everything, leaving nothing out, and she listened until I was finished.

"None of that makes sense," she said when I had finished.

"To us," I said.

She appraised me for a long time, then walked toward me, shaking her finger. "I was so worried, Rhodes. Scared to death." She poked me in the chest with her finger. "You're never leaving me again, Rhodes. Do you understand?"

"Yes, dear." It never occurred to me that I could be the one left alone.

Buzz was in the sacristy of his makeshift church. "The prodigal returneth," he said. He opened a cabinet, took out a bottle of red wine and two glasses, and filled them up. "The sacredotal grape. To your safe return," he said, lifting a glass. I did not reach for mine.

"You were their connection," I said.

"They're harmless."

"They're psychos. Gentry tried to kill me."

The priest nodded. "I'm sorry. I went to see them, told them that if they ever let anything like that happen again, I would not only no longer help them but also bring the wrath of the law down on them."

"Why *did* you help them?"

Buzz sighed. "It's what I do. Besides, God most loves fools and fanatics."

"Even if the devil breeds them?"

"That's one side of the argument. You played dumb with the sheriff."

"Maybe I've spent too much time around you," I said, reaching for my glass.

"Better with me than with souls lost to obsession."

PART III

Everything that lives, lives not alone, nor for itself.
—William Blake

23

TROUT are classified taxonomically in the family Salmonidae. The oldest fossils go back fifty million years or so, though some experts estimate one hundred million as closer to year zero. There is a line of scientific opinion that in our millennia, *Homo sapiens* has not mutated as much or as effectively as might be expected, which may suggest the difficulty the so-called superior species faces in quest of its piscine elders.

Base genes persist. Males are built for sex with our females on all fours in front of us and we are programmed to perform quickly, a question of guards dropped and readiness for collective defense. We continue to be attracted to fire, though we have little need for the raw form anymore. The modern concept of romantic love is thought to have the strength needed to override our baser urges; but it is modern marriage that is the glue, as couples find themselves enmeshed in matrixes of obligations and expectations. Man was not made to be alone, though by and large, we have no choice in the matter, one way or the other.

Ingrid and I were married by Father Buzz in early October. We did not honeymoon. Our home became our refuge. We wove ourselves into the fabric of Grand Marais and it into ours. *Sports Afield* offered me a monthly column and I accepted. We were happy and life was full and I was certain that this would go on forever. We hardly noticed the winter.

In May we had fine spring weather. The trees were blooming, ferns were eagerly peeking from the forest floor, and early wildflowers were radiant. Ingrid was in East Lansing for a weeklong seminar at the Michigan State Police Training Center. She was supposed to return late Friday afternoon. I filled vases with forget-me-nots and cooked spaghetti sauce all day. I couldn't wait for her to get back, but evening came and there was no sign of her and no word. Cops lived peripatetic lives and I was getting accustomed to it. Sooner or later I knew she would slip into the house in darkness, float into bed, and cover me with her love.

There was a knock on the back door just before eleven P.M. Sheriff Donal Hammill and Father Buzz were outside. I remembered when two lawmen came to my sister, Lilly's, door to tell her Roger was dead. My blood went cold, my brain numb. I smiled like an idiot.

"It's Ingrid," the sheriff said. "I'm sorry."

People can talk about death with specificity in the abstract or when it applies to strangers, but when it refers to people close to us we can rarely say the word. The more personal it is, the more circuitous the language. We expect our parents to die before us, not our spouses.

"It was instantaneous," Hammill said.

Wasn't all death instantaneous? One second you were among the living and the next you were somewhere else. I felt strange, more confused than shocked. I wondered if Ingrid had a map for where she was. She loved maps. I walked back to the bedroom to see if she was there. I even said her name. Buzz followed me. She loved hide-and-seek.

"She stopped at an accident near Topinabee. She tried to direct traffic around the mess, but a truck lost its brakes." Hammill mercifully skipped the remaining details.

I sat on the edge of the bed and patted the covers. Not there. I went to my closet, then her closet. I needed her scent close to me.

Buzz added. "Do you want me to stay?"

"Sure, we can have spaghetti. Ingrid will be here any minute."

I heard Father Buzz say, "Donal."

The house filled with people, Karla and Van, Janey, Fred Ciz, others. "The pasta's for Ingrid," I told them.

Somebody gave me pills.

If Ingrid wore clothes at all around the house, she wore a ratty gray sweatshirt. I had bought it for her in Key West. I found it, rolled it up, lay with it under my head, and wondered how long it would be before she came home.

We buried her west of Grand Marais, in a remote area where voyageurs had allegedly buried their dead in unmarked graves three centuries before. It was one of her favorite places to picnic and make love. Hemingway was close to her.

When the funeral was over, I took my gear and hiked up the No Trout from the mouth. I did not bathe or shave and hardly slept. I did not want to remember the past or think about the future.

Buzz, Fred Ciz, and Janey came out to the river after I had been there nearly two weeks.

"Fish biting?" the priest asked.

I had no idea if I had been catching or not.

"We couldn't find your camp," Fred said.

There was no camp. When I was exhausted I simply got out of the water and slept, a hyperactive animal lacking purpose. I was covered with blackfly and mosquito bites.

"It's time for you to come home," Buzz said. "Grief is natural. Grief heals. This doesn't. You need to be with people." Fred nodded agreement and he and Janey took my arms.

I did not argue with them.

I spent the summer in the house. Janey stopped in every day to bring food. On Independence Day there were fireworks over the harbor and Janey came with fried chicken and slaw and three-bean salad and cold Strohs. I ate in the dark while she sat across from me and the windows flashed spectacular colors. Sometime that night I crawled into bed and Janey took off her clothes and slid in next to me, whispering, "You can call me her name if that helps." I couldn't do it.

My editor at *Sports Afield* was named Vairo. He was in his early sixties and nearing retirement. He loved scatterguns and dogs, wingshooting and people who wrote crisp sentences. He was an artful blend of patience and insistence. In August I started writing again. On Labor Day I had dinner at Staley's. Donal Hammill and his wife drove up from Newberry and Janey's kids and Karla and Van and their children joined in. I had little to contribute to the lively conversation, but the company gave me strength and when Lilly and her kids made a surprise appearance, I sobbed, not for what I had lost, but for what I still had. Buzz called this progress, adding, "About damn time."

Janey continued to hover close by and I was glad to have her there. She slept with me occasionally. In bed she said, " Maybe if you make your body happy it will help your mind." The motto of animal trainers and behaviorists. Therapeutic sex. But I could not do it. Janey was an affectionate and caring woman, and I suspected she was curious about Ingrid and me, but she did not ask and I did not volunteer.

I led a mostly solitary life. I fished and I wrote. In October Buzz went to Wyoming for a month's retreat and vacation. Snow came the day he left and it kept coming and the air turned frigid and the ground froze six feet down and winter settled on Grand Marais six weeks earlier than customary, and some weeks before the *Farmer's Almanac* had predicted it. I taped plastic over windows to seal them and spent days in the woods sawing deadwood and hauling it back until I had enough for two winters.

At night I wrote and read and stared at the radio. On Sundays Fred, Janey, her kids, and I ice-fished and watched the Packers. Lombardi was gone and with him the pride and edge of the Pack and it struck me how much impact one man could have on so many strangers. Some people are gifts, people like Fred and Buzz and Lombardi. And then there were the rest of us who tend to take far more than we give.

Ingrid had gotten me into the habit of going around the house without clothes. I wrote in the nude at the kitchen table. Sometimes Janey would drop by for a visit and find me this way. She just laughed as I scrambled. Clothes encumbered me. I knew it was a silly notion, but writers tend to indulge their idiosyncrasies as sops to creativity. Clothes took my juice. I thought Papa would understand that we each had to do what worked for us.

It was in the third week of November, six months after Ingrid's death, and I was writing a column about jigging for winter walleyes. I wrote on tablets of legal paper. False starts got wadded up and dropped on the floor. I discarded a page and saw it flit across the linoleum as a frigid breeze filled the room.

My eyes shifted to the open door.

Raina Chickerman stood in the doorway, wearing knee-high white mukluks, black cords, a white parka, white mittens that reached up to her elbows like medieval gauntlets, and a huge gray-white fur cap with snow on it. She took off the hat and whacked it on her leg, spraying snow on the floor.

She looked at me and said, "Nice outfit."

She had never been one for social conventions, like knocking on doors. Queen Anna had thought her rude, but it wasn't that. Punky simply did not recognize arbitrary boundaries.

I was too startled to speak.

She circumnavigated the kitchen, walked over to me, and looked at my lap. "Looks like puberty finally caught up," she said.

"Nice to see you, too."

She rubbed her hands together and blew on them. "This is the year," she said.

"Go away," I said. "I'm done chasing."

Marriage is a wonderful institution and the bond of love an endless source of comfort. But marriage does not erase the baggage you carry into it. I had fought hard to forget the snowfly; you cannot suppress the irrational. Some of us have things inside us that cannot be explained, urges that boil continually in or out of our genetic soup. I had kept my gear packed and ready since Buzz and Fred found me on my river after Ingrid's funeral. I did not look at it and never went into the room where it was stored, but I knew it was there and could feel its presence and spirit. The room had been like a mine waiting to be stepped on.

Raina went to the door. "If you stay, you'll always wonder," she said sharply. "The only regrets are for things not done." She left the door open. Snow billowed in.

I had walked away from Ingrid without a word. This would be different. I wrote a note to Janey and the others and told them I had gone away to fish.

I pulled on my clothes and grabbed my gear and went out to Raina's black truck. I stood in the snow beside the passenger window. She came around, took my gear, tossed it in the back, and I got in.

"I was sorry to hear about your wife," she said.

"Just drive," I said. I thought again about how I had left Ingrid and then lost her. Had that been my fault, some sort of divine retribution? Now I thought of Janey and my friends and felt a shudder, but I could not turn back. I had to do this.

Snow swirled around us. There was little traffic. Raina stuck to back roads, which were icy and rutted. She drove fast, with one hand on the steering wheel, but she kept a sure and steady line.

"It's real, you know."

"If so, it would be better known."

"One's existence is not predicated on somebody else knowing it. There are millions of unknown species of insects that live and our not knowing about them does not change the fact."

Of insects, of cats, of fish, I thought.

When we were children, Raina's delicate features had reminded me of the porcelain dolls my mother collected. She was still beautiful, but in the dim light of the cab I saw that hard lines were forming. The light made her face into a mask.

"Do you know of Shoumatoff's hairstreak?" She glanced at me.

"A new beauty aid?" I said laconically.

"It was discovered by a Russian in Jamaica in 1933. The locals, of course, already knew of them, but the butterfly was not officially found until science classified and named it. Before the Russian came, did it exist or not? Mankind imposes its order on nature, but that doesn't mean the order is real."

When we were children, Raina and I had lain in fields at night and watched for shooting stars and, when we saw one, we would give it a name. "Like our stars."

"Which weren't stars at all," she said. "Hairstreaks have azure wings, which makes them distinctive. In nature bright or unique coloring usually points to a mating scheme, but hairstreaks mate by scent, not by color." She looked over at me. "I confess, I still have your scent, have been able to recall it all my life. Can you still smell your wife?"

"No."

"I don't mean her soaps and perfumes. I mean *her.*"

I didn't want to talk about Ingrid. Raina had always been adept at going directly to my innermost thoughts.

She said, "There's an erudite psychologist in Australia who studies forms of ignorance. He talks about denial, meaning hurtful things that we will not allow ourselves to think about. Then there are taboos, all those things our tribes say are too dangerous for us to know. From there it gets gray. Tacit knowledge refers to all sorts of things that we know, but aren't really aware of. Error is another level. These are the things we think we know, but don't. Then there are known unknowns, all the things we know for sure that we don't know, and finally, at the pinnacle of ignorance, the unknown unknowns, all the things we don't know that we don't know. Most of our ignorance resides there."

"The snowfly?"

She smiled. "It's real."

"You've seen it?"

"No," she said matter-of-factly. "Not in the way you mean."

"Maybe you're wrong."

" 'The irrationality of a thing is no argument against its existence, rather a condition of it,' " she said, adding, "Nietzsche."

She had always been an intellectual show-off. I countered, "Nietzsche also said, 'Without beer, life would be a mistake.' I'm thirsty."

"You made that up."

"Prove it," I said. It felt almost like we were children again.

We stopped at a crossroads village at an establishment called the No-Moon-Saloon, a name open to several interpretations. The walls were covered with deer heads with glass eyes. The menu was a litany of high fat. Though technically in the Temperate Zone, our annual temperatures could swing through 170 degrees, whereas equatorial climates seldom varied 20 degrees in a year, these facts strong evidence of the weakness of labels. In the Temperate Zone ectomorphs have a low life expectancy. Up here you ate fat and died slow from accumulated arterial plaque or you ate sensibly and died young and thin, vehicular mayhem and bar brawls notwithstanding.

Raina ate deep-fried pork rinds, a burger with the works, onion rings, fries, and a wedge of chocolate silk pie, all of this washed down with two bottles of Strohs and three cups of coffee loaded with sugar and Pet milk from a can.

I sipped my beer and watched in amazement.

"I don't eat breakfast," she said by way of addressing my disbelieving stare.

I offered to drive.

"I do my own driving," she said. "Get in."

We eventually got to a village called Trout Creek and veered off on a two-track in the hump of a bend in the road and hustled down the narrow track, throwing white rooster tails. Branches whacked the sides and roof and we glanced off several small trees. I had a premonition of death.

"You get your license out of a Crackerjack box?"

"Same principle as life, keep moving or bog down," she said, clearly enjoying herself.

We finally stopped at a cul-de-sac carved out of an area of tightly packed hemlocks.

We had no sooner come to a halt than she was out and strapping on her pack. I didn't ask questions; I quickly collected my gear and followed her into the trees. She moved with the grace and speed of a pronghorn.

The river was fast, its flow broken by huge granite boulders. The water flowed heavily and fell over a series of steps to form frothy cataracts and an immense din that drowned all competing sounds. Raina stayed back from the river's edge and trotted sure-footedly along the icy rocks. I followed as best I could.

I smelled wood smoke before we topped a low ridge. On top, under some cedars, there was a line of lean-tos and canvas tents.

Raina entered the camp without hesitation and headed directly to a large tent.

Red Beard and Val stood when we entered.

"So," Val said. "It's true."

Raina beamed aloofly.

"We figured it was here," Red Beard said. "Your presence is proof."

Raina only smiled.

We ate and drank and talked. There was only one topic: A few white flies had been seen at several locations on the river. The tone was respectful and reverent and, as I listened, I understood that all of these men had walked away from whatever lives they once had to singularly pursue the same myth that had pulled me in starts and stops the better part of my life. I had leaned in and leaned out and only circled the fire, but they had stepped into the flames and had been consumed. Was this my future? It was a disconcerting thought.

We were given a small lean-to near the river. Balsam boughs were piled on the floor for insulation. A sheet of stiff canvas hung down the front as a door and flapped in the gusting wind. The roar of the nearby water was oddly soothing.

Raina unrolled a large sleeping bag.

I started to unroll mine.

She patted her bedroll. "Us," she said. It was cold. Breath vapor hung in the air. Raina took off her clothes and slithered into the bag.

"Now you," she said. "Keep your clothes on."

When I slid in with her, I let my hand graze her buttocks and felt desire leap in me. She jerked in surprise, shifted away, and growled icily, "This is only for warmth."

But I could still feel the warmth of her flesh in my hand.

Raina and I slept for three hours before returning to the main tent.

The men had peculiar names. The man with the distinctive beard was Red Beard, for obvious reasons. Foot Long was a former butcher. Numbers had been a CPA. Wheelie had owned Ford dealerships in central Illinois. Silk was a retired army Green Beret. Test Tube had been a pharmacologist for Parke-Davis in Ann Arbor. Funnel had been the *Today Show*'s weatherman in the early 1960s. There were others as well, all with similar stories of previous lives in more or less normal jobs and careers, and Val, whom they called Comrade.

"I saw a pair two nights ago and six last night," Test Tube informed the assembly.

Some had seen none, others had seen more, but there seemed to be general agreement that tonight there would be more white flies. Test Tube gave us a brief lecture on progressions and probabilities. His observations were crisp and clinical, his tone dispassionate. I thought it odd that a man so devoid of emotion would be so obsessed with something as soft as trout and hatches.

"How long you been doing this?" I asked him.

"Full time? Seventeen years. It only counts when it's full time," he said. "You quit your job for this?"

Test Tube looked surprised. "Quit? Of course not. It's more in the nature of a sabbatical. When this is done, I'll go back."

After seventeen years? I had heard once that the half life of a new post-doc was two years, meaning half of what he had learned in almost thirty years in school was obsolete in those twenty-four months. Did he really believe what he was telling me?

Red Beard had been "in," as they put it, twenty-five years. Foot Long, twenty-one. Val was the newest of the group. I saw no sign of York Gentry and didn't ask about him.

Together the men talked through their tactical plan. The river was the Mibra Onty. The watch would run from one A.M. until an hour or so after sunrise. I asked the reason for this timing and was ignored. Each of us would have an assigned stretch. If a sustained hatch came off, we were to signal the others. I understood: After years of failure on their own, the men had bonded together out of shared obsession and sheer desperation. The myth of strength in numbers.

Only Test Tube seemed calm. The others were restless, antsy, jacked up, and trying to contain their anxiety. They were like grunts setting up a night ambush, their nerves raw and exposed, plugged into the universe at an atomic level where there was only energy begging release.

Raina and I were assigned adjacent positions. I started to assemble my rod when we got to the river, but she stopped me.

"Don't bother," she said before she walked away.

I thought she was telling me to avoid stringing the rod until I needed it. I took my position above a long, flat slick.

The trick in winter fishing is to dress in layers under your waders and get into the water as quickly as you can. Extremities tend to freeze first, but if you're dressed right the constant temperature of the water stabilizes the lower limit of cold for your lower body. Your upper torso still has to contend with windchill, but half of you is constant. I didn't know what else to do. You take what edge you can get. In winter safety and comfort margins were shaved thin.

Only we didn't get into the water and I felt the chill before my feet went numb. I was not insulated for standing on the bank in snow. I walked around stamping my feet, earning only a periodic and faint tingle, but the outcome was already decided. If I didn't find a way to warm them, my feet would freeze. I gathered dead branches from under the trees and dug down through the snow to pine thatch and deeper yet to find dry material and nursed a small fire to life between some rocks and put my feet over the flames and withdrew into myself. I had met a grunt in Vietnam who said he would write a novel based on where his mind traveled when he was on guard duty. I wondered if he had lived to write his book.

Raina come down to my position after it was light. My back ached from the cold. I offered her a cigarette.

"Coffin nails," she said. "I quit. I've got too much life left to live."

Invincible as a child, she remained invincible as a woman.

The men had prepared a huge breakfast of sausages, eggs, and biscuits the weight of sinkers. I was starved, but Raina did not eat. Instead she drank several cups of black coffee. Afterward, the group dispersed. It had started to snow hard.

"I like this," Raina said, catching flakes on her tongue.

We went back to our tent, burrowed into our bag, and slept again. The heat of her body ignited long-held lust in me, but I had to be content with the warmth our bodies created.

It snowed all day and the wind picked up and blew across the rift where the river cut through the hills. Trees rattled against each other, squealing under the assault, and Raina got out of her sleeping bag and pulled back the flap of the lean-to and stood naked in the face of the wind and looked over at me.

"Just what the doctor ordered," she said.

We met the others again after dark. The wind was hard out of the north and it was nearing a whiteout. There was no way to fish in such conditions.

The white fly count from the previous night was assembled. I reported no sightings. Raina reported at least two dozen and four rises. Had she gone after them? No, not time yet, she assured the others. This earned some discussion. Clearly, she was the expert and her words excited them. Flies had been seen above Raina's position, but not below. Tonight all positions would be adjusted upriver. Raina and I would anchor the downstream boundary. I thought it likely we'd all freeze to death before the night was over.

"How are we supposed to see?" I asked them.

They all looked at me.

"White fly, whiteout. How do we see a hatch?" No response. "How do the fish see it? They can't see a hatch in rain."

As before, they ignored me and went back to talking among themselves. People with obsessions tend to ignore details that don't fit their expectations.

"Eat big," Raina whispered to me when food was ready.

We repaired to our shelters after the meal, walking past our own twice before we located it. I had to look at my feet to keep my eyes from freezing.

In the bag she turned her back to me. "Conserve energy," she said. She was breathing evenly and asleep almost immediately.

Queen Anna had always told us that people who slept fast were either all good or all bad. Which was Raina?

"This is crazy," I told her before we went out to our icy stations around midnight.

"Think of it as part of the allure," she said.

"I still don't understand how the fish can see a hatch in zero visibility. Or us see the fish." Much less how a hatch could happen in such extreme weather.

She ignored my remarks. "Let's go."

I lasted only minutes beside the river, then gave up and climbed uphill into a grove of balsams and cut and piled branches to give me a mattress and air space for insulation. I curled up in the fetal position and slept in fits.

Raina was suddenly there beside me, a ghost poking at me. It was still dark and snowing hard, the wind roaring through the trees like an oncoming locomotive. "Time to go," she said, shouting to be heard over the wind.

"Is there a hatch?" I looked around. "It's not light yet. What about the hatch?"

She plopped my pack beside me and yelled, "I'm going. You do what you want."

I grabbed my gear and followed her though the drifting snow. We immediately left the river and veered into the forest. When I caught up to her, she gave me the end of a nylon cord.

"Wrap it around your wrist." To be heard, she had to put her mouth against my ear and shout. Her breath was hot against my freezing skin. I was too tired and numb to resist. I did as she said and followed like her prisoner. We were tied to each other by shared insanity. Or something. There is no way to describe the effect of a whiteout. Eyes and ears die. Your inner compass spins endlessly, unable to fix. My whole world was in my wrist. Raina led and I followed, the same as it had been when we were children. Queen Anna would scold me: "That girl would tell you to jump off the roof and you'd do it." I stood mute in the face of such charges. It was true: I had always been mesmerized by Raina. I had no idea how she could see, much less maintain a particular direction. Or keep the pace. I had no choice but to cling desperately to the umbilical.

I was certain we were going to die, but we didn't. Once again Raina brought us through.

In her truck the heater fans blasted us. I was semiconscious. Her headlights made circles in the wall of blowing snow ahead of us. Watching made me dizzy. When I closed my eyes, I slept.

It was still snowing hard at daybreak, but the wind had died down. We were nosing our way along a narrow two-track, plowing through drifts. The snow fell straight down.

"Where are we?"

She didn't bother to look at me.

She got out of the truck and ran up the road and out of sight. The wipers loudly flicked back and forth, leaving slushy arcs. When she came back, Raina jerked open the door and said we should go.

"It's warm right here."

She glared at me. "I'm not going to tell you twice."

"You like getting your way," I said.

"No," she said. "I *insist* on it."

I walked stiff-legged up the drifted lane behind her. The sky was beginning to lighten. We came to a trailer with an unpainted plywood entry shed attached. Somebody had nailed a board to the vestibule and painted MANIAC MANOR on it. The trailer's interior was cool, but there were space heaters clicking busily and the edge was coming off the air quickly.

"Nice place you've got."

"It's not mine," she said. "Let's sleep. We'll worry about food later."

"Not yours?"

"We're borrowing it," she said. "Forest Samaritan Rule."

I thought for a moment. "You mean we're breaking in."

"You're the wordsmith," she said. "I need sleep."

She threw her sleeping bag on a double bed. When I started to get on the bed with her, she squeezed down the opening to the bag. We were standing next to each other.

"I sleep alone," she declared.

"What about the other nights?"

"Different place, different rules."

There was the sharp edge to her voice that Punky's used to have, only now the edge was like a razor. I had always backed down when we were children. Not this time.

"We abandoned the others at the river."

She looked at me and yawned. "We all choose to be where we are."

"We just left them there."

"There's no rule against that."

"The big hatch isn't going to be there, is it? You didn't see any flies, did you?"

"There were a few," she said. "There are some on most rivers this year."

"You deliberately misled them," I said.

"You figured it out," she said, turning her back on me as she undressed.

"They could die out there!"

I was tired, disgusted, dumbfounded, and sick of her lies. I grabbed her and spun her around. She fought to get loose and we fell onto the bed. My hands wrapped around her throat.

"Goddamn you!" I screamed at her.

Her eyes locked on me as she began to gasp for air. I wanted to hurt her. She had driven me to this.

"Key's manuscript," I said, trying to regain my composure. "Why did you have to have it?"

"It was my father's work. It was supposed to be published, but the OSS stopped it because they feared it would somehow get linked to what my father was doing from Germany. The OSS killed it and they got what they thought was the only manuscript, but a copy got made and ended up in England. They belonged to my father," she said angrily. "To me."

"Two copies," I said. "I found one and you got the other. What's in the manuscript?"

"Not codes," she said. "No government secrets." She flopped in the other direction, and was immediately asleep.

I knew she was lying about the manuscript. There might be no government secrets in the document, but I knew that it contained something about the snowfly that she was determined to keep from the world, and to herself. This was the Raina I had always known, interested only in herself and using everyone for her own purposes. I lay down on the other bed and fell into a troubled sleep.

I had a strange dream. Three angry, bearded men were pointing deer rifles at me. I opened my eyes. It was not a dream but a bone-chilling version of reality.

"Look what I found sleeping in my bed," one of them said. I used my eyes to search for Raina. Her bed was empty, her things gone. She had misled the group and, now, she had bailed on me. *Goddamn her!* I kept thinking, "Maniac Manor." This was not the moment for histrionics.

"Forest Samaritan Rule," I said, groping for something, anything.

"What the fuck is he talkin' about?" one of the men asked.

I said, "People in dire trouble have the legal right to use any cabin they need. It's law."

"Only law here is what I say it is," the first man said. He thrust the rifle forward for emphasis.

"Failure to comply is two years in jail, twenty thousand dollars, and confiscation of the property. Ignorance of the law is not a legal defense." I was desperate. Bullshit against a gun feels absurdly inadequate.

The man took aim. "Fuck your law," he said. "This is *my* place."

I closed my eyes.

"Wait, Harry." Another voice. "He ain't done no harm. Maybe he's tellin' the truth."

"You shoot him, Harry, and I'm tellin' the cops." Another voice of reason.

I opened my eyes.

"I can't have jerk-offs takin' over my camp."

"I was just using it," I said. "I was freezing."

Two of the men pointed their rifle barrels at the floor.

"Let him get dressed and get out. We came to hunt, not fuck with cops."

I said, "Sorry, Harry. If you were me, what would you have done?"

The one called Harry had a thick black beard and shaggy gray hair. "I sure as hell wouldn't be walkin' the boonies in a blizzard."

"Leave him be," one of Harry's companions said.

Harry lowered his rifle. "Get your shit and get out."

There was only one set of tire tracks in the lane, and they attached to the hunters' green pickup truck, which meant Raina had been gone a while. When I got out to the road I turned east, glad to be free and full of rage, Raina's sucker again. She had spun such a tale about her parents that now I wondered what was real and what was not.

I walked a long time before I managed to hitch a ride to town. I had a lot of time to think. Gus Chickerman didn't want the manuscript. If it had been that sensitive, the government would not only have stopped the project but also confiscated the materials, the original, and all copies. I doubted even that Gus had written it. It seemed more likely to have come from the pen of the original M. J. Key, somehow ending up briefly in Gus's hands. Why, I had no idea, but I was certain Raina wanted it for one reason: She was addicted to the snowfly and determined to do what her father had once done. If she had the secret, she wanted to keep it to herself. I thought of the huge fish at Sturdivant's. And just as Gus had misled Sturdivant, Raina was misleading everyone, me included. The mysteries surrounding the manuscript would have to wait. Raina was not going to beat me. I found a telephone and called Fred Ciz.

"Where are you?"

"Sidnaw."

"It's going to take me some time to get all the way over there. Are you all right?"

"Time is only the arithmetic expression of position in the space-time continuum."

"Stay inside," he said. "It sounds like your brain's froze."

24

DURING World War II, there had been a camp near the village of Sid-naw housing thousands of Nazi POWs. A handmade sign on the door of the town's only restaurant proclaimed WHITETAILS FOR JESUS/WE MAKE OUR OWN PASTIES AND KRAUTS. I did not seek an explanation; we are not intended to understand some things. I had a "special breakfast pasty," which tasted like every other pasty I'd ever eaten: dry and bland. Cornish miners had warmed their pasties on shovel blades. Almost all the mines in the U.P. had gone belly-up. The miners and their shovels were gone; only pasties remained. Pasties and me. Raina was gone, too. White flies remained a jump ball.

Why had Raina come to me this time? This time was neither accident nor coincidence. She had intentionally sought me out and knew about Ingrid. She had been keeping track of me and she had come to get me, not because she wanted me with her. For years she had blocked my way. Maybe Gus had helped her. There was no way to tell on that count. She had misled Val and the others, then gone out of her way to get me out of her way. Why?

As a child, the Raina I felt I knew did everything with a purpose.

I had a good idea what she intended. If I was here, I couldn't be elsewhere. Raina wanted the snowflies to herself. There was no other conclusion.

"This is the year," she had said in Grand Marais.

There had been a few snowflies on the Mibra Onty, but there would be no hatch. "A few on most rivers *this year,*" she'd said.

Not on the upper reaches of the Lesser Trout.

Nor on the Dog. Sturdivant was sure it would be there this year, but he had been duped by Gus. Like father, like daughter, I guessed. Sturdivant was headed for more disappointment.

When we were kids Punky could outperform us all, but she always begged for a head start, an edge. Not from a dearth of confidence. Rather, as insurance. She played all angles.

We are who we are after a certain point in life, which is more or less how the Jesuits viewed it. Raina was evidence. What had she asked me? Had I ever gone all the way in anything?

She had seized me on the No Trout. Her captive. The others had been unhappy with her, meaning my capture had been her idea. Again, I had to ask why. What exactly was she up to? Head start? Misdirection? Getting to know the competition was more likely. Sizing me up, taking my measure.

The Mibra Onty was near the Wisconsin border.

Wanted an edge. Me, out of the way.

As kids it had been Punky and me, neck and neck in love and competition. I had only twice beaten her at anything, getting the senior writing award and beating her in the fourth-grade spelling bee, and after that she had not talked to me for a month. We had always been in competition, but outcomes had always seemed more important to her than to me.

She had come after my old man's funeral, seen me, and gone. Why?

Had ignored the death of her parents. Some absences are easier to explain than others. I couldn't get it out of my mind that she had set the fire that killed her parents; she said only that it was what her parents wanted. They were dying. What a terrible decision to face. I felt sorry for Raina. And I was beginning to loathe her.

The Soviets read *Izvestia*, which means "truth," of which it was largely devoid in the standard sense. The real truth was in what was not written. A captain I'd met in Vietnam had told me the best read on the enemy is where they didn't seem to be.

What was between Raina's lines?

She liked to have the biggest advantage she could manage. She thought she knew where the snowfly would hatch and wanted me as far away as possible. She had been in the U.P. for months, Fox, No Trout, Mibra Onty. Putting down her scent? All in the U.P.

Then it hit me. She had steered entirely clear of the Lower Peninsula and the best trout fishing was there, not here. Always had been.

None of this was an accident.

Fred arrived late that afternoon. I borrowed some money from him, got change, called information, got a number in East Lansing, and made the call. When I hung up I told him we needed to get back to Grand Marais to get my car.

"We found the door standing open, you gone, and only a note. Janey was worried, Bowie. We all were."

"It couldn't be helped," I said. My stomach churned. I did not want to hurt Janey, but this had to finish. I wanted it over, once and for all. And I had to hurry.

The sky was clearing when we reached the coast of Lake Superior. The snow and lights made Grand Marais look like a storybook village.

"Where are you going?" Fred Ciz asked.

"All the way," I said.

Lloyd Nash had introduced me to M. J. Key's work. Key-Chickerman, former agricultural college professor. It had been Nash I called long distance from Sidnaw.

"M. J. Key," I said to him.

"You can't be him."

Nash was shouting like he had gone hard of hearing. "This is Bowie Rhodes. White flies, remember?"

"Which Bowie Rhodes?"

"How many have you known?"

"I don't like telephones," he shouted.

"I cleaned the specimen room."

"And did a damn lousy job," he said. "It was still a hopeless mess the last time I saw it."

"Professor, where was M. J. Key from?"

"In what context?"

"Where was he born?"

"I don't know when."

"Where, not when," I shouted.

"Stop Thirty-Six," he bellowed. "Are you deaf?"

One of us was. "Where's that?"

"Upstate, on the railroad."

"Are you sure?"

"Beulah Reddiger is from Cat's Breath, Indiana."

An unexpected tight turn in an enfeebled brain. Who the hell was Beulah Reddiger?

"What's that got to do with Stop Thirty-Six?"

"Cat's Breath, Stop Thirty-Six, you don't forget names like that. There's no file in the brain to lose them in. Tend to stick and stand on their own, even when the memory turns to mush. Are you with the bank?"

"Thanks," I said. Poor Nash.

What had Raina said? That I had gone to a lot of trouble to learn something I should have known on my own. I stopped at the library in Gaylord on the way south in the morning and checked old maps of the region. The answer had been literally out my back door, which maybe explained all the drownings above the house. Stop Thirty-Six was subsequently named Whirling Creek and then Pinkville. I had never known. There all the time. Born on it, to it, with it, ignorant of it. The real Key had been born there. That's why Chickerman settled there. For the snowfly, which he had learned about from his friend Key. Raina said Key was American. I had always assumed he was English. He went to Europe all the time. Something I should have known on my own, Raina had said repeatedly. Whirling Creek had been home, an extension of my existence, home ground, my spawning waters, the crucible where the old man and Queen Anna had shaped my sister and me.

But Raina was not up the creek. Instead, there was a small Airstream parked on the flats between where my old house had been and where the floater had hung up on the rocks.

Gus had come to Whirling Creek for a reason, because it had been Key's home water and Key had written about the snowfly. It had to be this way. Only this scenario made sense. Roger Ranger had seen Gus Chickerman prowling upper Whirling Creek in the dark. The answers were in the past and closer to the present than I ever imagined. Every fisherman had his home water, the place he knew best, the place where secrets unfolded under constant vigilance.

Whirling Creek had been M. J. Key's home water, Gus Chickerman's, Raina's, *mine*.

I wanted to shout at her, "I've figured it out and I'm still dogging your ass!"

City and country clans alike have little sense of the night skies overhead, one because it's obscured by too much light, the other because there's too much there to comprehend. It was one of those nights that could shrink you into nothing if you looked up too long. Relativity as leveler: I doubt Einstein had this in mind with his theoretical tinkerings.

I was warmed by anticipation. Too often we end up in places without purpose. In Song Lai I had asked a Marine how he felt about where he was. "Everybody's gotta be somewhere," he said.

I built a primitive shelter in the woods and watched the trailer for two days. Raina stayed mostly in her Airstream. Several times each day she came out, walked to the river, and stood there with her arms crossed. Each time she stomped back and slammed the door. She was visibly perturbed. Each slam reverberated like a rifle report.

Before Queen Anna died she got clear headed. "Those fish he put back all those years," she whispered to Lilly. "Someday they'll get big." Prescience?

The dull sun showed itself through cloudy gauze in the southern sky late in the afternoon, then, without warning, popped out, hot and white. Raina came out in her waders and stood, assembling a two-piece rod. The glare off the snow was white as an atomic core and equally blinding.

Afternoon and still light. On the Mibra Onty she'd led the others to believe that the hatch would be after midnight. She had set us all up masterfully, being ever careful, the commander of all details, focused on getting her edge. She had Key's manuscript.

But now the edge was mine.

When she came out of the trailer and headed upstream, I followed at a discreet distance.

Maybe she was overconfident, maybe not. It would not be out of character for her to double back on her track. I would not underestimate her. Not this time. I veered away from the creek and paralleled it by a quarter mile. There were several places upriver where there was high ground with secure views. I found her below the first overlook.

She was squatting on a mound of upturned tree roots. Ice was stacked along the bank. She was watching something.

Flies were rising. Black, not white. And small, though they fused into smoky clouds. Midges, I guessed. I saw fish rise, but they were small. The old saw: Small flies, small fish. Besides, big fish fed almost exclusively on other fish, white flies the possible apparent exception to the taste for cold flesh.

When the sun went down, it got dark fast. I had to get closer to maintain my watch and carefully climbed down to the river.

Raina remained where she had been. Her concentration was eerie.

Later, the moon crawled up, illuminating the snow, casting pale light.

Still she squatted.

By the time I saw more flies I realized they had been hatching for a while. They were white, but nowhere near as large as I had anticipated. More plentiful than on the Mibra Onty, but not anything like a full hatch. Here and there, now and then, sporadic, almost teasing. But I could hear fish after them.

Raina stood, then squatted again. Stretching, I guessed.

I studied the water. There was a long run across from her and, below us, the stream shifted ninety degrees to the right and narrowed, gathering speed, the force giving it voice.

Hours went by. I could hear her talking to herself. Cursing. The hatch continued sporadically, never getting heavy, often ceasing.

She prowled anxiously back and forth along the bank like a cat. Each time the hatch restarted there were several minutes of splashing, slurping fish.

I smiled. It was not at all what I had imagined, and, just as obviously, not what she had imagined. I could feel her anxiety, but felt no sympathy. I thought of Red Beard, Test Tube, Val, and the others looking for something that did not exist on the Mibra Onty. How many wounded were left in the wakes of her lies and their own misshapen dreams?

Finally Raina had waited long enough. When a hiatus came, she splashed into the current. When the flies began to rise again, she began to cast. She caught three fish and each time shouted unintelligibly, slapping the creature angrily against the water, stunning it, killing it. Her actions sickened me. Raina was a headhunter, a killer.

I had followed her to confront her. I had dreamed all day about such a potentially triumphant moment, but the thought of besting her was suddenly gone. She was pathetic to let a myth drive her life and I was not any better. The shame was mine as much as hers.

I decided to leave and climbed back up the rocks.

Below me I heard her screaming, "Goddammit, goddammit." The echo of her voice flew up and down the creek.

I left her with her anger, crossed the ridge above her, and cut back toward the river. I didn't care anymore if she saw my tracks or even me. I was done with this insanity. I hoped Ingrid could not see me.

When I got downriver, I stuffed my gloves in my jacket and lit a cigarette.

Then I heard splashes.

To my left, then past me. Flailing arms. A dark shadow under a white moon, breaking the surface of fast water.

Raina.

I ran frantically along the creek, but she was out of reach. Once her head came up and I felt her eyes lock on mine and she shrieked, *"Mine, mine!"*

It was instinctive to want to go in after her, but I knew this water would put both of us in jeopardy. The safest place to get her was at the pool below the old house. If she lived that long. I ran, thinking of the floater hung on our rocks when I was a child and imagined Raina there and ran harder.

I would get only one grab at her. If I could catch her in the upper pool and hang on, I could steer us both to downstream safety. *If* is always the hooker in risk.

I waited much longer than the time she needed to drift down to me. Had she managed to get out? Or had she gone under and gotten hung on a snag? I kept turning my head, but the moon was nearly down and the light was failing fast. I waded closer to the channel and reached out with my arm. If I didn't see her, I might snag her by feel. It was down to luck, pure desperation.

I felt something smack my arm and instinctively clawed it with my hand and held tight. It was a fly rod. When I lifted it, the end of the line suddenly peeled out like a runaway freight, and the rod snapped out of my hand as the leader broke with a distinct crack. It had been not just a fish, but a huge one.

Raina Chickerman did not float down Whirling Creek that night and she did not walk down and, when the sun began to rise, I was alone with the fact that those who sought the impossible often found it. I felt empty and sick.

There was nothing to be gained by searching alone. I drove out to a phone, summoned help, and returned to the homestead to await its arrival. While I waited, I went through her Airstream. Key's manuscript was on a small table. I remembered some words of Izaak Walton: No man can lose what he never had. I did not open the manuscript, but a hardbound copy of Richard III was open to this line: "And therefore, since I cannot prove a lover . . . I am determined to prove a villain." Why? I would never learn. I took the manuscript to the river's edge and used it to start a fire to keep me warm. I no longer wanted to know what was in it. I had seen its terrible effect and that was enough.

There were a couple of dozen people in the search party. Raina's body was found close to where I had last seen her. She had gone under and gotten stuck under a sweeper. There would be a coroner's report, but scientific observation would not tell us more than we already knew. She was dead.

I only glanced at the body, which had turned blue. Sitting in the open air, her hair had iced and turned white, like some sort of monster. Her face was frozen in fear and anger.

A conservation officer in a green uniform came over to me.

"She was fishing out of season," he said.

"Back off," I told him.

"The law is the law," he said.

He had a thick red nose. I punched him with all the anger I could raise, which at that moment was considerable.

I didn't want a lawyer, but the court appointed one anyway. Striking an officer was a felony. My lawyer advised me to apologize and throw myself on the mercy of the court. I told him to fuck off.

The judge asked how I would plead.

The conservation officer had pink skin, two black eyes, and an annoying smile. He was enjoying his moment.

I looked at the judge. "I'm not sorry," I said. "I should've killed the bastard."

I was a local. The felony was dropped to a misdemeanor and I got fourteen days, including an afternoon under escort for Raina's funeral, shackles on my ankles and wrists. There was a small turnout. There was no sign of Val or the others who I had last seen on the Mibra Onty. I had expected this.

But there was one man there I had not expected to see.

Lawyer Eubanks wore a black cashmere overcoat with the collar turned up. He fingered the brim of a black fedora as he walked over to me.

"Raina lit the fire that killed her parents," I said. "M. J. Key was a professor in England, but he was an American."

Eubanks nodded solemnly, but avoided looking at me. "Gus bought Key's property in Pinkville."

"I'm sorry about Raina," I told him. And I was.

"She had her strengths," he said, "but mercy was not one of them. You did what you could," he said.

"Did I?"

"She was a sick woman. She had a splendid education and a future, and threw it all away. For nothing."

"The snowfly," I said.

"Fiction," he said. "Deadly fiction." There were tears in his eyes, and mine.

The night before the county released me, I had a dream.

There were no visual elements, just a fragrant and intoxicating scent that awoke me and left me blinking wildly, my nostrils flaring.

When I walked out of the jail, Janey was waiting. She was driving Buzz's old station wagon and looked tiny behind the giant steering wheel.

"I'm sorry about your friend," she said. We hugged hard and drove north.

I said, "I like how you smell."

"I'm not wearing perfume," she said.

"I know."

Some things become obvious when you least expect them.

Valoretev and the group had moved to the Mibra Onty after Heming-way's death but I had no idea where they were now. I suspected Buzz would never allow himself to lose touch with his flock, crazies included. It was his job, he said. I say it was his life.

"Where are they, Buzz?"

"Near the source of the Tahquamenon, a place called Eagle's Nest."

"Take us," I said. "Janey and me." From that point forward I never wanted to be apart from her again.

We hauled snowmobiles on a trailer and drove west to a railroad spur called Serendipity. There we left the truck and rode the snow bugs west into the wilderness. We pulled supplies on toboggans. Buzz knew right where to go.

The men were living in shelters built under uprooted cedar trees. We stopped the machines and turned the motors off. Gas fumes lingered in the frigid air. The silence was heavy and penetrating.

Valoretev came out of one of the shelters. He was wearing snow goggles made from a piece of canvas wrapped around his head.

"Key's dead," I said.

The Russian removed his jury-rigged goggles and squinted at me. His eyes were red from smoke, his skin ashen.

"She went after the snowfly and drowned. I was there. She set all of us up to keep us away from where she thought the hatch would be, but I found her. There was no hatch, only some flies, small. She died for nothing. It's time you stopped, Val. There is no life to be had here, chasing and living a lie." I did not tell him about the fish that had broken off Raina's line.

I never told anyone about that, until now.

The Russian went to speak to his compatriots. Buzz, Janey, and I unloaded supplies.

Val eventually came back. He had his gear with him.

"Where are the others?" I asked.

"You cannot kill a dream with a fact," he said.

"What about you?"

"It is time I found another dream," he said with a weary sigh.

Val came back to Grand Marais with us and remained there. He died not long ago, a proud husband, father of three, grandfather of five, and fished nearly every day until the very end. We were friends.

PART IV

He who doubts from what he sees will ne'er believe, do what you please.
—William Blake

25

THERE are a lot of theories about what makes a marriage work. I don't put much stock in theory, but in retrospect olfactory attraction seems as reasonable an explanation of success as any.

Janey and I were married in Grand Marais one year and four months after Ingrid died. We lived with her children in the apartment over the Light and became a family. Hannah Wren managed to clear her claim on her father's estate and together we resurrected the column. Hannah visited often and became one of Janey's closest friends. I traveled most summers and spent winters in Grand Marais. Angus had been right about headhunting and I took sublime pleasure in meeting people who loved fishing for its simplicity and inherent beauty.

Despite the travel required by the column, I made it a point to fish Whirling Creek several times a year. Janey and I even built a simple one-room cabin where the old house had stood. We built it ourselves, with no outside help. Janey didn't care for fishing, but her kids did and I made a concentrated effort to teach them what I could. Carl, our eldest, loved it as much as I did and was often with me. Sometimes I took one of the kids with me on my trips. And sometimes Janey and I met alone together for a couple of days at the cabin. The fires that burned hot in us from the beginning have remained so all these years.

We were at the cabin together late one September. There was a hurricane in the Gulf of Mexico and a mass of warm air had pushed north in a singular weather pattern that left Michigan drowning under monsoonlike conditions. The fishing was awful; we stayed inside, which was all right with me.

We made love that afternoon and later she went out for a walk while I toyed with some columns. When she came back, she shook off her rain slicker, spraying me.

"Isn't it late for lightning bugs?" she asked.

"Did you get into the beer without me?"

"I'm serious, Bowie. There are some lightning bugs down by the river," she said.

They were usually done by July, August at the latest, but it was unseasonably warm and humid and nature frequently violated man's expectations. I had never seen lightning bugs in heavy rain, much less in autumn.

Janey tossed me my raincoat. "I'll show you," she said.

I didn't want to go out, but I had questioned her veracity and she would not let up until her honor was restored. All marriages pivot on such conventions.

"Is this really necessary?"

She pushed the jacket at me again. It was.

We walked down to Whirling Creek and then I saw. *Some* lightning bugs? There were clouds of them blinking wildly and brilliantly. I had never seen so many in one place.

"*See,*" she said, sliding her arm around my waist. "We might have missed this."

The lightning bugs were stretched up and down the stream, but they seemed to be concentrating over the pool, forming a ball that grew brighter and brighter until it was nearly overhead. The amount of light it shed was stunning.

The ethereal cloud began to flatten on the bottom and dissipate into a thin layer of flickering mist. I was so focused on the light that I did not see the first white flies rise off.

It was not like the night Raina had drowned. The insects rose to the surface like white bubbles and lifted straight up, wildly flapping their wet wings. And they were huge, some of them as large as my hand.

Dozens turned to hundreds, turned to thousands, turned to a solid wall, filling the air, denser than a whiteout, and the water began to boil below them as trout slashed at them, slapping their tails, twisting, surging greedily, their mouths open, all caution gone, the water alive with flies and trout, illuminated by a layer of lightning bugs. I sank to my knees in disbelief on the bank and felt Janey pulling on me and handing me my fly rod, which I took numbly and stared at the fluffy snowfly on the end of the leader and looked at her.

"Where? How?"

She pushed me toward the water. "Fish," she said. I waded in, dumbfounded. The yellowed, dusty fly was one of those that Hannah Wren had given to me many years before.

"Throw, hon," Janey said. "*Throw.*"

And I did, upstream and across with a little lift at the end to create a mend. I felt a strike immediately and snapped the tip upward with a firm flick and the fish took off upstream. Janey squealed and I held on as the line peeled out of the reel with a pained clatter and I thought, I can't stop it, and started upstream in pursuit and Janey ran beside me when the fish turned and shot back downstream. I turned with it and reversed direction and the flies continued to hatch and covered me like huge feathers, and the trout danced upstream again and I went blindly with it, unable to see the umbilical in my hand, the muscles in my forearm searing. When I thought it was lost, it turned again and sounded and parked and I slid to my knees and there we sat, at an impasse. My chest heaved.

When I tried to move the creature, it resisted.

"Is it there?" Janey asked from nearby. Her face was lit white by the light of the insects but began to fade, and I looked at the water and the lightning bugs were beginning to blink out and the surface began to calm and something heavy rammed hard into my thighs and splashed like a depth charge and I tried to lift it again, but without effect. The river that had boiled with trout was calm.

"I don't know what to do," I told Janey.

"Just hang on," she said.

I did. For two more hours, by which time night had asserted itself and it was black around us, but I could still feel the bend in the rod and the incredible force beyond.

"It may have wrapped me," I said. "Circled around a limb or rock."

"No," Janey said resolutely.

I don't know how long it was after that, that I felt the rod tip communicate life stirring.

"It's moving," I said. It had descended into the hole and current and had held me off. I was in awe.

But it did not move far. Its weight had the rod nearly doubled. I pawed at the reel, lifted the rod, felt sluggish resistance, took in line. Was it coming in? I lifted again and recaptured more line. Progress. Not a lot, but some. Statistically significant. How much torque could the rod handle? Or the reel? Or me?

"It's not done," I said, more to warn myself.

"Net?" Janey asked.

I fought a laugh. What net could handle this? I kept cranking slowly. Despite all the force at the start we were down to finesse and determination.

Line came in steadily.

"Can you see it?" Janey asked.

I didn't answer her. It had to be out of the hole. Now and then it swam a couple of feet backward and took line, but these were feeble efforts compared to the earlier thrusts.

"How will you get it?"

"Maybe it will get me." I remembered the sharp pop of Hemingway's line. It had broken his ancient heart.

Suddenly, I had slack line. I backed up and began cranking wildly.

"What?" Janey shouted. *"What?"* She had left the bank. "I'll get a light!"

"Coming at me," I said, reeling furiously, my arms extended high, behind the curve, beaten.

I couldn't reel fast enough and never caught up to it. It swam almost lazily to my feet and between my legs and swung downstream in the current, head toward me, so close I could reach down and touch it, a slick black form, its shoulders as wide as my thigh. I could only imagine its length and girth. More than the thing on Sturdivant's wall. Much more. Frighteningly more. A thing that could not be.

It moved slowly around me again and let itself slide past again, looping me. All it had to do was dart for deep water and the leader would tighten on my legs and break.

It had won.

I dropped the rod tip and let the line go slack. Surrender.

A light beam danced on the grass tops beside the water.

"Don't," I said when Janey got to the bank. "Turn it off, please."

Darkness again.

"Is it there?" she asked.

"Yes, beside me." For how long? Why didn't it go?

I heard Janey ease into the water.

I looked at the majestic fish. It rose to the surface. I saw the fly embedded in the side of its mouth.

Janey was beside me. "Is it hurt?"

"No."

I tossed the rod backward and bit the leader in two.

I took my wife's hand and guided her to me.

I ran my hand down the leader to the fly.

Janey knelt beside me and touched the trout; it did not move.

"My God," Janey said.

I wiggled the fly until it loosened and came free.

The fish remained.

Janey gently slid her arms under its massive belly and urged it toward deeper water.

The fish still did not flee.

I reached down and turned its head into the current.

It submerged into the blackness, then reappeared upstream of us, held itself broadside to the current, as if it was measuring us, and after a brief pause flashed around and behind us and in a blink leapt completely out of the water and hung there in our minds, imprinting itself and, finally, plunged into the hole with a clean splash and disappeared.

Forever. What could not be never would be again in my lifetime.

EPILOGUE

ALL of this was a long time ago. I did not intend to write about it, any of it, but Janey convinced me I should. Most of the time, I suppose, I couldn't write about it. There were just no words. I thought of it as a curse, but Janey insists that all things have a purpose and it's what we do with them that matters. The snowfly had brought us together, she said, which made it a gift. Ours.

Maybe.

Curiosity is also a gift, but too much, and it becomes something else. There is much in our world yet to discover, but discoveries always extract a price.

I once asked Father Buzz how I could separate passion from obsession. He thought for a while. "Do what's inside you and let God keep score."

We are different people at different times in our lives.

I was driven to search and almost missed what is most precious.

Life, I discovered, is not about the unknown. Life is defined by what we make out of what is and the comfort that comes with such knowledge. It's hard enough to take care of what you have, and simplicity is the most complex thing in the world to maintain.

But sometimes, when the air is dry and dust devils soar, or when lightning bugs hover over the ground like frail votives, I close my eyes and see the Rathead drinking pure water or feel the weight at the end of my line and see a snowstorm of white flies and that magnificent fish defying gravity, and I think it turned out better than I might have hoped. Certainly better than I deserved.

Those who've gone up the creek and returned will know what I mean.